the island house

the island house

A NOVEL

nancy thayer

Ballantine Books
New York

Published in the United States by Ballantine Books,
an imprint of Random House, a division of
Penguin Random House LLC, New York.

BALLANTINE and the HOUSE colophon are
registered trademarks of Penguin Random House LLC.

Library of Congress Cataloging-in-Publication Data
Names: Thayer, Nancy, author.
Title: The island house : a novel / Nancy Thayer.
Description: New York : Ballantine Books, [2016]
Identifiers: LCCN 2016005078| ISBN 9781101967041 (hardback) |
ISBN 9781101967065 (ebook)
Subjects: | BISAC: FICTION / Contemporary Women. | FICTION / Sagas. |
FICTION / Romance / Contemporary. | GSAFD: Love stories.
Classification: LCC PS3570.H3475 I86 2016 | DDC 813/.54—dc23
LC record available at lccn.loc.gov/2016005078

Printed in the United States of America on acid-free paper

randomhousebooks.com

2 4 6 8 9 7 5 3 1

First Edition

Book design by Elizabeth A. D. Eno

To

Ellias, The Prince
&
Adeline, Star Shine
&
Emmett, The Coochie
&
Anathea, Bright Eyes

acknowledgments

In an absolutely perfect world, I would have as my editor the editor I have now, the gifted Linda Marrow. She is smart *and* wise, and her guidance and intuition made this book the book I wanted it to be. Linda, thank you.

Thanks, also, to Dr. John West, who talked with me and loaned me many helpful books and one of his own monographs. Thanks to my sister, Martha Foshee, a nurse who helps me in more ways than I can mention and she knows why I say that. Thanks to Jill Hunter Burrill, Tricia Patterson, Deborah Beale, Mark Beale, CurLette Anglin, Charlotte Maison, Jean Mallinson, Sofiya Popova, Katie Kaizer, Mary West, Josh Thayer, David Gillum, Sam Wilde, Neil Forbes, Julie Hensler, Joe Vargas, and Superwoman Sara Manela. Thanks to my UMKC friends Nicole Leone, Karen English, Gina Kauffman, Vice Chancellor Curt Crespino, Dean Bonnie Postlethwaite, Jane Greer, and Dean Wayne Vaught.

Thanks to Will Clift, who knows about the ocean at night and inspired part of this book. Thanks and a huge hug to Lucy Breed, who told me one evening about her "summer children."

Meg Ruley, you are my rock star agent and my Downy Flake best friend. DFF! Thank you for everything. Christina Hogrebe, I don't think I can live without you. Enormous thanks to Danielle Sickles and the brilliant crew at the Jane Rotrosen Agency.

I am so fortunate to be with the excellent people at Ballantine. I'm very grateful to Gina Centrello, Kim Hovey, Christine Mykityshin, Maggie Oberrender, Paolo Pepe, Elana Seplow-Jolley, and Penelope Haynes.

Hugs and kisses—XOXO!—to my delightful Facebook friends. Your friendship keeps me writing—and smiling.

In an absolutely perfect world, I would be married to Charley Walters. Oh, wait! I am!

Where shells lie thick it is often those that are broken
that have the greatest beauty of form.

—Gavin Maxwell, *Ring of Bright Water*

who's who in *the island house*

The Vickerey Family

Alastair Vickerey, the father, also known as Dr. V
Susanna Vickerey, the mother
Henry Vickerey, the oldest child
Robin Vickerey, the oldest daughter
James Vickerey, the second son
Iris Vickerey, the second daughter

The Vickereys' Summer Children

Valerie Whitman, Henry's friend and true love
Jacob Barnes, Henry's best male friend
Courtney Hendricks, Robin's best friend
Callum Findlay, James's best friend
Pearl Schwartz, Iris's best friend

The Family Friends

Quinn Eliot
Christabel Eliot, Quinn's daughter

The Cowboy

Monty Blackhorse

the island house

Courtney always took the slow ferry to Nantucket at the beginning of the summer. It was a sort of ritual for her, watching Hyannis with its docks, wharves, beach houses, and sailboats slide slowly into the background until the ship was surrounded by water, with no land in sight. It was the gentle disconnecting from the mainland that made it possible for her to let go of the real world and everything it contained. For two hours, she would sit at a window, staring out at the infinite blue sea, its white-tipped waves, its oddly serene seabirds bobbing blithely so far from land, and in the distance, like a child's first drawing, a fishing trawler sputtering along with its nets sinking down and down into the mysterious watery unknown. Suddenly, Courtney would catch a glimmer along the horizon. Low and flat, it shimmered like a mirage, and as the steamship *Nantucket* rumbled along, an intense point of light would flash and disappear, flash and disappear—the first sign of Nantucket, the Great Point Light. As soon as she spotted this, Courtney would rise from her seat, walk down the aisle, and push her way out through the heavy door to the bow. Here the wind whipped her hair into her face and the sun shone into her eyes and the air smelled of salt. She was almost there, and she wanted to be alert and watchful, to feel herself being borne closer and closer to the island she loved.

She was standing on the deck now, scanning the horizon for landmarks—the water tower, the cluster of rainbow sailboats daringly leaving the harbor, the buoys.

This year, this summer—this would be a time she would always remember. She was sure of that.

"Have you been to the island before?"

An older woman had come to join her, and stood next to her, her age-marked hands holding tight to the railing.

"Yes, several times, actually, for about ten years," Courtney replied. "And you?"

The deeply tanned creases of the woman's face readjusted themselves as she smiled. "Growing up, my family summered here. My parents left me their house, and my husband and children and I summered here. This summer our grandchildren are visiting."

"How lucky you are," Courtney said wistfully. She wanted what this woman had, she wanted to marry the man she loved and raise a great pack of children on the island.

The woman studied Courtney. "And where do you stay when you're here?"

Courtney paused before admitting, "With the Vickereys on the cliff."

"The Vickereys!" The woman stood back a pace, the better to scan Courtney up and down, appraising her. "Are you a Vickerey?"

"No, no," Courtney hurriedly assured her. "I went to school with Robin Vickerey. We were roommates at Smith, became good friends, and I've just fallen into the habit of visiting a lot." Even as she spoke the words, Courtney could hear the style, the blasé cadence of the Vickerey family: *I've just fallen into the habit* . . . As if she were one of the Vickereys and belonged in that enormous rambling house as part of their accomplished, complicated, turbulent, family.

The older woman arched an eyebrow. "I'd say you're lucky, too, then. You're one of Susanna Vickerey's summer children."

Summer children: that was what Susanna called her four children's best friends who spent every summer in the Vickerey home, even though those "children" were adults and had been for years.

"Yes," Courtney agreed happily. "I am."

The first summer Courtney Hendricks spent on Nantucket, she was eighteen years old, a naïve, book-smart optimist who didn't know what the world would throw at her but was sure she could handle it.

And after all, look at what had happened: even though she was from little ol' Emporia, Kansas, she'd been accepted by one of the finest women's colleges, Smith College, in Massachusetts. Even better, best of all, her roommate was Robin Vickerey, who became Courtney's dearest friend.

Robin had long flaming red hair that curled like party ribbon and green eyes and adorable freckles spattered across her nose. With looks like that, you'd think she'd be kind of wild, but Robin was cool, calm, and collected, a quiet, studious, organized person who was a gem at stopping quarrels in the dorm. Robin and Courtney had become friends immediately. They shared the same sensibility. They were truly engrossed with their studies. They weren't geeks, but they didn't do quite as many stupid things as the other girls in their dorm. Courtney knew she was considered a goody-goody, which she probably was. She assumed her Midwestern upbringing was responsible for that, so she was surprised to find the same kind of careful, helpful, Girl Scoutish attitude in Robin. After she came to know the entire Vickerey family, she understood why.

On a long spring weekend of their freshman year, Robin had invited Courtney to her home on Nantucket. She'd mentioned that summer jobs as retail clerks, waitstaff, and landscapers paid outstanding money and Courtney wanted to check it out. Courtney's parents did all right for themselves—her father owned a pharmacy for which her mother did the books. But Courtney wanted to help soften the blow of college tuition and expenses. She'd worked after school and on weekends in Emporia—why not work on Nantucket, where the pay was so much better? So she went along with Robin. They caught a ride to the Cape, took the fast ferry to Nantucket, and Susanna Vickerey, Robin's mother, met them at the boat and drove them out to 'Sconset.

When Courtney first saw where the Vickereys lived, she was dazzled. Anybody would be. It was a huge old house with lots of bedrooms, set on a bluff overlooking the Atlantic Ocean. Dr. Vickerey was a surgeon in Boston; the Vickereys kept an apartment in the Back Bay, but the family home was Nantucket. They had four children, and their house was always jam-packed to its literal rafters with friends. The mother, Susanna, liked it that way. She said it filled her soul to have guests around. She called some of the guests her "summer children," even after they turned twenty-one.

"Stay for the summer," Robin had coaxed Courtney. "There's always room for one more."

Courtney had gone into town that Saturday afternoon and looked around. The town was sweet and old-fashioned yet had excellent restaurants with famous chefs and fabulous clothing stores. Lots of places needed summer help. She talked to her parents, her parents talked to Robin's parents, and it was agreed. She went for the first summer and fit right in. She borrowed one of the Vickereys' bikes for the ride to work and back. On rainy days, someone was always in the house and willing to drive her into town. On her days off, she went to the beach with Robin. Some nights, when the moon was full and the breeze was inviting, she and Robin wandered down to the beach parties. They drank some, but not much; it didn't interest them. During those years they were just as interested in curling up with a good book on their time off as partying. Or simply staying at home, lounging on the back patio, drinking lemonade, having easy lazy conversations and watching the white curtains flutter as the sea breezes blew through the open windows of the marvelous great house.

That first summer was eleven years ago. Courtney had come here every summer since then. In many ways, Nantucket felt like her second home. She had graduated from college and come here to work for the summer. She had gone to grad school in Boston for a master's in English literature and come here to work for the summer. She'd gotten a job at UMKC teaching English lit and composition, and still, as an adult, for five more summers, she had returned to this island, this house, this family. She told her parents and Kansas friends it was because she made so much money working summers in Nantucket.

But this year making money wasn't enough of a reason for her to continue to go back East. Thank heavens it was Susanna Vickerey's sixtieth birthday. Courtney *had* to be there for that. The Vickereys were throwing a huge party, and Susanna had been so wonderful to Courtney for so many years.

But even the party wasn't the real reason.

James Vickerey was the real reason.

Courtney had been in love with him since she first met him eleven years ago. Since everyone in the Vickerey family seemed to know, share, and have opinions—which they discussed openly at the dinner table—about everyone else's secrets, Courtney had kept her feelings fiercely private. Not even Robin knew. Courtney seldom saw James, anyway. She was always working and James was often gone, backpacking in Europe when he was in college, working with a techie start-up group in Boston after graduation.

But last year . . . Courtney gripped the ship's railing. After what happened between them last year, she knew she had to return to the island for one more summer.

She hadn't expected Monty Blackhorse to add to her confusion.

You would think, Courtney thought, that a woman as versed in literature as Courtney would not be surprised by anything that happened between a man and a woman.

You would think that any woman, no matter what she did, couldn't be shocked by any man if she had grown up with a father, a brother, and a male best friend.

On the other hand, on the spectrum of men and emotions, Courtney's father and brother were way over on the placid-headed-for-comatose end. They were strong, silent men. Not mysterious. Just silent. Her father was a gruff man's man who came home from his pharmacy expecting dinner on the table and the television tuned to some kind of game—football, baseball, hockey—he'd even watch the fishing channel if necessary. Her brother, Donnie, was five years older, a pharmacist working with their father and planning to take over the family business someday. He was obsessed with Legos when they were small, and as Courtney became a lover of books and literature and what Donnie called "fussy stuff," what little interest Donnie had in her faded away. Now that he was a father, he'd softened a bit, but his children were both boys whose favorite video was of monster trucks in muddy fields.

And Monty, her best Kansas male friend, had never done anything that shocked her in all the sixteen years since that first day she met him when she was trespassing on his property.

For her thirteenth birthday—her admittance into adolescence, although she'd tried to convince her parents she was an adolescent the moment she hit double digits—her parents had given in and bought her a horse of her own. Star was a buckskin mare with a white star between her eyes. They boarded her at the Schmidts' ranch, so until she got her own car at sixteen, she had to bike out there unless she could catch a ride. She could usually pester Donnie into driving her. Her birthday was in early May. That first summer, she had the entire summer stretching before her, day after delicious day of riding.

The first time she rode Star on the Schmidts' land, Courtney entered the stable, Star's new home, and smooth-talked and gentled the horse as she put on the blanket and saddle. Star stood at seventeen hands. Courtney might have appreciated a stepladder, but she wasn't going to admit it. Awkwardly, she got herself up onto the gracious old roping saddle. It was padded, with wide leather stirrups, a rocking chair of a seat. Courtney had kept Star at a gentle trot as they explored the Schmidts' pasture, getting to know the horse, sensing how she and this horse were going to take to each other. She'd ridden Star before, and liked her, but the horse was in a new stable, and horses could be quirky. Still, Star was seven years old. She seemed easygoing and content, no kind of diva.

The next time Courtney hoisted herself up into the saddle, she relaxed a bit. Beneath her, Star nickered and fidgeted, clearly announcing that she was bored.

Courtney nudged the buckskin horse with her knees and dug her heels into Star's sides, and they were off, galloping over a shimmering sea of sweet green grass. Never in her life, Courtney thought, would she experience anything to top the sheer soul-soaring joy of galloping across a field on the back of this horse. She and Star became one creature, united by speed, motion, bliss, and on Courtney's part, a thrilling smidgen of terror. Star loved to run, and Courtney let her have her head. She felt the huffing of the huge animal's lungs beneath her, the silken glide of the powerful muscles carrying her.

In the distance, she spotted a stand of cottonwood trees. Easily jumping over a fallen white rail fence, she headed Star in their direction. As they drew closer, she saw a narrow creek winding along just a few feet from the trees. It was shady there, and Courtney was glad, because even with the temperature only in the low eighties, her clothes were sweat-soaked from the ride. When they reached it, she reined Star in, took a moment to lean forward and pet her and whisper endearments to her. Her horse muttered and tossed her head, white saliva flying. Courtney dismounted and held the reins in her hand as Star drank from the creek.

She'd knelt at the edge of the creek, scooped the water in her hands, and patted it over her neck and face, letting it drip down past her shoulders, cool and refreshing. She was a jangling bundle of sensation, physically elated and exhausted by the full-out gallop, thrilled to know this horse was *her* horse now.

"Hey. You're trespassing."

The voice came from behind, sudden and arrogant.

Courtney, startled, almost lost her balance and toppled into the creek. Turning, standing, she looked up at the speaker.

Monty Blackhorse sat there on his huge coal black stallion. For a moment, she stared at him. He was definitely something to stare at.

He wore jeans, a blue denim shirt with the sleeves rolled up, and roughed-up cowboy boots. No hat. His coal black hair was long, tied

into a tail down his back. She knew he was at least part Native American. He was big and he wasn't smiling. He was riding bareback.

The Blackhorses were famous in the area. They raised the finest
Black Angus on the planet, and they were rich from doing it. In Strong
City near the Tallgrass Prairie National Preserve, the ranch was about a
twenty-minute drive from Emporia, and a good two hours from Kansas
City. But everyone in that part of the world took driving long distances
in stride. It was part of living in such big open country. The speed limit
for driving on the rural highways in Kansas was seventy-five miles per
hour and most people drove faster.

The Blackhorses' enormous house and barns were on the south
side of their land, close to Emporia, so they attended church in Emporia, and bought their groceries and every day stuff there. They used the
Hendricks Pharmacy, and Marie Hendricks and Evelyn Blackhorse were
friendly, friendly enough that Marie knew that Evelyn went into Kansas
City's elegant Plaza area to buy her clothes.

Rich as they were, the Blackhorses had sent their children to a private school. Monty had the distinction of being kicked out of that
school this spring. Everyone in Emporia knew about it. Monty was kind
of a celebrity.

Confronted by the real-life legendary Monty, Courtney took a moment to consider her options. He terrified her, but he was only a kid,
and the rumors about him made him seem like he'd be fun to know.

Courtney's long brown hair was clipped back under her cowboy
hat—no two ways about it, this design protected the skin from the
spring sun like no other hat could do—jeans, boots, a sports bra because everything was going to be jounced around, and a light cotton
shirt. No makeup. It would be just silly to wear makeup riding. She was
not dressed to impress.

Monty was thirteen, but he held himself like a man—like an arrogant, wealthy, challenging man. Courtney was fascinated—and chal-
lenged.

"I'm trespassing? I didn't see any signs." She held her chin high and
stared back at him, her gaze unwavering, giving him as good as she got.

Monty shifted slightly, obviously surprised by her spunk. "Where do you stable your horse?"

"Where do you stable yours?" she shot back.

His black eyes glittered with momentary irritation—how could anyone not know instantly who he was? As he stared down at her, though, his mouth quirked upward. He knew she was playing a game. "This is my land. I'm Monty Blackhorse."

"Monty Blackhorse," Courtney echoed. "I've heard about you."

He frowned. "What have you heard?"

Courtney cocked her head. "You got caught in the school after hours with a fifteen-year-old girl."

A lazy smile crossed Monty's face. "We were just messing around."

"Really," she replied sarcastically. "So you'll be going to my school next fall?"

Monty shrugged.

"What grade?" she asked, although she knew.

"Eighth." His smile was gone.

"That's the grade I'll be in. I know a lot of stuff you should know. About teachers, other kids."

His eyes narrowed. He didn't reply. Courtney guessed he was weighing how much he wanted to know stuff against how much he wanted to seem cool.

"I didn't know this was your property, by the way," she told him. "I jumped an old decrepit fence back there . . ." She pointed. Star knocked Courtney with her head, impatient to move. "Tell you what. *Forgive me for trespassing on your land*"—she said this in a tone that clearly meant *like she cared*—"and I'll tell you some stuff about the teachers and the principal at our pedestrian little public school."

Monty took one long minute to decide. "It's a deal."

Courtney hoisted herself up into the saddle. Star nickered and fidgeted, wanting to get going.

"We can talk back at the house. Wanna see the rest of the land first?" Monty asked.

"Sure."

"Can you keep up with me?" Monty asked.

Courtney did a fake girlie-girl simper. "I'll certainly try."

Monty turned and let his horse amble away from the creek. Courtney followed. Before them stretched an eternity of rolling pasture, with a blur of trees far in the east.

"Race?" he asked.

She nodded, and they were off.

Quickly Monty was ahead, but that didn't bother Courtney. Star loved to run, and Courtney let her go and soon they were side by side. They thundered across the pasture, whooping and laughing with excitement, slowing down as they approached the Blackhorses' big white house.

"Told you I could keep up with you," Courtney bragged.

"You can ride," he admitted as he urged his horse through a gate into a corral. "Come on," he said. "Let's get some lemonade."

In the kitchen, he poured them each a glass of sweet lemonade from a pitcher in the refrigerator. "Let's go in the den."

The den was at the back of the house, one wall shelved with books and games. Clue. Monopoly. Scrabble.

Courtney studied the television, which wasn't even as big as the one in her own home. "Don't you have an Xbox? Or Wii?"

Monty wouldn't meet her eyes. "My parents won't allow them in the house. They're kind of strict about that."

Courtney drew back, as if he'd said something really terrible. "Gosh, we have Xbox and Nintendo. I thought everybody did. You should come over to my house sometime."

"How about now?" Monty suggested eagerly.

"I've got to get Star back to the Schmidts'," Courtney told him. "But maybe tomorrow?"

His face fell. "Tomorrow's Sunday. I've got to go to church and stay home on Sundays. And during the week I have to help with the ranch . . . maybe next Saturday?"

"Sure," Courtney said easily. "Absolutely."

Their friendship had begun that day. It might never have happened at all if she hadn't accidentally trespassed on the Blackhorses' land.

Monty's parents were stern and standoffish, looming over their son's life like ogres from a Grimm's fairy tale. They were ready to punish Monty severely at the slightest offense, and when he started at the local school, he kept to himself for the first year. He was allowed to go to Courtney's house on Saturdays—they didn't know about the videogames. After the first few weeks, Monty satisfied his electronic fix. He and Courtney would walk around town, get sodas in the ice cream store, bike around town, or sit in the air-conditioned house and play cards. Courtney's parents liked Monty. They invited him to dinner and the Blackhorses allowed him to come.

Any insecurity Courtney might have felt from being in the presence of the infamous and utterly dreamboat Monty Blackhorse was balanced out by her knowledge of what kind of freaks his parents were, so harsh, so suspicious. Monty had an older sister who was in boarding school and then in college, headed for a career in law. Monty was the chosen one. He had to take over the farm, stop acting like a fool, behave like an intelligent teenage boy, and be responsible. With Courtney, he could be a normal kid, laughing till milk shot out his nose, making ridiculous fart jokes, eating enormous sundaes from the ice cream the Hendricks kept in the freezer.

When school started, that first year, Courtney casually drew Monty into her crowd, which was, she had to admit, the cool crowd. Monty effortlessly became one of them, although he seldom spoke about himself. When Courtney's friends asked her about him, she gave bland answers. She'd never betray him about his weird parents, and Monty was aware of that, and their friendship grew stronger. By the time he was a sophomore, he was picked for junior varsity football, and after that, varsity football his junior and senior years. He seldom came to her house on Saturdays in the fall, but once the snow fell, he came again, regularly.

Days passed, months, and then years. Years of Saturday afternoons when Monty played videogames in the Hendricks's den, while Courtney curled up in a chair, reading. Her parents called her a bookworm, and worried about her being too introverted, so they were always delighted when Monty stopped by, never realizing that while Monty was annihilating monsters, Courtney was in Russia with *Anna Karenina* or in France with *Madame Bovary*. Her tastes were wide. She read *Huckleberry Finn* one weekend. The next weekend, she read *Rebecca*. She read Ernest Hemingway; she read Georgette Heyer. She read Danielle Steel; she read Edgar Allan Poe. She read every bit of *Gone with the Wind*, even though Scarlett's taste in men made her impatient and frustrated. Why on earth did Scarlett love that wimpy Ashley? She wanted to throw the book across the room. Monty sat on the sofa exploding buildings while Courtney wept over a romance.

When she read *Peyton Place,* she got so embarrassed, even though Monty didn't know the book, that she carried it out of her room, shut it in her desk drawer, and returned with a copy of *Oliver Twist*.

Of course, when the weather allowed it, they went riding. Her parents or brother would drop her at the Schmidts' stable, and she'd rocket off to the creek where Monty would be waiting. They'd let their horses have their heads and race over the pasture, until they came to one of the white board fences corralling the Black Angus. If the herd was over in another pasture, they'd dare each other to jump. They jumped over fallen trees, they jumped over tractor tires. Courtney knew she had no proper seat or form, not like a show jumper, but she didn't care a fig about that. When Star jumped, Courtney was heart struck with terror and ecstasy. She'd land inelegantly back in her saddle, let Star slow down, and circle around to meet Monty. They'd grin at each other like they possessed the secret of happiness, and maybe they did.

In the long golden sun of late afternoon, they took their time riding back, allowing their horses to amble side by side while they talked. Out here in the open air, they chatted about all sorts of things they never spoke of in her den.

In the early months, they kept their conversation light, speaking of the dogs and cats living on the ranch, and Courtney's parents' ancient golden retriever who by law shouldn't be allowed in the pharmacy but was always led in the back door so she could lie in the office at the back with her head on one of Courtney's mother's old coats. Courtney told

Monty about her brother, Donnie, who had his own truck and drove Courtney to and from the stable on Saturdays.

Monty told Courtney about his Native American heritage. His great-grandmother had married Joseph Blackhorse of the Wichita tribe that was scattered across Kansas and Oklahoma. Their son had homesteaded the land that now belonged to the Blackhorses and married a young orphaned Irish girl from back East. Their son was Monty's father. By the time Monty's father came of age, the Blackhorse ranch had hit prosperity, what with the stockyards in Emporia and Kansas City.

"Lots of people have some kind of Native American blood," Monty said. "I'm fortunate to have coal black hair." He grinned. "Girls seem to like that a lot."

"I guess modesty comes along with that gene," Courtney teased.

But it was true, girls liked Monty. Almost every girl in the high school flirted with him and absolutely every girl in the school envied Courtney's easygoing friendship with him.

When Courtney was a sophomore, she started dating. Not Monty—that would have been like dating her brother. She enjoyed flirting with the guys and the occasional make-out session in the cab of a truck, but she never spent time giggling or weeping over some boy like her girlfriends did. She read. She had plans.

During the high school years, Courtney and Monty had less time to ride together. When they did, they didn't spend as much time riding as they did talking. They let their horses idle along over the pasture, sometimes stopping to eat the sweet green grass, and they talked. It was easy that way.

Her junior year, Courtney got serious with Tanner Warren, a big guy, defensive guard on the school's football team, the same team Monty played quarterback for. She didn't actually have sex with Tanner, but she did get naked with him. Once or twice she gave him oral sex, because he was kind of desperate, and all her friends were doing it with their boyfriends, and it made him so happy.

That spring, once the snow melted and the air softened, Monty insisted they go riding. They were halfway to the creek when he said to her, "You'd better watch yourself with Tanner."

Courtney's neck nearly snapped off, she turned so fast to stare at Monty. "What are you even talking about?"

"Don't be stupid. Tanner talks in the locker room."

Embarrassment coursed through Courtney, turning her face red, scalding her blood way down to her toes. "What has he said?"

"Hey. Guys talk. You'd better be careful."

"I haven't had sex with him," Courtney snapped.

"I'm not saying you have. *He's* not saying you have. I'm just saying, be careful."

"Monty, you ought to know by now I *am* careful." Tears filled Courtney's eyes and she was glad they were riding side by side, so Monty couldn't see her face. "You know I want to go to college, I want to *teach* in college. I most certainly do *not* want to get knocked up!"

"I hear you," Monty said, uncomfortable around her tears. "Come on. Let's race to the creek."

She wept bitter tears that flew backward as she let Star gallop over the field, and once at the creek, Monty didn't bring up the subject again. But she was grateful for his warning. That week she broke up with Tanner, and for the rest of her high school days, she kept herself away from guys and concentrated on making the best grades she could. She wanted to go East to college. She was determined.

She gave Monty his own warning, too, when he started dating one of her good friends, Donna. Donna had fallen fast and hard for Monty. She was having sex with Monty every chance she got. She begged Courtney to find out if Monty loved her.

"Don't be crazy," Courtney told Donna. "We don't talk about stuff like that."

But the next time she went riding with Monty, she said, "I wish you'd stop messing around with Donna. She thinks you two are serious. As in wedding bells serious."

Monty was quiet for a few minutes. After a while, he said, "Yeah, no, that's wrong. I want to get married and have a herd of kids—but not with her. I've got someone else in my sights for marriage, for the long haul."

"Maybe you've *said* that to Donna, but what's that ol' saying? Actions speak louder than words?"

Monty kicked his horse and raced off. Courtney didn't try to keep up with him. She could tell he was angry. That week Monty told Donna he didn't want to see her anymore. Donna lost ten pounds, she was so heartbroken. The way things worked in high school, Courtney had to choose between them and she chose Donna. Their senior year of high school, Courtney and Monty ran with different crowds and never went riding together.

Then Courtney went off East to college. Monty went to the University of Missouri at Columbia, playing football every year. During school vacations, Courtney and Monty slowly became best friends again. They emailed each other, had long walks at Christmas vacation, and sent silly pictures of themselves through their cellphones. After college, Monty took over the ranch. Courtney got her master's degree and started teaching at UMKC. They kept in touch, but not as often. They were only a couple of hours away by car, but they were separated by their adult lives. They never went riding together anymore.

So Courtney was shocked this morning when Monty phoned to tell her he wanted to drive her to the airport.

She was amazed at what he said when they got there.

2

The first time Robin met Courtney, she wanted to lie down and cover her face with her pillow. Courtney was as optimistic and glossy as a cheerleader—which of course she'd been back at her Kansas high school. With long, shiny, dark brown hair, huge brown eyes with thick lashes and exquisitely arched velvet eyebrows, and an athletic, energetic, slender body, Courtney went through the world liking everyone she met and expecting everyone to like her right back. She was the most *enthusiastic* person Robin had ever met.

Courtney and Robin were both eighteen, freshman at Smith College. They'd been thrown together as roommates in the dorm. Courtney was as friendly and eager as a Labrador puppy, almost wriggling in her excitement to be starting college. She knew she wanted to major in English literature so she could eventually teach at a university; she wanted to go on for a master's, but she didn't know where; she was nearly foaming at the mouth with excitement because a famous authority on contemporary literature was a guest professor and although

Courtney hadn't found a place in her class yet, she was going to attend the woman's open lectures.

Robin had no idea what her major would be. She had no idea about what she wanted to do. She was desperately homesick for her beautiful island with all its weathers and all her friends, and especially for her family. Iris was only eleven years old, a darling little girl who adored Robin. Who would braid Iris's hair before she went to school in the morning? Who would ride bikes on the moors with her and show her the secret places? Who would play paper dolls with her when she was sick or sit on the sofa on long winter evenings reading *Anne of Green Gables* to her in front of the fire?

Her mother would do all of that, of course, and it was probably time that Iris got to be alone with her parents instead of the tagalong pet of her older siblings. Robin missed her mother, too, enormously. Her mother was radiant, nurturing, funny, *alive*.

Her father she wouldn't miss so much. He was, well, almost a shadow. Alastair Vickerey was a genius surgeon practicing at Mass General, and when he wasn't actually at the hospital, he was in his study at home, writing up cases. Robin could remember him being more present in her life when she was little, but he was never a tickle-the-baby, throw-the-baseball kind of dad with any of his children. As the years passed, her father became increasingly obsessed with his work.

These days people often referred to Dr. Vickerey as Dr. V, even, sometimes, his children. They had started doing it as a gibe, reminding their father they existed, that not only patients and body parts needed his attention. He didn't even notice. Tall, portly, his red hair streaked with gray and white, his shaggy white eyebrows growing thicker, his back rounding into a hump from too much time over the operating table, the computer, his books, he resembled some kind of musk ox stuffed into a suit. His basic means of communication was a sniff, a snort, or a growl. No, she couldn't say she'd really miss her father.

Her older brother, Henry? He was three years older than Robin. She had adored him when she was small, and even though they both had changed, she still did. He was her handsome, magnificent big brother. He'd carried her on his shoulders, he'd taught her how to swim and sail, he'd gotten taller and more handsome every year. But when he was in high school, he lost interest in his younger siblings, and then, when he was nineteen, he'd had a kind of nervous breakdown. Different doctors were working with him on diverse therapies and medications, but Robin never knew what to expect from him, and she worried about him constantly.

She would absolutely miss James. He was a year younger and already six inches taller than her five foot eight. As a kid, he'd been a clown, a rascal. He'd just finished his senior year in high school. He'd done well—there was no doubt that he was smart—but he was restless. People said James was "too smart for his own good." He got A's in all his courses and did his homework in about two and a half minutes. Their mother had hired a computer whiz to teach James about computers; that kept him occupied for much of his free time. He played baseball and soccer and had plenty of friends, but still he seemed filled with a kind of irrepressible energy that drove him mentally as well as physically. One summer he announced that he was going to learn Japanese from an elderly man who had retired to the island. Robin had overheard her parents discussing this.

"Ridiculous idea," Dr. V had grumbled.

Susanna had countered: "It's perfect. Japanese is almost impossible to learn. Just what James needs to keep his brain busy."

So Robin worried about James, too, and because he was her younger brother, being away from him made her feel guilty in an illogical way. She never actually took care of him, but she watched him. She sort of monitored him. She didn't want him to go through the craziness Henry did—as if she could control that!

Her first year of college, she missed her Nantucket friends, too, the ones off at other colleges and the ones who remained working on the island. She missed her bedroom at home. She missed the huge, rambling, sun-filled rooms of her home. Every day she thought of the island, its mists and gales, its expanse of moorland and secret coves, its plunging hawks and sweet-eyed seals. She missed the arrogant splendor of the sea. She knew she had to go to college, but it felt like something she had to endure.

Courtney changed all that. Courtney was fun and silly and intelligent and good-hearted. When snotty, ultra-reserved Eastern girls ridiculed Courtney for her twangy accent and called her a hick, Courtney just tossed her sleek mane of dark hair and ignored them. When Robin felt comfortable enough with her to ask her if the other girls' snobbery didn't bother her, Courtney answered with a shrug, "Oh, I was expecting much worse than this. I prepared myself for coming East. Whenever I get insulted, I make myself conjure up my horse and the feeling of riding her bareback and I feel just fine."

Robin might not have made it through her first year of college if not for Courtney. The classes were challenging, and the teachers were so intense about their subjects that Robin felt like some kind of lower life form because she didn't want to become president of the United States or the scientist who cured cancer. Her grades were mediocre and she spent a great deal of time alone in her room. It amused her that she got the reputation for being aloof and stuck-up. Courtney fell in with a group of super-bright English majors and brought Robin into that group. Often when that gang went into Northampton to the movies or a restaurant or went to Mount Tom for an all-day hike, Courtney insisted that Robin join them. Gradually and halfheartedly and in spite of herself, Robin began to feel at home.

By spring, Robin and Courtney were best friends. Robin invited Courtney home for a long weekend, hoping to lure her to the island for the summer. Susanna loved having people in the house. The more the merrier! During that first long Easter vacation weekend when Robin brought Courtney to the island, Henry was in Boston and James in Washington, DC, on a class trip, so Courtney didn't see the Vickerey family in all its normal nutty glory, and Robin was glad. Certainly she'd warned Courtney about her charming, disruptive, clever, whirlwind brothers. Courtney had said she couldn't wait to meet them, but Robin had worried. From all Courtney had told her, she came from a calm, stable family. If she ever saw the dark side of Henry, Courtney might get freaked out.

But that spring vacation was perfect. Even the weather cooperated. Usually it could be dreary on the island in April, with low gray skies and bitter winds. That April the sun blazed from a robin's-egg blue sky, and the seas were deceptively calm. They biked into town together and checked out the shops and restaurants with HELP WANTED signs. When Courtney heard how much these places paid, she called her parents to say she wanted to work here in the summer.

Robin worried all over again the last day of their freshman year. If only, she thought, if *only* Henry could be his normal wonderful self for the first few days of Courtney's stay, so Courtney could get to know the *real* Henry. For the past three years, ever since Henry had had his first episode, his moods had gone up and down as the psychiatrists tried to find the right fit of meds to keep Henry stable. Robin had told Courtney about this, but not in all its terrifying detail. She really wanted Courtney to spend the summer with them, and she didn't want to scare her friend away.

That year, when the dorms emptied and Robin and Courtney were all packed up, they caught a ride from Northampton down to Hyannis to catch a ferry. Robin's mother met the girls at the dock, helped them pack their luggage into the back of the minivan, and told them how happy she was to see them both. She chatted away cheerfully, asking the girls about their courses, and Robin saw no telltale sign of worry on her mother's face, heard no tension in her voice. Maybe things were okay, she thought. Maybe Henry was all right.

Her mother pulled into the driveway of their house. The front door opened and Henry came out. Robin held her breath. Then Valerie stepped out behind him, and Robin gave a sigh of relief. Usually if Valerie was with Henry, things were all right.

"Hey, baby rabbit," Henry called, coming down the slate path to the car. He was six three, whip thin, with red hair, large green eyes, and horn-rimmed glasses.

"Hey, guys." Valerie, possessed of a mellow personality, hung back, satisfied to give them all a wave. She was a hair short of six feet tall, thin, with blue eyes and blond hair worn short—she was athletic like Henry and headed to med school, too. "Look at you, you big old college girl." He wrapped Robin in a warm hug, and she hugged him back, savoring her big brother at his best.

"Who's this beauty?" Henry asked when Courtney stepped out of the car. "Mom told us she was a looker, but wow. The island will never be the same."

Courtney blushed.

Valerie thumped Henry on the shoulder. "Cut it out. You're embarrassing her." She held out her hand to Courtney. "Hi. I'm Valerie Whitman, Henry's friend."

"Friend?" Henry asked. "Don't listen to her, Courtney. Valerie's the love of my life, and she knows it. She likes to downplay it to make me keep reminding her."

Maybe Henry is a bit manic, Robin thought, biting her lip, but he opened the back hatch, lifted out their suitcases, and carried them into the house and up the stairs. *Maybe,* Robin thought, *Henry is simply happy*. He and Valerie had both been admitted to Harvard Medical School. They deserved their sunny moods.

That summer everything was perfect, or as perfect as a house could be with a thousand people coming and going. Robin's younger brother, James, had just graduated from high school. He and his sexy wacko friend Christabel spent most of their days working for the Department of Public Works, going around the island picking up trash on the beaches and sidewalks. It was their community service handed down by a judge for the idiotic prank they'd pulled that spring. Often Christabel and her divorced father, Quinn, came for dinner. Robin's younger sister, Iris, was still a kid, twelve years old and carefree. Henry and Valerie were like twins joined at the hip. Together they volunteered at the hospital and quizzed each other on anatomy, preparing for med school. Every evening they went for long runs and on Sundays they took the kayak over to Coatue and back. Friends of Henry and Robin and James came for a week or two to enjoy the island, and Robin and Courtney gladly helped Susanna cook for the suntanned, laughing, salty-mouthed mob.

Robin spent the summer volunteering at the Maria Mitchell aquarium. Most of her days involved patiently teaching visiting children about the small creatures in the touch tank. The best days she got to collect specimens as she snorkeled around the inner harbor. She wasn't making any money, but she didn't need money. She was seriously in love with the island and the water around it. She didn't know where this passion would lead her, but she was ready to follow. When she wasn't working, she was racing around buying groceries for the circus at home, and in her free time, she and Courtney ran down the steps to the beach and swam. As for men? She couldn't be bothered. College guys did not show off their best selves at the all-day, all-night, deafening-rock, drink-till-you-puke beach parties. Besides, Courtney worked so hard that summer, by night she had no desire to do anything but collapse.

The great thing was Henry. He remained stable, cheerful, on track. At the end of the summer, he and Valerie even treated Courtney and Robin to dinner at Topper's. He engaged Courtney in a heated discussion about literature and doctors, insisting Emma Bovary's husband was a much maligned doctor, and suggested Courtney read the works of Walker Percy. Courtney glowed from his intelligent attention.

Robin was grateful for Henry's beguiling charm that evening, although an envious gremlin at the back of her mind was jealous that Courtney admired Henry so much. *You should see him when his meds aren't working,* she wanted to say. *You have no idea how much time I've spent trying to talk him down or cheer him up!*

But that was mean-hearted of her, and she honestly hoped Courtney would come back to the island next summer, so she shut off the gremlin in the back of her mind and pretended to be totally fascinated by Valerie's excitement over what she'd read about some newly FDA-approved antibiotics. Valerie was as clueless as Henry when it came to mixing dinner conversation with appropriate topics. As Robin ate her delicate sea bass and nodded and umhummed to Valerie, she remembered the terrifying first time Henry had been in psychiatric trouble.

Henry had been a sophomore at Harvard. All his classes were in advanced science and math. He was so far ahead of everyone that two of his professors were privately working with him on a paper in biology. Susanna stayed at home on the island with Robin, who was sixteen,

James, who was fifteen, and Iris, who was only nine. Their father came to the island every weekend. During the week, he performed surgery at Mass General hospital, just across the Charles River from Harvard and yet, somehow, and not surprisingly, he never had time to visit his oldest son. Not that Henry wanted visitors. When Susanna and her daughters and James went up to Boston, they called Henry and offered to take him out to lunch or dinner. He was always too busy.

The Friday before Thanksgiving vacation was to start on the island, the three kids were sitting at the kitchen table—the kitchen table Robin looked at now—while their mother leaned against the sink drinking coffee and supervising their breakfast. This had been almost fourteen years ago, and Susanna had still been as lithe as a girl. The phone had rung.

"Your father!" Susanna guessed as she reached for the phone on the wall. They were not yet using cellphones, that's how long ago it was.

It was like a movement in a ballet. Susanna held the phone to her ear and pivoted and stretched to reach her coffee cup on the counter. Her face had been young and filled with light.

In an instant, the light faded, the youth vanished, Susanna's hand dropped away from the coffee cup, and she turned away from her other children to face the wall.

It seemed to Robin a very long time before Susanna said, "I see." She listened again to the voice on the other end of the phone. "No, Dr. Vickerey's in Sweden. At a conference. He won't be back until the weekend. But I'll come."

Robin stood up. "Mom?"

Her mother ignored her. Her fingers found a pencil on the small desk beneath a chalkboard used for lists. She wrote something on a pad of paper. She said, "I'll be there as soon as I can."

When she turned back to face her three children, it was as if, for just a moment, she had no idea who they were.

Iris, oddly enough, was the one to offer helpful advice. "Mom. Take a deep breath."

Her words seemed to break the spell. Susanna actually took a deep breath. She flashed a smile at her youngest daughter. "Thank you, Iris. Children, that was Mass General hospital. Henry is—ill. He's ingested a complicated mix of drugs—he's okay now, physically. I need to go there right away." But she didn't move.

Robin said, "I'll go with you, Mom."

"Let me think. I need someone to stay home and take care of Iris."

Iris objected. "I can take care of myself!"

James offered, "I'll come with you, Mom."

Susanna studied James for a moment and all the children knew she was pondering the possibility that while she was gone, James would pull more adolescent stunts. Robin had always been the practical, reliable, sensible one. Everyone in the room knew this.

"I think I need Robin with me," Susanna said.

So there it was: if Susanna needed Robin, the news about Henry was very bad. Her children were given a view of their mother they almost never saw, the face of a woman tormented with indecision, anxiety, and fear.

"I need to leave as soon as possible. James, can I leave you in charge of the house and Iris?"

"Sure." The look he gave his mother was a guarantee of his best behavior.

"Thank you," Susanna said. To Robin, she said, "Get your purse and any extra money you have—we might need it for a cab. We can't take time to stop at an ATM. Let's go."

Robin gently pointed out: "Okay, Mom, but I'm dressed and you're not."

Susanna didn't even smile. She looked down at her body in its pajama bottoms and T-shirt as if she had never seen it before. "I'll dress. Call the airport, reserve a flight on the next plane to Boston."

"Maybe we should pack in case we have to spend the night," Robin suggested.

Susanna blinked. Her jaw fell open. She looked completely helpless.

"Mom." James, who was already taller than his mother, gently urged her into a chair. "Drink some of your coffee. Tell us who that was who called. What did they say?"

Obediently, Susanna sipped her coffee. "Dean Winters," she said slowly. "He said Henry was found on the grounds of the university in the middle of the night, bleeding from a cut in his arm, and"—she tilted her head down, averting herself from the word she finally managed to whisper—"raving. Henry was raving. He was incoherent, inebriated, and probably full of drugs. They don't yet know what kind. They don't know where he got the drugs or alcohol from."

James made a noise. "Mom, it's Cambridge. Anybody can get anything in that town if they want to."

"They tried to help him settle down . . ." Susanna's eyes widened, filling with tears. She wrapped her arms around herself as if she'd suddenly caught a chill. "They had to—" A low moan gusted from her throat. "They had to put him on a stretcher in an ambulance. They strapped him down."

Iris burst into tears. Robin hurried to wrap consoling arms around her sister.

"Hey." James's voice was calm but as powerful as their father's. "Think of people hit in car accidents. Women who've fallen in the streets and broken their ankles. Everybody who goes in an ambulance gets strapped down. It's no big deal."

Susanna lifted hopeful eyes to her second son. "Really?"

"Really." James wrapped an arm around his mother's shoulders. "You're doing it again, going straight for the worst-case scenario. Is that all they know? Is that all they told you?"

Susanna nodded numbly.

"Okay, well, maybe Henry had some LSD and is having a bad trip. Everyone tries LSD sooner or later." Immediately, James said, "I haven't. I won't. I'm not saying Henry did. Maybe he just got shit-faced drunk."

It was almost more than Robin could bear—seeing her competent mother nearly paralyzed. She took charge. "Come on, Mom, let's pack for overnight and get to the airport. James, make reservations now. Iris, make us each a bag of munchies for our purses. We don't know when we'll get the chance to eat." Robin didn't care about eating ever again in her life, but she knew it would relieve Iris to be part of the solution, not to stand helplessly watching.

Robin followed her mother up to her room. Susanna looked around in confusion.

"I don't know what to wear. It's kind of funny, isn't it? They never covered this in motherhood manuals: What to wear to visit your son in the loony bin." Susanna tried to laugh.

On Nantucket, Susanna had developed a wardrobe much like all the island mothers who spent their days driving children to football games or play rehearsals. Jeans, a white button-down shirt, sneakers, an L.L.Bean vest. For going out to a casual event, jeans, a crisp white button-down shirt, and a Hermes scarf. Less casual: a cashmere sweater and pearls. Low-heeled shoes because of Nantucket's cobblestoned streets.

"Put on your navy wool suit with a white shirt," Robin told her. "It's almost Thanksgiving. It might be cold up there." As she spoke, she dug out her mother's Lilly Pulitzer duffel bag. Moving efficiently, she put in her mother's pajamas, some clean underwear, a white T-shirt, and a colorful wool shawl. "Mom, get your toothbrush and face cream and stuff like that. I'm going to go to my room and change. I'll be ready in five minutes."

As Robin and her mother waited at the airport for the next flight to Boston, they paced the floor together, unable to speak, caught in a helpless fluster of distress, like bees batting at a window screen.

"I'll phone home and see if anyone else has called with an update on Henry," Robin said to her mother.

"Oh, what a good idea. I'll do it!" Susanna hurried off to the pay phones.

For a moment, Robin was miffed. It was her idea after all. Yet she knew it would be helpful for Susanna to do something, anything. As if she could somehow be useful.

Susanna came back. "Mass General called. Henry's been transferred to McLean's. And Jacob Barnes phoned. He's Henry's best friend. You remember him, he's stayed here before. He was the one who alerted the campus health service about Henry. He's driving out to McLean's after his last class."

"Jacob Barnes? Is he the short fat one we met at lunch when we were up in Cambridge in October?" Robin knew she would get a rise out of her mother and she did.

"What a terrible way to describe that perfectly nice young man!" reprimanded Susanna. "That's not like you at all, Robin."

Robin breathed a sigh of relief. Her real mother was still there, hiding behind the zombie.

The flight to Boston took forty-five minutes. Robin suggested they rent a car instead of taking a cab because who knew how long they would stay in Boston. They were given a small gray Toyota sedan. The kind rental clerk asked if they would like a map but Susanna assured him she knew the area well. Once Susanna was behind the wheel of the car, she became more alert and in charge. In the passenger seat, Robin breathed a sigh of relief. She was sixteen. She could drive, but she didn't possess a driver's license. Boston traffic was infamous and after the narrow, lazy lanes of the island, the route to Belmont was almost futuristic in its complexity and velocity.

More than that, right now she wanted her mother to get back into her supermom self. The division of labor in their family had always been crystal clear: their father provided the funds to run their large household. Susanna was in charge of everything else, especially the welfare of the children. Many years had passed when the four Vickerey children had whined to their mother, But why can't Dad come watch me in my ballet recital, or baseball game, or father and daughter school dinner, or award ceremony, and had received the same reply: You know your father is a very important surgeon. He is saving lives. If he can't come, it's because he's operating on a person right now, saving someone's life. You should be proud of your father. And I'm here.

Sooner or later, each of the children learned not even to bother asking the question. They saw their father on holidays and often at dinner in the evening and sometimes he actually paid attention to them, but mostly he was preoccupied with his own medical thoughts. Robin didn't hate her father but she didn't love him, either. Did she want him to be different? Even the question was encased in guilt. Did that mean she didn't care if people lived or died? How selfish was she?

By now, at sixteen, she had seen enough of life and other people's families to know that it was probably a good thing that their father was in Sweden at a conference today. Any kind of family difficulties sent him into a kind of hypertensive, red-faced, barely controlled rage. He did not like to be interrupted. More than that, he didn't like being told what to do. He was uncomfortable unless he was the authority in the room. Henry was his oldest son, off-the-charts intelligent, and planning to follow in his father's footsteps as a surgeon. Henry had always excelled at everything. Their father would not be amused to find his son shuttled off to a mental institution.

At the hospital, Susanna pulled into a parking space, shut off the motor, and put the keys in her purse.

Then she sat frozen, staring straight ahead.

"Mom?" Robin prompted.

Susanna cleared her throat. "I'm sorry to tell you this. I know a mother should be strong. But I need you to be aware that I might pass out in there. All my life I've been terrified of entering any place where doors lock behind me. It's ridiculous, I suppose, but I've always been certain that if I went into a prison or a mental hospital, once I got in, they would never let me out."

For the first time, Robin wished James were in the car. He had the kind of oddball humor that would turn their mother's fears into laughter.

"You'll be fine, Mom." Robin tossed off the words automatically. She wanted to get to Henry.

Susanna didn't move, except for the trembling of her hands.

Possibly that was the moment, sitting in a rented car on a late November day, that Robin, aged sixteen, became an adult. Until that moment, she had unconsciously assumed that her mother was nearly superhuman. Susanna dealt with scrapes, cuts, and bloody noses with effortless competence. Diaper rash, eczema, black eyes, high fever, stomach flu, middle school broken hearts, and chaotic birthday parties with a wild-eyed herd of nine-year-old boys, all that was a walk in the park for Susanna. She gloried in it.

But this.

Henry.

Not a simple case of a college sophomore getting drunk with friends. Not an accidental overdose of NoDoz before exams. Something more serious, something that had brought Henry here. No one had yet said he was in a locked ward, so the dean had told his mother or Susanna had guessed.

And what she had guessed had nearly turned her to stone with fright.

What could Robin do? She put her hand on her mother's shoulder and said, "I'm here."

Susanna nodded. "Thank you, darling."

In the main building, they were directed to another building, where they were shown to someone's office where they sat waiting for Dr. Someone—they were told the name only once and it blurred in their minds—to appear. He arrived, shook hands, sat at his desk, pulled out a folder. An attractive man, middle-aged, gray-hair cut close to his head, a wedding ring.

"Henry Vickerey. Alastair Vickerey's son, right? And Dr. Vickerey is at a conference in Sweden. Ahem. First of all, Henry will be fine, physically. He was found on the grounds of the college at two in the morning, brought here. Blood alcohol: 0.27. Irregular heartbeat. Low body temperature. Tox screens showed a mix of Benadryl, Valium, and Ecstasy in his blood."

"Ecstasy," Susanna whispered, horrified.

The physician made a kind face. "Ecstasy is not that bad. Lots of kids take it. It's not heroin. Not cocaine. Not meth. In Henry's case, the mix of alcohol and drugs caused his collapse. The hospital administered charcoal to induce vomiting."

"So he's okay?" Susanna whispered.

"He's going to be fine, physically. He's exhausted from the experience, from the vomiting. Emotionally, psychologically—that's why he was brought here. We need to ascertain whether this was an accident or a suicide attempt."

"It wasn't a suicide attempt!" Robin said angrily. "Henry would never do that."

Her mother made a slight whimpering sound. She put her hand to her throat.

"Henry's friend, Valerie Whitman—" The psychiatrist paused for them to indicate whether or not they knew her.

"Yes, of course, Valerie stays with us during the summer," Robin quickly informed him.

"She told us what I'm sure she'll tell you, so it is not confidential information. Your son has been seeking help at the university therapy clinic."

Susanna cried out, "Why?"

"We don't know. Henry didn't tell Valerie. At this point, he's not talking."

"Not talking?" Susanna echoed.

"He won't speak to us."

"I want to see him," Susanna said.

"Of course." The doctor rose. "Come with me."

Numbly, Robin and Susanna followed the doctor out of the building and into another building. He spoke with a woman at a desk, who directed them down the hall to another office.

"This is Philip Wiseman," the doctor said. "He's in charge of your son's case. He'll provide the information you need, and he'll be the contact person for you while Henry remains in the hospital."

Philip Wiseman was around forty, with a shaved head, gold-rimmed glasses, and a goatee. He held out his hand for both Susanna and Robin to shake.

"I'll be taking you into the ward where Henry is at present. Don't be alarmed that he's in a locked ward. Until he allows us to discover whether or not he is a danger to himself, this ward is where he needs to be. Henry is stonewalling us—not unusual. You should be prepared that he might not speak to either of you. Also, at this moment, Henry does not have the reserves to handle your emotions. If possible, try to be positive."

"Please," Susanna said, "just let us see him."

"Of course. Come with me." The counselor led them down a hallway to a door with a glass window that had a grid of wire between the two panes. He slid a card key chained to his belt in the slot and the door opened with a loud buzzing noise.

Susanna and Robin followed the counselor inside. The door slammed behind them and Robin understood her mother's fears. They were trapped.

They were standing in another corridor with doors on either side. Philip Wiseman led them to a door, knocked sharply, and opened the door.

Inside, on a bed, Henry lay, fully clothed, except that instead of his shirt he wore a hospital gown. His eyes were closed and his arms were folded tightly over his chest. He was very pale. He was a block of marble.

Robin stayed by the door while her mother went to the bed, sat on the edge, and put her hand lightly on her son's hand.

"Henry. We're so glad you're safe." When Henry didn't respond with so much as a blink, she continued, "Robin's here with me. James stayed home to take care of Iris, and of course Daddy is in Sweden. We got the phone call this morning. Robin and I flew up at once. Darling, I'm so sorry you had this—episode. You know we will all do anything we can to help you. You know we love you." Susanna's voice broke.

Henry did not respond. Robin could see the rise and fall of his chest. Once he moved his arms slightly; behind his closed eyes he was awake.

Taking the other side of the bed, Robin sat down next to her brother, her beloved, wonderful big brother. She adored him, and he knew it, and she knew he adored her. She could get a smile out of him. She knew she could.

"Hey, Henry. It's me, Robin, in case you can't tell with your eyes closed." No reaction. Not even a twitch. "You're so full of surprises. I thought stunts like this were James's specialty." No response.

Robin chewed her lip, thinking desperately, fighting back a terrible fear. It was a moment like one of those nightmares where a train is coming straight at you and you wake up gasping. If this silent, obstinate guy pretending to be Henry didn't care about Robin's feelings—couldn't force himself to open his eyes and tell her it would all be okay—if that was true, then her world had changed forever.

One more time. One more try. Robin leaned close, put her hand on his arm, and whispered, "Come on, Henry, help me out here. Tell us what happened. We know you've been drunk before. You know I've been drunk before—don't tell Mom."

Her attempt at humor didn't work. Despair rushed through her and it was almost angrily that she said, "Henry. I love you. We all love you."

Henry didn't respond. Behind Robin, Philip Wiseman cleared his throat.

Robin turned hopelessly to the counselor. Tears blurred her eyes.

Philip Wiseman said calmly, "We should let Henry rest. I assume Dr. Gardner explained that we would like to keep Henry here to evaluate him. This is up to him, of course. He is free to go whenever he feels ready."

Robin looked at her mother. "Mom, we can take Henry home!"

"I don't think Henry wants to come home now, Robin," her mother said quietly.

Frantic, Robin joked, "Okay, Henry, it's up to you. Blink once if you want to leave here. Blink twice if you want to stay."

Henry didn't blink. Robin choked back a sob.

"Henry," Susanna said, kneeling next to the bed and speaking quietly. "Robin and I are going to stay in the Boston apartment tonight. We'll keep in touch with Mr. Wiseman and if at any time you want us to come pick you up, we will. You know we will. It might be that this hospital is a good place for you to be right now. It might even be that people in this hospital can help you in ways that I can't. I trust the professionals here at this hospital. You are in good hands. Don't rush. Remember, we love you."

Henry didn't blink. Robin stared at her mother in awe. Somehow, from deep within, Susanna had managed to find, if not the perfect words—in this event, there were no perfect words—the best words possible.

Susanna leaned forward and lightly kissed her son on his forehead. "Take care. See you soon."

"It's been great talking to you, Henry." Robin couldn't resist one last

attempt at humor. She wanted him to know that she still thought he—
her Henry—was there, in that immovable body, somewhere.

"We'll let you rest," Philip Wiseman said to Henry. He ushered Robin
and her mother out of the room and into the corridor.

They walked down the hall. Philip Wiseman magically opened the
terrible door and they were set free. At his desk, he took Susanna's
Boston phone number. "You said exactly the right things. Sometimes a
good rest is what a person needs."

Susanna shook the counselor's hand and the two women went out
into the sunshine. When they reached the rental car, they got inside.
Robin looked over at her mother.

Susanna began to cry in a way Robin had never seen her cry. She
laid her arms on the steering wheel and rested her head on her arms
and sobbed while her shoulders shook.

That had been thirteen years ago. For thirteen years, Henry had wrestled with his bipolar demon. Psychiatrists helped, therapists helped,
medications helped. Valerie helped. After he entered med school, his
intense concentration on work and the praise he got from his teachers
had seemed to pacify the ogre within him. Robin's parents had helped
her understand how to cope with Henry in all his states, and most of
all, they helped her understand that Henry was not her charge; she was
not responsible for him.

What her parents couldn't deny was that being bipolar was genetic.
It was in her parents' genes, it was in Henry's temperament, and to a
lesser or greater degree, it was in her own psychological makeup as
well. So far, Iris seemed untouched by it. James, Robin thought, could
be an idiot, but she didn't see any signs of the disorder in him.

And in *herself*? She read and read about the illness, about the way
the mind worked, and heaven knew she heard enough of it at the dinner table, with her father, who was, after all, a surgeon, holding forth
on every possible medical glitch. Still, she couldn't make up her mind
about herself. She knew she *appeared* untouched, *normal*.

But no one knew about her secret passion and the risks she took to satisfy it. If she told anyone, she'd be forced to stop. So she kept her secret close to her heart, even though it terrified her as much as it elated her.

Focus on now, she reminded herself. Focus on the fabulous fact that she was driving her old Jeep to the Hy-Line ferry to pick up Courtney, who was arriving for another summer. This weekend was Susanna's birthday, and there were a million things to do to prepare. Robin was good at parties; all would go well. And Henry would be all right.

3

Courtney stayed on deck as the ferry slowed. They were gliding into the harbor, rounding Brant Point with its squat lighthouse, wending between sloops, motorboats, and launches. Gulls swooped, mallards splashed, and black cormorants unfolded their wings like banners. It all began: the grand mansions facing the harbor, the green sweep of the yacht club lawn, the gleam of steeples and windows, the lush towers of trees. Great white yachts awaited their captains while smaller boats bobbed near blue stanchions. The ferry slid into its berth. Crowds of people in bright summer clothing waved from the pier.

All around Courtney, people scrambled to gather their belongings and hurry to the exit ramp. Courtney remained in place. The summer boats were always crowded. She had no reason to rush. If this were to be her last summer here, she wanted to savor every moment.

She gazed down at the redbrick dock and the waiting crowd, searching for her best friend.

Robin. With her pale freckled skin, her appearance was unusual, especially because Robin had the Vickerey profile, too—that slight, charming overbite caused by her two front teeth just a millimeter too large. Susanna, the mother, was also tall, red-haired, and athletic, but without the overbite. Still, she could pass for her husband's sister. They were striking, the Vickereys, athletic and easy in their bodies, powerful, graceful. When the family got together, all six of them, it was impossible to deny the authority of DNA.

DNA—the crux of the matter. The hidden golden loop, part blessing, part curse. The Vickerey family couldn't deny the presence of the family's genetic kink. It was most obvious and troubling in their oldest son.

In the early years, when Courtney first spent the summers working on Nantucket, Henry and Valerie, three years older, might as well have been in their forties. They were so different, so adult, so aloof. While Courtney was drifting around memorizing grammatical terms, Henry and Valerie were med students at Harvard Medical School in Boston. They lived in the real life-or-death world, and when they escaped to the island in the summer, they crashed, sleeping, exhausted. Over the years, Courtney got to know them both a bit, enough to see that Valerie was the calm one, intelligent and industrious, her energy a steady light.

Henry was the shooting star, the volcano, his mind like the sky on the Fourth of July. It helped that his father was a surgeon, that he'd learned concepts like *hyperplasia* at the dining room table. But that couldn't explain the speed of his mind, the startling leaps of deduction when diagnosing, or the intense, nearly superhuman focus he could bring when working on a surgical procedure. With his younger siblings, Henry was kind in an absentminded way, as if they were household pets, docile and somewhat interchangeable. Robin, James, and Iris worshipped him, grateful for the slightest smile he tossed their way. Valerie was nicer. She remembered their names and she remembered Courtney's name, too, and asked about her college work. When they all ate together at the dining room table, Valerie often mimicked Henry, sending the entire table into howls of laughter. Henry was so preoccupied he didn't even notice.

•   •   •

One summer Henry spontaneously organized an all-night picnic on the fifth point of the long sand bar at the end of Nantucket. A pack of Vickereys and their friends sailed to Coatue with bags of munchies, coolers of beer, soda, and wine. That was a night Courtney would always remember—the full moon rising over the ocean, the sand transmuted to silver by the high August moonlight, Henry's CD player blasting out wild music as they all danced barefoot around a small, and illegal, fire, the laughter, the singing, the twinkling lights of town in the distance, the ridiculous hilarity of peeing in the bushes, wading out into the warm water, lying on her back, idly kicking her feet, floating free in the water in the exotic *dark,* knowing she was young and free and among fabulous friends.

When Courtney went to Nantucket that Christmas vacation, Henry insisted they all had to dive into the cold Atlantic to welcome the new year. Fewer summer children were there. Iris was still a kid and hadn't started college or met Pearl yet; she was tucked up in bed with a cold. But James was there, and Robin, Christabel, and Valerie. At eleven-thirty, they began making their way down the steps on the bluff. It was very cold. Snow coated the handrails, steps, and beach. When they reached the bottom, Henry handed around open bottles of champagne to give them all courage. They'd been eating, drinking, and playing foolish games all night, so they were already silly with laughter. At five till midnight, Henry held up his wrist with its gleaming waterproof watch: "Clothes off NOW!" he shouted. They stripped off their coats, hats, gloves, and boots, their dresses or slacks and shirts, until they were all hopping up and down on the icy sand, shivering with cold, wearing only their underwear. "HAPPY NEW YEAR!" Henry shouted, and led them racing into the cold foamy waves and plunging into the dark frigid water.

People shrieked. All around Courtney, bodies became blurs of dark movement as they thrashed out into the indescribable, searing, breathtaking cold. Frantically, with numb limbs, she swam to shore and staggered up toward her clothes.

"Here." James held up her coat and wrapped it around her.

For one ecstatic, surprising moment, Courtney was in James's arms, feeling the warmth of the coat and the strength of his embrace. *He sought me*, she thought, as a delirious hope flared inside her.

"James, help me!" Christabel stumbled toward him, arms clutching her thin torso for warmth. "I can't find my coat."

And the moment vanished. James found Christabel's coat. He handed it to Christabel; he did not wrap it around her as he had with Courtney. Courtney noticed that and cherished the image in her heart. But quickly Christabel had shoved herself against James. "Put your arms around me! I'm freezing!"

Henry continued to swim in the glacial water, stroking far away from shore. All the others had returned, gasping, shuddering, and screaming at Henry to come back. When he did swim back and walk up to them, he held his arms out triumphantly.

"I am Henry Vickerey, master of land, air, and water!" he shouted. "The universe is wide and far, and I am its most shining star, I spend my light on all who trust, and conjure magic out of dust!"

This was not the first time Henry had gotten grandiose and poetic, certainly not the first time Courtney had witnessed it. For a few moments, he *was* gleaming and magic, but Courtney knew how quickly he would become repetitive and boring. She gathered up her clothes and scurried barefoot up the wooden steps to the warmth of the house. She heard Valerie, remaining on the beach, pleading with Henry to put on his coat, cajoling him to calm down, go up to the house, and celebrate the new year there. When she reminded him the rest of the champagne was in the house, Henry finally conceded.

When Henry was good, he was very very good. He organized scavenger hunts that taught them the history of the island as they raced around in pairs searching for the clues. He prepared marvelous clambakes on the beach and dance parties in the house with a live island band. When he took the time to focus on Courtney, he *got* her, telling her about the vices of the authors she was studying, quoting Coleridge or Lamb as if his mind was a computerized encyclopedia. He brought his mother flowers.

But when he was bad, he was horrid.

The times he was depressed weren't the worst times, at least not for most of the family. Henry would gradually slump into a kind of adolescent contempt with the world, not bothering to answer when spoken to except in monosyllables. He'd refuse to eat, or swim, or play a board game. Courtney could almost see the light inside him dimming, as if his dazzling good humor were set on a sliding switch. Then Henry would subside into his bedroom, not coming out for days. Susanna or Valerie would slip quietly into the room, carrying a glass of iced tea or a plate with a sandwich on it. The house would fall quiet. It was restful. Courtney had blithely assumed it was restful for Henry, as well.

But some days, which Courtney came to recognize were during Henry's ascent into a manic state, he would buttonhole Courtney as she cleaned up the kitchen or folded laundry, describing to her with wild excitement a new surgical discovery or the historic decision to use ligation or emollients instead of cauterization to mitigate bleeding from wounds on the battlefield. Courtney could scarcely understand one word out of five. That didn't matter. Any live person became his designated audience, so no matter how she moved around a room, Henry would track her, talking incessantly, trying to make her meet his eyes, shoving his face toward hers. Usually, after a while, Valerie or Susanna would rescue her, and then Henry would monopolize them, ranting exuberantly, waving his arms, shouting.

"Sorry about that," Robin told Courtney one day. "Henry's getting manic again."

"Aren't there medications for that?" Courtney asked.

"Yeah, but they have side effects. I've learned to keep away from him when he's like this. Just walk away, leave the room, shut a door in his face. You can't hurt his feelings."

"You're very relaxed about this," Courtney remarked.

"I've lived with him all my life, remember? I'm used to him. Don't look so worried. I'm not manic-depressive. I'm almost tediously normal."

"I wouldn't say tedious." Courtney paused. "How about James?"

"What? You think he's manic-depressive?"

"He certainly gets involved in all kinds of tomfoolery."

"Tomfoolery." Robin smirked. "No one uses that word on the East Coast, darlin'. Why? Are you interested in James?"

"Don't be silly," Courtney answered.

But of course she had been interested. She had been in love. What was that expression? *Madly in love.*

For eleven years, Courtney had seen how this inherited knot unraveled itself in the oldest child, Henry, and maybe in James, a year younger than Robin and Courtney. Iris, the youngest daughter and baby of the family, so far appeared unhampered by the gene. Robin, too, seemed to have escaped it, although she was an unusual person. Very secretive, even from Courtney. Number 10 on her list of why she, Courtney, was returning for the summer—numbers one through nine were all about James—was that Courtney wanted to find out what it was that made Robin so determined not to leave the island.

Now she had arrived. Now it could all begin.

The passengers filed down the ramp off the boat, onto shore. The Hy-Line workers rushed back and forth, pulling the heavy blue-curtained luggage racks from the hold and into line in front of the children's shop, The Toy Boat, tucked away in one of the old fisherman's shacks next to a couple of T-shirt shops. Courtney picked up her backpack from the blue plastic seat and made her way through the cabin to the stairs down to the lower deck. A man in Nantucket red slacks with a Labradoodle on a leash was ahead of her. The ramp to shore was steep today, because the tide was out.

Then the familiar bliss of arriving—Robin rushing to hug her, crowds milling around looking for their luggage, the sudden internal adjustment to stable land after the rocking boat, the stream of unadulterated sunshine on Courtney's shoulders, a sense of *beginning*. The beginning of summer!

"Let's get your luggage," Robin said, tugging Courtney's hand.

Most of the racks were emptied now. Suitcases thump-thump-thumped as passengers pulled them toward taxis and cars. People talked and kissed and laughed. Dogs barked.

Courtney spotted her two big cases on a rack at the end, headed toward them, yanked them onto the ground, and lifted the handles.

"Give me one," Robin demanded. Charging ahead of Courtney, she led her down the wharf, past the island tour buses, past Straight Wharf Restaurant and the gazebo, and left, past Old South Wharf, down to Commercial Wharf where one of the Vickereys' old Jeeps was squeezed into a parking spot. Lifting the hatch, she hefted Courtney's case in. Courtney tossed in her other suitcase and backpack. Robin slammed the hatch shut.

"Okay? Get in. Let's go!" She hopped in the driver's seat, fastened her seatbelt, and back-and-forthed the Jeep out of its spot. "The house is a *carnival*. My fault, I suppose. But it's Mom's sixtieth birthday, and she's taken care of everyone else forever. I want to give her a fabulous weekend she'll always remember. So lots of people are coming."

"I'm glad," Courtney said. "A crowd is the perfect present for Susanna. She wouldn't be impressed with diamonds or cruises." Courtney adored Susanna for the way she made everyone feel at home, as if Susanna were a mother hen, sweeping even the most gawky or grumpy chick into her warm, affectionate embrace. Courtney had wanted to be like Susanna even before she met her—she'd always dreamed of having lots of children, and now as an adult she could see that she could have that, she could have both of her dreams come true: a large family and a job teaching English in college. She imagined herself curled up in a fat chair beneath the warm glow of a lamp, reading *The Once and Future King* and Robert Frost's poetry to her children.

"You'll be with me in my room for the weekend, by the way." Robin broke into Courtney's reverie as she steered the Jeep into the stream of traffic on Washington Street. "Sorry about that, but Mom's cousin and her husband are coming, so we have to squeeze in. Iris will have Pearl with her, which will undoubtedly make that spoiled little New York miss shudder, having to actually share a room. James's got two friends bunking with him—you know he's home for the summer, right?" Without waiting for an answer, Robin continued, "Henry's living in the apartment over the garage. Which is a pit, I've got to tell you. When he gets home from the hospital, he falls fully dressed on his bed and sleeps a hundred hours, then showers, stumbles down to eat whatever we'll fix for him, and goes back to work. Two other of Mom's old friends recently emailed they're coming. I think Quinn has offered to put them up, but Mom wants them in the house with her, so I don't know what they'll do."

"Is Susanna loving this?" Courtney asked when Robin paused for breath.

"You know her, she loves a party, as long as it's not for her. She hates being the cause of such a fuss."

"She'll be happy when everyone gets here."

"Maybe. She's a royal pain right now. When she found out we've booked a tent and a band, she totally freaked. She's insisting on making her own birthday cake!"

"Susanna does make fabulous cakes," Courtney reminded Robin.

"Yeah, but making her own cake for a grand slam sixtieth birthday? That's demented. She wanted to cook the dinner, too, a formal dinner for a hundred people, are you kidding me?"

"It's not like she hasn't done that a thousand times—"

"But we told her we'd already hired caterers and it was a done deal, *shut up*. So this is, what, Thursday, and the party's Saturday night, but guests start arriving tomorrow—"

Courtney smiled to herself. Courtney was not a *guest*. She was one of Susanna's summer children. She asked, "Is Henry back with Valerie?"

"No. Breaks my heart. Henry's got a new girlfriend now, a nurse named Lisa. She's been dating him for two or three weeks. Poor girl, she's got a lot to learn."

"Valerie . . . ?"

"Valerie still refuses to marry him unless he tries the lithium Dr. Olson suggests."

"That's really sad. They've been together for fifteen years."

"I know. She's put up with him through all sorts of meltdowns and medications. But she really wants him to try lithium."

"Why doesn't he take it? He must hate these black moods as much as everyone else does."

"The side effects. Lithium can cause trembling of the hands. Just think what *that* would mean for a surgeon. Also, impaired memory, unsteady gait, confusion, vomiting, diarrhea—you can understand why he won't risk it."

"But those are only *possible* side effects, right?" Courtney pressed.

"Right. But he's stubborn."

"You Vickereys are extremely stubborn." Courtney knew this from experience, from her conversation—her argument—with James last year.

"Valerie is, too. She won't take his calls, won't see him."

"So he's started dating Lisa?"

"Lisa's a very nice girl. She's a nurse. Pretty, too. My guess is Henry wants to remind Valerie she's got competition."

"Henry and Valerie are both working at Nantucket Cottage Hospital?"

"Yeah, but he's a surgeon in the ER and Valerie's a general practitioner. Different hours. Crazy hours for Henry, car wrecks, nighttime heart attacks, and with summer coming, there will be moped crashes and surfing accidents and all that. That's Henry's reason for living over the garage. He says in the winter he'll buy himself a house here, but he's probably hoping by then Valerie will have changed her mind."

Courtney nodded. "So who are *you* inviting to the party?"

"Well, duh, *you*."

"You know very well what I mean."

Robin shifted uncomfortably in her seat. She glanced in her rearview mirror, as if checking the traffic, as if she needed to on this seven-mile two-lane road out to 'Sconset and the bluff where the Vickereys' house overlooked the ocean. The speed limit on this road was forty-five miles per hour, the fastest speed allowed on the island.

Courtney let her question hang in the air.

After a moment, Robin admitted, "I didn't invite a date. I'll pair up with Jacob."

"Jacob Barnes? Henry's friend? I thought he got married."

"He did. Then he got divorced."

Courtney laughed. "I'd love to see your mother's address book." Courtney knew she was letting Robin off easy, but this wasn't the time for a good ol' heart-to-heart. Courtney would have the whole summer to find out what was up with Robin and this year she was determined to succeed. "How's Christabel?"

"She's having an exhibition of her paintings in Boston this August. She's become very drifty in gauzy gowns and bare feet."

"She always was very drifty in gauzy gowns and bare feet. When is she going to grow up?"

"Why should she? This medieval maiden persona works well for her."

Robin waved her hand at the main street of the small picturesque town of 'Sconset. A straight avenue of lush lawns and large houses, with distinguished old elms and maples towering on either side, their green leaves arching toward each other, forming a canopy of shade. "How does it look?"

"Like heaven." Courtney sighed.

They came to the world's smallest rotary by the post office and the Sconset Café.

"Robin?" She turned to face her friend. "Could we drive down to the beach first? I want to tell you something, and I don't want to be interrupted."

Robin arched an eyebrow. "Well, that's intriguing."

She wrenched the steering wheel to the right and headed down the hill. She parked in the small lot by the beach, switched off the engine, and looked at Courtney, squinting her eyes as if she could read Courtney's mind.

"Ready to hear your confession, babe."

"It's not a *confession*," Courtney said, quickly adding, "but it *is* a secret. It just happened, and I'm—disturbed—and I don't want anyone to know about it except you."

"Well, *tell* me!" Robin ordered.

Courtney took a deep breath. "Okay. You know Monty Blackhorse."

"The man I met last April when I came out to Kansas to visit you? The sexiest man I've ever set eyes on? Yes, Courtney, duh. I do know

Monty Blackhorse. I'd go to bed with him in a minute if—" Robin gasped. "Oh my god, did you sleep with Monty? Are you pregnant?"

"Stop it," Courtney said. "It's nothing like that. Well, it is *something* like that . . ."

"You're torturing me."

"Monty asked me to marry him this morning!"

Robin's jaw fell open. "Get out of here."

"He did, Robin. It was totally unexpected, and *no*, I haven't slept with him, he's always been my friend, my *pal*." She undid her seatbelt so she could face Robin. "He phoned me last night and said he'd like to drive into Kansas City from his ranch today. He said he'd pick me up at my apartment and take me to the airport. I said sure, I mean, he often had to come into the airport to pick up shipments for the farm, feed or a tractor part . . ."

"Never mind the tractor part, what about Monty?"

"All right. He said he'd just broken off with another woman—Jackie Monroe, you should see her, she's gorgeous—and yesterday he realized he was never going to be happy with any woman because he's in love with *me*. He's been in love with me for years, he said, but we've been such good buddies, and we've both been so crazy busy in our lives, yet he's always felt something was missing in every relationship he's ever had, and what's missing is *me*. He loves me. He wants to marry me. He wants to have babies with me. *Lots* of babies." Tears filled her eyes. "You know I've always wanted to have lots of children."

"They don't have to be Monty's children!" Robin protested.

"I don't know," Courtney said sadly. "Maybe they do."

"I'm stunned," Robin said. "But, Courtney, for god's sake, you should have at least thought about it. You should have at least had sex with the man!"

"I had a plane to catch."

"You should have changed your reservations, you moron! Man, what an opportunity you missed."

"Robin, I don't *want* to have sex with him. We've been best buddies for so long. I mean, there are all kinds of love. I just don't feel that way about him."

"You're hopeless. All right, then, what did you tell Monty?"

"I told him I was absolutely shocked, that I cared for him, but I couldn't get my head around even the *thought* of marrying him. And then—" Courtney buried her face in her hands so her words came out muffled. "And then he kissed me."

"Was it wonderful?"

"It was—*confusing!*" When Courtney raised her head, her eyes were full of tears. "Robin, I love Monty so much, but he's my best old Kansas buddy. I can't even think about having sex with him."

"Maybe you need time to get used to the idea," Robin suggested.

"Oh, Robin." Courtney put her face back in her hands again, because she didn't want Robin to catch the slightest hint of her real feelings.

She didn't want Robin to know she was in love with James even though Robin *wanted* Courtney to be in love with James so they could be sisters-in-law, connected forever. And Courtney couldn't tell Robin about what had happened between her and James—she hadn't told anyone yet, it was all too precarious, like a dream that could vanish at any moment. Besides, Robin would get her hopes up, and she'd blab about it to Susanna and Iris, and she'd start nagging James, and it would become a Vickerey family drama and it would all be even more of a mess than it was now.

How could *love* cause her such a heavy burden of confusion and guilt?

"How did you leave it?" Robin asked.

Courtney reached into her purse for a tissue and wiped her eyes. "I told him I was flabbergasted, and flattered, too. I told him he had to give me time to think, that I'm spending the summer here, that I've never thought of him romantically, because he's always been my best friend." She smiled at Robin, adding, "My best *Kansas* friend. He said he's not in any hurry, he understands how I feel, but he knows we're right for each other. He reminded me that if I married him, I would be near my family and friends, and I could still teach at UMKC until I started having babies . . ." Courtney took a deep breath and said, as if surrendering, as if yielding, "He said with him I could have a happy, stable family."

Robin stared out at the ocean, surging and rolling up against the beach. "He's right, I guess. I mean, about all those positive benefits of marrying him. And gosh, you and I are both getting old. We're almost thirty. We're almost old maids." She turned back to Courtney. "But damn, I want you to live *here*."

Courtney said bleakly, "I'm from Kansas, remember? My family's there."

"And your other family's here."

Courtney started to object, but really, she felt it was true, that the Vickereys, all of them, were as much family to her as the people she'd been born to and grown up with. But that didn't mean she could move to the island just to be near them. "My job's in Kansas City."

"So teach here."

"There's a university on the island? I hadn't noticed."

Robin leaned over and wrapped her arms around Courtney. "You have to live here. I want you to."

Courtney said softly, "It isn't that easy." Restless, she shook herself away from Robin. "I don't want to talk about it anymore. I don't want to *think* about it anymore. Let's go home."

"*Home*," Robin echoed smugly. She turned the Jeep around and headed up the hill and around the rotary toward the bluff.

They drove slowly past the sweet little cottages already smothered with roses, and out and around until they were on Baxter Road, where the grand old summer houses rose from behind privet hedges, their chimneys and gables and widows' walks and second-floor dormers just visible. Strangers could imagine the view they had on the other side— the sweep of the blue Atlantic. Courtney knew the view well. Her knowledge was a treasure she clutched close to her heart.

When they arrived at the Vickereys' huge old house, Robin steered the battered Jeep between the hedges and up the driveway. Robin had often joked that someone could do a psychological evaluation of the people in the house by studying the vehicles in the driveway.

First, Dr. Vickerey's Jaguar, a sleek silver beast that he believed made people think he was famous, which he was in his field, and arrogant and dictatorial, which he wasn't. He was really a lot like Greta Garbo: he only *vanted to be alone*. His years of intense work as a surgeon at Mass General had left him exhausted, although not defeated, because Susanna, the love of his life, pampered and protected him. Made him take his blood pressure pills. Made him take them when he'd forgotten them or didn't realize he needed them.

He seldom drove the Jag. Apparently he simply enjoyed having it in the driveway.

Susanna Vickerey drove a much used Toyota minivan to haul around her ever-changing pack of passengers to the beach, the library, the ice cream shop, the boat, or the airport, and often to the emergency room.

At the back of the driveway, near the garage with Henry's apartment above it, sat Henry's 1969 Chevy Camaro convertible.

The moment Courtney glimpsed the Camaro, she was time-warped back to a day three years ago, when Courtney had flown into Boston from Kansas City to spend another summer on Nantucket. Robin had insisted that she would pick Courtney up and drive her to the Cape; Courtney should absolutely *not* take her usual mode of transportation, the reliable Plymouth & Brockton bus to the ferry.

When Courtney got to the baggage claim in Boston, she found Robin waiting for her, smiling ear to ear.

"What's going on?" Courtney demanded.

"Wait and see," Robin told her. Sliding a duffel bag over her shoulder and picking up a suitcase with the other hand, Robin led Courtney out of the terminal, across the busy lanes of traffic, and into the parking garage.

Henry was there, leaning against a bright blue, convertible Chevy Camaro, as American and groovy as any car could possibly be. Henry had just finished med school and rewarded himself by buying this American classic. It had been updated and repainted to make the wide white stripe down the front of the hood shine as white as snow against the glossy blue.

Stepping forward, he took Courtney's roll-on suitcase from her and hugged her hard. "I'm your chauffeur for the day," he announced.

"Is this your car?" Courtney was amazed.

Henry patted the car fondly. "It is. It's my present to myself for getting my MD. Like it?"

"It's amazing!"

"It's ridiculous," Robin teased. "Like he needs a muscle car on Nantucket where the fastest you can drive is forty-five miles per hour."

"That, dear sister, is why I offered to escort you to collect Courtney. And on the way, we're stopping at the Taj in Boston. I'm taking you both to lunch." Henry began piling Courtney's luggage in the trunk.

Courtney glanced at Robin, silently asking for reassurance: was Henry manic?

"No worries," Henry said, reading Courtney's mind. "I'm sane and stable. But I have a week off before I start my surgical internship on Nantucket, and I want to have fun."

"Where's Valerie?" Courtney asked as she squeezed into the back-seat of the car.

"Visiting her family in Connecticut for a week. She's going to start as a family practice intern at the hospital." Henry settled in behind the wheel. Looking over his shoulder, he asked, "Ready, girls?"

Henry had been so very much himself that day. Not manic, not depressed, but happy, relaxed, and proud of his achievements. He'd been amazingly unself-absorbed. At lunch, he'd asked Courtney how she liked teaching freshman English, what her apartment in Kansas City was like, if she'd gotten serious with any man in the past year, and he *listened* to her answers. Happiness was contagious that day. Henry's levelheaded composure made Robin glow with pleasure, and seeing both siblings calm and content filled Courtney with a quiet joy.

For so many summers, she had seen these two during good times and bad. She belonged to them in a way, and they belonged to her.

•   •   •

"Whose new Jeep?" she asked as she pulled her suitcase from the back hatch.

"James rented it for the summer. He wants to work from home as much as possible, and the Internet makes it possible."

A car she'd expected to see wasn't there: Christabel's geriatric, coughing, faded blue Citroën. Christabel loved that car. She'd had it retrofitted with seatbelts and the necessary lights, but the seats were old, flat as boards, and uncomfortable. Still, the car was unusual, if not unique, and Christabel identified with it.

Finally, Courtney looked past all the cars to the great rambling house she was about to enter. Her heart said, quite clearly: *Home*.

She shook it off. This was not her home. Not really.

At least, not yet.

Together Courtney and Robin hauled Courtney's luggage into the house and up the stairs to Robin's room. Robin had a large corner room, the biggest one on the second floor, and she'd arranged it like an apartment, with a desk at the window and a thirty-two-inch flat screen television perched on top of her ancient mahogany chest of drawers.

Courtney dropped her suitcase on the floor and flopped on the bed. She put her hand over her eyes. "Oooh. Give me a few moments. It always takes me a while to recover from motion sickness."

Robin unzipped Courtney's suitcase and started hanging her dresses. "Aren't you ever going to get over that?"

Courtney moaned. "Seasickness pills put me to sleep."

"Have you tried those wristbands?"

"Yep. They don't work for me. Not the electronic ones, either."

"But the seas were calm today."

"I know, but I can get motion sick riding when you drive." Courtney smothered a grin in the pillow.

"Ha ha." Robin dropped onto the bed next to Courtney, putting her hand on Courtney's forehead. "You're such a fragile flower."

The door flew open and Iris clomped in. The youngest Vickerey, just graduated from Smith, she wore a plaid flannel shirt and a batik skirt and clogs. Her purple hair was gelled and spiked. Her lipstick and nail polish were black.

"Hey, lesbos," she yelled, "get out of bed and come help with dinner."

"Lovely to see you again, too, Iris," Courtney said.

Iris threw herself down on the bed on Courtney's other side so the three women were squashed together. "Oh, did I hurt your feelings, my lil' ol' country mouse, my hillbilly honey, my Kansas cutiepie?" She smooched kisses all over Courtney's face, making Courtney giggle.

Courtney had met Iris when she was eleven. She'd seen her sweep through various transformations, personalities, hair, and clothing styles throughout the years. She'd watched Iris grow from sweet to silly to angry to intellectually contemptuous to peace-to-the-world loving. She had flown up for Iris's college graduation this May. Iris was the baby, the beauty, the family pet.

"Stop, stop." Courtney giggled. "You're tickling me."

Squashed between Robin and Iris on the twin bed, Courtney felt herself blend back into this family, so different from her own.

The first summer Courtney spent at the Vickereys after her freshman year at Smith, Iris had turned twelve, obsessed with fingernail polish and hair styles. Whenever Courtney wasn't working as a waitress at the Brant Point Grill, Iris used Courtney as her own living doll, trying to coax curls into Courtney's thick brown hair, painting Courtney's nails green with sparkles, begging Courtney to paint her own nails black or blue or yellow. If Courtney had a day off, she'd wake to find Iris in bed with her.

"Scratch my back," Iris would demand.

At night, when Courtney was drop-dead tired after a long day, Iris would open Courtney's bedroom door, walk into the room unannounced, and crawl into bed with her. She'd wrap her arms around Courtney. "Just keep your eyes closed. I'm going to rub your back and sing you a lullaby."

Iris was the most like Susanna, Courtney had decided. Iris loved people, was naturally happy and busy and buoyant. As she grew older, she went through all sorts of adolescent transformations, but she never exhibited any signs of the manic-depressive gene that shadowed the family.

"I'm so glad you're back home," Iris cooed at Courtney now, snuggling close to her, nearly lying on top of her. "I've missed you. Did you bring me anything?"

"Iris, for god's sake," Robin said, "you just turned twenty-three years old, you're not a kid."

Courtney allowed herself another moment of indulgence in this warm smash of sisterhood, soaking it all in like a vitamin.

Robin rolled off the bed and strolled over to Courtney's other suitcase. Iris went to study her reflection in the mirror. "I'm a college graduate," Iris announced, more to herself than anyone else. "I'm sophisticated now."

Robin snorted. "As you've just demonstrated."

Courtney sat up, smoothing her ruffled clothes and hair. "Is Pearl here?"

Pearl was Iris's best friend from Smith, a posh New Yorker, as cold as Iris was warm. *Go figure*, as Pearl often said.

"Tomorrow," Iris told them. "I'm picking her up at the airport." Clonking in her uber-eco clogs to the door, she said, "So we have to help with dinner. Come on."

4

Courtney had been in love with James from the first moment she saw him stomping in from the outdoor shower with a towel wrapped around his waist. True, James was a year younger than she was, but like all the Vickereys, he was tall, clever, and charismatic. And even that first year, when he'd just graduated from high school, he had the body of a man and a smile that made Courtney's heart gallop.

That first meeting, Courtney and Robin had just settled in for the summer. Valerie had gone for a run with manic Henry. Susanna had driven off to buy groceries. They always needed more groceries at the Vickerey house. Robin showed Courtney through the house—the washer and dryer, the kitchen and pantry, and all the rooms, including the basement where the fuse box was kept.

Robin and Courtney had dragged their stuff up to the bedrooms and unpacked. They were both giddy with excitement at being here, on the island, at the beginning of the summer. Tomorrow they'd start work at their jobs in town, and later today Courtney would borrow Iris's bike and follow Robin into town to get the fastest and safest route memorized. But for now everything was new and sparkling like the sun on the ocean. The day was hot and humid, but they stayed in their travel clothes—easy, loose summer dresses and sandals.

"Let's have some iced tea," Robin suggested. "Then we'll have a swim."

"In the ocean!" Courtney had squealed. "I've never swum in the ocean before."

"It will be cold," Robin warned her. "This side of the island it's always cold, but it will warm up over the summer."

They trotted down to the kitchen. Courtney took out the ice tray while Robin brewed a pot of peach tea. Robin had forgotten to show Courtney the outdoor shower, which many island houses had so people could rinse the sand off instead of tracking it into the house. So she was surprised when James entered the kitchen, dripping wet, nude except for a towel around his waist. The tall, red-haired, gorgeous hunk of man casually walked across the kitchen, picked Robin up right off her feet, and hugged her.

His towel slipped slightly, showing a section of untanned, muscular bum.

Courtney blinked. Her family was demonstrative, but not quite so flamboyant. Over the years, she came to learn about the Vickerey family's careless ways. They were all so active, so athletic, wet from swimming or sweating from tennis, in a hurry to get to a cookout—they didn't care, they didn't even seem to notice their state of dress. Or undress.

James was a year younger than Robin and Courtney. He'd just graduated from high school. He'd gotten his physical growth early, so at six foot two, he towered over the women. Even in early June, he was already tanned, his long muscular limbs burnished by the sun, his red hair sun-streaked with blond.

"Hey," he said to his sister as he set her back on the floor, "who's this?"

"Courtney. My roomie from Smith. She's going to live with us this summer."

"Well, all right." James cocked his head and gave Courtney a frank head to toe inspection.

Robin slapped James on his muscular hairy chest. "Stop it. She's way out of your league, sonny."

Courtney thought, For sure. She was a Shetland pony. James was a Lipizzaner stallion.

James nodded to Courtney. "Hey."

Her throat was dry. "Hey," she managed to squeak back.

"So you're joining us in the madhouse for the summer, right?"

"James." Robin almost growled.

James grinned his sideways "gotcha" grin, and left the room. Courtney and Robin were left in a bubble of stillness as they listened to him take the stairs to the second floor, two steps at a time.

"Wow," Courtney breathed.

"He's an idiot," Robin told her.

"Is he—like Henry?"

"You mean manic-depressive? The jury's still out on that one. He certainly pulls a lot of stupid stunts, especially when he's with Christabel. But hey, he's just graduated from high school. He's a child."

Eleven years ago, Courtney had kept her feelings for James strictly to herself. That first summer, she had been certain it was just a crush, like going all girlie gooey over a movie star. And she would have seemed like a nut job herself if she'd told Robin or anyone about her infatuation, because during the next four years, James had been like a typical frat boy buffoon, getting drunk at beach parties, missing his summer job because he woke up asleep in the sand without a ride home. When he was in college in Boston, he pulled stupid pranks like swimming across the Charles River with an inflatable Loch Ness Monster strapped to his back at five in the morning as the sun was rising. That had nearly caused a traffic accident on the Lars Anderson bridge and won James a misdemeanor charge with a thousand dollar fine.

James was bright, energetic, mischievous, but kind. Like all the Vickereys, he had a quirkily prodigious mind. In James's case, he had a rare facility for languages. The most athletic of his family, he won medals and silver cups for swimming and sailing. In college he played soccer, but it was the water he loved. He loved riding the waves the way Courtney loved riding her horse.

When he graduated from college, he spent several months in Japan and then, because of his familiarity with medical jargon and his ease with languages, he started a medical translation firm based in Boston. He worked hard, was seldom on the island, and when he was home, he sequestered himself in his room, working at his computer. When he came down for meals, he extolled the discoveries in medical technology, from the software in computers to laboratory tests on humans, that were appearing at firecracker speed. He told them that the usual FIGS languages—French, Italian, German, and Spanish—were no longer sufficient to meet the demands of all the emerging countries. The business of translation, software localization, revising websites and apps for foreign language use generated over thirty-seven billion dollars a year. And it was a growth industry.

By the time James was twenty-seven, his Boston-based firm had a dozen employees. He traveled everywhere, to conferences, to hospitals, to exotic countries, and he traveled first class.

Of course he had girlfriends. In his early twenties, he'd had an ever-changing parade of gorgeous girlfriends. In his later twenties, he seemed to have become a monk. He wasn't on Nantucket the entire summer, so possibly he had relationships he didn't talk about, but when his siblings teased him about his lack of love life, he'd responded with a good-natured smile that he didn't have time for romance.

James treated Courtney as he treated Robin and Iris and Henry's fiancée, Valerie, with careless indifference and offhand compliments. They were comfortable with each other. In that house, no matter that it was spacious, people were forever bumping into one another coming out of a bathroom or bedroom.

Courtney had watched James change from a madcap kid into a serious and competent man. It was two years ago, when she was twenty-seven and James was twenty-six, that she realized her feelings for him had not changed, but deepened.

• • •

It happened at the beginning of the summer when he strode into the house straight from a conference in Brussels, still in his lightweight gray summer suit, his tie loosened, his shirt collar open, a briefcase in one hand, and a suitcase in the other. He was tired and jet-lagged and grown-up and gorgeous. He kissed his mother and sister, and because Courtney was in the room, he kissed her, too.

"Hey, Courtney," he said. "You're here! Let the summer begin!"

When James leaned over to kiss her cheek, the bristles on his jaw lightly, briefly, scratched her skin. He smelled like jet fuel and gin and coffee, and the touch of his lips to her cheek sparked a mysterious, delicious conflagration that blazed fast as a wildfire through her body.

He felt it, too. She was certain of that. He jerked back as if burned, and stared down at her for a moment with a puzzled look on his face.

Susanna, oblivious, asked, "Want some coffee?"

"No, thanks, Mom. I'm going to shower and collapse. I think I'll sleep for about a month." He left the room.

That summer Courtney worked long hours at the bookstore and James worked long hours in his room. Most of the time when they saw each other, they were with the rest of the family and summer children. There was the moment—a flash—when she walked out of the ocean onto the beach in her new bikini and saw James staring at her as if he'd never seen her before. She smiled at him. He blushed. James blushed! But he turned away to get another beer or talk to someone, and the moment vanished and Courtney could do nothing more than remember it every night when she fell asleep.

James didn't touch her that summer two years ago, but he paid attention to her, handing her his sweater when they were sailing and a chilly mist swept over them. Asking about her family, her job, her horse, when they were all together at the dinner table. And watching her. So many times she'd caught him looking at her. Each time she smiled and he quickly glanced away.

Two years ago, at the end of the summer, she had been certain that something was going to happen between her and James. She wasn't wishing for anything spectacular—she could never dream that he might love her. But he might make love to her. That could happen. Even that would be a dream come true.

It was a hot night at the end of August. Courtney was wearing a blue sundress, her long hair twisted up and held with a clip at the back of her head. No makeup. Flip-flops. She had biked home from a house on Atlantic Avenue in 'Sconset, where she'd babysat for a litter of cousins while their parents went to The Chanticleer for dinner. Earlier that day she'd packed most of her clothing, possessions, and gifts. Her summer job at the bookstore was over. Her teaching position at UMKC awaited her, as did her family, her friends, and her horse. She was in that peculiar state of anticipation and regret that occupied her at both the end and the beginning of the summer, the times when she was making the transition from one home to the other.

She'd stowed her bike in the garage and meandered around to the back of the house. She had nothing in her hands—she carried nothing, needing not even a book to read when the children were in bed, because her heart and thoughts were full. The babysitting money was tucked in her dress pocket.

She intended to sit in one of the deck chairs on the long porch and let things settle as she stared out at the calm ocean, down below the bluff, murmuring rhythmically to itself as it touched the shore. Lights shone from inside the house, upstairs in the bedrooms, only a few illuminating the first floor.

The soft glow fell over a figure seated in one of the deck chairs. Her heart tripped, letting her know before her own mind said the words that it was James seated there.

"Oh, hi," she said. She stopped a few feet away from him.

"I was waiting for you." James stood up, as if this were a formal occasion and she was returning to a dinner table. He wore board shorts, a white button-down shirt hanging down, sleeves rolled up, flip-flops. His red hair burned rose-colored in the light.

She'd had no intuition of what he was about to say. Years ago, she'd made her peace with the hopelessness of her love for James. "What's up?"

"I want—" James stopped. Started again. Said it all in a rush. "I want to make love to you."

Surprise—shock, really—made her laugh. "James. Stop messing around."

"I'm not," James said seriously. He held out his hand. "Will you sit down and talk with me?"

Courtney stubbed her toe into the ground a few times. She was distrustful, slightly offended, definitely cautious. "I don't know. What do you want to talk about?"

James took another step toward her. He was so near her she felt the heat of his body. He put his hand on her waist.

She had loved him in silence and in secret for so long, for years. Her heart went wild in her chest. But she had some pride, some amount of self-control.

Stubbornly, Courtney said, "James, I don't want to be just another quick roll in the hay for you."

He moved his hand down to her thigh. His hand was warm. "Oh, it won't be quick."

He leaned close to kiss her.

"Darlings! What are you doing out here?" Pearl Schwartz, James's little sister's best friend, staggered up, plopping down on a wicker chair facing them. She was just twenty-one, and had celebrated by getting drunk in as many ways as possible all summer. Her lipstick was smeared, her hair a mess, her dress stained. Her shoes were in her hand. "God, I would die for some water. I don't suppose either of you would bring me some water?"

It was always the way things went at the Vickerey house. No privacy. Constant interruptions. And, because of Susanna, because they had become one large clumsy family, the instinctive need to take care of ones who needed it.

"Pearl, are you okay?" Courtney asked, leaning toward the younger woman.

"Sssure," Pearl slurred. "Jus' drunk." Even hammered, blurry-eyed, stinking of alcohol, Pearl was a stunning beauty.

Courtney said, "Pearl, let's go into the kitchen. You can have a nice drink of water, and I'll help you get up to bed."

"Fine here." Pearl slid down in the chair so that her long legs stuck out and her bum rested precariously on the edge of the seat.

"No, you're not." Courtney stood up, leaned over, and took the other woman by her upper arms. "Come on. You can't sleep outside. You need some water in you. Come on, Pearl, stand up."

James came around to lift Pearl. "One—two—three." He hoisted her to a standing position.

They managed to get Pearl into the kitchen. Only the stove light gleamed, and even that hurt Pearl's eyes. Courtney ran a glass of water. "Here, honey. Drink." She held the glass to Pearl's lips as if she were a toddler.

Pearl took a sip, shuddered, and hurled all over Courtney's dress.

Courtney automatically stepped back. Pearl sagged as James held her beneath her arms. She hurled again, sinking to her knees, managing to splatter Courtney's feet and legs this time. Vomit was on Pearl's clothes, too, and in her hair.

"Want to sleep," Pearl muttered, rolling onto the floor.

"Let's get her into the outdoor shower," Courtney told James. "I'll shower with her, and strip off our clothes. You go find some robes, big shirts, something. Two things, one for her, one for me."

James managed to pull Pearl to her feet. Together Courtney and James maneuvered Pearl back outside, off the porch, around the corner to the outdoor shower. They propped Pearl against a wall. James went off. Courtney turned on the water, dialing it as cold as she could tolerate, grateful it was still August and hot.

"Damn!" Pearl cursed. "That's cold!"

Courtney held Pearl against the wall with one hand. With the other, she aimed the shower nozzle at Pearl, who moaned and cursed and shouted until gradually she sobered up, only slightly, but enough to understand what was going on.

"I'm fine," Pearl said, knocking Courtney's hand away.

"Use the soap." Courtney handed her a shrunken, used bar of Ivory.

While Pearl stripped and washed, Courtney slid her own dress down to her feet and stepped out of her underpants. She wore no bra, nor did Pearl. They weren't shy about their nakedness in front of each other. All the summer children, male and female, had seen the others in every stage of dress and undress. There was nothing like getting caught in a rainstorm while sailing to cause sodden bathing suits to cling to a body, exposing every bump and crevice.

Still, when James arrived with towels and robes, he handed them over the shower wall. Pearl was steady enough, and chilled enough, to pull on the robe and wrap a towel around her head. She stumbled out of the stall.

"Going to bed," she announced.

"Let's be sure you get there," James said, and took her arm. They bumbled away into the house.

Courtney slid her arms into the welcome warmth of the robe and made a turban of the towel. She put her dress and Pearl's into the washing machine in the laundry room off the kitchen, then set about cleaning up the vomit from the kitchen floor. She didn't mind doing it—years ago, when she was in college with Robin and had too much to drink a few times, she knew others had taken care of her in this way.

But it did dull the atmosphere of romance.

By the time she'd finished cleaning up, it was after one o'clock. She climbed the stairs slowly, exhausted and pissed off at Pearl for ruining an amazing moment in Courtney's life. Peering into Pearl's bedroom, she saw James moving the wastebasket to the bed where Pearl lay collapsed and pale.

Pearl was young and indomitable. "Want to have sex, James?" she croaked.

James pulled a blanket over her. "As enticing as your offer is, Pearl, no, thanks." He spread a towel on the bed next to Pearl's shoulder. "I put a wastebasket on the floor for if you get sick again, and a towel."

"James, you're so nice. You're so handsome. Come on, James—"

"Sleep it off, Pearl." He turned away and left the room.

Courtney was leaning against the wall, eyes closed.

"So that pretty much ruined the mood, right?" James asked.

Courtney laughed. "Pretty much."

"Still, I could come visit you in Kansas City. We could have some privacy away from this"—James held out his hands—"*zoo.*"

"I love it *here,*" Courtney told him. She walked toward her bedroom, James at her side. She was tired, and angry at Pearl, foolish beautiful Pearl, who had interrupted a moment Courtney had been waiting for for years.

James read her thoughts. "I should have taken you out to dinner. At least for a walk on the beach where we could be alone. This isn't the way I pictured it." He sniffed the air. "I've got barf on my shirt, right?"

Courtney smiled and nodded. "I should go to bed. Let's talk tomorrow."

He touched the side of her face lightly. "Tomorrow."

But the next day was full of packing and people saying goodbye and a nerve-wracking weather report of an approaching hurricane-force wind. Courtney caught a late boat to the mainland and took a bus up to the airport in Boston so she wouldn't be trapped on the island by the storm.

Courtney returned to her normal life, the life she thought of as "real." She taught at UMKC and graded exams. She drove down to Emporia on the weekends to see her family and friends and ride her horse. When blizzard conditions prevailed, which was often, she curled up on her sofa and read. Alice Munro. Edith Wharton. Joanna Trollope.

And about once a week, she received an email or a text from James. Nothing romantic or even tantalizing. Stuff about work. *How are you? Christmas is great this year. You would love it. Norway is awesome; here I am near the top of the world.*

She emailed back, keeping it light and friendly. *Work is fun. Some students excellent, some have heads stuffed with hay. I've been riding my horse a lot, even in the snow.* The most intimate she dared was: *I'd love to see Norway sometime.*

Last year, Courtney was twenty-eight. Suddenly all her Kansas friends were getting married, or already married and having babies. Monty had taken on all his father's responsibilities for the ranch and her darling Star was twenty-two—old for a horse, and not as enthusiastic about racing long rides as she once was—so Courtney didn't spend one day that May riding with Monty. Her parents didn't understand why Courtney continued to go to Nantucket for the summer. She could always teach a few summer courses.

When she arrived at the Vickerey house last summer, she was determined to let James know how she felt about him. The worst that could happen would be that he'd tell her he didn't return her love, he only liked her as a brother. That would be terrible, and humiliating, but she decided it was better to be heartbroken than to continue in such an emotional limbo of longing and hoping and loving all by herself.

But when she had settled back into the Vickerey house, she discovered that James was different. He was intense, serious, almost brooding. Robin called him *Heathcliff*.

Christabel, his childhood buddy, was the first one to say anything. "James, you're just no fun anymore!" she blurted out during one dinner at the Vickereys. They'd had lobster, and Christabel had put the claws on the ends of her fingers and snapped at James, who had jerked his head away from Christabel and muttered, "Cut it out." Courtney had met Robin's eyes across the table when the little incident took place, and Courtney knew without words that Robin feared that James was spiraling down into a depression like the ones Henry often had.

As the summer continued, James hadn't seemed depressed. He'd just been very busy. He secluded himself in his room or in Dr. V's library, reading texts and typing notes into his computer. When he went for a swim, he did it at odd hours, and alone, instead of going out with the gang as he always had before.

He stopped talking to Courtney. He absolutely *ignored* her. This made her sad, and it made her mad, and it was some consolation that he also ignored Christabel, who complained about him all summer long. Courtney had always known that James would never love her. That was simply the natural law of life, that the man she adored so ferociously would never love her back. But one of the reasons she came to the island for the summer was to see James, to be around him, to laugh at his jokes, listen to his rambling explanations of his work, to

warm herself in the glow of his presence. Well, and to finish the conversation James had started at the end of last summer. Then he'd said
he wanted to make love to her. What had happened?

The day before she left for Kansas City, Courtney decided she
couldn't take it anymore. She *wouldn't* take it anymore! Was he in a
depression? Was he undergoing some kind of personality alteration,
transforming from a man who enjoyed life and laughter and people,
especially his family, into a grumbling recluse? Had he decided that
with all the specialized academic knowledge he had gained, he was
suddenly too high falutin' for them all?

She had to know, and she wanted to give him a great big loud piece
of her mind. But she wanted to do it with some degree of privacy, when
no one else could interrupt.

That morning, she knew it was now or never. Robin and Susanna
had gone into town to shop for groceries. Iris had already returned to
college. Henry was at the hospital. Even Dr. V was gone, off in his precious Jaguar to meet an old friend and colleague for lunch.

Courtney was packing for the wrenching transition away from Nantucket and back to Kansas City when she suddenly knew that this was
the time.

She'd gone out of her room and down the hall. James's door was
shut. She knocked. Twice. Hard.

James looked surprised when he opened the door. "Hey," he said.
"What's up?"

He wore only board shorts and a T-shirt. He was barefoot and his
red hair stood out in all directions—he often ran his hands through his
hair when working.

"I want to talk to you," Courtney told him. "I want to come into your
private lair where I haven't been *all summer*. I want to sit down and
have a conversation with you."

James had looked wary. "Um, okay . . ."

She shut the door behind her. They might be alone in the house
now, but at any time someone could return. She wanted privacy.

James's room was piled with books and papers, journals and scientific periodicals. Courtney could spot only two places to sit: on the chair by his desk, or on the bed. She chose the bed, because she didn't want to appear to be spying on the papers on his desk, although she'd like to.

James took the chair. He swiveled it around to face Courtney.

All her courage, all her outrage, all her eloquent sentences vanished the moment Courtney looked at James. He was so handsome, and she loved him so much, and she could see how tired he was, how stressed, and suddenly she didn't want to be angry or demanding or accusatory. She wanted to hold him in her arms.

"James," she said, and she could scarcely get the next words out. "I miss you."

His face changed. Softened. "Courtney," he began.

"No, stop. Listen to me. I know I've *seen* you this summer, but every single day you kept yourself closed off from me. I don't know if you're depressed, like clinically depressed, or just overwhelmed with your work, or if you've decided you hate me and you're sick of me coming here every summer, or—"

"Stop it, Courtney, don't you know?" James interrupted. "I love you."

She stopped talking. She lost her breath. Her mind raced. Did he mean he loved her as if she were a sister? He surely meant he loved her as if she were a sister.

"That's why I've stayed away from you," he continued.

"Because you love me?"

"Because I love you."

"That doesn't make any sense," Courtney argued.

"If you think about it, it makes all the sense in the world. Courtney, you've been part of our family for ten years. You've seen us at our worst. You've seen Henry depressed, and Henry manic, and you know how hard it is on our parents, on us."

"Yes, James," Courtney rushed in, foolish and craving his touch, wanting to ignore everything she knew except her own desires. "But you're not like Henry. You aren't bipolar."

James spoke softly. "Maybe. Maybe I'm on some sort of spectrum. But I do carry the gene. If I ever had children, they might inherit the gene. I won't let that happen."

Courtney drew back, as if slapped. She had never thought this through, that her love for James might lead to marriage and children, children with a shadowed inheritance. Of course she hadn't thought this far ahead, because she had never guessed that James might love her.

"Wait." Courtney held up a hand. "Give me a moment here, James. Did you just say that you love me?"

James smiled. She smiled back at him, and for one long warm delicious moment they moved outside of time and space and hung suspended in their own world.

Courtney wanted to touch him. Hug him. Kiss him, kiss him sweetly and fiercely. "Do you mean you love me like you love Robin and Iris?"

"I mean I love you like I love no one else in the world, Courtney. I've loved you for years." James's smile faded and his eyes grew shadowed.

"But why haven't you said anything? Why haven't you—we—why haven't we made love?"

James rose from his chair and walked, not toward Courtney, but away from her. He stood with his back to her, staring out the window at the ocean.

"Don't you think I've been wanting to make love to you for years? Don't you—"

Courtney interrupted. She stood up, nearly shaking with nerves and hope and fear. "No, I *don't* think that. I've thought you loved Christabel!"

James turned to face Courtney. He looked haunted. "I do love Christabel. I care for her deeply. She was my comrade when we were adolescents, getting into trouble, trying to be wild and different and free from our families. And we've had sex, too, I won't lie about that, but it was part of that madcap phase we were in. We wanted to be Zelda and Scott Fitzgerald, we wanted to be anybody except who we were. When I went off to college, I grew out of that whole period of my life. I moved on."

"And Christabel?"

James shook his head. "Christabel will move on when she meets a man whom she can trust."

"And she can't trust you?"

"She can't trust me to love her, because she knows I don't. Not the way she wants. I haven't slept with her for years, probably six or seven years. God, Courtney, why are we even talking about Christabel?"

Courtney took a few steps toward him. "Because I love you, James. Because I need to know how you feel about her. So that I can understand what you mean when you tell me you love me."

James stared at Courtney for a long moment. Then he closed the empty space between them and took her in his arms. "This is what I mean when I tell you I love you."

His kiss was so sweet, it was like warm honey surging through her blood, and Courtney wrapped her arms around him, pulling him hard against her, and James cupped the back of her head in his hand and with his other hand brought her hips against his. She pressed against him. His kiss was a kind of possession—and suddenly he broke away. He thrust her away from him and shook his head angrily.

"No, Courtney. That's what I'm telling you. We can't do this."

"We can't make love? But it will be wonderful!"

"Yes. And it will break our hearts. It will make it even more painful to leave each other. It will mean that when you marry someone else, I'll be fucking miserable. It will mean—"

"But I won't marry anyone else, James!" Courtney broke in.

He stood apart from her, taking deep breaths. "Well, you'd better, because I'm not going to marry you. Think about it, Courtney. Do you want to go through life afraid, afraid that your own children might be cursed?"

"Cursed? Don't be dramatic—"

"You've seen Henry! You've seen what he's put our family through. Courtney, I'm not being dramatic, I'm being realistic."

He was on the verge of tears, and because she loved him, because she understood him, Courtney backed away. Everything he had said was true. The worst part of it was that Courtney could not promise with one hundred percent of her heart and mind and soul that she would marry James no matter what. People said that, they sang songs about true love forevermore, they said it in their marriage vows: *in sickness and in health.* Courtney knew she loved James. She had thought she loved him enormously, passionately, and without reservation. She had never thought of the consequences of being with him for life, for his life, and her life, and the lives of their possible children.

"I don't want to be a coward," she whispered, more to herself than to James.

"There might be a way," James said softly.

"What do you mean?"

"I mean . . . look, Courtney, you have to remember I've spent my life hearing you rave about how fabulous my mother is, and how you want to be just like her, you want to have thousands of babies of your own. Even last year, you were constantly talking about your Kansas friend Donna, and the whole birth thing, and how you wanted to hold your baby in your arms and nurse."

"I don't remember telling you all this."

"Of course you didn't, but you talked about it to Robin and Mom constantly. I couldn't help but overhear."

"Okay, all right, but how does that become a problem?"

"Because . . . what if the only way we could be together would be if we promised to adopt children. Or you could have in vitro, we could have some other guy's healthy sperm fertilize your eggs."

Courtney stepped back, hugging herself, protecting herself. "I don't know what to say. This is all so . . . so *scientific.*"

"I know it is. It sounds cold and analytical and unromantic. But lots of people do it, Courtney. We could do both, we could adopt and do in vitro. You could have that pack of children you want."

"But, James. I want *your* babies. It's *you* I love. Your red hair, your body, your intelligence—all of that, I can't explain it, I can't separate you into parts, but come on, imagine what a baby of *ours* would be like! Your family has some kind of difficult gene, that's true, but they also have such brilliance, such zest for life, such—such *radiance*! I want your babies and no one else's, James."

He shook his head. "And I'm certain that I don't want to pass on my genes."

Courtney stared at James, and he stared, unflinchingly, back. She saw the determination in the set of his jaw, and she saw the sadness, the resignation in his eyes. She had never loved him more, and at the same time, she wanted to shake him. He was so *wrong*.

It would not be easy to change his mind. She knew she needed patience. She wasn't giving up, but she needed to do this cautiously.

"Well, I'm stunned, James. I'm heartbroken. And I have to leave tomorrow." She kept her voice calm, as if she were gentling a nervy horse. "I'll leave. And I'll think about it, about adoption, about *in vitro*. Okay? But you need to agree you'll reconsider your decision about having your babies. Our babies."

"I can't promise you that." He had shut down on her, his face was stiff, his voice controlled.

"James—"

"I won't change my mind, Courtney."

She touched his arm. He stood as still as stone.

"Okay, then. But we can keep in touch, can't we? Email?"

"I suppose. I'll be working."

"Well, I will, too!" She wanted to kiss him, she wanted to shake him. He was not going to budge. Nor was she.

That had been nine months ago. Since then, they had communicated via email and Twitter, but not often.

Courtney had told no one, not her best Kansas girlfriends, Donna and Jean Anne, not her mother, and certainly not her closest BFF Robin, about what had happened last year with James. She had kept the knowledge to herself, turning it around and around in her mind like rubbing a worry stone or a bead in her fingers, trying to make sense of it all.

Now she was back on Nantucket. Something might have changed.

James might change his mind—or she might change hers. She was unsettled, restless, as she followed Robin down the stairs to join the family.

And the thought came to her like a shooting star: *Monty Blackhorse* would give her lots of children.

No one could ever be sure exactly how many people would be dining on any given night. Often the whole family was there: Dr. Vickerey, his wife, Susanna, children Robin, James, Iris, and of course Henry—unless he was called to the emergency room.

James's friend Christabel was often there and sometimes her father was, too. Quinn Eliot had been divorced years ago. He taught at the public high school and had standing invitations to dinner at many homes, but over the years he'd become part of the Vickereys' intimate sphere.

The dining room and kitchen were one combined open space with a counter between where Susanna or whoever cooked could set out the food buffet style. Everyone helped himself. Courtney had come one time for Christmas when the dining room was arranged much more formally with the Vickereys' old silver, china, and crystal set out on an antique linen tablecloth. The table itself was an antique with several leaves. At the beginning of June, Henry and Robin opened up the table, inserted all the boards, and left it that way, full-length, for the summer.

Robin went to the sideboard to choose one of the many tablecloths Susanna kept there. Courtney helped her swoop and smooth it over the table, then found matching napkins and put them around while Iris set out the silverware.

"Courtney, I've made paella in honor of your arrival!" Susanna was at the stove, stirring. Tall, plump, naturally, helplessly lovely, with tumbling red hair, she was Maureen O'Hara, Ann-Margret, Julianne Moore wearing L.L.Bean and an apron. She pulled her hair up and back to keep it out of the way while she cooked. Once they found her hair held with two children's twirly straws. All her guests adored her, and she adored them. Most of them.

Courtney went around the counter to say hello. "I'm so glad I'm here. Thank you for having me."

Susanna put down her spoon and embraced Courtney in a warm hug. "Let me look at you." She smoothed Courtney's hair back from her face. "You're lovely as always, Courtney, but too thin, too pale. You've spent too much time with your books. We've got to get you out on the water."

"Mom," Iris commented, "you think everyone's too thin."

"Look"—Susanna waved a hand at the colander in the sink— "I picked mussels especially for you. Went to the Jetties at low tide this morning." Susanna herself was not too thin. She was plump, though not fat, big-busted, big-hipped, full-bodied, and sturdy. She wore one of several pairs of ancient frayed khakis with a blue button-down shirt. Her strawberry-blond hair was streaked with white and tied up behind her head in a ponytail with a red scarf around it. No jewelry except for her wedding ring. No makeup except for lip balm. Her face was already rosy from being out in the sun.

"Oh, thank you. I haven't had mussels since I was here last. What can I do to help?"

"Toss the salad? The olive oil's in that cupboard."

"Mother," Robin persisted, "Courtney is *not* pale. She *goes* outside. She rides her horse. But she wears this astonishing new invention the world calls *sunscreen* so she won't get skin cancer."

Susanna said, "I think use the red wine vinegar tonight, Courtney. No spice."

"Fine. Pay no attention to me." Robin set out wine and water glasses on the table.

"I'll go fetch Dad," Iris said. "I told him once already." Muttering, she left the room.

"Let me dump the food into the troughs, Mom," said Robin.

"I hate it when you call them that," Susanna complained. "It's quite elegant French pottery, you know."

Robin nudged her mother out of the way as she spoke. "I know, you're right, I apologize. Just reminding you how much food you cook every evening." Robin had become a self-appointed guard and assistant for her mother. At Easter, when she visited Courtney, she'd discussed what to do about her mother. Susanna was a fiend for cooking, always eager to try new recipes, growing herbs and vegetables in her small back garden, and never happier than when the dining room table was crowded with people eating her delicious food. No one but Robin seemed to notice that Susanna was showing signs of aging: some swollen arthritic knuckles, the white in her hair, a few age spots on her face and hands, and a tendency to slouch, even to limp as if her back bothered her.

"She needs to take a yoga class," Courtney had advised.

"Of course she does," Robin had answered. "But you know my mother, she'll never do anything for herself."

Courtney assumed that Susanna's health was one of the reasons Robin had moved back here after graduating from college. More and more, Robin was taking over the running of this huge house. Robin volunteered for several of the island's nature organizations, too. She seemed quite happy and Courtney knew that Robin was attached, heart and soul, to the island's natural beauty. Yet something else kept Robin here, some secret—some secret love? This year Courtney was determined to discover what it was.

Courtney held one of the French porcelain bowls while Robin scooped half the paella into it and then into the other, trying to divide the mussels, shrimp, and clams equally between the two. Susanna opened one of her two ovens and, hands tucked in oven gloves, brought out long loaves of garlic bread, already neatly sliced and buttered. She settled the bread into two wicker baskets and put them on the table.

Dr. V entered the room with Iris right behind him. Tall, big-boned, he wore his Nantucket red trousers with a blue and white striped crisply ironed button-down shirt and startlingly white tennis shoes he bought new every summer. His children chided him that he looked like the American flag. He paid no attention. He liked order. He liked knowing he could reach in his closet and take out exactly what he needed without worrying about it. His red hair had turned white and so had his bushy eyebrows. He had a habit of pushing his reading glasses up onto his forehead and walking around the house that way, in spite of his family's derogatory comments.

Courtney ran to greet him. "Dr. Vickerey, hello. I just got here for the summer. I'm so happy to see you again." She dared to lean up and peck his cheek with a kiss.

"Very nice, very nice." Dr. Vickerey patted Courtney's shoulder as if she were a familiar dog.

"Sit down, Dad, and I'll bring you some wine," Iris said.

James walked into the room. He wore a pair of baggy board shorts with a clean, ironed, but ancient white button-down shirt hanging down, and deck shoes so old the front soles flapped like a pair of ducks' beaks. He was already tanned.

"Courtney! You're here!" James pulled her to him and wrapped her in a hard but brotherly hug.

Courtney had no time to do more than inhale James's aroma of sunshine, salt air, and delicious male, because right behind James came Christabel.

"Christabel!" Smoothly Courtney moved from James's embrace to hug Christabel. If anyone on the island were too thin, it was this restless island beauty, all long bones and the big eyes of a child painted on velvet. Today Christabel wore a tattered 1950s gingham shirtwaist resurrected, no doubt, from the town dump. She'd braided her long blond hair into two pigtails and tied them with red ribbons to match the cherries in the fabric of the dress. Courtney could see that Christabel wore white cotton underpants but no bra—Christabel was too skinny to need a bra. On her feet were a pair of someone else's red high heels that made her taller than Courtney. The shoes were too big for her and she tottered around, laughing at herself as if she were a drunk.

"My Lolita look," Christabel announced, turning in a circle for everyone to admire.

"Ridiculous," Iris retorted. "You're twenty-seven, Christabel."

"Darlings, grab a plate and some wine and sit down and we'll have dinner." Susanna dished up a plate and set it before her husband, who was drinking the wine Iris had given him.

Susanna had a multitude of crowd-size recipes she varied over the days to keep the throngs in her house satisfied. Macaroni and cheese, often with lobster baked in. Lasagna. Seafood chowders thick with potatoes, onions, and bacon. Rice tossed with all sorts of fresh veggies and shredded cheese. Enormous meatloaves that could do double duty the next day in sandwiches.

All of Susanna's summer children had worked during their college and post-grad summers, making fantastic money as waitstaff, landscapers, babysitters, and construction workers. All of them had at various times offered to pay some kind of rent for their rooms and meals but Susanna wouldn't hear of it.

"Nonsense! What else would we do with all the rooms in this ridiculous house?" Susanna would reply and that would be the end of it.

Fifteen years ago, when Valerie was Henry's best friend and girlfriend and the first official summer child, she devised a way to help. She arrived on the island with cartons of flour, packages of yeast, and boxes of baking powder and salt. At least once a week, on her day off, Valerie made pastries for breakfasts and pies and cakes for dessert in the evening. They were delicious and helped keep the crowded household fed.

Courtney was more practical. She went online and ordered prodigious amounts of toilet paper, paper towels, bath soap, shampoo and conditioner, tissue, laundry detergent, dishwashing detergent, and clear plastic trash bags from Walmart to be delivered to the Vickereys' house.

Callum Findlay, James's best friend, arrived with what seemed like wagonloads of liquor—everything bought in the "real world" was much cheaper than what could be procured on the island. Callum satisfactorily stocked the house with beer, tequila, margarita mixers, and wine for the summer, which was appropriate since he and James and their gang drank most of it.

Pearl outshone them all. She had her mother's housekeeper send up several cases of champagne and boxes of exotic cheeses and caviar sheltered in ice.

"Caviar and champagne?" Christabel had scoffed. "Trust you."

"Everything else was already taken," Pearl had answered haughtily.

Quinn Eliot, Christabel's father, was divorced. He prepared most of his own meals and had gotten rather good at it. In the summer he came over often with offerings of striped bass and bluefish he caught out sport fishing with friends, or great slabs of beef brisket and short ribs or simply about a thousand pounds of ground beef for hamburgers. He'd fire up the grill on the patio and cook dinner for everyone, his way of repaying the Vickereys for the many times his daughter dropped into their house for meals.

Quinn was relatively young, around forty-five. His wife had given birth to Christabel when they were both still in college. They had moved to Nantucket, where Quinn taught science at the public high school. Desiree had left him for another man when Christabel was only ten. She'd not only left him but her daughter, too. She moved to Europe and seldom bothered to communicate with Christabel. It was as if her first husband and child had simply never happened.

Quinn had seldom dated since then, even though he was a handsome and amiable man. He'd focused on teaching, sitting on community committees, and most of all, trying to help his daughter. Like his Christabel, Quinn had blond hair, now fading to brown, and blue eyes flashing behind glasses.

He could have easily fit in with Henry and Valerie, who were only about thirteen years younger, but he selected the company of Dr. Vickerey and Susanna, who were fifteen or more years older. Courtney thought this was because he spent nine months of his year teaching adolescents and wished for more mature company. And over the years she'd noticed how young women who visited the Vickerey house often developed crushes on Quinn or, like Pearl, acted flirtatiously around him just for the hell of it. Quinn ignored them, acted like an absentminded uncle.

Tonight Quinn wasn't there. Only seven people sat at the long dining room table: Susanna and Dr. V holding down the ends, James and Christabel on one side, Robin, Iris, and Courtney on the other.

Susanna started the meal by raising her wine glass in a toast. "Courtney, we're glad you're here!"

"I'm so glad to be back," Courtney said. "Thank you, Susanna." Quickly she added, "And Dr. Vickerey."

Dr. V had already started eating. Sometimes he engaged in conversation with the others and sometimes, as now, he seemed preoccupied with whatever medical journal he'd been reading. Several years ago, Courtney had been present when Susanna, in one of her rare rages, told her husband he could not bring reading material to the family table. They were a strange couple, the Vickereys, Susanna with her rumpled clothing and elegant manners and Dr. Vickerey, with his perfectly ironed clothing and rumpled behavior. Yet it was obvious that they loved each other and that their marriage worked well.

Courtney's head was bent over her plate, focusing on her paella, when she sensed James looking at her over the table. She took a fortifying sip of wine, and raised her head and met his beautiful green eyes.

"So," James asked Courtney, holding her gaze with his. "How did the teaching go this year?"

For one long moment, Courtney allowed herself to indulge in the pleasure of simply viewing his face.

She answered brightly, casually, "It was great. I had several mandatory freshman English classes with troublesome students. Kids these days who are so used to cellphones and email they rebel at the thought of punctuation. But I had a couple of super bright stars in my literature classes. I'll have them next year in world literature. I'm looking forward to that."

"But you're not teaching this summer, right?" James asked.

"Right. I'm not teaching any summer courses, so I'll be here for three months." A pang struck Courtney's heart. When she was away from Kansas, she missed her horse more than she missed her friends, her parents, and even Monty.

"How's Star?" James asked.

Courtney blushed. She knew James was really saying: *I remember everything about you. I think of you.* When she had her breath back, she answered, "She's getting old, I'm afraid. And the weather wasn't cooperative this summer. I usually rode bareback, near the stable, just to be with her."

"That reminds me. I've been saving a quote I found for you." James closed his eyes for a moment as he remembered. "'There is no secret so close as that between a rider and his horse.'"

"Oh, lovely! Who said it?"

"A fellow called Robert Surtees, a nineteenth-century British sporting gentleman."

"I've never heard of him," Courtney said carelessly, when what she wanted to say was: *James, don't do this. Don't make me want you.*

"I don't think many people have," James said.

Christabel, who always got restless when the attention was focused on someone else, broke in, "So did you bring your cowboy boots?" Her question implied, as Christabel often did, that Courtney was a rather amusing hillbilly.

"Of course not, Christabel," Courtney responded mildly. "I couldn't afford to keep a horse on this tiny little island."

"There are several stables on Nantucket," Iris offered, "but I think they're all private."

"Where are you going to work this summer?" James asked.

Courtney shrugged lightly. "At Murray's Toggery. An adjunct professor of English does not make a glorious salary. And I'll sign up for babysitting at the hotels," Courtney told them. "The money is too spectacular to miss."

James spoke up. "I was wondering if you'd help me edit an especially dense translation. I need a good proofreader."

Courtney couldn't look at him. She imagined them, side by side, James bending over her shoulder, as they studied the manuscript together. A powerful wave of hope swept through her. "Sure. Sounds like fun."

Outside, a horn honked. Iris jumped up. "That's David. Gotta go, hot date." She pecked a kiss on her mother's head, hurried her plate and glass into the kitchen, and raced for the front door, winking at Robin as she went. Her old boyfriend was helping Iris make "Happy Birthday!" banners to hang tomorrow all over the house and the tent.

As Iris went out the front door, an adorable young woman wearing blue hospital scrubs burst in through the kitchen door. It was often like this at the Vickereys' house, people coming and going. Henry had threatened to install a revolving door.

"That's Henry's new girlfriend, Lisa," Robin whispered to Courtney.

Lisa had brown hair cut Miley Cyrus style and large brown eyes beneath strong brown eyebrows. "Susanna? Oh, good, Robin, you're here. It's Henry. I've been trying not to come, but now I'm getting worried."

Everyone at the table froze. The temperature of the room plummeted. Because she'd lived here for so many summers, Courtney knew what the problem was: when Henry was smothered in the suffocating black folds of depression, his moods could be terrible, frightening conditions. Worse, Henry could be stopped like a watch with a run-down battery. Paralyzed.

Wringing her hands together, Lisa explained. "Two days ago, a thirteen-year-old boy, a summer visitor, stole someone's Jet Ski and went for a joyride. He ended up crashing into the rocks at the Jetties. He totally tore himself up. By the time the ambulance got to him, he had almost bled out. Blood out of his head and internal bleeding. At the hospital, Henry opened him up and tried to stop all the bleeders. But the boy died on the table."

Susanna whispered, "Dear god."

"Henry held it together in the hospital. I drove him home—here."

Looking at Courtney, she explained, "I live in town with a bunch of other nurses, but I stay here sometimes. Once we were in the front door, Henry went ballistic. Cursing. Throwing things. I couldn't get him to settle down. He thought it was all his fault that he couldn't save the boy." Tears streamed down her face. "I couldn't convince him that no-body could have saved him. Henry—I've never seen anything like this. Well, except in the psych wards."

"Oh, honey," Robin said.

"I tried to get him to drink some water, some beer, but he wouldn't take anything. He cried like a little boy. I sat and held his head and tried to soothe him. After a while he got very quiet. Since then, he hasn't spoken a word or eaten anything. He won't respond. I went to work today, and when I came home, he was in the same place. Not moving."

Susanna said, "I'll go—"

"Mom, you know what the doctors said. You can't run to him every time he gets depressed. Besides, you need to rest up for this weekend."

Christabel suggested, "Get Valerie."

"Valerie said she's done with it," Robin reminded her.

"I'll go see what I can do with Henry." James pushed back his chair.

Robin stood up, taking charge. "James, you went last time. I'll go." She wrapped Lisa in a hug and steered her to a chair at the table. "So scary for you. Here, sit down and let me pour you a glass of wine. You could probably use something to eat, too. This casserole is pure com-fort food."

Lisa fretted: "But Henry—"

"—is lying comatose on the sofa," Robin reminded her sensibly. "He's not going anywhere."

This one is not going to last, Courtney thought as she watched Robin pour the wine, fill a plate with casserole, and pat Lisa's back. If Valerie hadn't been able to deal with Henry, this sweet young thing certainly wouldn't be able to.

Robin arched an eyebrow at Courtney.

Courtney got the message. Leaning over, she held out her hand.

"Lisa, hi. I'm Courtney, Robin's friend from college. It's lovely to meet you. I just arrived today from Kansas."

"Courtney knows how to square dance," James added with a teasing smile and a sidelong glance at Courtney. "She owns cowboy boots and probably a Stetson, too."

Courtney rolled her eyes at James. "Cow*girl* boots," she corrected.

Christabel added in a twangy accent, "Yeah, Courtney's a true straw chewin' hillbilly gal. Robin met her when Courtney was a foreign exchange student at Smith."

"*Christabel,*" Susanna said disapprovingly. She'd been trying to improve Christabel's manners for years.

"What?" Christabel opened her eyes in fake innocence. "I'm joking." Pouting, she added, "Anyway, I can't understand what she says half the time. Her accent's worse than any European's."

Robin changed the subject. "Lisa, how do you like working at the cottage hospital?"

"People are really nice," Lisa said. She forked food into her mouth. "Helpful. Funny. I guess—neighborly. So different from Boston, where there were so many doctors and nurses and administrators I couldn't keep them straight. That was kind of overwhelming. On the other hand, Nantucket in the winter is kind of"—Lisa looked around the table at the faces of the family who'd chosen to live here, some of them year-round—"quiet," she finished.

Christabel snickered. "Darling, you're dating Henry. He should be enough of a roller-coaster ride."

Dr. V grunted, tossed down his napkin, pushed back his chair, and left the room, his plate and his wine half-finished.

"What?" Christabel said, widening her eyes in pretended innocence. "Did I say something wrong?"

"It's fine," Susanna said. "Robin, thanks for dealing with Henry. I'll go be with your father."

"I guess you're learning we're not the Brady Bunch," James said to Lisa with a rueful smile.

Looking at Lisa, Robin added, "Don't worry about Dad. He's frustrated because he can't fix Henry. He's a surgeon. He expects quicker results. Henry goes up and down, and we're all used to it." She turned to Courtney. "Want to go check him out with me?"

"Absolutely," Courtney answered. "Lead the way."

"I'll go with you," Lisa said.

6

The three women went out the back door and across the lawn. They hiked up the stairs to the door over the garage. It opened into a large room: living, dining, and kitchen combined. Doors led to the bath and small bedroom.

Henry Vickerey lay on the sofa, face hidden against the cushions, back to the room. He didn't so much as twitch a muscle when the women entered. The tallest of the tall Vickerey family, he seemed like a giant child, his auburn hair sticking out all over, his shoeless feet looking naked and bony and vulnerable.

"Oh, honey." Robin sat on the arm of the sofa and stroked Henry's head. To Lisa, she said, "Is he on any meds?"

Lisa frowned. "I don't know."

Courtney went through to the bathroom and checked the medicine cabinet. "Nothing but NyQuil and aspirin," she called.

Robin snorted. "After all these years, you believe Henry keeps his stuff in the *medicine cabinet*? They're probably in a stoned wheat thin box in the cupboard."

"*Stoned* wheat thin," Lisa echoed, giggling a bit.

Robin slid onto her knees on the floor next to the sofa and gently shook Henry's shoulder. "Henry. This is the weekend of Mom's big party. You've got to pull out of it. At least pretend. You promised to be in charge of drinks tomorrow night for the dinner. I don't know what wines to get, and I can't mix drinks. Come on," she begged. "You promised."

No response.

Robin glanced up at Courtney. She motioned with her head for Courtney to join her. Courtney sank to her knees and touched Henry's back.

"Hey, Henry. I just got here today. For the party. Well, for the summer." She felt the warmth of his back beneath his shirt, the slight rise and fall as he breathed. "Remember I've got a cowboy friend back in Kansas? I think I'll phone Monty and have him come up here and hogtie you and drag you around the yard a few times to wake you up."

Robin threw Courtney a grateful smile. Courtney was babbling, but she'd been here before, trying to fill up the room around a depressed Henry with the liveliness of words, any words, like bringing heat to a cold empty place. Plus, the normalcy of it all was making Lisa relax.

No response.

Robin puffed with exasperation. "Henry, you are not allowed to do this. Mom's party is the day after *tomorrow*."

No response.

"You helped us plan it, Henry. Remember? We've got planes to meet, food and booze to buy, and the tent people will set up tomorrow, but someone has to be there. Did you take this weekend off?"

"He d—" Lisa began, but Robin waved her silent.

No reaction from Henry.

"When does Jacob arrive?" Jacob Barnes was Henry's best friend from med school, working in the ER at Mass General. Short and given to plumpness, with frizzy brown hair and thick glasses, Jacob was smarter than all the Vickereys combined, and incomprehensibly mild-tempered and steady, which frustrated Robin, who wanted to believe that brilliance was indisputably linked with mental instability.

"You'll feel better when Jacob's here. You know what he sees in the ER is a lot worse than what you see here. Plus, Jacob's always good for some off-color jokes."

No comment.

Robin turned to Lisa. "Honey, I think you might as well go back to your place. I'll toss a blanket over Henry and let him sleep. He'll be better tomorrow morning."

Lisa frowned. She had a room in a house near the hospital, owned by the hospital for nurses and technicians. She stayed there when she had to be at work the next day; some nights she stayed with Henry. No hiding Henry's love life, not in the Vickereys' garage, where anyone who came or left could be spotted from the house. "I wish I could do something."

"You've done so much already, staying with him for all that time," Robin assured her.

"If Henry doesn't . . . if he's still—should I come to the party anyway?"

"Absolutely," Robin assured her. She didn't like talking about Henry as if he weren't in the room. "Susanna and the rest of us want you to come."

"I bought a new dress, it's kind of expensive . . ."

Robin wrapped a gentle but firm arm around Lisa and moved her to the door. "I can't wait to see the dress. You will be ravishing in it. And, Henry, if you don't get your flat ol' ass up by then, there will be plenty of other men happy to dance with Lisa."

"Oh, good. I don't want to be all by myself . . ."

Robin opened the door. "Go home. Take a bubble bath and relax. If Henry changes, we'll phone you. And absolutely come to the party!"

Lisa left. Robin went into the bedroom to fetch a blanket. She tucked it around Henry's motionless form. She smoothed his hair. She found his cellphone on the coffee table and set it closer.

"Sweetheart, take as long as you need. If you want something, your cell is right here, and I'll come right away."

No response.

"Try to remember all the lives you've saved. Try to remember your office walls, smothered with thank-you notes and pictures by little children. Remember how much we all love you." Robin crouched in silence, her hand on her brother's back. "Okay. We'll check in tomorrow."

She motioned for Courtney to follow her and went out the apartment door and down the stairs.

Courtney said, "You're so good with him, Robin. So patient."

"We've talked about this, Courtney. You wouldn't think I was *patient* if he'd broken his ankle. No one would expect him to get up and walk on it. He's broken his heart and his mind a little bit. Healing takes time."

They were back at the house. James and Christabel had disappeared, leaving their plates and glasses on the table instead of carrying them into the kitchen. "I swear, when James is around Christabel, his age plummets to about five and his IQ to about fifty."

Courtney laughed. "I'll help you clean up."

They worked in the companionable silence of friends who had done this very thing many times before. When all was tidy and shining and the dishwasher had begun its reliable gurgling and churning, Robin said, "Let's walk down to the beach."

In the darkening evening, they made their way across the front lawn, through the small white gate, and descended the zigzag of steps down the steep dune to the beach where the sea rolled to the shore. The sky was cloudless, the moon was bright. The edges of the dark waves glowed white. The sand was inviting. They took off their shoes and walked barefoot.

"So," Courtney said, as if they'd been interrupted in a conversation, "what else? What about *you*?"

"Let me think. They asked me to co-chair the Science Association gala, but I refused. I agreed to be their secretary, but I hate that fancy-schmanzy glamour stuff."

Courtney was silent.

"Go ahead. Say it." Robin nudged her friend with her elbow. "'Robin, you ought to get out more often! Take that gala job. You're almost thirty years old, no job, no beau, you're stuck in a rut.'"

"Well?" Courtney asked. "You *are* living at home with your parents like some Victorian virgin."

Robin shrugged elaborately. "I like it here. I love the island. I work for the conservation association, I organized the annual bird count, and I'm taking online courses about island water quality. Why should I move? Mother and Dad go back and forth between here and Boston, and someone needs to be in charge of this house. Plus, I forgot to tell you. Dad's writing his memoirs and he wants me to take dictation, type them up, and edit them."

Courtney stopped dead in the sand. "Oh, Robin, that's just sad."

"Dad's going to pay me."

"Robin!"

"If he weren't my father, you'd be happy for me. You'd think I'd gotten a decent job."

"But he is your father."

"Yes, and he's had an amazing life. He never talks about his work, but, Courtney, believe me, over the years, he's seen so many significant changes in surgery. Plus, he's got heartbreaking anecdotes, and hilarious ones, too." Robin started walking again. "The truth is, Courtney, I think we'll get a publishable book out of this. When Dad starts talking, he's absolutely eloquent. He knows about surgery from practically the first account scratched on a cave wall with a clam shell. Do you know, for example, that as few as one hundred years ago, it was common practice to pack a sutured wound with earthworms?" Robin shuddered.

"Gross. Robin, I don't doubt everything you're saying. But what is wrong with this picture: lovely bright woman living at home, working for her parents, dating no one, going nowhere?"

"I came to visit you in Kansas this Easter," Robin pointed out.

"You know that's not what I meant."

"Courtney," Robin said with quiet intensity, "we've talked about this before. Not everyone has to move all the time. Some people already are where they're meant to be. I—"

"Yes, and you've filled your life up with so many volunteer duties, so many committee meetings and associations, that it seems like you have a life, but I think you're *hiding* from life!"

"Oh, Courtney, don't you know me at all?" Robin demanded.

She stopped to stare at Robin. "I don't think I do. And that's terrible. You're my best friend, but you keep too many secrets."

Robin averted her eyes. Courtney was her best friend in the world, had been for over a decade. And she was right—Robin did keep secrets from her. From everyone.

Reaching over, she took Courtney's hand. "My secrets are so humdrum, if I tell you, you won't believe they're secrets."

"Try me."

Robin sighed, gathering her thoughts—concocting her smoke screen. "Well, then, first of all—I don't ever want to leave this island. Of course I'll travel now and then, like I did to see you, or go up to Boston to stay with Mom and Dad for a symphony or something. But this island is my home, and I feel—don't you dare laugh—I feel a *calling* to remain here and do what I can to tend it." She stopped and stared Courtney in the eyes. "If I am in love, Courtney, I'm in love with Nantucket, and I can't imagine loving anyone more."

Courtney nodded. "Okay. I get that."

Looking doubtful, Robin began walking again. "You want a home, husband, family. I really truly don't care if I have children."

"That's because you have your hands full with your own parents and siblings. You're slipping into Susanna's shoes."

"Okay, if I am, is that so wrong? Everyone adores my mother, and she's the happiest person I know."

"But she's a mother and wife! That fabulous house, the four amazing children, they are *hers*, not yours!"

A little hit. A punch to the diaphragm. Robin let her thoughts settle. "True. Still, with all our guests, she's glad for my help. And Dad's still passionate about his work in Boston, plus, he really wants to write this book about the changes in surgery. So much is done now through technology. There aren't enough hours in the day for him. His book—"

Courtney interrupted, "But *you* don't have to be the one to help him write that book. He could hire a secretary. For that matter, your mother could hire help."

"She has a housecleaning service come once a week. And come on, Courtney, you know how she loves cooking."

"Oh, you're getting my thoughts all tangled. I guess what it comes down to is when, *how*, are you going to meet a man?"

"Who says I have to, Courtney?" Robin shook her head. "I don't mean I'm gay. I mean—what do I mean? Let me think. I mean, first of all, in college I had quite a decent number of romantic experiences to fill my memory bank but no one made me dizzy with love. I've *seen* guys I like here on the island now and then, but I've never wanted to be serious with them. Meeting someone new just isn't a priority of mine."

Courtney crunched an empty crab shell lying in her path. "Let's turn around and walk back. I apologize if I've insulted you. It's that I worry about you. But I suppose I do understand what you're saying. For one thing, I don't love Kansas the way you love Nantucket. I don't feel like a *custodian* of it like you feel about the island. More a, well, member of a tribe, I guess. Not the people so much as the land, the grass, the sky—my horse."

"And Monty?"

Courtney was silent for a few moments. "Yeah, of course, Monty."

"Now *you're* lying to *me*."

Courtney's head snapped toward Robin. "Why do you say that?"

"Because you love James."

"I never said that."

"Um, duh. I've only watched you drool over him for eleven years."

"Please tell me I don't *drool* over him." Courtney didn't wait for Robin to respond. "Anyway, James is bound at the hip to Christabel."

"Christabel." Robin bent down to pick up a pebble and toss it into the ocean. "Now there's someone who really needs to get off island."

"She went to college—"

"—and dropped out sophomore year. She tried art school, and ending up taking drugs. Quinn had to send her to rehab for six months, remember? She settled down once she got back home. I worry about her, too, Courtney, more than I worry about Henry. Whatever's going on with him is genetic, I think, chemical, with a chemical solution.

Henry made it through med school. He's a genius surgeon. You and I both know that if an emergency call came in right now, he'd probably rise above his funk and set to work."

"But Christabel?"

"She's a broken spirit. It's not just that her mom abandoned her when she was so young, although that's part of it. It's as if—I don't know how to express this, but you've seen her over the years, you know what I mean—Christabel has to live her life on high all the time. Normal life bores her. Take daily meals, for example. She's twenty-seven years old. She lives at home with her father and spends her time making herself look extraordinary and painting in her studio, which used to be Quinn's garage. Quinn, who spends all day teaching, has to come home and cook dinner. He has to buy the groceries. He cleans the house. Christabel has no interest in that sort of dull, demeaning thing. She wants to be *discovered*. She wants to live a fantasy."

"Well, she is an amazing beauty. And her artwork is interesting."

"That's true. So with any luck one day a wealthy summer man will sweep her off her feet and take her away." Robin stopped and took Courtney's arm. "Because believe me, Courtney, James is not going to marry her. He's not even sleeping with her."

"That's none of my business."

Robin continued as if Courtney hadn't spoken. "James and Christabel were a cute couple when they were teens and in their early twenties, but James has grown up. He has his medical translation business and with his facility with languages, he's riding the tide into the future. He's making money and meeting deadlines. Christabel's still drifting around in her underwear hoping she'll shock people. If James feels anything for her, it's pity, not love. Not desire."

"Listen to you," Courtney said, softly joking, "talking away about love and desire. Who do you desire?"

Robin stared up at the sky and it seemed as if she were falling into a well of longing as deep and complicated as the darkness above them. Maybe sometime she could tell Courtney, but not now. She said, "This weekend I *love* my family and I *desire* the achievement of a marvelous celebration in my mother's honor, with all her children and her summer children gathered around her. That's enough for now, don't you think, Courtney?"

Courtney conceded. "It is." She yawned. "Sorry. The sea air . . ."

"You must be whipped from traveling across the country today."

"You're right. I am. I'm going on up."

"I'll stay down here for a while. Enjoy the quiet while I can."

"Good night." Courtney kissed Robin's cheek and headed toward the wooden steps up the cliff.

R obin sauntered back down the beach, hoping her body language spoke of ease—in case Courtney looked down at her. Alone, free from the others, she was torn, pulled by the need to be out on the water and that need balanced by the necessity of climbing the steps, checking on her parents, and getting some rest before this weekend began.

Always, *always*. Her obsession with her secret, and her wish to be normal.

She sat on the sand—it was cool and damp in the night air, and she shivered. She wrapped her arms around her knees and watched the water in the moonlight. Waves, regular and tranquil, not tugged tonight by the moon's whims or driven by the wind, rose and broke as they rolled toward the shore.

It would be a lovely night to go out. A perfect night.

Robin sat very still, listening.

Oh, this was ridiculous, *she* was ridiculous! If anyone in her family had the slightest inkling of the unnatural, dangerous risks she took, they would say *she* was the crazy one. No one could know. No one. Ever.

Courtney would probably understand, but she couldn't count on Courtney not to let the secret slip to someone who would let it slip to someone else, and soon her parents would know, and then all hell would break loose.

Why the devil did her life have to be so conflicted? Why were her wildest, dearest loves unacceptable, *wrong*? She rose, pacing down the beach, fighting off tears.

Much of her life Robin had understood how a kinky, twisted hidden gene of manic-depression twined through the synapses and ganglia of the Vickerey brains, wreaking different degrees of havoc. Because . . . if she were given to depression, she would be sorely depressed. Most days she reminded herself to be grateful for all she had. Most days she was thankful to be in love and to be loved. Some days she even thought it best that the man she loved could never be the man she lived with, because then he would have to know about her other secret.

But some days . . .

Some days she yearned for a home of her own, with a loving husband coming in the front door to squeeze her, kiss her hello, ask her about her day, tell her about his. She caught herself hypnotized in front of menswear in department stores, wishing she could buy this soft cashmere sweater, or that nautical raincoat, or—sweetest of all, most intimate and necessary, men's briefs.

What would it be like, to sleep all night long in the same bed with a husband snuggled against you, to bring him hot soup when he was ill, to wave casually to her friends as she entered a restaurant with him at her side?

Robin was four years old when Quinn Eliot arrived on the island with his wife, Desiree, a stunning and extravagant woman. She grew up hearing people gossip about the couple.

Quinn and Desiree had married young. Too young. Desiree got

pregnant accidentally when they were dating their sophomore year in college. They married, had a baby, and lived with Desiree's mother until Quinn finished his degree.

With their two-year-old daughter, Christabel, they moved into the ranch house near Surfside Beach that Quinn had summered in and inherited from his parents. Quinn taught history at the local high school. Desiree joined every organization she could tolerate, hoping to meet "interesting" people. She threw parties. She chaired galas. She loved the busy six months of the year and was bored to literal tears in the winter. The "interesting people," Desiree felt, left at the end of August.

Christabel grew into winsome childhood, with the Icelandic blond hair Desiree paid money to have. Susanna worried that Desiree treated her daughter as an accessory and a playmate. Desiree dressed them in matching outfits to call attention to their mutual prettiness. She took Christabel with her everywhere, most memorably off island to Boston for shopping expeditions. They stayed in posh hotels, saw ballets and theater, rode the Swan Boat in the public garden. She gave Christabel lavish, exotic birthday parties to which the parents were also invited.

The summer Christabel was ten and already beginning to blossom into the intensely female beauty she would become, Desiree ran off with a wealthy German. She filed for divorce, telling Quinn to take full custody; she didn't want their daughter "confused" by the different language and customs of another country.

By then, Robin was twelve, hearing chatter about Christabel and Quinn from her friends as well as from her mother over the dinner table. It was a sad tale: Christabel became emotionally paralyzed when her mother left. She stayed in bed, not willing to eat, not surrendering to tears, asking no questions of her father about what had happened—even though Quinn explained it to his daughter in the best, most gentle way possible, over and over again.

Desiree left at the end of August. When school started, Christabel refused to go. Quinn, who was now known by his peers as "poor Quinn" and by his students as "poor Mr. Eliot," talked with friends about how to help his daughter. Several women, mothers of Christabel's friends, even Susanna, went to the house to sit on the bed and attempt to chat with the mourning girl. Quinn sought professional help, but Christabel refused to speak with anyone.

But one morning, Quinn came home from teaching to find his daughter sitting on the sofa in the living room, watching a soap opera. Christabel's hair was matted and tangled, her pajamas wrinkled, her face expressionless. But when he made peanut butter toast for her and set it on the table with a glass of juice, she ate and drank. He understood that she was, in her own inarticulate way, coming to terms with her new life. Quinn told Susanna he was appalled by the frothy soap operas his daughter watched, but it seemed to work: therapy by television. He was sure Christabel wasn't the first person to try it.

Another week later, Christabel walked into the elementary school wearing a scarlet dress of her mother's. She had sliced off the hem so it fell at her knees, and wrapped an orange scarf around and around her torso to bind the larger garment to her own body. She looked wondrously strange, magnificent, even regal. She did not appear pitiful or sad. Somehow Christabel had swallowed the black seed of her grief and it had transformed her, as in a fairy tale, into a princess.

In the community, Quinn was considered a good man and a loving father. He had the counsel of many teachers and parents to help him through this difficult time. He also sought professional help, mainly because he was troubled by Christabel's appearance as she became a teenager. If he bought her—with the help of mothers—new clothes, Christabel ignored them. She insisted on retaining the cast-offs of her mother's wardrobe, every scarf, skirt, and sparkle of it, and fitting it somehow to her body. Otherwise, she seemed okay, maybe quiet, but stable. She attended class, maintained reasonable grades, hung out with friends, and did the household chores Quinn assigned her. When she became a young teenager, she was about as normal as any of her classmates, except for the weird dressing habit.

When her behavior began to change, it was slow, almost unnoticeable, and all the other junior high girls were changing, as well—wearing too much makeup, sassing their parents, rolling up the waistbands of their skirts, riding in cars with boys. By high school, Christabel was skipping class, missing her curfew at home and her deadlines at school, and smoking. And drinking. And seeing older guys.

One of the older guys was James, which wasn't surprising, given his talent for mischief. He was a year ahead of Christabel in school, only one year older, but in high school that year was significant. James had been blessed with the same careless glamour that shimmered around Christabel. With his mass of auburn hair, his long heavy-lidded sea-green eyes, and his lanky height, James was the handsomest boy in the school.

One Saturday, a sophomore girl saw James and Christabel walking on the beach together. Not holding hands, but touching shoulders, talking intensely, obviously *together*. The girl called a friend who called a friend. Within minutes everyone who counted—everyone in high school—knew about this alliance.

And then it was as if a great collective sigh of satisfaction rose up from the high school students. They had known this would happen. Exquisite Christabel Eliot and dreamy James Vickerey together? This was perfection. This was the stuff of which legends were made. Their imaginations soared.

Robin was sixteen that year. She had a crush on a baseball player named Drew. He was dating someone but often stopped in the hallway to talk to Robin, facing Robin so that her back was against her locker while he stretched one tanned muscular arm above her shoulder, creating an intimate space between the two of them. She knew he liked her. Lots of guys liked her. She was good-looking. She had long, wavy, strawberry-blond hair, green eyes, dark lashes. But that had never mattered much to her.

Being with her family mattered to her, and being on the island. Her family was different from other families, she thought, although she never expressed her opinion aloud. Her father was an important surgeon in Boston. Her oldest brother, Henry, was nineteen and a sophomore at Harvard. Henry was on his way to med school with plans for becoming a surgeon like their father. Robin, James, and Iris were just as intelligent, just as capable, their parents reminded them. Robin knew she didn't have the same virtuoso scientific mind her brother possessed, but she did have—*something*. She was quick to learn, always easily making A's in school. She knew she could have all the friends she needed, boyfriends, too. But she didn't really need them, or even want them very much. She loved being alone—she *treasured* being alone.

Her mother never let Robin be as solitary as she wanted. They lived in a *community,* Susanna reminded her children. She made them attend church with her every Sunday. She encouraged them to take part in the Christmas pageant, in the school plays, in the Green Team that went around the island picking up trash. They should take part in community events—Daffodil Weekend, the Halloween parade, the Christmas Stroll. They should learn about town government and what it meant to be well-informed, year-round citizens.

"Yawn," Robin complained to James one day. "Gigantic snot-sucking yawn." She would never speak that way in front of her mother.

"Oh, I'm not sure I agree with you, Robber," James said with a mischievous gleam in his eyes.

"Tell me!" Robin sat up from where she'd been lying on the floor. "What are you going to do?"

All James would say was: *Wait and see.*

Nantucket Island had a winter population of around ten thousand involved, and argumentative, citizens. The annual town meeting took place in April. The high school auditorium was filled, the board of selectmen sat alert at a table in the front, and the moderator had a time clock to help keep order. Citizens, sane and otherwise, who had been shut in their homes all during the long windy winter, flocked to the gathering to voice their concerns with all the righteous indignation they'd been squirreling away like nuts over the winter.

That year, landscaping regulations were the hot topic. Landscapers used pesticides, herbicides, and fertilizers that sent toxins into the harbor and ocean, injuring the health and abundance of the fish and shellfish that gave fishermen and scallopers their livings. The town had to vote whether or not to ban the use of certain chemical products.

On the day of the town meeting, Robin was puzzled when, just as school was letting out, she heard her brother's name mentioned in excited whispers.

Before she could find out what was going on, her mother arrived to pick her up. Iris was already in the car. James was nowhere to be seen.

"Hurry up," Susanna told Robin. "Get in." She peeled away from the line of family cars, her mouth tense.

"What's going on, Mom?" Robin asked.

"I'm not sure," Susanna said. "Carla Townsend phoned me—she lives on upper Main—but I can't believe what she said is right. I really can't believe it."

For sunny Susanna to be sputtering like this was both frightening and amusing for the Vickerey daughters, who sat in the backseat sharing wide eyes and suppressed giggles. Susanna drove just over the speed limit through the narrow streets into town, parking on Main Street in front of Nantucket Pharmacy. It was, in fact, the only space she could find, which was unusual for an April day when the tourists hadn't yet arrived. Dozens of vehicles, especially contractors' vans and carpenters' trucks, slanted toward the curb where crowds gathered. Robin, Iris, and Susanna stepped outside to join them.

Susanna nodded toward the cobblestone road next to the stately brick Pacific National Bank. *"No,"* she whispered.

Proudly walking down the street came James, wearing a placard that said, NO PESTICIDES. He'd ripped a pair of jeans and cut and frayed the cuffs. He wore a sort of linen tunic that was also torn. He was barefoot.

In his hands he held the reins of a placid roan gelding. Seated in the saddle was Christabel, her long blond hair woven with daisies, her lithe fourteen-year-old body completely naked except for daffodils placed at strategic points—over her nipples, her loins, and two on her bum.

"Dear Lord," Susanna murmured.

The crowd cheered.

Christabel did not respond. She didn't look left or right, but straight ahead, her poise regal, her nakedness stunning in its purity and beauty. She was fourteen. The sun seemed to shine out of her pale skin. She resembled a queen on a royal pilgrimage rather than Lady Godiva.

"They're beautiful!" Iris exclaimed, bringing her hands up as if in prayer.

They *were* beautiful, Robin realized. For a few moments the two did not resemble a pair of foolish teenagers, but a myth come to life. How old was the original Lady Godiva? Robin wondered. Back in the thirteenth century, or whenever it was, people died earlier, married earlier, were adults earlier. James walked steadily, eyes straight ahead, his chin held high as he led the horse, and Christabel also held herself proudly. Maybe those two really did care about the state of the oceans. Maybe this wasn't only a prank, something to wake up the townsfolk after a long cold winter.

Cameras began to flash.

"Hey, that's my horse!" a man yelled. "They stole my horse!"

Sirens sounded, shrill, coming louder, and the spell was broken. The horse jerked his head up and down nervously. James had to pause to steady the animal. Two uniformed officers approached James and Christabel, stopping their progress.

"You stay right here and don't move," Susanna instructed her daughters. She fought her way through the crowd and down the street, but before she could reach James, the policemen had gently taken the teenagers into their car. The horse's owner climbed into the saddle, steered the horse into a U-turn, and headed back out of town. This occasioned several "Boos" and a few more camera flashes.

The crowd quickly dispersed. Robin's mother returned.

"Get in the car. We're going to the police station."

Christabel and James were arrested for stealing a horse, indecent exposure, and inciting a riot. They were allowed to return home in the custody of their parents.

Their father was still in Boston, at the hospital. Susanna was white with anger as she drove James and his sisters back to their house. She told Robin to get a snack for herself and Iris and take it to the TV room, then shut herself and James into the living room. A few minutes later, Quinn Eliot's Jeep turned into their driveway. Lady Godiva, now wearing jeans and a sweatshirt, and her father, Quinn, knocked on the door and entered the house.

From the upstairs front hall window, Robin peered down at the fa- ther and daughter coming up the walk. She meant to scrutinize Chris- tabel for signs of anxiety, but found herself mesmerized by Mr. Eliot instead. She'd seen him around school. She would take one of his his- tory courses next year. She'd heard other girls talk about how gorgeous he was, but hadn't paid attention. Now she paid attention.

Mr. Eliot was tall, slender, and blue-eyed, with a mass of thick sandy blond hair neatly combed into place and spilling over his forehead in spite of his grooming. He wore jeans and sneakers, a blazer and tie. He looked angry and sad. Next to him, Christabel strolled as if on her way to lunch.

Later, Robin would learn the consequences of her brother's antics. James and Christabel were sent before a magistrate who ordered them to perform one hundred hours of community service. Susanna and Quinn agreed privately not to ban the two teenagers from seeing each other—that would only lead to more mischief. Susanna began to invite Quinn and his daughter for dinner several nights a week, and to join the family on excursions out to Great Point to see the seals, or on their boat to sail to Coatue. Possibly Susanna was attempting to provide some feminine guidance for Christabel, because the young girl slowly became part of their family. Maybe, Robin thought in her most private, wicked, imaginative heart, her mother was in love with Mr. Eliot. Who wouldn't be, especially if she were married to a grumbling curmud- geon like her father?

After the Lady Godiva affair, Susanna loosened her own reins on her children's activities. She welcomed her children's friends into the house and let them run around freely. Undoubtedly she was hoping to be able to keep an eye on their activities, but it did feel as if the true Susanna was emerging.

Then—the catastrophe. In the fall of that year when Robin was six- teen and James was fifteen, Henry, the first son and the family's most sharp-witted child, a shining star at Harvard, had his first real struggle with depression.

•   •   •

Robin shook her head, as if shaking off the memories, and the fear, and the sorrow. *She* was nuts, stomping around here on the beach talking to herself!

She forced her mind back to the present. Tomorrow, more guests. Saturday, the birthday party. She'd left a list for herself in the kitchen, but she wanted to go over tomorrow's schedule with her mother. She walked back to the zigzag steps, climbed them, and crossed the lawn to her house.

The lights were on in her parents' bedroom on the first floor. A few years before, when Susanna slipped on a pile of magazines when she was getting out of bed and broke her ankle, they decided to move from the master bedroom on the second floor and turn what had been a conservatory into a first-floor bedroom. Now Robin was often the lone occupant of the second floor with its many bed- and bathrooms. When Henry got his MD two years ago, he moved back to the island but to the apartment above the garage. James took over the second-floor master bedroom for his own bedroom and workspace when he wasn't in the Boston quarters of his medical translation firm. Iris had kept her bedroom as her definite very own when she was in school at Smith, where Robin and Courtney had gone. Iris had graduated last month and taken up residence on the island until she could figure out her next step. That left two extra bedrooms for guests. Courtney had had "her" own bedroom for eleven years, and Iris's friends or their parents' buddies had used the other guest bedroom. The attic was turned over to the boys and their friends long ago and still used for sleeping guests when necessary. It was probably ridiculous to own such a large house, but sometimes it didn't seem large enough.

She knocked on her parents' bedroom door.

"Come," her father ordered.

As always, her mother and father were sitting side by side, tucked up in bed, reading. They were very organized and cozy, sheltered by the fat U-shaped reading pillows Robin had given them one Christmas. The pillows supported their backs and had pockets for their books, reading glasses, and in Mom's case, tissues; in Dad's, a small notebook and pen. Susanna had a pillow beneath her legs to help her back and her feet stuck out from the light summer quilt. She hated hot feet. Her father's feet were covered. He hated cold feet. Separate reading lights mounted on the bed behind them illuminated their books and their heads, and Robin couldn't help but notice how her father's snowy white hair was thinning, her mother's strawberry-blond hair darkening and streaked with silver. Her father wore his neatly ironed blue checked summer pajamas with ink stains on the pocket. Susanna wore a pair of Henry's old running shorts and a T-shirt saying, SAVE THE WHALES.

"Can I get you anything before I go to bed?" Robin asked.

Susanna patted the side of the bed for Robin to sit. "We're fine, darling. How's Henry?"

"Sleeping. I told Lisa to go home. She's kind of a lightweight, don't you think?"

"Let's not judge her too quickly," Susanna advised. "Henry takes some getting used to."

"True. Anyway, tomorrow's another day, as you always say. We'll see how he's doing then. I could use his help. We've got a long list of to-do's before the party Saturday, and some guests are arriving."

Her father grunted eloquently.

"I'll make my cake," Susanna mused, tapping her lips with the stem of her glasses. "Plan a time when you won't need the kitchen."

"Morning. The tent people will be here at ten to start setting it up."

Her father moaned.

Robin continued, unfazed. "I've got an appointment with the caterers and I need to go grocery shopping. If you're making the cake, you won't want to cook, so Courtney and I are going to make dinner tomorrow night. There will be a crowd."

"Thank you, darling. What would I do without you?" Susanna murmured, stroking Robin's cheek.

Robin kissed her mother's forehead, went around the bed, and smacked a loud wet kiss on her father's cheek. He muttered something that sounded like "Good night," in reply.

8

Friday morning, Robin opened her eyes and saw Courtney snoring away in the other twin bed. She allowed herself a moment to be pissed off at Courtney for criticizing Robin's lifestyle and another moment of being pissed off at herself for not sharing her secrets with her best friend.

But a moment was all. She had errands to run. She threw back the covers, tossed herself out of bed, and raced down the hall to the bathroom for a quick shower. The June day, like many early summer days, was starting off cool, but Robin knew she'd be spinning around like a rat in a maze marathon and it would heat up quickly, so she pulled on shorts, a T-shirt, and flip-flops, then stuck her long hair to the back of her head with a clip.

She was glad to be the first into the kitchen. She made a huge pot of coffee for the household, poured a cup for herself, and sat at the table going over her list as she ate a cup of yogurt from the refrigerator.

She cherished moments like these, when she was alone in a full house. She scanned the kitchen, enjoying the sight of the clean slate counters, efficient appliances, and the sun slanting in the window be-neath checked gingham curtains, illuminating a stripe across the an-tique pine table. She was grateful to her mother for all this. It was Susanna who transformed the family's white elephant into a smartly electrified and heated year-round home with plenty of beds and hot water and attics to play in on a rainy day. Their apartment in Boston was pleasant enough, but Susanna had always summered on Nan-tucket. She wanted her children to live near the sea, to ride their bikes safely for miles in any direction, to climb trees, to invite guests— Susanna had wanted to give them all a storybook life, and she had.

But some things even Susanna couldn't change. Ever since Henry had his first breakdown, there was a cloud over the storybook life, a troll lurking beneath the bridge.

James wandered into the kitchen, breaking into Robin's thoughts, pulling her back into the here and now. He poured himself a cup of coffee and sat down at the table. "Hey, sis."

"Hey, James. Thank heaven you're up! The tent company will be here at ten. If you could hang around and kind of supervise, answer questions, that sort of thing, that would be great. Also, before then, do you think you could go up and see how Henry's doing? If he won't or-ganize the drinks for tonight, you have to."

James nodded, but Robin sensed his reluctance. James, like every-one else in the family, adored Henry, but also was afraid for him when he was hit hard by depression, and also guiltily frustrated by him.

Robin charged ahead. "Mom's going to make her birthday cake this morning. She'll put it in the refrigerator in the back hall. I'm going into town for groceries—I've checked the weather forecast on my phone and the day promises to be fair, so I think we'll have a cookout tonight. You'll help with that, right? Hamburgers, hot dogs, sausages, shrimp? I'll have Courtney help me make a ton of potato salad, coleslaw, mac and cheese, and a big green salad." Robin stared at the ceiling a mo-ment, tapping the pencil against her lower lip. "I still haven't decided what to make for dessert tonight. I was waiting to see how many people would actually be here."

"Don't drive yourself crazy, Robin. Just buy some ice cream and cookies and let people serve themselves." James reached into the fruit bowl in the center of the kitchen table and took a banana. "What about picking up people from the ferries or the airport?"

Robin consulted her lists. "Callum and Pearl are flying in at around the same time this afternoon. You and Iris can take Mom's minivan and meet them at the airport."

"Why don't *you* pick up Callum?" James's eyes glinted over the top of his cup.

"James. Don't start." Callum had been James's best friend all through college. Tall, good-looking, and elegant, he'd developed what James insisted on calling a crush on her. A polite fellow, he'd never pressed Robin, although he was always at her side if she needed something. She tried to keep away from him. She liked him, but didn't want to lead him on, because that was it, that was all, she simply *liked* him. Her love was elsewhere.

"I'll never understand you." James glared at her, then changed the subject. "I'll take my Jeep to the airport."

Back on safe ground, Robin said, "You'll need the minivan because Pearl's bringing tubs of flowering vines to wind around the tent poles. They might be in water. Don't ask. You know Pearl. You'll want to put the tubs in the back." She looked at her list. "Mom will have Dad's convertible to pick up her friends around noon. Dad will be hiding away in his study. I've already checked about the car with him. I'll take the Jeep to get the groceries — if Courtney ever wakes up, she'll go with me and help me lug things around."

"Is Jacob coming?" Jacob, Henry's best friend from med school, worked at the ER at Mass General.

"Damn, I forgot about him. He was going to call to let us know if he could take a couple of days off. I hope he can, he'd be good for Henry."

James stared out at Henry's apartment over the garage. "If Henry goes into some kind of meltdown this weekend, I'm going to hit him over the head with a club."

"James," Robin objected.

James stood up and scrounged around in the ancient cookie jar, taking out a couple for his breakfast. "I don't mean I'll kill him. I'll just knock him unconscious for a while." He grinned mischievously at Robin. "And these are oatmeal raisin, *health Nazi,* so no lectures."

"I want Henry to be conscious and in good form tomorrow, for Mom's sake," Robin said.

"That's what we all want," James agreed.

Susanna came into the kitchen, freshly showered, wearing shorts and a T-shirt.

"Mom! You're not going to pick up your friends dressed like that, are you?"

"No," Susanna answered calmly, "I'm going to make my cake dressed like this. I'll change later." She poured herself a cup of coffee and sat down at the table with Robin, bringing the familiar fragrance of Ivory soap with her. "You look organized."

"I think I am. I hope I am. James is going to be in charge of the tent people. I'll take Courtney with me to get groceries."

"Do you have eggs on the list?"

"Of course I do, Mom. Look, don't worry about one single thing. Enjoy the day. You have to pick up your friends at the airport, then you can all go for a walk on the beach or anything you want. We are totally on the case."

Susanna embraced Robin. "You are an angel."

"Then I'd better fly," Robin quipped. "Off to make miracles happen." She kissed her mother's cheek and left the kitchen.

Upstairs, Robin found Courtney's bed empty and heard the sound of the shower running. Good. She wouldn't have to wake Courtney up. She needed Courtney to ride along this morning and help her with her errands.

While she waited, she peeked into Iris's room. Iris was standing by the window, still in her pajama bottoms and T-shirt. In the slanting morning light, Robin's younger sister's face was pensive, almost sad. *She's changed,* Robin realized. *She's a woman now.* A rush of protectiveness surged through Robin. Iris was her little sister. What had happened to her in the past four years to make her look so much older? It wasn't just the purple hair.

"Hey," Robin said from the doorway.

Iris smiled. "Hey."

Robin entered the room, went to her sister, and wrapped her arms around her. "Damn, girl, you're getting tall."

"Not as tall as you," Iris murmured.

Robin laughed a low wicked laugh. "You'll never be as tall as I am." That was, after all, the simple truth.

"Where's Courtney?" asked Iris, still staring out the window.

"Showering. Mom's in the kitchen starting to make her cake. James has put on his SWAT gear and gone out to see Henry."

"So do you have a minute to talk?"

The question surprised Robin. It had been years since Iris had sought Robin out.

"Of course." Robin gave her sister a little squeeze before walking over to the unmade twin bed and sitting cross-legged on the end. This was their time-honored tradition: sitting on the bed, Iris leaning against the headboard, Robin leaning against the footboard, relaxed and comfortable. In no hurry.

Iris settled herself and for a long time she was quiet. "Have you ever had a friend you wanted to—I don't know, get rid of?"

Robin was so startled by the question, she laughed. "Well, there have been some boyfriends I might have wanted to murder."

Iris didn't smile but shifted restlessly. "That's not what I mean. I mean, how do you say to someone that you don't want to be her best friend anymore?"

"You're talking about Pearl." Robin wasn't surprised and she certainly wasn't upset. She had never liked Pearl or understood Iris's friendship with her. But she knew from her relationship with Courtney how a college roommate could become part of someone's life.

Iris nodded. "She's so glamorous, Robin. She's so *all that*. I can never match her. I can't keep up."

"Oh, honey, thank heavens for that." Robin tried to gather her thoughts. She didn't want to tell her sister what she really thought of Pearl—that the wealthy young woman was an alcoholic and a slut.

After all, Robin had slept with her share of men and spent her share of time throwing up in the toilet or standing in the shower with a pounding headache. Iris and Pearl had been together for the past four years. Pearl had stayed here every summer, not to make money like the other summer children, Pearl didn't need money. She had plenty of that. It was the parties that drew Pearl. It was the endlessly changing parade of young men, friends of Henry's or James's or male friends of Robin's who made the Vickerey house an irresistible oasis to Pearl.

"Pearl wants to go to Europe this summer." Iris began to peel the polish off her toenails. "I told her I didn't have the money to go. Even though I know, if I really wanted to, I could get Dad to cough up the funds. I just—I don't know how to explain it."

Robin tried to help her out. "Maybe you want to be here because you love the summers here."

Iris shrugged. "That's the thing, Robin, I don't have any idea *what* I want to do." Iris suddenly lifted her head and aimed an accusatory beam at Robin. "*You* know what *you* want to do. You want to stay on the island all your life and be part of the community and help out Mom and Dad. James has already built up a major company because of his facility for languages. Henry's got his wacko mind to deal with and he's a freaking *surgeon*. Valerie is already a physician. Courtney is a college professor. Callum's going to join his family's import/export business. And me! What do I want to do? I have no idea. Robin, I think my head's going to explode."

Robin ached to scoot down the bed and wrap her little sister in her arms. But she knew Iris would wriggle out impatiently. Iris could be mercurial. Sometimes she still acted like a child and suddenly she would be furious because she wasn't treated as if she were a grown-up.

"Lots of people your age don't know what they want to do."

"But I don't want to be like, *lame*."

"You know you don't want to go to Europe for the summer," Robin offered. "That's a start."

"I suppose." Iris lifted her head and leaned forward. "I don't even want Pearl to be here for Mom's party. Pearl will drink too much and try to seduce some inappropriate man. When she's here, I end up being her watchdog." Iris's face squeezed up in misery. "I don't know what has happened to me. I used to have so much fun with Pearl. I've never laughed so hard with anyone. We could talk about everything. When I stay with her in New York and we go to a museum or a play or restaurant, I almost get high from being so sophisticated. I mean, Pearl doesn't use cabs. She uses her father's driver. Robin, I have seen so many things in New York. Really wild partying."

"Oh, honey, have you—"

Iris shook her head impatiently. "No! I see enough crazy behavior at home. I don't need to take drugs. I don't want to, either. You know, Pearl wants to go to Amsterdam because of the pot houses." Iris lifted her head and her face was shadowed with weariness. "I said to Pearl, when I was mad at her, you just want to go to Paris to find a fresh gutter to vomit into."

"Oh, Iris." Robin closed her eyes as if she could block out the image.

"And do you know what she replied? She laughed at me, she said, 'True. Plus, I want to find some fresh men to fuck.'" Iris had tears in her eyes. "She wasn't always this way, Robin. You know that. She was sweet when I met her. I mean, she was way more sophisticated than I was and she'd had way more sexual experience, but she was sweet."

"What about her parents?" Robin asked.

"What about them? Her father's never around and all her mother does is shop. Our family is like the flipping Brady Bunch compared to them and we're all crazy."

Robin tried to lighten the mood. "I wouldn't say we're *all* crazy. There's still hope for you."

Iris took her sister's words seriously. "I think so, too. That's why I just want Pearl to go away."

"Didn't you say she's going to spend the summer in Europe?"

"Yeah, but she'll be here for the party and who knows how long she'll stay."

Robin tapped her lip with her fingernail as she thought. "Tell you what. I'll stick with you or Pearl this weekend and give you a break."

Iris sighed deeply. "That would be brilliant of you, Robin."

"And for the rest of it, I'll help you work it out. Me Tonto, you the Lone Ranger."

At last, a smile from Iris. She launched herself across the bed and hugged Robin. "You are the best sister in the world!"

Courtney tapped lightly on the open door. Her long brown hair was shiny and wet, skimming the fragrance of her strawberry-scented shampoo into the room. She wore shorts, a white T-shirt, and Keds. "Am I interrupting?"

Robin spun about, keeping an arm around Iris. "Not at all. I was just waiting for you. We have a thousand things to do today."

"Do I have time to grab a cup of coffee?"

"Of course. Iris, do you want to come with?"

"No, thanks. I've got to get the room ready for Pearl. Her plane gets in this afternoon. Can you go with me to pick her up, Robin?"

"Sure. See you later." Robin headed for the stairs, Courtney following.

"The weather's super today," Courtney said as they hit the first floor where the sun streamed in the windows. "I checked my phone—it's supposed to be perfect tomorrow, too."

"I know. What luck."

"Your mother's karma."

They reached the kitchen door. Susanna held the large mixing bowl in her arm as she poured cake batter into several pans. At the kitchen table, miracle of miracles, sat Henry, wearing yesterday's clothes. James was preparing two cups of coffee.

Courtney absolutely waltzed into the kitchen. "Good morning, everyone! James, is there enough coffee for me?"

Robin stood watching, soaking it all in, this family moment illuminated by morning sun, emotions winking around the room like Tinker Bell's light. James's face when he saw Courtney—happiness, love, *vulnerability*. Why? Was something going on? She'd tackle Courtney and find out.

And Henry, slumped at the table like one of the walking dead, but present. At least physically present. James set a cup of coffee in front of him. James had a hematoma on his jaw. Henry had a swollen eye.

"So what happened to you boys?" Susanna asked casually, never taking her eyes from the cake pans.

"Yeah," Courtney added. "You look like you spent the night brawling in bars."

Henry grunted.

James replied archly, as if he were simply a mischief-maker, the goofy little brother, "We bumped into each other getting out of Henry's door."

In those frivolous words, Robin saw the truth of it, the way it had happened so many times before:

James entering Henry's living room, finding his brother lying in deep depression on the sofa.

James starting off by good-natured wheedling: "Hey, bro, it's almost the big day, tomorrow's Mom's birthday party, we've got a ton of things to do and I can't do them without you. Jacob flies in this afternoon. You've got to pick him up from the airport. Some of Mom's friends arrive, too. And the cousins—whoa! Get ready! Maybe Uncle Eddie still has that bunion he wants to show you."

After a while, after no response from Henry, James would get physical. He'd attempt pushing, rolling, pulling Henry off the sofa. Henry would freeze. Go wooden. James would do something like climb on the back of the sofa and use the power of his legs to shove Henry onto the floor. Maybe Henry hit his eye on the coffee table. Something. Something enough to jar Henry out of his lethargy into action. Henry would slowly get up from the floor, rotate toward James like a bull facing another bull, and charge. The brothers would tussle, but James would win because he had emotion behind him, the desire to please his mother, the need to get Henry to move out of his stupor, and Henry would be weakened by his depression.

There would be shouting. Cursing. Name-calling. Probably the brothers would wrestle all the way down the stairs. But the moment they stepped outside, James would have said: "Henry, you self-centered brat, get a grip. Make your hair lie down, you look like Einstein. Don't let Mom see you so freaky. Stand up straight. You're an overeducated, spoiled, *fragment* of asshole, not even the entire asshole, just a small wrinkled red bit of skin, and for once in your life you're going to pretend you're a real person so Mom won't kill herself in despair."

Something like that. James would say something like that—he had before; Robin had heard him. When he got angry at Henry, James got graphic and colorful. Inventive. It was a device he'd learned as a toddler stumbling in the footsteps of his utterly cool older brother. Boys were so different from girls, Robin thought. She had adored baby Iris from the moment she was born, all pink and helpless. She had held her, dressed her, given her the bottle when she was old enough, and later, bathed her, played with her, read to her. Iris had worshipped Robin. When Robin braided their hair and tied them with matching ribbons, both girls giggled and raced around the house showing off.

Boys, at least the Vickerey boys, thrived on rivalry. When they were young, Henry ignored James, when all James wanted in the world was a speck of his big brother's attention. Robin could clearly remember Henry, six, sitting on the floor in the playroom, building something out of Legos, while James, two, stood behind Henry, hitting him on the back and shoulders over and over again. His small chubby fists pounded on Henry until Henry rolled his eyes and lost his patience and threw his younger brother on the carpet, tickling James while he squealed with triumphant laughter.

When they were older, Henry was always reading, studying, comparing drops of ocean water with drops of rainwater under the microscope he kept set up in the basement. Still, Henry taught James how to toss a baseball, aim a basketball, whack a tennis ball. Henry loved his younger brother and stood up for James countless times against their parents. When James got into trouble for one of his stunts, Henry championed him against their parents. As teenagers, Henry snuck James out several summer nights to get him shit-faced drunk, so James would know his limits and learn how to drink intelligently, at least for his age. When Henry caught James smoking, he gave him a black eye and promised to do it again any time he so much as caught a whiff of cigarette smoke on his clothing. He shared his girlie magazines with James. Taught him about condoms and STDs. Shared his knowledge about girls with James.

Somewhere along the way, when Henry was in med school and James out of college, translating medical journals and websites into different languages and making a fortune, the power balance shifted. James didn't have more power than Henry, but they were equals. They trusted each other. As hard as it was for Robin to comprehend how these two males who had pounded each other with fists could trust each other completely, that was the way it was.

As a teenager, Robin had longed for her big brother to adore her, to protect her, compliment her, introduce her to his friends while at the same time insisting he'd murder them if they as much as looked at her legs. That was the way it was in books. In movies. In many of the families she knew. But Henry was, first of all, passionately absorbed in medicine, devoted to becoming a surgeon, with no interest in anything else. Henry shadowed his father, and back in those days, when Dr. V was a busy, powerful surgeon, he favored Henry, the oldest of his children by three years, the one who could stand quietly and fervently worship his father. Every opportunity he had to learn from his father, Henry seized. In a crisis, Henry would wrench his attention onto James. But it seemed to Henry that both his sisters, Robin and darling little Iris, were not much more interesting than a pair of Jack Russells.

James, only a year younger than Robin, had taken on the role, like a superhero donning his cape, of protector for both Iris and Robin. It helped that he was tall and witty and smart. Ironically, the only real protection Robin needed was from Henry in the instances when she'd needed to talk him down during a manic episode. There were days when Henry, in his manic state, plunged into the water, planning to swim across the Atlantic to Portugal. Or decided to fly from the roof of the garage. Or dragged all his books out into the yard, preparing to start a bonfire, because he didn't need the books anymore; he knew it all. Robin at her best wasn't physically strong enough to wrestle Henry away from his schemes. James could do it, and after that, he'd challenge Henry to a race to the 'Sconset post office, or all the way into the rotary by *The Inquirer and Mirror*. James had sat up thousands of nights listening to Henry expound on theories that would mystify Stephen Hawking. Those, Robin knew, were the hardest times. Henry depressed was sad but easier to handle. Dealing with Henry in his worst manic states was exhausting and sometimes even dangerous.

In the past three or four years, Henry's psychiatrist had found a mix of prescription medications that kept Henry free from the worst of his manic states. It wasn't perfect yet, and Henry still had to fight the demon of depression, which was why Valerie was so insistent that he try lithium.

Yet, Robin thought, with fond amusement, Henry and James would always be rivals. Now as Robin watched, Susanna put the large bowl with the remains of the batter in front of Henry, also giving him the spatula to lick.

"Hey!" James protested.

"You get both beaters, sweetie pie," Susanna said to her second son, handing him the batter-dripping beaters.

As her mother turned back to the sink to rinse her hands, Robin imagined all the diplomatic, delicate negotiations Susanna had had to make over the years between these two alpha males.

Something else was going on, Robin realized. Courtney was skulking around the edges of the kitchen, her back turned to the table as she took down a mug, poured her coffee, added a drop of milk and a spoonful of sugar, and remained standing, leaning against the counter, instead of sitting at the table as she usually did.

James held out one of the batter-covered beaters to Courtney. "Want to lick one?" Of course, being James, he made it sound erotic.

Courtney blushed. "No, thanks. Just coffee for me this morning."

Why did Courtney blush? Robin wondered. Courtney was used to James's silliness. *Something was going on!*

Was she right? *Was* something happening between James and Courtney? Robin had dreamed of this for years, so she was surprised at the thump of jealousy that hit her right in the stomach. Courtney was hers, her best friend, not another groupie drooling over James.

"Great," she said. "Bring your cup with you. We've got a lot to accomplish today."

"Okay," Courtney answered easily, and walked past James without looking at him. "Bye, y'all," she said over her shoulder.

So maybe Robin was overreacting again. It was hard not to in this household.

9

The June evening was balmy, warm, and slightly humid. All around the patio, terra-cotta tubs of flowers spilled their colors and fragrance into the soft air. The wide green lawn where they often played croquet or badminton had been transformed into a modern Camelot by the great white tent that had been installed today, ready for tomorrow night. Tall green privet hedges lined the boundaries of the Vickereys' backyard, turning the space into an extension of the house, another room with the sky as ceiling. James had set up a CD player programmed to play songs from his mother's younger days and the music floated into the air, bubbles of sound drifting around the conversation and laughter.

Everyone was there. Everyone had been met at the airport, brought to the house, shown to a room, and invited to meet on the patio for a casual cookout. In the more comfortable, cushioned, wicker chairs, Dr. V sat with friends from Boston. On a floral-cushioned glider, Susanna was squeezed between her two best friends from college. They had already had a couple of James's peach and Prosecco cocktails. Their cheeks were rosy and they were giggling like children.

At one of the round tables, Quinn chatted with Susanna's cousins, while his daughter, Christabel, barefoot and clad in a sailor costume she'd found at the thrift shop, danced by herself to the music. Henry's best male friend, Jacob, talked with Valerie, probably about something involving blood and guts, their favorite topic, while Henry sat listening to whatever Lisa was babbling about. Robin and Courtney, Iris, and Pearl floated around the edges of the party, refilling wine glasses, putting out extra napkins, and making their own insignificant banter. Pearl was marvelously chic in four-inch heels and a little violet dress that set off her black hair and pale eyes. Courtney grinned as she watched Pearl's eyes flick from Callum at the grill with James to James and over to Quinn, like a colorful raptor idly choosing her prey.

Courtney tried not to look at James.

The food was set out buffet style on one of the long tables, so people had to take a plate and serve themselves. When everyone was seated, Courtney noticed with amusement that while Lisa had taken a seat on Henry's left side, Pearl had alighted on his right side, and was ignoring her food to turn her seductive attentions on Henry. Pleasant, good-natured Lisa had never met Pearl before, had no idea of the games Pearl liked to play. For a brief moment, Courtney thought of asking Lisa to help her in the kitchen where she could tell Lisa not to worry— Henry knew what kind of flirt Pearl was. He'd known her for years. But the thought passed. Courtney didn't want to disrupt the table, and really, she needed nothing from the kitchen. Plus, Lisa needed to step up to the plate.

Courtney sat next to Susanna's cousin, a pleasant, slightly dowdy woman who talked relentlessly, as if no one had listened to her for years. It was actually restful to be blathered at, Courtney thought. She could concentrate on her food and simply nod at Gwen every so often. She knew James was at the other end of the table, with Christabel on his left and Valerie on his right. Christabel allowed herself to be entertained by Henry's friend Jacob, who sat on her other side . . . Jacob, chubby, genius Jacob, who with surgical precision ate his hamburger with fork and knife.

Candles had been placed down the length of the long tables and in the center of the round ones, but it was still daylight, that expansive summer light promising full harvests, sunburned shoulders, and hints of heaven. Conversation muted as people ate.

Quinn called out, "Excellent hamburgers, James! Well done!"

Susanna stood up. She rose, and stayed there, at the head of the longest table.

"Hello, everyone," Susanna said with a slightly nervous tremble in her voice. "I'm so glad you're all here tonight. I want to thank you all for coming to my birthday party, but tonight I want to take the opportunity to say something especially for the group gathered here. Tomorrow evening will be a crush, I know, and what I have to say—" she paused.

Courtney glanced at Robin, who shrugged her shoulders and looked worried. *Dear heavens,* Courtney thought, *don't let Susanna be sick.*

"I want to tell you all how much this birthday weekend means to me," Susanna continued. "And especially, I want to tell my summer children how honored I am they left their busy, adult lives to come here this weekend. You all—Valerie, Jacob, Courtney, Callum, and Pearl—know I've called you my 'summer children' and I'd like to talk about that. I never meant to imply that you were *my* children. I know your own parents did all the hard work of supporting you, teaching you, turning you from squalling infants into civilized human beings. They had the responsibility, the burden. I had—well, I had the *summers.*"

Courtney relaxed in her chair, and sensed how the rest of the party also surrendered their alarm and settled in for a pleasant speech.

"I had you for the summers, and not to wax poetic, but it seems I had you for the summers of your lives, when everything was lush and bountiful, growing, flourishing, and playing. I've been able to watch you over the years as you changed from callow youths into students and then into the capable, admirable, generous grown-ups you've become."

Some people started to clap, but Susanna held up her hand.

"Wait. I'm not finished." Leaning forward, she said, "Jacob. Valerie.

You two were my first summer children. You came home with Henry and worked for the summer and brought such pleasure to our lives." Susanna took a piece of paper from her pocket and unfolded it. "Jacob, I hope you know I've been baking oatmeal cookies every morning just for you—"

James burst out, "Oatmeal? More like raisin–pecan–coconut–cranberry–chocolate chip cookies! They were as big as these hamburger buns."

People laughed. Susanna nodded. "True. You all took them with you for your lunches, and I knew you were getting some fuel for your active bodies. Jacob, I watched as you grew stronger and stouter over the years—"

"Stouter!" Callum yelled. *"There's* a euphemism! How about *fatter!"* Jacob blushed but beamed happily.

"—and I want to say this to you: I know you are working on pediatric surgical instruments and techniques I can't even begin to comprehend. I'll miss you this summer, and I'm so pleased you found the time to come today. And if you ever crave cookies, let me know at once, and I'll make a batch and express-mail them to you."

Jacob nodded several times, fast, almost squirming beneath the attention from the table.

"Now. Valerie. When you arrived that first summer with Henry and Jacob, you were a string bean, too. Such an intense girl. Well, you've grown into such an accomplished woman. I'm thrilled that you're a general practitioner here on the island. I want you to know that I never told Henry about the man you had a crush on your junior year. Since it's safe to mention it now, let me just say, what a relief that you escaped his clutches. With your brains and beauty, you'll go far. But not, I hope, off the island."

The table went quiet. Valerie rolled her eyes and murmured, "Oh, Susanna." Henry stared stonily at his plate, Lisa glanced beneath her eyelashes at Valerie, and finally James broke the tension by saying, "Good job, Mom, tell us all the secrets!" People relaxed and laughed. Courtney smiled smugly. She was certain she knew exactly what Susanna was doing: making Henry jealous of the man whom Valerie liked in junior year, reminding Henry that Valerie was an attractive woman who wouldn't hang around while Henry behaved stubbornly.

"Courtney." Susanna turned her attention to Robin's best friend. "I'll admit I was quietly concerned when you arrived with Robin. You're such a natural beauty and so clueless about it that you had men flocking around you like bees to honey."

Courtney knew she blazed beet-red all over her face and neck. She felt James's eyes on her and went even hotter.

"I loved all the rainy evenings when you stayed at the house and shared some of your studies with me. I never knew much about medieval literature, or, frankly, any kind of poetry. You taught me so much. You enriched my life. I'm proud of you for having a position at a university but at the same time I'm sorry you won't be here in the East. I'll miss you so much."

"Thank you," Courtney replied softly. Oh, she *would* miss Susanna if she returned to Kansas. And maybe she wouldn't have to. Her heart twisted with conflicting desires.

Susanna moved on. "Callum. I think I should thank you for keeping James out of trouble, but if I did that, I'd have to admit that when James got into trouble, you were probably his partner in crime. I'm thinking of the Sunfish you swamped off Coatue and the Jeep that either you or James wrecked more times than I can count."

From the foot of the table, Dr. V grumbled incomprehensibly.

"Now I think it's safe to tell you that your parents and I were always in touch by phone or email."

"Good god," Callum moaned while everyone else laughed.

"You two boys got into so much trouble I couldn't possibly make all the decisions without help from your parents. But we did a good job, don't you think? You're a significant force in your family's firm. If you wreck our Boston Whaler, you can simply buy us a new one." Susanna paused for the laughter. "So you see, you all, I've been able to keep more than one secret." She aimed her gaze at Pearl. "Pearl. You'll be glad to know that I did not tell your parents about all the times you came home at three in the morning looking, shall we say, a little under the weather."

All around the table, eloquent glances were exchanged. The children and the summer children were well aware that Pearl drank too much and equally aware that it was almost impossible to get in touch with her parents, who were always busy in some exotic country.

"You and Iris have just graduated from college," continued Susanna. "Your futures are ahead of you. I know you plan to travel around Europe this summer, but I want you to know you'll always have a home here, summer or winter."

For once in her life, Pearl did not respond sarcastically. She very quietly said, "Thank you, Susanna."

"So that's it!" Susanna glanced at her list, then put it on the table. "Thank you for letting me warble on. I want you to know that having summer children has been one of the most exciting, challenging, memorable, and wonderful times in my life. I love you all, and I'm old enough to be wise enough to know that love is rare and loving someone is a gift." She lifted her wine glass. "Here's to you, my summer children."

Everyone at the table toasted and drank. Susanna sat down, beaming at everyone.

With a dramatic screeching of chair legs against the patio tiles, Christabel shoved her chair back, stood up, and with her chin high, strode away from the table. Every inch of her radiated fury. She went around the side of the house and disappeared from sight.

Courtney couldn't stop herself from glancing at James. Was he going to go after Christabel? Did he feel he needed to take care of her, to soothe and calm her? If so, anything he said last night didn't matter.

James was looking at his mother. His own face held a slight frown. All around the table, people murmured to one another, wondering what had happened to make Christabel storm away, and wondering what should be done now, and by whom?

Quinn half rose from his chair. "Sorry, everyone, sorry. I apologize for my daughter's rudeness. Please don't worry—it's just a, um, feminine kind of thing, you know." By the time he finished speaking, he was bright red.

But his awkward apology did the trick. Susanna smiled and nodded

and the other women all made reassuring noises, and no one left the
table to run after Christabel.

Still, a tinge of discomfort tinted the atmosphere.

Courtney spoke up. "Would you like to hear a really bad joke?"

Everyone nodded and yelled, "Yes!"

"Okay," Courtney said. "A girl came skipping home from school
one day. 'Mommy, Mommy,' she yelled, 'we were counting today, and
all the other kids could only count to four, but I counted to ten. See?
one, two, three, four, five, six, seven, eight, nine, ten!' 'Very good,' said
her mother. 'Is it because I'm blond, Mommy?' 'Yes, it's because you're
blond.' The next day the girl came skipping home from school.
'Mommy, Mommy,' she yelled, 'we were saying the alphabet today,
and all the other kids could only say it to D, but I said it to G. See? A,
B, C, D, E, F, G!' 'Very good,' said her mother. 'Is it because I'm blond,
Mommy?' 'Yes, it's because you're blond.' The next day the girl came
skipping home from school. 'Mommy, Mommy,' she yelled, 'we were
in gym class today, and when we showered, all the other girls had flat
chests, but I have these!' And she lifted her tank top to reveal a pair of
36-Cs. 'Very good,' said her embarrassed mother. 'Is it because I'm
blond, Mommy?' 'No, it's because you're twenty-five.' "

It was a terrible joke, Courtney knew that, and she couldn't have
told it with blond Christabel there, but some people laughed, and
some moaned, and conversation started again.

But Courtney peeked beneath lowered lids at James. He was staring
right at her, smiling. She had done a good thing. She'd turned the party
back into a party.

After dinner was over, people remained around the table, sipping another glass of wine, watching the sky slowly darken, talking, laughing,
relaxing in the summer air.

Courtney helped Robin and Valerie clear the table. Lisa stuck posses-
sively to Henry's side. Dr. V disappeared into his study. The kitchen was
almost overpowering with brightness, and each time Courtney stepped
back outside, it took her eyes a moment to adjust to the fading light.

"Candles," she murmured, trying to remember where the Vickereys kept them. She decided she didn't need them—everyone had left or gone inside. She was alone in the velvet darkness of the summer night. And suddenly the richness of the sweet air, the infinite sky above her, and the salty breeze off the ocean overwhelmed her. She leaned against the side of the house, hugging herself to hold herself together, struggling to calm her emotions.

She loved it here so much. She loved James so much. But what could she do? She couldn't force James to trust the future and let her have *his* babies. She had no magic words or wand. She did have that astonishing proposal from Monty. Should she consider it rationally, unemotionally? Monty was a good man. He was handsome, and strong, and reliable. He loved her. Couldn't she change the way she felt about him? Certainly she was fond of him, she loved him—*in a way*. Couldn't she come to love him sexually and romantically? She'd read of that happening . . .

As if summoned by her thoughts, James strolled up next to her. She knew that it was too dark here for him to see her face, and he had no idea that she was riding a wave of desire and despair.

He leaned next to her against the house. "That was one of the worst jokes I've ever heard," he teased.

"Come on, give me some points for trying," Courtney said, softly knocking his arm.

James inhaled sharply when their arms touched. Simply that, bare skin touching bare skin, made her body beg for more. She knew his did, too. She could feel his longing. The simple connection was powerful between them.

Courtney took his hand, and her need increased. She held his hand, palm to palm, as she said, "James, Susanna's speech tonight was wonderful."

"I know. It gave me a lot to think about."

Courtney moved closer to him. Hurriedly, urgently, she said, "Yes, me, too. Susanna said that love is rare. That loving someone is a *gift*. I love you, and I know you love me. Please, James, if I'm brave enough to want marriage with you, and children with you, why can't you be brave, too?"

Calmly, James retorted, "Mom talked about her summer children. How she loves them. We could adopt children and love them as much as our own."

Courtney countered, "We could do both. Have our own children and adopt."

"I won't take that risk. You haven't seen Henry in his worst states. I wouldn't want my child to go through that. I wouldn't want adopted children to live with that."

"Oh, so you think your family is the only one with kinky genes? James, everyone has eccentricities."

"Henry is more than eccentric. There's a wide spectrum of how people are affected by bipolar disorder. For all we know, Henry's right in the middle. I mean, it could be worse for . . ."

"You can't say it, can you? *For my children.*" Courtney's romantic mood had vanished, replaced by anger. "You've been so fearless, living in foreign countries, starting up your own company. Why are you so cowardly about your *life?*" As soon as she said it, Courtney wished the word *cowardly* back in her mind. It was an insult, it was name-calling, and she wasn't surprised when James dropped her hand and walked away from her.

She stood still for a moment, wondering whether to go after him, and decided against it. She'd gotten herself into the wrong mood for this wonderful evening.

She went into the house where she found Robin in the kitchen mixing up an enormous egg and cheese and veggie casserole that could be popped in the oven tomorrow morning.

"Did you like Mom's speech?" Robin asked. She wore an apron over her party clothes and had flour on her nose.

"Um . . ." Her heart had taken possession of her mind and Courtney mentally slapped her own face for being so self-absorbed. She forced herself to stop thinking about James. "Susanna was wonderful," she replied. "I love her so much." She took an apron off the hook and tied it on. "I want to help. Give me something to chop."

She heard the front door open and close. She heard heavy steps to the second floor. *James,* she thought. Going up to bed. Alone.

Later that night, after she'd helped Robin clean the kitchen, Courtney lay in her own bed, miserably trying to fall asleep, getting mad at
herself because sleep wouldn't come. James was so *obstinate*!

If he only knew—she wanted to tell James, she *would* tell James,
about the time Monty took her to a hotel in Kansas City.

During the years she was in college, Monty kept in touch with Courtney. He'd phoned her occasionally, emailed and texted her. His conversation was light and factual, mostly about his herd of Black Angus, the
weather—always significant in Kansas—and his new pickup truck. She
could sense a slight amusement on his part when she told him about
her fall. Her studies, her teachers, *poetry*. She knew he considered her
interests sweet but boring. She didn't dislike him when he gently made
fun of her—they had always kidded around with each other.

Her senior year at Smith, she returned to Emporia for Christmas
vacation and Monty surprised her with tickets for a performance of
The Nutcracker in Kansas City. The drive to KC was over an hour. The
ballet would be at least two hours. They'd go out to dinner afterward.
He suggested they spend the night in a Kansas City hotel instead of
making the long drive home on icy roads in the dark.

He told her that over the phone. All she'd been capable of replying
was: "Well."

"Tell your parents I'm reserving two separate rooms," he said.

He knew how to rile her and that worked. "I don't have to tell my
parents anything," she said, but she felt queasy in her stomach. Monty
was her friend. Agreeing to go to a hotel with him—was that some kind
of promise she'd go to bed with him? She knew how guys worked when
it came to sex—they could be romantic, devious, or flat-out challenging. And Monty was a man.

The ballet was glorious, but all Courtney could take in was how it
felt to have Monty sitting next to her, not even trying to hold her hand.
In his coat and tie, with his long black hair tied back, he resembled
Johnny Damon, the baseball player who had been born in Fort Riley,
Kansas, and first played for the minor league team, the Wichita Wran-

glers. The contrast of his elegant dress and his elemental warrior mag-
netism made the women around them stare—stare, they practically
drooled. Courtney had to admit it to herself, she loved it, being here
with this big handsome man, and she knew he was doing his best to
please her, because ballet was not Monty Blackhorse's kind of enter-
tainment.

Afterward, as they filed out of the auditorium with the rest of the
crowd, Monty said, "I got us reservations at Café Aixois. We can walk
there from here."

As they ate, they chatted comfortably about the past fall: the semi-
nar Courtney took on teaching, Monty's loss of a prize bull. His parents.
Her parents. What had happened in Kansas while she was gone.

After dinner, she waited while Monty raised a hand for a taxi—he'd
left his car at the hotel. She smiled at how sophisticated he was, this
man whom she'd known since he was a boy.

But as they settled in the back of the cab, the atmosphere thick-
ened. She smiled nervously at him.

Monty put his arm around her and pulled her next to him. He drew
her close to him. Then he kissed her. He *seriously* kissed her.

He wore a black wool coat with a black collar of some extremely
soft fur—mink? He'd taken off his black Stetson once he got in the car,
but he still wore his leather gloves. His embrace was a kind of coaxing,
a physical sweet-talking. It made her think of all the times she'd
watched him handle a nervy Thoroughbred, gentling the animal down
until she stopped backing away to the full length of the rope and stood
still next to him, huffing with anxiety. The thought that she was even
thinking about a horse right now was so ridiculous she almost laughed
right into his mouth, but she controlled herself. She ordered herself to
enjoy this moment, but a small giggle escaped from her mouth, and
she pulled away.

The taxi stopped in front of the hotel. Monty escorted her through
the lobby to the elevators. Their rooms were on the same floor. He
walked her to her room and waited while she slid in the key card.

She looked up at him. "Monty, thank you. This was a wonderful evening."

"It doesn't have to end now," he told her. His black eyes were gleaming.

"What?" She wanted to laugh and she kind of felt like throwing up. "Monty. Come on. We're *friends.* I'm not going to bed with you. Don't be ridiculous."

His face flushed. He flinched as if she'd struck him. It was not even possible, she had thought then, that she could hurt his feelings. He was *Monty.* Her sense of amusement was replaced by dread.

Then he smiled, a crooked half smile that she knew so well. "Well, *amiga,* it was worth a try."

He leaned toward her. She froze in place like a doe sensing the scope of a hunter's rifle.

He pecked a kiss on her forehead. "Sleep well." He walked away to his room.

She hurried into her room and into the bathroom where she stood gawking at herself in the mirror. Her lipstick was smeared.

"What in the hell was that about?" she asked her reflection. She didn't want to believe Monty was like so many college guys she'd dated, guys who assumed she'd drop into a bed with them after a hot meal and a hot kiss. Monty wasn't like that, she would not believe that of him.

Which meant what? If he didn't want a roll in the hay, did he want to *make love*?

In the mirror, her reflection laughed. Monty Blackhorse was as likely to love her as he was to fall off his horse. And after all, he was only a guy, and the first thought in any guy's head was sex. She was getting herself all worked up over nothing.

The next day as they drove back to Emporia, she felt no tension between them, no sense of embarrassment. They were easy with each other, joking, talking, listening to the country western station on the radio.

Monty hadn't tried to get her in bed since then, and that was a good eight years ago.

But now as she lay in bed remembering that night, illumined by the

light of Monty's marriage proposal, a powerful emotion—love, gratitude, admiration for the way he'd handled that December date. He had
not pressured her. He'd somehow understood how the timing was all
wrong for her to take him seriously. Maybe he had been in love with
her way back then, eight years ago, and had waited for her to be ready
for him. Could she ever be ready for him?

A ripple of salt air breezed through the open window, and she pulled
the sheet up to her shoulders. She should go to sleep. Tomorrow was
the big party for Susanna.

She closed her eyes, wondering which man she would dream about.

10

After dinner, Susanna and her friends and relatives curled up with Irish coffees in the living room. Iris and Pearl drove off to the Box to dance. Henry had brightened up and even laughed during dinner; now he sat at the round patio table with Valerie, Lisa, and Jacob. Robin wished she were a fly on his shoulder to see how he would handle having his first true love and his newest squeeze together.

James was talking with Courtney as they leaned against the house beneath the shadows of an old maple. *Interesting,* Robin thought. She lazily began clearing the table, carrying dishes into the kitchen.

"I knew I'd find you here." Callum entered the kitchen, holding several plates.

"Am I that predictable?" Robin asked, laughing, knowing that yes, actually, she was. She opened the dishwasher door and slid out one of the racks, effectively separating herself from Callum.

Years ago, she'd had a crush on Callum, even though he was a year younger. Tall, broad-shouldered, dark hair, dark eyes, and *quiet*—that was Callum. His calm presence in the midst of all the squabbling Vickereys made him seem mysterious to Robin. His family ran an import/export business in Boston, so when he came for the summer, he always brought some exotic offering for Susanna—a Chinese vase, a silk kimono.

When they were younger, in college, Callum went along with James in his idiotic escapades. They slipped out of the house at night to take the small motorboat out to sea and ran aground on a sandbar. They spent the night drinking and singing until a friendly fisherman towed them back into the water. They took the top off the old Jeep, packed it with guys, and drove along the stretch of sand to Great Point, where they ran out of gas, stuck at the water's edge as the tide came in. They went to innumerable beach parties, they drank too much, they received endless phone calls from girls they'd wooed and forgotten. But Callum never exhibited the adolescent carelessness that drove James. Callum was like the silent lieutenant standing at the side of the reckless monarch. He was the guard walking two steps behind, watching, prepared.

After Robin got over her crush, she wondered why James was friends with Callum. The men were so different. Callum was a rock, James a fox, an eagle, a traveler, impatient to go on his way. She decided that just as she had her own secrets from her siblings, so did James. Who knew what Callum was like when he and James were together off the island? Who knew what Callum was like as an adult?

Now, as Callum stood in the bright kitchen light, watching Robin clatter about putting stuff in the dishwasher, he said, "I know what you're thinking."

"You do? *I* don't know I was thinking," Robin joked.

"You're thinking you wish I would go away and leave you alone." When he said the words, he didn't sound pathetic or self-pitying, just factual.

"I'm *not* thinking that!" Robin protested. "That's awful."

"Then stop building your dish barricade and give me a moment of your full attention."

Robin stopped shuttling dishes. She dried her hands on a towel. She forced herself to look at Callum. He was good-looking, and he was looking serious. Lightly, she said, "Well, that sounds ominous."

"Come outside with me for a few moments," Callum said.

Robin blinked.

"I'm not going to ravish you on the patio table, for god's sake, Robin. I just want to talk to you. I want to tell you something."

Maybe he was getting engaged! Robin was surprised by a sting of jealousy. "Gosh," she joked, trying to cover her emotional turmoil, "don't tell me you're dying."

"I'm not dying," Callum replied. "It's nothing like that. Come on outside."

They sat at the round table farthest from the house, darkened with shadow. Callum poured them each a glass of wine before sitting down not next to Robin, but as far away as he could. So that was another surprise.

"Don't keep me in suspense," she said. "Tell me!"

"I'm moving to Singapore," Callum said.

"What?"

"We're expanding our business. I've got to establish a branch in Singapore. Find office space, interview for employees, get communications in place."

Robin couldn't take it all in. "How long will you be gone?"

Callum shrugged. "Don't know. A year, at least. Maybe two, three."

"Will you be coming back a lot?"

"I doubt it. I'm going to be responsible for continuity. It's a big expansion for our company."

"What about summers? Won't you come here in the summer at all?"

"Not for the first few years." Callum smiled and looked into the distance. "I'm not one of your mother's summer children anymore, Robin. I'm in a new part of my life."

Robin nodded. "The end of an era."

Callum let the silence last. He cleared his throat. "And the beginning of one."

Her heart did a strange blip. In the past few years, she'd realized that James was right, the tables had turned, and Callum was the one with a crush on her. He'd never so much as asked her to go to a movie or concert with him. Of course, if he had, James would have teased him mercilessly. But at some point, maybe three years ago, maybe more, Robin had become aware of his eyes resting on her during dinner. He was there to open a door or hand her out of a boat. He complimented her when she knew she didn't look half as good as Iris, Courtney, or Christabel.

"You're very quiet," Callum said.

"Sorry." She waved her hand. "Sorry. It's just, you got me thinking, about endings and beginnings. This summer children thing Mom talked about—I guess we'll always be children to her, but really, we have to face it, we're adults. It's true," she mused aloud, "I don't pay a mortgage, my parents give me money for groceries, but they're groceries for the entire house . . . I suppose to some people I must seem, well, *stuck*." She turned the bracelet on her wrist at the thought. "Courtney thinks so. Courtney thinks I'm stuck."

"Maybe you are stuck. Or maybe you're right where you want to be."

Robin nodded slowly. "I do love it here. Not just the house, or my family, but the island, and—"

"And Quinn Eliot."

Robin flinched as if he'd slapped her. "W-Why . . ." she stammered, and felt heat break out along her neck and cheeks. She was grateful for the darkness. "Why do you say that?"

"Robin." Callum's voice was gentle. "I've been watching you for years. I think I might know when you're going to sneeze before you do. Don't worry. I'm not going to tell anyone else and I don't think anyone else has guessed."

After the first sharp stab of fear had passed, a kind of ease flowed through Robin's veins. "It's hopeless," she whispered. "I know that." It was a relief to talk about this with someone.

"Why?"

"He's so much older than I am."

"Does that bother you?"

"It would bother my parents. My family. Eighteen years is a large difference."

"And what would Christabel think?"

Robin snorted. "She's gorgeous. I'm sure she'll get married some-day, and then . . ."

"You're willing to wait? Take what you can get?"

Robin winced at his words. Over the years, Callum had seen Robin in every conceivable guise—angry at her parents, silly-drunk, take-charge capable, sentimentally loving. They'd gotten swamped on a Sunfish together, their bodies slick with water as they collided, swim-ming up to the air, choking and spitting water and gasping. They'd danced together in glamorous clothes at wedding parties, they'd helped James or Iris or Courtney or any of them stumble into bed after too much booze and hot summer fun. They'd celebrated birthdays, the Fourth of July, New Year's Eve. They'd kissed—casual, nonsexual kisses saying hello, goodbye, happy New Year. If anyone asked, Robin would say she *adored* Callum. And she did. But she didn't love him, and she couldn't take it in, couldn't grasp it, that he might feel something like love for her.

She had remained quiet, lost in her thoughts, for too long. Callum stood. "I'm going to find James."

Robin started to call him back, but stopped herself and simply watched him walk away. What had just happened? Sinking back in her chair, she admitted to herself that she knew what had just happened: Callum had told her he was going away. He had hoped she would ask him to stay. Instead, she had confirmed his guess, that she was in love with Quinn.

Callum had said he thought no one else knew. She hoped he was right. Courtney had never hinted or speculated. When Courtney talked freely about what a spoiled brat Christabel was, what a weak, lame father Quinn was, Robin always agreed and changed the subject. As much as she longed to confide in Courtney, she kept her silence. It was complicated. Probably it would always be complicated, a rope of inflexible knots.

Her love for Quinn was, at first, a delicious secret, a private game. It was more than enough simply to possess this secret—it was a matter of fierce pride, it transformed her love into something mythic because it was so concealed. Each clandestine meeting with Quinn was sharpened with a heart-pounding anxiety that someone might see them. That Quinn—*Quinn!*—was willing to take the risk made their love seem more profound than others, more important.

Did the secrecy fuel her passion? She had to face up to that possibility. She couldn't envision a time when her family and friends knew.

Recently Quinn was pressing her to bring it all out into the open, to tell her family and Christabel, to perform the romantic ritual, the engagement ring, the wedding plans, the wedding itself. And he wanted them to move off island, to start their married life away from Nantucket and all its powerful memories.

Quinn had been patient with her for so long. Well, and she had been patient, too.

One hot August night three years ago, the Vickereys were having a lavish barbeque. Courtney was there, and several of their summer friends, all of them tanned and relaxed, enjoying the summer night, the food, light talk, silly jokes.

For the first time ever, Quinn arrived with a date, another teacher at the high school, named Essie Holdgate. She taught English, and she and Quinn were collaborating on an interconnected honors course. Essie was small, tiny-boned, with a tiny waist. Her dark hair was cut in a no-nonsense bob, but her face was lovely. She was the first sign that Quinn was recovered from his wife's betrayal, and the first time he had looked so very happy. Christabel never showed up that night. Probably she was boycotting the couple's public appearance; later, they'd find out that she'd gone to a bar, gotten drunk, and picked up a man to spend the night with.

But that night, that first night, when Robin was twenty-six, three years ago, when she worked for a clothing boutique while she tried to figure out what she wanted to do with her life—college had not answered that question for her—when she was dating no one special, but Henry and Valerie were almost engaged, and Courtney was all about her teaching job and not very interested in men—that night Robin had watched Quinn with that china doll Essie Holdgate, and arrived at the horrible revelation that she was in love with Quinn.

Quinn was eighteen years older than she was! He hung out with her parents! His daughter was only two years younger than Robin! This was absurd!

Robin had never asked much of life—why should she? She had so much, she knew she was fortunate. She'd never cared much about all that love stuff, and she had a tranquil personality; she didn't long for celebrity or wealth, she enjoyed each day as it came.

Suddenly, *this*! Such a wrenching, burning, ambush of her heart, such an unexpected revelation. *Quinn!*

All right, he was handsome, and smart, and he was kind, and the kids he taught adored him, and he clearly did the best he could with his troubled and troubling daughter. But love? Robin *loved* him? Where did that come from? She'd always admired him. She'd been fond of him, she thought of him often, and the thought made her happy—but this was more than that, this was insane, this was an emotion too strong for her to tolerate.

Especially because there he was, his entire body leaning toward the precious Essie, his face lighting up when she spoke, and when they sat at the table, he casually draped his arm around her shoulders as he and the exquisite Essie—who was undoubtedly, since she was also a teacher, his soulmate—talked about books.

Well, damn it, *Robin* read books! And that had no bearing on anything, it was as if she were completely invisible, and she knew, she *knew* that Quinn was going to marry Essie and they'd be coming over all the time, holding hands, cooing and gooing, god, they'd probably even have babies!

Robin managed to make it through the meal, but when dessert was served, she slipped away. No, she *ran* away. She had terrified herself, and she had no idea how to survive this. She'd thought she could live on this island for the rest of her life. She loved the island, it was her home, and one way or the other, she'd thought, in her idiotic vague way, that she'd find a way to live on the island for the rest of her life.

But if Quinn married that adorable teeny-weeny Essie, Robin knew she couldn't bear to remain here, to see them together, to witness their love. And what *was* love? If it was this desperate frightening whirlwind of emotion, she didn't want it.

She'd sequestered herself in her room. When Courtney came to check on her, Robin said she had a stomach bug.

For the rest of the summer, she lived in a kind of haze, overwhelmed by the crazy new sensation. To others, she seemed normal, if slightly absentminded. Only she knew her heart had become a Tilt-A-Whirl.

When September came, the island slowly emptied of tourists. Susanna's summer children left for their real jobs. School started. Quinn didn't drop by the Vickerey house as often.

Christabel left to attend art school in Boston.

One morning the wind shifted, the air was dry, and pots of burgundy chrysanthemums were set out on people's front porches. The hint of winter, the lift of briskness—the way nature changed overnight gave Robin courage. She was determined to be brave. She had changed overnight, and she wanted to talk to Quinn.

Friday afternoon, she biked over to his house, sat on his front porch, and waited for him to come home.

When he pulled into the driveway in his old and compulsively well-maintained Volvo, he was shocked to see her. He nearly threw himself from the car. "Robin! Is everything all right?"

Quinn was wearing black jeans, a tartan shirt, and his beloved corduroy jacket. His blond hair was mussed and he'd pulled his tie loose and undone the top button of his shirt. To Robin, he was irresistible.

She rose and slowly walked toward him. "Everything's fine, Quinn. I came over because I'd like to talk to you in private."

"Oh. Oh, well, okay. Let me get my—" He reached into the car for his briefcase and backpack. "Are your parents okay? Henry?"

"Everyone's fine." She followed him back to the porch and into his living room. Her heart was flipping. She had the oddest, most adolescent need to giggle, but managed to restrain herself.

Quinn walked into the dining room to drop his stuff on the table—he did most of his work at the table, even though one of his bedrooms was an office. Robin followed him, and when he turned to her, she said quickly, because that was the only way she could say it: "Quinn, I'm in love with you."

He had laughed with relief. "Robin, that's really sweet of you to say. But—"

"Sweet?" she interrupted. "No, not sweet." She flung herself at him, clutched the lapels of his corduroy jacket, and yanked him toward her for a kiss.

It was not a magical kiss. He was not prepared and she was too nervous, too eager, trying too hard to seem passionate. Her mouth hit his mouth too hard, knocking his lips against his teeth. Even so, they *connected*.

Quinn stared at her, amazed. Then he put his hands on her face and bent his mouth toward hers and pressed a long, tender, and ragingly sexual kiss on her mouth.

When he lifted his head, Robin gasped.

Quinn turned away. He stalked into the living room. "No. No, Robin, that was wrong. I'm sorry."

His face was flushed, and Robin followed him, on fire. "Not wrong!" she insisted. "You know it was right, that kiss. Quinn, I mean it. I'm in love with you."

"You're a child," he said.

"I'm an adult," she argued. "I'm twenty-six years old."

"And I'm forty-four. My daughter is only two years younger than you are. This is completely inappropriate."

She grinned, cocking her head. "I think if you'll take me to bed, you'll find it's *extremely* appropriate."

Panic flashed over his face, then vanished, and she knew without a doubt that Quinn had thought that Christabel might walk in on them, and fortunately remembered that Christabel was off island, in art school.

"Robin," Quinn reasoned, "you've got to realize we can't possibly have a future together. Your parents—Christabel—my colleagues—the superintendent of school—" He sounded desperate.

"I don't need a future," Robin told him. "I want this day. I want you now."

He shook his head. "I don't think—"

Robin pressed herself against him. "Don't think."

That first time they had not made it to the bedroom. They did not make love so much as they *took* each other, wrestled and devoured each other, dropping down onto the carpet in front of the sofa, moaning and shoving and pulling and arching, and then collapsing side by side.

They lay there for a long time, catching their breath. Robin rolled onto her side and buried her head in his chest, sniffing his scent like an animal. She had seen him in bathing trunks, but somehow, as he lay beside her wearing only a tartan shirt, unbuttoned to reveal his tanned and naked chest, somehow he seemed naked to her. She was certainly naked to him, in body and soul.

Quinn smoothed her hair back from her face. Lifting himself over her with his weight resting on his elbows, he told her, "That was lovely."

"Lovely? That was phenomenal."

He smiled sweetly. "Oh, you eloquent Vickereys." He pulled on his trousers and buttoned his shirt, but left it hanging out, a rakish look for such a well-groomed man. He rose, went into the kitchen, and returned with two glasses of cranberry juice.

Robin barked with laughter. "*Cranberry juice?* You know I'm twenty-six, don't you?"

He sat in an armchair and put his glass on the table. "We need clear minds, Robin. We acted foolishly enough without liquor. We don't need to add it to the mix."

She dressed. She curled up on the sofa and took a sip of the cranberry juice. It was cool, sweet, and refreshing, and exactly what she needed.

Tilting her head, she said, "So you like me, too."

"Of course, I do, Robin. I desire you. I've always been attracted to you, but I've also always known it's an impossibility. I'm a teacher, a public figure, a man who works with young people. I can't even be seen with a woman young enough to be my daughter."

That was how it began, their love affair. With passion and desire and good humor, and an agreement to keep what was between them secret until the time was right to share it with everyone else.

That was three years ago. The first year, Quinn had to gently, kindly extricate himself from his relationship with Essie. Robin understood his reasoning for doing it slowly, but each time he was with Essie—at the high school homecoming dance he'd promised to chaperone with her, at a mutual friend's wedding and reception—each time jealousy had built a bonfire in Robin's heart, and when she finally, secretly, met Quinn, their lovemaking was a conflagration. By Christmas, Quinn was no longer dating Essie, but Christabel returned home for the holidays, and when Quinn and Robin met, it was at holiday dinners and gatherings. They did not touch each other. They scarcely looked at each other. And the restraint became a kind of delicious game.

When Christabel dropped out of art school and returned to the island, Robin was the one to suggest to Quinn that they keep it a secret for a few more months. She cared for Christabel and didn't want to cause her any more pain.

So Robin met with Quinn in secret. Their meetings were of necessity brief, taking place in hidden locations, and their longing for each other increased the desperation of their need. Each time they met was shocking, brave, and exquisitely rich with emotion.

During the past year, Robin and Quinn had spent more time talking and less time making love. They didn't feel comfortable speaking on the phone when others were around, but they texted each other.

Quinn wanted to tell the others. He was tired of secrecy; it was beginning to feel like game-playing to him. He didn't like keeping a secret of such magnitude from his daughter and from Robin's parents, who were close friends.

Quinn wanted to go public with their love, and more than that, he wanted to leave this island, move away from the house where Christabel's mother had abandoned her, and start life over in some mainland Massachusetts town. Christabel would have a new start there, meet new people, breathe fresh and healing air. Quinn could find a job teaching at another school. He and Robin could marry, and all their neighbors and his colleagues would know him and Robin as man and wife, not Quinn and the Vickereys' oldest daughter.

Robin argued with him. She loved Nantucket. She wanted to live here all her life. She had an identity separate from her family's. She volunteered for several organizations. She had friends who didn't care two figs that she was a Vickerey. As for Christabel, she was also happy here. She felt safe here. Hadn't she dropped out of art school to return to the island?

She was simply running back to her father, Quinn argued. It wasn't healthy for his daughter to be so attached, he knew that. She needed to strike out for herself, to be in a broader, less claustrophobic world.

For the past six months, Robin and Quinn had argued more than they had made love.

She knew she had to tell Quinn about her other secret. Then he would understand why she had to stay on the island.

Yet she had not found the courage to tell him. She knew that once she revealed her secret to him, he very well might recoil from her, he might think her as mad as her own brother had been sometimes in his life. She needed to tell Quinn, and soon, but she was afraid.

11

The day of Susanna's birthday party was sunny, bright, and warm, with only the gentlest of breezes stirring the air. Courtney followed Robin everywhere, helping her with the thousand details needed to make the evening perfect. The caterers took over the kitchen. The tent rental company had raised the poles supporting the white sailcloth tent and laid the hardwood floors yesterday. Today they set up the tables and chairs and laid out the starched white tablecloths. The florist arrived with centerpieces. The bartenders lugged in barrels of ice and cases of wine and champagne. Courtney helped Robin set out the place cards Robin had so painstakingly handwritten. Dr. V hid in his study. Susanna's friends took her out to lunch and kept her out as long as possible. The children—biological and summer—took time to go down to the beach to swim and tan.

The glitches were minor. With so many people taking showers, the hot water ran out. One of Susanna's friends discovered the dress she'd brought had a tear along one seam. Susanna, ever handy, mended it. A married couple, longtime friends of the older Vickereys, had RSVP'd that they were coming, but phoned at the last minute, sending their regrets because of a family situation. Courtney helped Robin rearrange the place cards. Upstairs, as they dressed for the party, Pearl slipped into such a brazenly seductive skin-tight orange dress that Iris burst into tears.

"You can't come to my mother's party looking like a whore!" Iris shouted.

Everyone on the second floor heard. Robin and Courtney, in Robin's room getting dressed, froze, listening with every cell of their bodies to see whether they'd have to intervene.

"Fine," Pearl said. "It would be a waste, anyway. This party's going to be full of old people."

"Sometimes I hate you, Pearl," Iris said.

Pearl laughed with her smoky low voice. "Yes, sweetie, but sometimes you love me."

She changed into a barely respectable lavender sheath. Iris, Robin, and Courtney wore bright summery dresses, and Susanna wore her mother's pearl choker with a lime green silk dress she and Robin had gone to New York to buy. The guys wore blazers with white shirts and ties, even Dr. V, who grumbled about the discomfort.

A knock at the door. James opened it. "Sonya! Richard! Come in!"

The party started, the bartenders got busy, and Robin and Courtney edged around the room, discreetly snapping photos on their phones. Not quite one hundred people crowded into the house and out onto the patio, and by dinner time, they'd enjoyed a drink or two and were a very happy bunch.

Robin, who had made the seating arrangements, had placed James next to Courtney at a round table. Jolly, rotund Jacob sat on Courtney's left, and Pearl was on the other side of James. Callum Findlay and Robin made the last pair. It was a good mix, full of jokes and laughter. While they enjoyed the entrée—marinated swordfish grilled to perfection—the conversation was general, but as they waited for their plates to be removed and the birthday cake to be carried in and the toasts to take place, Courtney glanced at James. He was studying her with a smile, and when their eyes met, she almost spontaneously combusted.

"Stop that," she whispered.

"Stop what?" James had perfected the sideways, slightly guilty smile.

"Be good, James. It's your mother's birthday party."

Beneath the table, his knee touched hers. James put his arm around her shoulder and drew her close. "What did you say? I can't hear in this crowd."

His lips didn't quite touch her ear as he spoke. His breath stirred her hair. Her dress was strapless, so his hand rested on her bare skin, and his touch made her breath come shallow and fast.

"It's your mother's birthday party. Be good."

"I can be very good," James assured her. "I can be excellent."

Well, this was something new! Her voice came out as a squeak. "Only last night you told me—"

"I've changed my mind."

"James. Don't mess around with me."

"But I've decided I do want to mess around with you. Everyone will be dancing. No one will notice if we're gone."

Lust ambushed her body and soul. She had asked for him to seize the day. Now he was ready to seize the night, and life was short, and the night was sweet, and she wanted him. Now he wanted her. He was next to her, this tall, strong, sexual male, offering her what she'd desired for years. Her body ached with need.

"All right," she whispered. "After the cake. When the dancing starts. We'll slip away." She put her hand on *his* thigh, close to his groin.

James drew in a deep breath. "Damn, Courtney, don't *do* that."

She laughed in a low, naughty voice. "You're touching me."

He removed his hand. "Yeah, but whatever you're feeling doesn't *show*. And I've got to give a toast. Move your hand or I won't even be able to stand up."

Courtney took her hand away. She let her head fall back so that her long hair slid around her shoulders as she looked at James. "Better?"

"You're killing me." James moaned, then pulled away and sat up straight in his chair. He took a sip of water. He took his notes out of his pocket and pretended to read them. "Talk to Jacob," he whispered. "Don't even *look* at me for a while."

Smug, Courtney laughed. "James, I think you've met your match in me."

"Courtney, I've always known that," he said. "Now leave me alone."

When the toasts began, Courtney leaned back in her chair and listened, applauding with the others, as friends, family, and neighbors told humorous or touching tales about Susanna. She relaxed, enjoying the moment, when all the planning and preparing was over, and the party had come off flawlessly, and for this small, contained time and space, everyone was content.

She was glad for the lengthy toasts and tributes made to Susanna. Courtney gazed around the room at the handsome, well-heeled crowd. Susanna sat at the head table, her lovely face glowing as people spoke about her, her red- and silver-streaked hair loose around her shoulders, so that she looked too young to be the mother of grown children. She accepted the accolades with blown kisses and applause.

James was at the microphone now, singing his mother's praises, making the crowd laugh. He was so handsome, Courtney thought. He took her breath away. She yearned to be alone with him, naked.

James handed the mic to someone else. He returned to his seat next to Courtney.

She whispered, "That was wonderful, James."

James smiled. "You ain't seen nothin' yet."

Three more friends toasted Susanna. She stood up and waved her thanks. Then someone, probably organized Robin, nodded at the band and the music began. Susanna pulled her husband onto the dance floor. He was scarlet and danced with his eyes looking toward the heavens for rescue, but he danced, holding his wife in his arms. Others crowded out to dance. Courtney took James's hand.

James warned, "If they play a slow dance, you and I are leaving."

And they did play a slow dance, one of Susanna's favorite melodies, the romantic "Unchained Melody." James pulled Courtney close. She laid her head against his chest, breathing in his scent of soap, sunshine, and starched cotton. His hand pressed her firmly against him. She closed her eyes and let him lead. This was heaven. Everything else fell away, all worries, all fears, even the chatter of the people in the tent, even the gazes of family and friends, and Courtney was alone with James, one hand against his neck, the other hand in his, her body sliding and brushing his body as they moved to the music. She wanted to kiss him. She wanted to kiss his neck. She wanted to touch him everywhere.

James stepped back, putting a few inches between them. He looked almost sleepy. "What?"

Courtney smiled up at him. "I don't want to wait any longer."

He spun in tight circles around the dance floor. "There's a problem."

"Really? I'm not aware of one," she teased, pressing her body against his.

He moaned low in his throat. "Where should we go?"

"Oh." All the bedrooms in the house were occupied, as was the attic. "I suppose all the hotel rooms are booked."

"They were probably booked last February."

"If we put the seats down in your mother's minivan . . ."

"We are not having sex in my mother's car. That's way too Freudian for me."

Courtney laughed. "There's the beach."

James slowed, so that they were really only swaying together. "Right. We could take a blanket down—"

"It's warm out. No rain, no wind."

"Let's go."

The sand stretched in a long line of silver beneath a tilted three-quarters moon. When they spread the blanket, no wind teased the corners. Down here, with the high bluff at their back and the Atlantic Ocean whispering up to the shore, they were alone. Not even a gull flew over them.

For a long time, they lay together, fully clothed, kissing. Courtney had wanted this for so long, she didn't want to rush it. She wanted to savor their closeness, the moisture of his lips, the mist of his breath, the brush of his cheek against hers. It seemed an extraordinary gift of the universe simply to be able, at last, to run her hands through his thick hair, to have his muscular shoulders and back right there, for her to touch, and when she brought her hand around to the front and pressed against the fly of his trousers, her groan of need was as deep as his.

She felt no awkwardness as she stripped off her summer dress and panties. She felt only an urgency to join her body to his. Their bodies were silver in the moonlight. The surging ocean was deep gray, with silver waves.

Then he was on top of her, fully in her. She whimpered, straining to get even closer to him.

James lifted his head, rose up on his elbows. "I love you, Courtney."

"I love you, James," Courtney answered.

He moved slightly, taking his time, and then he moved faster, harder. Everything else in the world slipped away.

"Good god," James said afterward. "What was that?"

Courtney smiled. "That was us. You and me, together."

They lay curled together, sheltered beneath the blanket, looking at the stars.

"I want to marry you," James said. "I want to marry you and make love to you every night for the rest of my life."

Courtney laughed in delight. "You sex maniac," she said. Immediately she knew the words were wrong. She almost bit her tongue. That word *maniac*. People used it so carelessly. *She* had used it so carelessly.

"James, I didn't mean—"

At the same moment, James said, "But the children thing is nonnegotiable."

She pulled away from him in order to see his face properly. "What?"

"We have to agree. Marriage, a life together, and we'll adopt children or do an in vitro thing."

"James!" She sat up straight. Her heels dug a hollow at the end of the blanket. Sand sifted in around her feet. "I want *your* children!"

James sat up, too. "I know you do. And you know how I feel about that."

Courtney burst into tears.

James turned his face away from her, but Courtney could feel his misery as they sat side by side.

"Courtney, I love you, but I don't know what else to say. I've seen Henry in his depressed states, I mean really depressed states, and I wouldn't wish that on any child of mine."

"But, James, you don't *know* your children will be bipolar. Think about it, think about how precious and generous your mother is, and how fascinating every single one of you is and how gifted, how funny, how kind. Your children will have all that, too."

"I don't know that." James stood up, holding out a hand to Courtney. "Let's go to bed. It's late, and we're tired and all we can do now is talk in circles."

Courtney shook her head, refusing his hand. "James, don't go up now. Stay here and talk with me."

"It won't get us anywhere, Courtney. I won't change my mind." He reached for his clothes and began to dress.

Courtney pulled on her panties and slipped into her sundress. She stood up, gathering the beach blanket against her for comfort. "I don't know what to say, James. I don't think I've ever been so happy and so miserable at the same time."

James reached out and took the blanket. Together they walked in silence to the steps and up to the long stretch of lawn. Lights were on in the tent, and shadowy figures danced, their laughter spilling out into the night air.

"Do you want to go back to the party?" he asked.

Courtney shook her head. "No. I'm going to go take a shower and go to bed."

James put his hand on her waist. "Courtney—"

She turned on a dime, full of hope.

He looked down at her, and his face was sad. "I won't change my mind. I can't."

"Monty Blackhorse wants to marry me," Courtney blurted out.

"If you're trying to make me jealous, you're succeeding. But that won't make me change my mind. And you'd be better off with him."

"What happened to you?" Courtney cried. "You used to be wild, a daredevil, a free spirit!"

"I grew up," James told her simply.

"Oh!" Courtney snapped. "I hate you, James!" She tore herself away from his face, from his touch, from the beach, and the enchanting dark ocean spreading past her sight or imagination. She strode across the lawn to the house, hoping to meet no one, not wanting to explain the state of her mascara, which probably had dripped down her cheeks with her tears. She raced into the house, up the back stairs, and into the bathroom. Locking the door behind her, she stripped off her clothes and stepped into the shower, letting the water pound down over her, covering the noise of her weeping.

12

Iris pulled an empty chair close to Robin. She'd been dancing all evening. A sheen of perspiration glistened from her skin. "Great party, Robin. Kudos."

Robin scanned the room. Some of the oldies had gone. Her mother and father leaned against the tent poles, chatting with friends as they took their leave. Callum, Jacob, and Quinn stood in one corner, talking about the Red Sox. Henry and Valerie danced slowly together, even though the music was fast. They were in a world of their own.

"Looks like Valerie's back with Henry," Robin whispered to Iris.

"Wow, you're right. Where's Lisa?"

"She left about an hour ago. I don't blame her."

"She doesn't have the balls to deal with Henry," Iris decided. "Valerie does. Valerie's strong. Valerie the Valkyrie."

"Come on. She's not a hefty babe."

"No. I just meant her temperament. You know what I mean."

Robin took a sip of ice water. "I do. Valerie's the best."

Iris leaned close to Robin. "Don't look now, but I think the Black Pearl has Quinn in her sights."

Robin looked. Pearl and Christabel were with the pack of men at the end of the tent. Christabel was chatting up Callum. Pearl was tugging Quinn out onto the dance floor.

"Pearl and Christabel." Iris laughed. "Together they could rule the world."

"Nah," Robin said. "Christabel's got too much invested in being the distressed damsel. Pearl wouldn't want to pair up with her. She'd roll right over her."

"Yeah, you're right."

For a while they watched Quinn and Pearl dance. Pearl was undulating like a mermaid, slowly shrugging a shoulder, tilting her hips, raising her arms above her head.

"Look at her," Robin said. "Pearl is a sex goddess."

"True. But Quinn's about a million years too old for her."

Robin objected, "Quinn's only forty-seven. Pearl's twenty-two."

"That's what I mean. Quinn's a dinosaur."

"I think Quinn's handsome." Robin couldn't help herself, she felt protective of Quinn, it hurt her to hear her sister's remark.

"I do, too, for an old guy." Iris took a glass from the table and sipped. "Ugh. Just water. Where's the champagne?"

"You've had enough. You'll feel awful tomorrow if you drink anymore."

"Yeah," Iris agreed calmly. "You're right. Plus, who wants to get drunk at her mom's birthday party?" She chuckled and poked Robin's arm. "Watch Pearl. What do you bet she and Quinn do the dirty deed tonight?"

Jealousy stabbed Robin. "Don't be ridiculous."

Iris ignored her. "And look around. Who's missing?"

Robin scanned the dance floor. "Courtney and James!"

"They slipped away quite a while ago. Three guesses what they're doing."

"Iris, is sex all you think about?"

"Is that wrong?" Iris teased.

"Why didn't you invite some guys?"

"Give me a break. I just got home. From a *women's* college, I might add. I don't even know who's on the island. Plus," Iris added, acting like a prim little girl, "I wanted to focus totally on my mother."

"Right," Robin scoffed.

Iris leaned close and whispered, "Hey, I have an idea. I'll go ask Callum to dance and you cut in on Quinn. We'll see how the great seductresses handle that."

Robin shrugged, but the idea was appealing. She seldom took the chance to dance with Quinn, to do *anything* with Quinn in front of other people, but Iris was offering an opportunity she couldn't pass up. "Great," she agreed, trying to sound halfhearted. "Let's go."

Iris squeezed Robin's arm — Iris was still so much a child, excited by the slightest game. "Cool."

Robin cut through the dancers to where Pearl slowly undulated, tilting her hips, while Quinn performed an awkward two-step.

"I'm cutting in," Robin said. She slid right between Pearl and Quinn. She put her hand on Quinn's shoulder and took his other hand in hers.

"Hey!" Pearl stopped moving and stood glaring. "We were dancing."

"You've been dancing all evening," Robin told the girl. "It's my turn now." She smiled sweetly. "Go ask Jacob to dance."

Quinn grinned as he whirled Robin away from Pearl. "This is a nice surprise."

"It's Iris's idea. She's trying to separate Christabel from Callum." As soon as she spoke, Robin bit her tongue. She didn't want to talk about Christabel. She was so done with talking about Christabel.

"Ah, so you two are simply being mischievous," Quinn said. His hand pressed her back, moving her closer to him as the music went down tempo into a slow dance.

"Right," Robin said. "I'm just playing with you." She wanted to press even closer, to feel the length of his torso against her body, to nestle her head on his shoulder, she wanted to wrap both arms around his neck and kiss his sweet mouth as they danced.

"I'll enjoy it while I can," Quinn told her. "People are leaving. It's probably time for me to go, after this dance." He pressed Robin closer, so their bodies touched. "Will you meet me tonight?"

A shiver of desire shot through Robin. "I can't. The house is full of people. Courtney's sleeping in my room."

"So you haven't even told Courtney about us?" Quinn asked.

"She just got here—" Robin knew her excuse was lame.

"You think I'll be content to go on like this forever? I'm not going to be satisfied with clandestine meetings." Quinn's voice roughened. "I want to marry you. I want to live with you."

"You want to move off island to live with me," Robin reminded him. "I want to stay here."

"That's childish of you," Quinn snapped. "You don't need to live with your family. We will be our own family."

Robin checked to see if anyone was dancing near enough to hear their conversation. "I can't talk about it at Susanna's party, Quinn."

"Fine." Quinn took his arms away from Robin and stepped back. Formally, he bowed his head. "Wonderful party, Robin. Thanks for asking me." He walked off the dance floor and, without speaking to Dr. V or Susanna, strode out of the bright lights of the tent and into the darkness of the night.

Waves of different emotions slapped at her so powerfully from all sides that she couldn't catch her breath. *Love*—that profound, intimate connection she had with Quinn, which had been like a warm current supporting her—and suddenly, *remorse, guilt, desolation*, because she was not brave enough to move forward. *Anger*—at everyone and anyone who could live a normal life without questioning, without decisions snapping at her mind like a rabid dog—and suddenly she could move, and she did. She needed succor, a reason to carry on, she needed to be in her sacred place, where everything came clear.

Without speaking to anyone, Robin fled the tent. She raced through the house where every light was burning bright. She heard water running in the upstairs shower she and Courtney used and decided not to go to her room to change her clothes. She didn't want to run into Courtney and have to explain her mood. In the back hall, she grabbed a life jacket, kicked off her high heels, and started out the back door, but she saw James crossing the lawn, alone, toward the house. *What's going on?* she wondered, but not enough to stop to talk.

Instead, she ran down the hall and out the front door. She ducked through the hedge between the Vickerey house and the neighbors'—the blessed neighbors with their homes in so many exotic places they were almost never on Nantucket. No lights were on in this huge mansion on the Atlantic. As Robin ran over the soft grass, music and chatter floated in the air and followed her as she went down the neighbors' stairs to the beach.

The beach was empty. The sounds of the party didn't reach here. She heard the ceaseless invitation of the waves as she hurried through the sand. She pulled on her life jacket. She found her small, wooden rowboat by a clump of beach grass and tugged it toward the water. She shoved off from the beach into the dark ocean, and rowed away from the land. After she was out far enough, she started the boat's four-horsepower Mercury engine. She would turn it off when she was further out, but rowing was hard work, and she didn't want the sound of the engine to alert anyone on shore.

She dipped her hand into the water. It was cold. Not frigid, but very cold. The lights of her house had become flickering candles. She switched off the engine and simply sat in the boat, in the quiet night, with dark sky above and dark sea below.

She didn't know if they would come. It didn't happen every time. She did not have a line of communication to the great creatures, but often, so often, when she waited patiently, quietly, they would come to play with her, the whales.

The right whales. Their species, over a hundred years ago, had been named the "right whales" because of all whales they were the ones who provided the best blubber for oil. Also, this species preferred to gather near the coastline, where it was easier for the whalers to reach and kill.

Whales were no longer killed for their blubber, except by a few northern countries. These Massachusetts waters had been safe for them for decades. In the summer, "whale watch" boats took tourists out into the ocean to spot the creatures, who skimmed plankton off the top of the water so that their dark heads often stood out like floating rocks.

They had first come to Robin three years earlier, when she was weeping with distress. She'd realized she was in love with Quinn Eliot and the knowledge had scoured her heart. What *was* love? Could it be this desperate frightening whirlwind of jealousy she felt when she saw Quinn with Essie Holdgate?

That night, like tonight, she'd needed to *move.* She ran down the zigzag steps and across the sand to the rowboat she kept there. She shoved it into the water, climbed in, and rowed away from the shore with all her might. Her rage gave her energy. She hadn't gone out this far at night, she knew it wasn't safe, and right then she didn't give a damn. Let her be swamped by a rogue wave, let her fall overboard, what did it matter to her, nothing mattered, she was nothing herself, she was a woman who was hopelessly in love with the wrong man.

When she was too exhausted to row anymore, she shipped the oars and sat there in the little rowboat, weeping. She wiped the tears with her hands, she let them fall, soaking her summer dress. She wanted to throw back her head and howl like a wounded wolf, but the rowing had tired her. She had no breath. She had only heartbreak.

Something knocked against the bottom of the boat.

She was startled out of her rage. She knew these waters well. There were no shoals in this spot. Had she rowed too far out? She looked back at the shore. The lights of her house were small globes of gold. She had rowed farther than ever before. This calmed her, oddly, because she knew she was going to exhaust herself rowing back.

Again, something knocked on the boat, this time setting it rocking sideways, heave-ho, heave-ho. Robin clutched the wooden seat. Her heart ratcheted in her chest. The moon was three-quarters full, illuminating the night, so that she could see herself, the boat, the water, everything painted with silver.

A third knock. She called out, "Who's there?" Of course no one answered, what could answer; she was alone in the water, but something was knocking her boat and she was too paralyzed with fear to seize the oars and row for home.

Her heart raced. Her mind tried to make some kind of sense. Perhaps it was a large piece of driftwood, a rudder, a box drifting in the water. Robin peered over the side of the rowboat.

An eye looked up at her. A living, inquisitive, moist, dark eye. Every hair on her body stood up. Sound would not come, breath would not come. She was stricken with fear.

As she stared, she saw how the eye was part of a head, an enormous black head covered with white callosities and a mouth curving upward. She was looking at a whale. A living right whale.

Who was looking at her.

Who was *seeing* her.

Her world changed at that moment. All that had gone before vanished, and this was the birth of her new life. She knew she was somehow caught in a miracle.

She was trembling so much her teeth were chattering. She managed to say, "Hello." Her voice was weak, she scarcely made a sound. She tried again. "Hello. You're a whale, aren't you? I'm a human. I'm Robin."

The utter absurdity of her words made her laugh. But exactly what does one say to a whale? The laughter opened up her throat, her chest, her heart. As she laughed, the eye disappeared, the whale sank from view. Less than a minute later, the whale breached, exploding out of the ocean into the air and landing again with a force that set waves surging toward her rowboat. Robin clutched the sides as her small boat tilted back and forth, managing to remain stable. Exhilaration swept through her, a joy she'd never before experienced. She was crying again, and laughing at the same time; she was in ecstasy. She couldn't wait to tell the others she had seen a whale, she had been visited by a whale, stared at by the creature, as if *she* were the odd one, living out in the air instead of inhabiting the glorious expanse of ocean.

Before she could pick up the oars to row home, another knock came on the boat. She looked down. There was the whale, and she knew it was *the* whale because of the pattern of the white clumps she had been taught in school—for in Nantucket, everyone was taught about whales—were called callosities. Each whale had a unique pattern.

She watched the whale with more attention and less fear. She knew they were curious.

"What must I look like to you?" she asked, as if the whale could speak. "I know you mate and have babies, but do you ever fall in love? What if your love is not returned?"

The whale floated next to her, the eye bright with interest. She was lying on her side, the length of her extending far past the length of the boat. The moonlight showed how the creature's body extended far below the surface, a blacker, darker shape than the silvered water. The whale was probably eighteen feet long, and weighed, Robin remembered from school, several tons. It wouldn't want to eat her, and it didn't seem hostile—what was happening?

"I'm frightened of you," Robin said. "Are you frightened of me?" She laughed again, because of course the whale had no idea what she was saying, she could speak French or baby talk or nonsense, it would be all the same to the whale. "You are wonderful," she said. "You are the most beautiful thing I've ever seen in my life."

The whale submerged. It did not breach again, and it didn't return, although Robin waited a long time. Finally, she rowed back to shore, slowly, steadily, her mind a white dazzle of memory and disbelief. When she finally stumbled up the steps, across the lawn, and into the house, it was late, and everyone was asleep, and the house was quiet. She unstrapped her life jacket, wrapped herself in the cashmere blanket thrown over the family room sofa, and collapsed on the sofa, falling into a sleep that was speckled with stars.

When she awoke the next day, hot in the cashmere blanket, disoriented to find herself in the family room, everyone else had already left the house. Courtney had gone off to work, pedaling on Robin's old bike. Her mother had left a note on the kitchen chalkboard: *Driving Dr. V to airport. Buying groceries. Lunch at club. XOXO MOM*

Robin was grateful for this space of solitude. As she showered, she worried: had last night been a dream? Or worse, a hallucination? She decided not to tell anyone about it. It would frighten and worry her parents, and her brothers would find something else to tease her about.

• • •

That was three years ago. Since then, she'd gone out countless times and countless times she'd been disappointed. But sometimes, the whale, *her* whale, appeared, floating beside her. Last year, her whale brought two other whales who lay sideways in the water, staring at her with their round eyes. Last summer, she'd seen the whales more than a dozen times. How they knew not to overturn her boat, plunging her into the ocean, *why* they didn't upend the boat, she couldn't imagine. No, she *could* imagine. She'd been reading about whales. They were mammals. They were intelligent. It was possible, even probable, that they had no wish to do her harm, that they chose not to endanger her life, even that they *liked* her.

Now, as she waited in her little skiff in the calm summer waters, she could see the dark mass of the bluff and above, the small, twinkling lights of her house and the larger glow from the tent where people, her parents, their friends, might still be dancing. The party had been a success, and she was glad, but Quinn's ultimatum that they leave the island overshadowed her happiness.

Could she tell Quinn? No. He would worry that her words, what he would understand as her *fantasies*, were signs of mania.

Tonight, the whales were not coming. Robin was exhausted from the birthday party. She was exasperated with her relationship with Quinn. The future loomed over her, more threatening than welcoming, a thundercloud, not a rainbow.

She started the engine and motored back to the shore.

13

The house was quiet. Most of the lights were off. Robin slipped in the back door and crept up the stairs. Along the hall, the bedroom doors were closed, but the bathroom across from her room was open and a light was on. She slipped inside and quietly brushed her teeth, then went into her room and tiptoed over to her bed.

"Robin?" Courtney whispered from the other bed.

Robin jumped. "Whoa! I thought you were asleep!"

"Can't sleep. I'd like to talk . . . can you stay awake awhile longer?"

"Sure. Just let me get out of these clothes." Robin dropped her party dress on the floor and slipped into a light summer nightgown. Crawling into bed, she plumped up her pillows and leaned against the headboard. "Okay. What's up?"

"I need to tell you something. And I need you to help me."

"That sounds serious."

Courtney said, "It is serious."

After a long moment of silence, Robin said, "Well, come on. You've got me on pins and needles."

"It's hard to talk about." Courtney sat up in bed, swung her legs over the side, and faced Robin. The lights were off but through the window moon and starlight gleamed in, dressing them both in silver. "Okay. Okay. Here it is. Robin, I'm in love with James and he's in love with me."

"Stop it."

"It's true, but don't get too excited," Courtney warned. "We talked about it last night and tonight, and he wants to get married. But he doesn't want to have children. It's a deal breaker, Robin."

"You're in love with James, really?"

"Yes. Really. The real thing."

"And he's said he loves you?"

"Yes. But, Robin, he's also said he won't give me children!"

"Oh, man, I've been hoping for this for years. Courtney, you're going to be my sister-in-law!"

"Wait, Robin. Calm down. I want children. James's children. James swears that can never happen. We can adopt. We can use someone else's sperm—ick!"

Robin pulled her knees to her chest and wrapped her arms around them. "Okay. Yeah. I can see where James is coming from. James has lived with Henry's bipolar problems—"

"I have, too," Courtney protested.

"True. But not quite as up close and personal as James and me. You haven't spent any time in psych wards or seen Henry zoned out on the wrong drug. We know it can be inherited."

"That's true, but I have seen Henry depressed, and I've seen him manic, and I am aware of the toll it's taken on your family, especially your mother." Courtney shifted position, tucking her legs under her, leaning out from the bed. "I've also seen you and Iris and James for eleven years. You're kind of bizarre"—she lightened her tone to joke—"but I don't see any signs of manic-depression."

Robin listened, taking time to absorb all of this. After a moment, she said, "Damn, Courtney, how could you be in love with James and never tell me?"

"Well, Robin, come on. I didn't admit to anyone, especially not to James, how I felt, and I only slept with him tonight—"

Robin almost achieved liftoff from the bed. "You slept with James? Tonight? Where? Why didn't you tell me?"

"Sssh. You'll wake the house. I am telling you now, I could hardly tell you before, did you want me to phone you from the beach?"

"The beach? You had sex on the beach?"

"Where else could we be alone? The party was going on. The house is packed with people."

"I don't believe this. I do not even believe this." Robin threw herself from the bed and paced around the room, pulling on her hair.

Courtney gestured to her laptop, lying on the floor beneath the bed. "I spent the past hour Googling *manic-depression*, Robin, and I've learned a lot. They know bipolar runs in families but they know very little about how it is inherited . . . they don't know the odds or what combination of parents it takes. They have yet to identify any specific gene, so there is no test. They don't know what combination of nature and nurture might be involved."

Robin nodded. "Yes. I've read about the syndrome, too. I've done lots of reading, as you can imagine. And so has James."

"But look at your own family, Robin. Four children. Only one shows signs of mania or depression."

Robin inhaled sharply. "I'm not so sure about that."

"What do you mean?"

Robin was quiet as she settled back in bed. She fiddled with her sheets and the light summer blanket, arranging them neatly over her knees.

"Robin? Are you okay? I mean . . . just *tell* me."

"You have to promise not to tell anyone else. Especially not Mom."

"I promise."

"Okay." Robin began pleating the edge of the sheet carefully as she talked. "You know my little boat down on the beach?"

"Yes."

"We go out in it sometimes."

"Right, okay."

"I go out in it at night, too. Sometimes. Way out."

"Gosh, Robin, do you wear your life vest?"

"Of course I do. That's not even what I need to tell you. When I get out, I don't know, fifty yards from shore, I turn off the motor and sit there. It's nice. Well, *nice* doesn't cover it. It's magical. I go out only if there's sufficient moonlight. And sometimes—not every time, but often—whales visit me."

Courtney didn't reply but sat in silence for a few minutes. Then she reached over and turned on the light on the bedside table.

"Robin. What do you mean, whales visit you?"

Robin made a bitter sound. "See? Now you think *I'm* crazy."

"No, I don't. I didn't say any such thing. But I want to know more. I mean, come on, Robin, a *whale* is well—*big*."

"I know. My whales are right whales. They're enormous. They come close to the boat and their size dwarfs the boat."

"Then what you're doing is dangerous." Courtney frowned. "Good god, Robin, they could capsize your boat."

"No. They're too careful for that. Sometimes they knock the bottom of my boat, I think they're letting me know they're there. Then they kind of float under the water near me. My special whale—I know, I know, that sounds insane—but there is one whale who likes to get close to the boat and look up at me and I look down at her and, Courtney, I swear on my life we connect. We look at each other, and that look is an entire conversation, it's *I see you, I'm glad you see me*."

"If what you're telling me is true, Robin, it's remarkable. It's even miraculous."

Robin turned toward Courtney. "Believe it, Courtney. It *is* miraculous. I'm aware of that. It does scare me out there, it makes my hair stand on end, I get goosebumps, I think I'm going to have a heart attack, I can scarcely breathe, and all the time I'm feeling so incredibly *blessed* by their visits. I talk to them, I even sing to them. I know it sounds weird, but whales sing to one another. We're just there, together, in the ocean, at night, in the darkness, and it's like this is how it is to be alive, on this planet, connecting somehow, and it's all a mystery."

Courtney said, "Would you take me out some night?"

Robin clasped her hands to her face. Helplessly, she broke into tears. "Yes," she said. "Oh, Courtney, yes." With tears running down her cheeks, she rose from her bed and sank down next to Courtney. She hugged Courtney tight. "You are so wonderful. You really are my very best friend in the whole wide world. I love you so much. I can't tell you how much it means that you want to go out with me." She dried her face with her hands and gulped a few times, settling down. "Now I feel brave enough to tell Quinn."

Courtney pulled back. "Quinn? Why would you want to tell Quinn?"

Robin took Courtney's hands in hers. "Courtney, I'm in love with Quinn."

Courtney frowned.

"He loves me, too."

"Gosh. I don't know what to say, Robin. I mean — isn't he kind of old?"

"He's eighteen years older than I am. I don't give a fig. I'm even glad. It's nice to be around someone mature after living with my brothers."

Courtney peppered Robin with questions. "Have you slept with him? How long have you been, well, together? How do you even manage to *be* together? Do your parents know? They must be totally freaked out. Oh my god! Does Christabel know?"

Robin laughed. "Yes, I've slept with him. It was wonderful — he was wonderful. He *is* wonderful. No, my parents don't know, and neither does Christabel. We've been meeting in secret for, well, for three years."

"Three years? And you're only telling me now?" Courtney moved away from Robin, scuttling up against the backboard.

"Hello, pot? This is kettle."

"I only slept with him tonight. Not three years ago!"

Robin swung her legs up and folded them under her as she faced Courtney. "At first we agreed to keep it secret. He's worried about his reputation, too, a high school teacher dating a woman so much younger. And Christabel, of course we have to take her emotions into account. She's so delicate."

"Have you talked about—the long term? Marriage?"

Robin sighed. "We have. Recently. We've got kind of our own problem there."

"Because of the bipolar thing?"

"No. No, that doesn't worry him, and we haven't really talked about having children." Robin sounded heavyhearted now. "No, it's that Quinn wants to move off island."

"And?"

"And I don't want to leave Nantucket."

"Why not, Robin? It's not as if you'd never be able to come back. You could come back whenever you wanted. You could see your family, your friends, your whales . . ."

Robin interrupted. "This is where I *belong*, Courtney. This is where I want to be. It's my home. The island is my home. I want to stay here."

"Have you told Quinn?"

"Of course I have. It's all we talk about these days. That and his precious Christabel."

"But you haven't told him about the whales," Courtney reminded her. "Why not?"

Robin chewed her lip, thinking. "I don't know. I mean, in a way it's too important to be shared. It's *sacred* to me, really, Courtney."

"And?"

Robin dropped her head. "And I suppose I'm afraid he'll tell me to stop going out, because it's dangerous."

"Well, that's understandable, really." Courtney leaned her head back, thinking. "Could you take him out there with you?"

"I don't know. I've thought about it. I don't know." Robin ran her hands through her hair. "Oh, Courtney, how can we be best friends when we've kept such secrets from each other?"

"I know. We're idiots. But if you think about it, Robin—maybe we're

both afraid. Afraid to make it real. I've had a crush on James since forever, but I never thought he could love me, too. What if I'd told him,
and he'd laughed at me, or been sweetly condescending to me—I
couldn't have come back to the island ever again. It's a big risk! Love is
a big risk!"

"I know," Robin agreed. "We've got to help each other be brave."

"Yes. Yes, you're right. You have to tell Quinn about the whales."

"And you have to tell Monty about James."

Courtney gasped. "Whoa, that came out of left field."

"Don't you think I'm right?" Robin pressed. "The man just asked
you to marry him."

Courtney buried her face in her hands. "Oooh, I hate this."

"You can't sort of keep him in reserve in case it doesn't work out
with James."

Courtney's head jerked up. "Come on! I would *never* do that."

"Then you have to tell him. You have to let go of him before you
can really be with James. Have you even told James about Monty?"

Courtney nodded, her face miserable. "I told him tonight. I kind
of—threatened him with Monty. James said he won't have *his* children
with me. And I said I want *his* children, and I really do, Robin. You
Vickereys are all so fascinating and generous and delicious and fun, I
would take the chance, I could live with whatever the Vickerey genes
gave me. Anyway, we argued, and I stomped off saying that Monty
wants to marry me and telling James I hate him." She met Robin's eyes.
"That was childish of me, wasn't it?"

Robin's voice was still low, sad. "Who knows what we'll say in the
heat of the moment? But it sounds like you aren't one hundred percent
sure about marrying James. What if he really won't change his mind
about this children business? What will you do?"

"I don't know." Courtney shook her head. "We need to talk more . . .
I suppose we could adopt . . . I don't know, Robin. But I am one hundred percent in love with James, don't doubt that. And you're right. I
need to tell Monty."

"Are you sure? He sounds like such a sweet guy."

"Sweet? Yes. And I care for him. But not *that* way."

Robin chuckled. "So you would never marry him, even if James weren't around?"

"No. I would never marry him."

"Then you've got to tell him."

"I will. First thing tomorrow. When you're telling Quinn about the whales."

14

The clock on the bedside table blinked at Courtney when she finally opened her eyes. 10:17.

"Ohhh," Courtney moaned. She and Robin had talked long into the night, but she hadn't meant to sleep this late. Glancing over at the other bed, she saw that Robin had already risen. "I need a cup of coffee," she said aloud, throwing back the bedcovers.

She'd achieved a standing position when her cellphone played its little ditty: Monty Blackhorse's name blinked at her.

Courtney didn't answer. She wasn't ready. What woman could ever be ready to reject Monty Blackhorse? He was so important, so successful, and the Blackhorse ranch was magnificent and famous. It could be her home if she wanted it.

But never mind the ranch, Monty Blackhorse was a deep-down, true-blue good guy. He was smart and kind and funny, and tall, dark, and handsome; she couldn't forget that. He had been her best friend when they were young, and as they grew older, Monty had looked out for her. He'd never pushed himself on her, not even that Christmas when he took her to the ballet in Kansas City. If he loved her, he had been patient, waiting for her to accept his love.

A memory surfaced: the two of them talking casually about the future. This spring, they had been watching a baseball game on television at her apartment. It looked like the Kansas City Royals were going to have a good year. They sat on the sofa, comfortable in their friendship, casually drinking beers and eating chips and salsa.

When a commercial came on, Monty asked, indifferently, "How long are you gonna be working at UMKC?"

"As long as they'll have me, I suppose," she replied. "I like teaching."

Monty dipped a chip and crunched it. "You could teach in Emporia. They've got a college."

"They don't have any openings," she reminded him.

"Well, then, teach in the high school."

She'd snorted and rolled her eyes. "Monty, why on earth would I want to do that? I love living in Kansas City. The university's awesome—you should let me show you around sometime."

"Yeah, but you don't want to teach all your life. You want to settle down and raise some kids, right?"

"Of course. Someday."

"I want some kids," Monty said. "I want a herd of kids. When I'm married, I'm gonna take my wife and kids to every national park in the country."

"Sounds like a great idea," Courtney had murmured vaguely.

"Thought you'd like it," Monty said—and the Royals hit a home run and they stopped talking.

Thought you'd like it. Had he been subtly implying that he was planning for her to be his wife? How thick she'd been, how clueless. But Robin was right. This was not a game, not for Monty. She owed him an answer.

She sank back down in bed. Could she do this without coffee? Yes. She could. And she would. She scrolled down, found his number, and hit it.

"Hey, girl."

The warmth of his voice woke her fully. Her body had raced from drowsy to red alert. He was such a good guy. Her dear old companion. She didn't want to hurt his feelings. "Monty, hi. How are you?"

"Fair to middlin'. We need us some rain out here. We're almost in drought conditions. But it's nice to hear your voice."

"Nice to hear yours, too . . . but, Monty, I need to tell you something." She hadn't planned what she would say. The words came rushing up out of her like a fountain. "Monty, I can't marry you. I'm incredibly flattered, but the truth is, I'm in love with someone else. I don't want to lead you on—"

He interrupted. "You think I didn't suspect some man was why you were so all-fired eager to get back East?"

"But that's not true!" Courtney protested, immediately adding, "Okay, it's partly true, but, Monty, I swear I never slept with him before . . ." She was making it worse.

Laughter rumbled over the line, surprising Courtney. Low, deep laughter, like the wind before a storm hits. "Before this summer?"

Courtney had a lump in her throat. "Monty, I never meant—"

He interrupted her. "Don't you say you never meant to hurt me, because the one thing I am not experiencing at this moment in time is *hurt*. I'm angry."

She ignored his words and pressed on with her own decision. "Monty, I'm sorry. I care for you, but I'm—" *Say it,* she ordered herself, *go on and say it.* "I love James Vickerey and I want to live my life with him."

"So what? You expect me to lie down and die?" Monty was even angrier; it steamed through the phone into the air around her. "You don't love James Vickerey, you're fooled by his fancy name and his fancy family. You've forgotten what you've got back here."

"Monty—"

"We're not done," he growled. "Not by a long shot."

He disconnected.

She felt sick. But she had tried. She'd told him the truth. Still, she knew it wasn't over. She could still change things.

Her heart said: *James. James. James. Any way you can have him.*
James.

Suddenly, without coffee, she felt awake.

"Courtney!" Robin tore into the room. "Courtney, such amazing
news, such great news! Henry's started taking lithium. It won't take ef-
fect right away, of course, but that he's even agreed to start on it is
wonderful! Plus, he's truly back with Valerie." Without waiting for a
response from Courtney, Robin did an about-face and headed out of
the room, still talking. "Come on downstairs and get some breakfast!"

She was *here*, Courtney thought. She was here with lovely Robin
who was practically her sister, here with this family who raced at break-
neck speed through life, here with *James*. James was probably downstairs at breakfast. Courtney went to join them.

Robin returned to the kitchen and for a while she leaned against the
door, just watching the spectacle.

James stood at the stove, scrambling eggs and frying bacon while
Pearl, wearing the clothes she'd worn the night before, leaned on the
counter next to him moaning about her headache and trying to get
him to look down the front of her wrinkled dress.

Susanna and her friends were cutting up melons, strawberries, and
peaches and tossing the juicy pieces into a large bowl.

On the other side of the counter, at the far end of the table, Henry,
Valerie, and Jacob leaned toward one another in serious conversation,
and Robin could tell by Henry's face that the mere decision to try lithium had energized him. Henry was calm, but content.

Iris sat at the other end of the table, chatting with her mother's cousins as they drank coffee.

Callum moved around the room, doing damage control, sweeping
used paper towels and egg shells into a trash bag, stacking abandoned
coffee cups and plates in the dishwasher, sponging off the countertops.

Her father, as usual, was nowhere around.

Entering the mob scene, Robin poured herself a cup of coffee. She
tried to ignore James because of all that Courtney had told her. She

wanted to grin with happiness because James loved Courtney, and slug him in the arm because he was being such a jerk. She toasted bread, found the blackberry jam she favored, and sat at the table.

Courtney appeared. She settled at the table next to Robin. "God," she whispered, "what time did we go to sleep last night?"

"Scrambled eggs?" James asked, approaching her with the skillet.

"Yes, please," Courtney answered, without looking at him. James spooned eggs on her plate and, when Robin nodded, onto hers. Without a word, he moved on to Henry.

Gradually, the breakfast ended, people drifted off to pack suitcases and head for the airport, and Susanna gathered her friends for a shopping trip in town. Robin carried cups and plates to the dishwasher, placed what was left of the fruit into a smaller bowl, covered it with plastic wrap, and put it in the refrigerator.

James lingered over his breakfast, watching Courtney. "Hey, Courtney," he called out, sounding lighthearted and casual, "want to ride with me to take Callum to the airport?"

"How soon are you leaving?" Courtney didn't look at him when she answered.

"In about thirty minutes."

"Yeah, okay, I'll go. Give me a sec to get ready." She left the room.

James followed but Robin could hear him in the front hall, talking to Susanna and her friends.

Robin began cleaning the kitchen. She was loading the dishwasher when Callum came in with more plates and cups.

"I'll do the skillets," he said.

"Thanks. I hate that job." For a while they worked without speaking, and Robin was grateful that Callum made no reference to their talk the night before.

As Callum set the cast-iron skillet to drip on the drainer rack, he said, "Jacob's already left. He told me he had to take an early plane."

Idly, Robin replied, "I wondered where he was."

"He slept up in the guys' room in the attic last night." Callum chuckled. "Slept on the floor and didn't complain. He was terrified of Christabel."

"Don't be mean, Callum."

"I'm not mean. You had to notice the way Christabel was with Jacob last night."

Robin didn't respond. She dried a pot with furious concentration.

"Poor Quinn," Callum said. "He has his hands full."

This was true, yet it annoyed Robin that Callum would say it. As if he were criticizing Quinn—*poor Quinn.*

"You may be right," she agreed through gritted teeth. "On the other hand, Christabel's an adult." Almost desperately, she added, "Quinn didn't run after her Friday night when Christabel made a scene because Susanna didn't name her one of her summer children."

Callum said, "That Christabel's a handful."

"Come on, Callum," Robin argued. "Give the girl a break. Her mother left her! To go off and live with some European! Has Desiree ever once invited Christabel to visit or come back here to visit Christabel? No, not once!"

"I know. That's terrible. I'm sorry for Christabel. I understand how that makes her frantic when people close to her pair off with each other."

Robin glared at Callum. He leaned against the stove, dressed in casual khakis and a red button-down shirt that accentuated the shininess of his thick brown hair. He was good-looking and brilliant and kind, and right now he was a pain in the neck.

She changed the subject. "You leave soon, right?" She made it sound like a demand.

Callum smiled. "You are so predictable."

Robin's chin jutted out. "Why do you say that?"

"Um, because I can tell you want me gone."

"Of course I want you gone, you're being a jerk." Why did she feel like crying? Why did she feel like *hitting* Callum right on his big muscular chest? She envied her father, who simply left the room if the emotional atmosphere got too thick.

"Yeah, you're right, I am being a jerk." Callum walked over and took Robin in his arms. Gently he hugged her to him, patting her back. "I'll leave when James comes down to drive me to the airport. I won't be coming back this summer. Too much work. But if you need me, Robin, call me, and I'll come. As a friend, no pressure, no more love talk, I'll come as a friend if you need me."

She rested her head on Callum's chest and let herself sink into his comforting embrace. It was hard, being the strong one, the sensible one, all the time, she thought, and then she remembered her night-time visits to the whales and mentally laughed at herself—she wasn't so sensible then.

"Thanks, Callum," Robin said. "I appreciate that. You're a good friend."

Callum released her from his embrace. He pecked a kiss on top of her head and left the room.

A moment later, she heard steps thunder down the stairs. James called out, "Ready to go, Callum?"

Courtney peeked in at Robin. "We're driving Callum to the airport. Wanna go with?"

Robin shook her head. "No, thanks. Things to do."

Robin went through the refrigerator and cupboards, writing a list of stuff she needed to buy in town. She heard people calling to one another as they left. Valerie and Henry had already driven to the hospital. Iris was driving the cousins to the plane, then going shopping in town with Pearl. Susanna had gone shopping with her friends. Dad was undoubtedly holed up in his study. Doors slammed. Car engines rumbled into action.

She was alone. Well, except for her father, but he didn't count, he was the invisible man. She was alone in the house, and the kitchen was clean enough, and her list was complete, and she could go to the grocery store or she could start vacuuming or washing sheets, and for a moment she felt like Cinderella. But no one had *told* her to do any of these things. She only wanted to help her mother. Plus, she loved this house, loved keeping it tidy.

Robin poured another cup of coffee and stepped outside to drink it. Sunshine would perk her up, and caffeine would help. For a few minutes, she watched the tent guys dismantling the tent, breaking down the poles, carting the wooden floorboards to their truck.

"Good, Robin," she said aloud to herself. "Sit all alone watching the tent come apart. That will cheer you up." She didn't care that she spoke aloud. No one was near enough to hear her.

Maybe they'd use the tent again when Courtney and James got married, because if the way they drooled around each other was any indication, marriage was in the future. And with *that,* like a thunderclap, she got what it was that weighed down her heart.

Courtney now belonged to James. James was first in her thoughts and affections—way first, so far ahead of Robin the distance couldn't be counted, and that was as it should be, your true love should be the heart of your heart, the person you would rescue in a fire, choosing that person first, always.

Still, Robin felt a bit like a chess piece that had been whapped right off the board to fall sideways, forgotten.

"Are you the *MOST* pathetic person in the world?" she demanded. None of the tent guys looked her way. But really? She had longed for Courtney and James to get together, to marry, so she and Courtney could be sisters-in-law.

She wasn't jealous. She was just tired. And totally not ready to face Quinn. But she'd made a pact with Courtney. So she would go—she would go, right now, to see Quinn!

Leaving her cup on the patio table, she raced through the house, found the keys to her car in the bowl, and jumped into the Jeep. She roared off, punching the radio to the classic rock station and singing as she went.

Quinn and Christabel lived on another part of the island, near Surfside Beach. By the time Robin had reached their house, she had calmed down. Christabel's Citroën wasn't in the drive, but Robin parked on the curb in case she came home and wanted to park near her garage-studio.

Quinn opened the door before Robin could knock.

"Robin." His face was stiff, wary; he was still angry from their argument on the dance floor. But he held the door open. "Come in."

"Thanks. I need to talk with you." Robin went into the living room. She stood near a chair, but did not sit down.

Quinn stood a few feet away from her, not close enough to touch her. He spoke formally, as if to a new acquaintance. "Great party last night."

She hated it when Quinn went cold on her. She was here to make peace with Quinn, not anger him, but she needed to break through his defensive shell. So she said, "Christabel seemed to enjoy herself."

Quinn's mouth twisted in annoyance. "You know Christabel enjoys being the center of attention." Quinn rubbed his hand across his forehead. "She needs to know she's liked. She will always need proof that people are there for her, because her mother wasn't, isn't. In a way— we've talked about this, Robin, you and I—in a way, your family takes the place of her mother. The other night, Susanna sort of disowned her—"

"Oh, please, Quinn, that's not the way to think of it, and it's certainly not the way Susanna meant it—"

"Maybe not. But I'm certain that's the way Christabel interpreted it."

"Quinn." She moved toward him. "I got us off on the wrong subject entirely. I don't want to fuss about Christabel."

Quinn's expression softened. "All right. I'm sorry to be so defensive. Let's start over. Here, sit down with me." He led her to the sofa. They sat side by side, but did not touch. "I'll go first. Robin, I love you. I want to start my life with you. I agreed to teach here another year so I can be near you while you make up your mind about leaving."

His desire, and his need, were so palpable, almost a color in the air, a swirl of darkness between them, and Robin could with one word make the darkness disappear.

And yet. And yet, there it was again, Quinn's attitude, his complete confidence that what *he* wanted—to leave the island—was the only possible choice for him and Robin to be together. His complete disregard—gentle, but disregard all the same—for Robin's continued insistence that she wanted to live on the island all her life.

Softly, she said, "I wish you could say 'while you make up your mind about leaving or while I make up my mind to stay.'"

Quinn gave her the look he might give a recalcitrant student. "We've gone over all this before, so often, haven't we, love?"

"We have." She rubbed her hands together, a nervous gesture, she knew. "Quinn? I need to tell you something."

"That sounds ominous."

"Not at all. Something wonderful. If I tell you, Quinn, you have to keep it a secret. You have to promise not to tell anyone, especially my mother and father. Not Christabel, either. No one."

"Are you pregnant?"

"God, no!" She felt his body recoil, as if she'd hit him, and in a way she had, almost insulting him with her reply. "No," she repeated softly, sweetly. "It's something you can't imagine. Well, I couldn't have imagined it before it happened. Quinn—let me tell you about it all at once." She took a deep breath. "Sometimes I take my boat out at night into the ocean, *far* out. I turn off the motor, and simply sit there, all alone in this amazing world of sea and sky."

"Okay. That sounds dangerous, but nice."

"It's amazing. So quiet, so unearthly. And, Quinn, sometimes, not always, but often, um—don't laugh, this is real—whales visit me."

"What do you mean?"

"They approach the boat. One of them—I know it's the same one because of the pattern of callosities on her head—likes to lie next to the boat looking up at me. I talk to her. She seems to listen. She likes me, I know she likes me—"

"For god's sake, Robin," Quinn scoffed. "You can't expect me to believe—"

"But it's true. And yes, I suppose it's rather dangerous and I admit being out in a small boat on the deep ocean in the night is kind of frightening, but it gives me a delicious sense of disconnection from the noisy, pretentious people world. It allows me to sort of enter a world humans don't often connect with."

"Robin. What you're saying frightens me for you."

"I can understand that. It terrifies me sometimes. But when I'm out there, out on the deep water, and I hear a knock on the boat and look down to see the whale, this mammoth, breathing, unimaginable being, when I'm connecting with her, I'm not afraid. I'm . . . I'm lifted up. Words can't explain it. It's like a zone of bliss—"

Quinn took Robin by the shoulders and smiled indulgently. "Stop it, Robin. That's the stuff of fairy tales, not real life."

"But, Quinn, it's true! It's real."

Quinn rose from the sofa. He paced the room, shaking his head. "My darling Robin. What you're telling me is, frankly, absurd. You sound like a little girl with an imaginary playmate."

Robin shot up off the sofa, hands clenched at her sides. "Are you saying I'm hallucinating? Making this up? Because it's true. Those whales are real."

Quinn turned from her and walked toward the window. He stared out for a long time before returning to Robin.

"If what you're saying is true, Robin, that is yet another reason you need to leave the island."

"What? Why?"

He held her shoulders so that she faced him as he spoke. "Let's say, for the sake of argument, that the whales are real. Do you not see how dangerous the situation is for you? What if one of these whales accidentally hit your boat so hard it capsized? What if you fell in the water out there, among your friendly mammals? Do you imagine that one of them will swoop under you and give you a ride safely back to shore?"

She caught the derision in his voice, and yet what he was saying was something she'd thought of herself. Accidents happened all the time, even among friends.

Quinn's voice became honeyed. "I love you, Robin. I want to marry you. And this is how much I love you. If you'll promise to stop seeing the whales, I'll stop pressing you to move off the island."

Robin gasped. He *did* love her, she realized, he must love her, to agree to remain on the island. Her heart swelled with hope, with love.

It would be crazy of her not to agree to this. Even she understood how she was romanticizing those few fortuitous and perilous moments out in the dark water when she saw the whales. What were those meetings compared to the chance to marry the man she loved and remain on the island she loved?

Still, she hesitated. To agree to this was like agreeing to shut the door on an experience so magnificent, so literally *awesome* it shone in her memory like a constellation of stars. She loved Quinn. But she loved that part of her life as well.

"It would make me sad to give up my nights out there," she said softly.

"Yes, I'm sure." Quinn smiled. "On the other hand, you could spend all your nights with me, here on the island, and I can provide you with a few sensations your fantastical friends can't."

Robin let him put his arms around her and hold her tight. He was strong, and warm, and good. He had made an enormous concession, agreeing to remain on the island. He loved her. "Okay," she said. "It's a deal."

15

Late in the afternoon, Courtney lay in bed with James, her nakedness covered by a sheet. A light summer breeze fluttered the air,
but here, in James's bedroom, even with the windows open, it was hot
and humid.

"I can't get up," Courtney murmured, her voice muffled by the way
she lay, facedown. "I can't even move."

"We ate too much at lunch," James said. "We've become a pair of
sloths. All we do is eat and have sex."

"Do sloths have a lot of sex?" Courtney wondered.

"I don't know. I'll Google it if I ever get out of bed."

Courtney slithered around to lie on her side facing James. She put
her hand on her stomach. "I definitely ate too much at lunch. If we
continue this celebrating, I'll look like Jacob."

James laughed. "What a terrifying thought. Will you get all hairy,
too? Because I can handle the weight, but the hair situation not so
much."

"We're both getting stupid, too," Courtney murmured. "Our conversational skills have plummeted since we started sleeping together."

"You said *plummeted*. That's a nice word. And conversational. Very cool. Five syllables."

"Maybe we should nap," Courtney suggested, snuggling into her pillow.

"We did that when we got back from lunch. It's almost dinnertime," James informed her.

"We could skip dinner."

"Right. So your plan is we'll lie here and sleep and have sex for the rest of our lives."

"Oh, what a good idea." Courtney nestled in James's arms. After a moment, she said, "Showers. We should add showers to our list." Smiling into his chest, she said, "I've never had sex in a shower with anyone."

"And that's not going to happen for you today," James told her. "You might be a rapacious, sex-crazy female, but males have a more elegant biology."

"You mean I've used you up," Courtney clarified.

"Definitely. I'm not sure I've got the energy to stagger to the bathroom."

"Mmm," Courtney cooed. "Then I'll get the first shower."

Courtney rolled away from his hot, sweat-slicked body.

In the bathroom with the cool water cascading over her, she regained her senses. She washed her hair. She laughed at how silly they were and closed her eyes and let her head fall back as she remembered having lunch at Cru and making love this afternoon. Twice. She'd entered a zone of pleasure, she was a child at a carnival, a kite in the air.

Dripping, clean, and fully awake, she wrapped herself in a towel and combed her hair out to dry naturally in the warm summer air.

James came into the bathroom as she went out. She heard the shower running while she pulled on panties and a sundress and brushed her hair. No makeup needed—her lips and cheeks were rosy from kissing.

James walked out of the bathroom, nude and clean. He pulled on his boxers and shorts and yanked a rugby shirt over his head. Dressed, he seemed different to Courtney. She looked at herself in the mirror. She looked different, too. Somehow in the last few moments they had become more adult, more *actual.* They were no longer merely lovers. They were lovers with decisions to make.

"James," Courtney said, "we need to talk. About where this is going—about your fears about children."

"We can talk," James said calmly, "but I won't change my mind, Courtney."

Her heart kicked in her chest. "But you should!" she protested.

"Courtney—"

"This is wrong. *You* are wrong! You say you refuse to have children, you won't even discuss it with me, but you *should* discuss it with me! I've read *tons* of articles about bipolar syndrome, and *I'm* not afraid to have your children. I *want* your children!"

"Courtney—"

"James, life is hard for everyone. Everyone is slightly eccentric one way or the other. Look at your precious Christabel! *She's* not bipolar, but she has been traumatized by her mother leaving her so abruptly and so very thoroughly. In a way, Christabel is traumatized every day, because every day her mother is still alive, still in Europe, still not in-terested in making contact with Christabel. So she's weird. She dresses like a child porn star. She causes scenes. And she expects *you* to take care of her."

"Is this about Christabel? You know she's like a sister to me. But if that's what's bothering you—"

"No, no, this isn't about Christabel. It's about being eccentric, being odd. It's about thinking we can control our lives. You don't want to have children because you're afraid they'll be bipolar, and—"

"Stop right there, Courtney, and think about what you're saying. Have you ever spoken with Henry about his illness? Have you ever sat down and listened to him? He has gone through years of trying differ-ent medications, and some of them have made his head feel like it's on fire, and some of them have made him drowsy, and some have made him nauseous. Maybe the same gene that makes him bipolar also makes him the genius doctor that he is, but Henry has had a hell of a hard time with this illness, and he's caused his entire family a lot of pain."

Courtney nodded. "Yes. I know that. I mean, I haven't spoken with him privately, seriously, at length, but I have read about it. I *get* it. Still, I've read the literature and there is no proof that you've got the gene or that you can pass it on to your children or whether it will be debilitating or merely bothersome. Look at all Henry has achieved! If I'm willing to take the risk, why aren't you?"

"I don't know," James said, his voice sad, his eyes shadowed. "I just can't, Courtney. I won't."

"James, listen to me." Courtney leaned close to him. "Do you think Susanna wishes Henry had never been born?"

James flinched. "Of course not. But I'm sure she wishes he weren't bipolar."

"But we don't get to pick and choose the qualities of our children, James. We can't order a child like a meal: *I want a tall blond with no freckles or moles or unruly tendencies.*"

James shook his head. Rising, he crossed to stare out the window for a while. He came back and sat on the bed next to Courtney, not quite touching her.

"Courtney, I love you. I want to marry you. I'm willing to adopt or try some kind of in vitro so we can have children. Isn't that enough?"

After a moment, Courtney said bleakly, "No. It's not enough, James. I love you with all my heart. But you've made up your mind, and so have I."

They sat in silence. Within her heart a tiny speck of hope still beat, flashing like a beacon, waiting to emerge into a full-blown explosion of joy.

But James simply stood up without speaking, and walked away, and left the room. She heard his steps going down the stairs. Courtney sat bereft, and the speck of hope shriveled and died.

16

Tuesday morning, life returned to normal, or what passed for normal in the Vickerey household.

Robin joined her father in his study to help him begin writing his memoirs. It was a daunting task. They had boxes of files, case notes, letters, and torn pieces of paper marked "absolutely necessary" and almost completely illegible.

Susanna planned to join a friend for lunch in town and then spend two hours on Main Street hawking raffle tickets for the church fair.

Henry and Valerie were at the hospital, working until late afternoon, when they vowed to return to Henry's room and sleep for three days straight.

Iris and Pearl coated themselves with sunblock and drove off to the *good* beach at Nobadeer for the day.

James secluded himself to work on his medical translations and deal with dozens of emails.

Courtney gave herself a lecture and biked to the library in town.

She'd find a good book to read, something to clear her mind. Maybe Kate Chopin's *The Awakening* or Anita Diamant's *The Boston Girl*.

The historic Atheneum with its white fluted columns had always drawn her to it, for books, CDs, DVDs, lectures, and especially for its hushed and tranquil rooms, so different from the Vickerey house. She scanned the new fiction arrivals, browsed through the stacks, checked out two books, and wandered upstairs to the Great Hall, where she settled at a table in a cozy nook.

She opened the book . . . and instantly flashed back to this morning, when she and James had made love. It had been hurried and intense, with no time for talking.

But there was nothing new to be said. He loved her. He wanted to marry her. She loved him, and wanted to marry him, to be with him forever and ever.

But never to have his children? Could she make that compromise?

Frustrated, she packed up her books and went back out into the sunshine. Sometimes walking helped her think, broke up the logjam of thoughts in her frenzied mind.

Outside, she sat on a bench in the library's garden. It was shady here, and on the velvet green lawn, children were playing with a Frisbee, or lying belly down in the grass, chin propped on elbows, reading. Two little boys were climbing on the crooked limbs of crab apple trees. Courtney had always marveled that these two trees, short and not very thick, could support the weight of children, but the trees seemed to flourish under their athletic attention.

They ran shrieking from each other, they yelled, they fell down, and from a stroller a baby wailed. They were noisy and spirited and as unmanageable as a herd of colts. They wore candy-colored clothing or spotless white with navy blue trim. Of course these were fortunate children, brought here on vacation or living on the island, being carefully watched by parents or nannies.

Courtney had always assumed she would have a family at some unimaginable point in her life. In her early twenties, she'd been focused on getting her master's, teaching, reading, riding her horse in Kansas

and swimming on a Nantucket beach. But later this year she would
turn thirty. A milestone. A turning point.

Restless, she rose and left the garden, strolling around the small
historic town, letting her thoughts idle while she walked past the neat
brick post office, The Hub with its windows full of seashells and toy
sailboats, Christmas ornaments of whales wearing Santa hats or wooden
doors with holly wreaths, up past the Bartlett's Farm truck with its
bounty of ripe red tomatoes, sweet sugar corn, heads of lettuce, and
broccoli, all fresh today.

Susanna was sitting outside the Nantucket Pharmacy, a card table
in front of her, a poster of a handmade Nantucket-themed quilt on the
table. She wore a floppy straw hat to shade her from the sun, and a sea-
blue sundress.

"Would you like to buy a raffle ticket for this quilt?" she asked
Courtney.

"Sure," Courtney said. And this was a freedom for Courtney, and a
sign of her adulthood, because when she first came here, she had
needed to save every dollar of her hard-earned money for school. "How
are sales going?" she asked companionably.

"It's early days yet. The real crowds come in July and August." Susanna checked her watch. "By now, most people will be on the beach,
craving a swim and a lie in the sun after our ghastly winter. What are
you doing?"

"I was trying to read in the library, but I couldn't concentrate. It's
such a gorgeous day. I sat for a while and watched the children climbing those hardy crab apple trees."

Susanna chuckled. "Oh, I love those trees. I used to bring my kids
in when they were little, to get books from the children's room, and
then to play in the yard. There's really no other public green space in
town."

Courtney hadn't planned to say it, and surprised herself when the
question popped out of her mouth: "Do you think Henry and Valerie
will have children?"

Susanna studied Courtney's face before she answered. "I hope they
will."

"Even with Henry's bipolar problems?"

Susanna turned to say hello to a passing friend. An older couple with a golden retriever pulling on its leash walked past, and a young man with a goatee rushed in the other direction, and then the space around them was quiet. Courtney chided herself for bringing up private matters in such a public space, but on second thought decided she might get more privacy here, with strangers strolling past and none of Susanna's children or summer children interrupting or overhearing.

"All my life," Susanna said in a hushed tone, "I have suffered from extremely painful periods and hideous PMS."

Courtney nodded. She'd been aware of this, of course, over the past eleven years. She knew it was one of the reasons that sometimes Robin did much of the cooking.

"I've tried over-the-counter medications, but none of them worked. I've tried exercise, walking, I've tried drinking so much wine it's made me dizzy, but nothing has really helped. Finally, *finally* I went through menopause, and the pains stopped. But now I've got excruciating hot flashes and night sweats. I can't fall sleep, and I can't stay asleep. No matter how little I eat, my body goes on its merry way, adding its padding of blubber to my bones."

Courtney objected with a smile. "You're beautiful."

Susanna shrugged. "My point is, Courtney, that I have a body and a mind, and both can be as perverse and intransigent as a kite in the sky. Would I change my body? Yes, there have been times in my life when I would have paid money to stop my periods, but our bodies, like life, are so *complicated* and everything is so intertwined, past our imagining. I'm stuck with this body of mine, and now that I'm sixty, I can look back at my life and say that I'm fortunate. I wouldn't change a thing—because changing one thing is like removing a piece of a jigsaw puzzle or one single block from a child's wooden tower. Change one thing, change everything."

An older woman carrying several parcels swept up to the table. "Susanna! Lovely to see you again! I'll take ten of those tickets. Maybe this year I'll win!"

Susanna turned her attention to the other woman, who clearly wanted to catch up with news of the winter.

Courtney murmured, "Thanks, Susanna," and strolled away.

A small park had been tucked in the corner across the street from Murray's Toggery and the grand, redbrick Pacific National Bank. No grass, but a sweet little fountain, several trees, lots of flowers, and a few benches. Birds chirped from the trees.

Courtney settled on a bench hidden from the sidewalk by halcyon blue hydrangea. She watched people walk past and let her mind drift. But her thoughts were interrupted by bits of conversation she couldn't help but overhear from people passing by on the sidewalk.

". . . thought your sister would like it! I did *not* buy an expensive Hermes scarf for her because I wanted to accentuate her double chin! Double chins, by the way!"

". . . I'm not saying he needs to go into assisted living, I'm just pointing out that he's got newspapers dating back five years and the inside of his refrigerator smells like dirty socks . . ."

". . . get the vegetables at the farm truck, and we've got pasta at home. Beazy and Karl are packing the Jeep with the beach chairs and coolers, so as soon as we get back we can get out to Surfside."

". . . not another doughnut. If you keep fussing, I'll turn this stroller right around and you won't get to swing at Children's Beach."

". . . he said if I really loved him, I'd have sex with him, so we did a lot of stuff but no *real* penetration . . ."

Courtney almost stood up and peered over a hydrangea bush to see how old the girl who spoke was. Instead, she gathered up her purse and library book and headed toward the side street where she'd locked her bike.

She lazily biked most of the way back to 'Sconset, but on the spur of the moment, took a detour down the Quidnet Road to Sesachacha Pond. Even here, on this relatively unknown and very tranquil spot, beach umbrellas were planted, staking out territory, and several children, wet and sandy, were making a fort out of beach chairs and towels.

She dropped her bike in the tangle of beach roses and walked up and over a high sand dune and there, spread out before her, was the ocean. This part of Quidnet attracted few families. The waves were strong, and sharks had been sighted here at the end of last summer. Never mind, she didn't want to swim, she needed to walk, to move, and not to overhear anyone else just for now. She needed to let her own thoughts sort out themselves.

Could she marry James, knowing she'd never have his children?

Her brother, Donnie, had gotten married young, at eighteen, to his high school sweetheart, Janice. They'd lived in a tiny second-floor apartment while Janice worked as a sales clerk, supporting both of them while Donnie spent four years getting his license as a pharmacist. For those four years, Janice had confided, they had lived in fear of getting pregnant. They couldn't have afforded for Janice not to work, and they were still young, not ready for a family.

"Wouldn't you know?" Janice had complained to Courtney two years after Donnie had gotten his license and joined Courtney and Donnie's father in the pharmacy. "For years we stressed about not getting me knocked up, and now it's been two years of trying, and I'm not pregnant yet."

They had eventually succeeded and had two little boys who were such tornadoes they weren't sure whether they could handle a third child. But it was something to think about, Courtney reflected, as she kicked off her sandals and sank her feet into the gritty, hot surface of the sand. Even in this super-scientific age, human beings didn't control their own destiny. One of her good friends from Smith, Lori Wallace, had drawn up a birth plan with her husband for the birth of their first child. It included a midwife instead of a doctor, a tub for a water birth, and tranquil music from one of Lori's yoga classes to keep Lori calm and centered during the birth process. Nature had decided not to follow the Wallaces' birth plan, and Lori had been rushed, wailing and weeping, to the hospital for a C-section. The baby had been fine and healthy, but Lori swore she'd never give birth again.

No one knew better than someone from Kansas how Fate liked to mess with human plans. Courtney called the Kansas four seasons Tornado, Drought, Hailstorm, and Blizzard. Maybe, she decided, she was less frightened of having a child with bipolar syndrome because she had been raised on the Kansas state motto: *Ad Astra per Aspera,* "To the Stars through Difficulties." She'd never thought life would be a sweet, strifeless ride.

Her sister-in-law, Janice, often stretched her arms out as far as they would go and said to her toddlers, "I love you *this* much!" Courtney faced the blue ocean, which was calm today, unrolling infinitely into the horizon. She held out her arms, forming the letter T, and smiled at how small she was compared to the expanse of water. But she did love James *this* much, she had always loved James, she loved his smell, his taste, the sound of his voice, and she loved his heart, his humor, his intelligence, and his kind and reliable strength.

She turned and walked back, for a while setting her feet into the indentations her own feet had made. Could she live without James's children? She loved this family so much, she loved every single gene that made them who they were. But if she couldn't have that and have James, what would she do?

She climbed back over the dune, brushed the sand off her feet, picked up her bike, and headed back to 'Sconset. The bike path along Polpis Road was broad and smooth, dipping in toward the cranberry bogs, winding through green tunnels of trees that sweetened her ride with moments of shade. She biked past the golf course, and saw on her left the great red and white Sankaty lighthouse rising from the bluff. Recent storms had eroded the bluff, causing massive chunks of sand to give way, thundering into the ocean. Some bluff-side houses had to be moved—or fall into the water. The Vickereys' house was closer to town, and the high bluff there had not been damaged by gale-force winds.

This afternoon, fog was drifting over the ocean, as it often did at this end of the island. Capricious, cool, and carrying tiny pinpoints of water, it made everyone's hair frizz or flatten as it moved silently, blown by invisible currents, over the land. The wind was coming from the east, and the fog swept and curled and unrolled over the land like a misty gray ocean. Courtney was glad she was almost home. It was difficult biking against the wind.

Cutting this way and that, through small quiet streets settled with summer houses, smelling the fragrance of the beach roses mingling with the last of the lilacs, Courtney wondered: *How much does anyone get?* She loved this island, and she loved the Vickerey family. She loved James. She *understood* his anxiety about having a bipolar child, but in truth, she was an outsider. She didn't *feel* his anxiety the same way. Did she love him enough to agree not to have his children?

Yes. She did love him *that much.* She loved him truly and with all her heart, and as she realized this, hope washed through her. She pedaled faster, eager to get home. To James.

The Vickereys' driveway was, as usual, congested with cars, with Christabel's Citroën parked on the street, halfway on the lawn. Courtney was hot and sweaty from biking as she walked into the Vickerey house. She wondered if she could dash down to the ocean for a quick cooling dip, although she wasn't keen on swimming in the fog.

In the cool front hall, she heard voices coming from the kitchen, and for a moment she froze, hallucinating Monty's voice among them. Had she gotten so immersed in her Midwestern memories that she was carrying them along with her into the present?

Iris, her purple hair sticking out like an excited cockatoo's, came racing down the hall, Pearl and Christabel sauntering behind, all of them grinning—*beaming.*

"Courtney! OMG! You never told us! He is so tall, and so huge and so gorgeous!"

This wasn't real, Courtney thought. This couldn't be happening. Monty Blackhorse could *not* be inside the Vickereys' house.

Pearl sashayed up to Courtney, pulling her close. "One thing. You have to tell us. Is his package as proportionally huge as he is?"

Courtney ignored Pearl. "Iris. Tell me Monty isn't here!"

Iris squinted apologetically. "He got here about an hour ago. He's looking for you. Mom invited him in."

Pearl refused to be left out. "Plus, Susanna's invited him to spend the night. She told him he won't be able to get a room on the island in June. She's invited him for dinner, too."

"Well, you don't have to look so satisfied about it!" Iris snapped at her friend.

Courtney wanted to sink through the floor. "Where's James?"

"He went down to the beach for a swim about an hour ago," Iris answered.

"So he hasn't met Monty yet?"

"No. Henry and Valerie haven't, either. They drove in a while ago and went straight up to Henry's apartment." Iris counted on her fingers as she spoke. "Robin went down for a swim with James. Dad's in seclusion. Mom made a lasagna for dinner tonight, so there will be enough food for everyone—"

Courtney dropped her laptop and notebooks on the front hall table. She spotted a leather satchel on the floor, embossed with the gold initials M.B. and a lightweight summer Stetson. Her heart sank. She was not ready to talk to Monty, not when things were so unsettled with James. And she didn't want to choose Monty on the rebound. That would be terrible of her—and *for* her.

She heard Susanna's charming voice moving toward them. "I think I hear Courtney coming in the door right now."

Courtney clutched Iris's shoulders. "Help me. At least go tell James that Monty's here and *I* didn't invite him!"

Before Iris could respond, Monty's big frame filled the doorway at the end of the hall.

"Hey, girl."

He stood almost six foot five, even without his Stetson. He wore a white dress shirt with a navy blazer and jeans that rode low on his hips in spite of his tooled leather belt. His black hair was pulled back and neatly tied to hang to his shoulders.

Even now, knowing she was deeply and truly in love with James, Courtney could not deny the tug she felt inside at the sight of this magnificent man.

"Monty." She was amazed she could speak. "This is a surprise."

He gave a slow aw-shucks smile that made Pearl, standing next to her, gasp.

"I think we need to have a talk," Monty said.

"Sure," Courtney replied, keeping her voice light. "Let's go out to the patio."

Susanna said in her helpful way, "I've invited your friend to dinner."

"That's so nice of you, Susanna." Courtney walked down the hall toward the kitchen, Pearl, Christabel, and Iris following so close behind she could feel their breath on her neck.

Iris angled in front of him. "Monty, would you like a beer?"

"Thanks, Iris, I would," Monty answered.

"I'll get it." Pearl rushed to the refrigerator.

"I think I'll get myself a glass of wine," Courtney snapped, since no one had offered her anything.

Pearl held out a beer. "Heineken," she purred. "Would you like a glass?"

Monty gave Pearl the full force of his smile. "I'm fine with this. Thanks."

Courtney poured herself a glass of white wine. A large glass. Almost full, and damn the etiquette.

"We'll go out this way," she told Monty, and headed to the back hall and the door to the patio.

She could hear his boots stomp as he followed. She was surprised he didn't wear his spurs, she thought, and smiled at herself and relaxed a little. She led him to the chairs farthest away from the house and sat down, gesturing with her hand that he should take the chair on the other side of the patio table. He ignored her and sat in the chair nearest her. Within touching distance.

Courtney took a fortifying slug of wine.

Monty waited, his black eyes concentrated on her like an eagle on its prey.

"Monty," she began, and when she realized that her voice wasn't trembling, not even a little bit, she sucked up some courage from the base of her spine, sat up straighter, and asked, "What are you doing here?"

"I came to talk some sense into you." Monty pulled his chair closer to Courtney. "Darlin', that's no way to do things, kissing me off over the phone."

"Monty—"

"I get it. I get it." Monty faked looking around. "It's scenic here. Nice people. Never Never Land—never have to work—"

"I've worked plenty here!" Courtney snapped. "I worked hard for eleven summers."

"Didn't mean to rile you," Monty said, although the twinkle in his eye told her he'd enjoyed getting under her skin. "All I mean is that it's a real picture book here, what with the ocean and the sweet little flowers and not a pile of horseshit in sight."

Courtney took another sip of wine.

"So I get why you'd want to live here. But, Courtney, this isn't where you belong."

"I think it is, Monty. I think it might be. I hope I'll find out this summer."

A flicker of light warned her that someone, probably Pearl, was watching from inside the house. Hell, Pearl was probably videoing this on her phone.

"Look, Monty, I'm not comfortable talking with you here. It's almost dinnertime. The house will be filling up with people—"

Monty began, "Susanna said—"

Courtney interrupted. "Monty, I want to talk to you more about this, but not here. Besides," she added, her thoughts piling up fast, "you can't stay here tonight." Monty *and* James sleeping under the same roof? The thought gave her heart palpitations.

"Susanna said all the hotels are full. She invited me to spend the night here."

"Oh. Right. She's probably right. Okay, you can spend the night here and I'll drive you to the airport tomorrow."

Monty's face clouded over. "I didn't fly all the damn way out here only to be sent right back."

"Well, I didn't ask you to come," Courtney reminded him. Softening, she said, "I know we need to talk, Monty. I want to talk to you about—everything. But I can't do it here. Let's go for a walk." She stood up.

Monty stood up, too. He took a step toward her. His dark eyes burned like coal. "Courtney—"

She held out her hands to stop him. She didn't want to hurt him, but she needed to make him understand. "Monty, please. You have been my best friend forever. You're wonderful, Monty. You are the Kansas catch of the century. I know that. I care for you and I admire you, and in a way I love you. But I love you as a friend. And whatever you feel for me, it can't be—complete. Because you don't know what my life is back here. You don't know the whole me, the real me."

Monty was quiet a moment, chewing on her words. "I think I do know you, Courtney. I know you're a sweet, good, smart woman who rides a horse like a Cherokee. I know you're all for gun control but you can use a rifle to put down a copperhead or a diamond-back rattler. I know you like to read your books, but you also have a fine talent for helping a heifer birth her first calf. You like to line dance and you own at least five pairs of cowboy boots—"

"Cowgirl," Courtney mumbled.

"You have more friends than we Blackhorses have stallions. Your *family* lives in Kansas. Forget me, think how *they'd* feel if you married and lived back East. And while you're at it, don't forget me, because you are the woman for me, and you are the *only* woman for me and you know that's true right down to the core of your heart."

In a strangled voice, Courtney begged, "Stop it, Monty." Tears welled in her eyes. Never before in all her times with Monty had he been so eloquent. Never before had Monty Blackhorse opened himself up like this. It was like being cut with a knife, because even if she didn't want to marry him, she cared for him, and she did not want to watch the man humble himself. She absolutely did not want to cause him pain.

Suddenly, Christabel stepped out onto the patio. Before Courtney could object, she said, "I thought I'd better point out that Robin and James are coming up from the beach. I mean, because it's obvious you two weren't aware, and I know you'd like a *private* conversation."

Courtney turned. Robin and James, both in bathing suits, towels flung over their shoulders, had come off the long wooden steps and were winding through the thicket of wild roses and stepping onto the lawn.

Robin was staring at Monty and grinning. That seemed to be any woman's normal reaction to Monty.

James was not grinning. He had a face like a thundercloud.

The back door opened again. Courtney heard Pearl and Iris come out to the patio. *Great,* Courtney thought, *it's* The Courtney's an Idiot Show *and I've got an audience.*

Robin and James strolled up to the patio.

"Hi, Monty," Robin said casually.

Monty flashed his killer smile. "Hi, Robin. Nice to see you again." He turned to James. "James, right? I've heard a lot about you."

James glanced at Courtney.

Courtney had to do it. "James," she said. "This is Monty Blackhorse. From Kansas. We have some things to talk about."

The men did not shake hands. Monty nodded curtly at James. James nodded curtly back.

"James," Courtney said, and the hell with kindness or good manners, "I didn't invite Monty here. He just showed up. Just now."

"But he's going to have dinner and spend the night with us," Pearl cooed, slithering over to stand close to Monty.

"The hotels are full," Courtney hurriedly explained. "No more planes or ferries."

"It's like some kind of heaven out here," Monty said. "I can sure understand why Courtney's come back every summer. This cool ocean air is sweeter than our hot Kansas sun. But Kansas is where Courtney was raised, and I'm trying to convince her it's where she belongs."

Courtney's breath caught in her throat.

James relaxed his stance. "Yes, thank you, it is nice here. And I appreciate your candor. But as far as Courtney goes, don't you agree it's up to her to choose where she wants to live, and who she wants to live with?"

Susanna, bright-eyed and innocent, came onto the patio, wiping her hands on her apron. "The lasagna's done. Dinner's ready in just a few minutes. Christabel, are you staying for dinner?"

To Courtney's surprise, Christabel's face brightened. "No, sorry, I can't stay. I have plans."

Susanna went back into the house, humming a little tune, seemingly unaware of the currents of emotion buzzing in the group.

"Christabel," James said, "if you'll give me a moment to shower and dress, I'll come stay with you."

"Great," Christabel said, a slight little smirk curling one side of her mouth.

"Hey, James, don't leave on account of me," Monty said. He tucked his thumbs inside his belt, lounging as he stood, easy and in charge.

"Actually, I think I will leave because of you," James replied, his voice calm, almost friendly. "Since my mother has offered you her hospitality, and there's no reasonable way to get rid of you, I'm going to stay at my friend's house tonight. You'll have plenty of time to convince Courtney to leave with you. All you have to do is to respect her wishes."

Monty flushed.

Courtney murmured, *"James."*

"And if she does choose to go back to Kansas, I'll accept her decision. If she decides to stay here, I hope you'll do the same." James strode into the house.

Monty watched him go. To Courtney, he said, "He's a straight-talking man. I like that."

Robin said softly, "Would you like another beer?"

"I absolutely would, thanks."

Robin went into the house, leaving Monty and Courtney alone.

"So he's the man you're going to marry?" Monty asked.

"I don't know. That's the truth, I don't know. It's complicated. Too complicated for me to tell you about now."

Behind Monty, Robin was acting silly at the dining room window, pointing at Monty and fanning herself with a napkin. In spite of herself, Courtney grinned.

"Monty, I want to go help Susanna get dinner on the table. It's what we always do here. Can we talk later?"

"Of course."

They walked into the house together.

"Shall I make a salad?" Courtney asked Susanna.

"That would be great, honey," Susanna said. She was bustling around the oven, unwrapping the foil around the garlic bread to see if the butter had melted.

"Smells delicious," Monty said.

"Thanks, Monty," Susanna said.

Pearl undulated up to his side. "Want to help me set the table?"

Courtney drew Monty to the counter with the cutting board. "He's going to help me chop vegetables," she told Pearl.

Monty grinned at Courtney's obvious act of possession.

For heaven sakes, Courtney thought, *when did every single thing get so loaded with significance around here?*

She handed Monty a knife. "Chop the tomatoes. Please."

As she tore lettuce into the bowl, Monty worked steadily beside her, cutting the tomatoes, and then the yellow zucchini. And it felt weird. Just plain *bizarre*, working in the Vickerey kitchen with Monty Blackhorse standing next to her. Fixing dinner was such an intimate, family kind of activity, it was such a friendly, normal thing to do, and Courtney's nerves were far from normal at the moment.

She could hear the water running in one of the showers on the second floor. By the time she'd dressed the salad and set the table, she heard James's steady step as he headed back downstairs.

Pearl came into the kitchen. She reached for the salt and pepper shakers, bending around Monty so that she brushed his arm. "Excuse me," she cooed.

"Anytime," Monty told her with a grin. He watched Pearl return to the table. It seemed to Courtney he was watching with interest and appreciation. She was surprised to feel a sting of jealousy beneath her breastbone.

James and Christabel came into the kitchen. James looked everywhere but at Courtney.

"We're going now," Christabel said. "See ya." She took James's hand and pulled him down the hall. Was Courtney imagining it, or did Christabel look triumphant, as if she had won James as a prize in a state fair?

She was losing her mind.

The front door slammed. Two car doors slammed. Courtney heard the peculiar tubercular noises the Citroën made as Christabel started it.

Automatically, Courtney helped set the table and carry in the salad, the lasagna, and the long basket of hot buttered garlic bread. For just a moment, the mingling mouth-watering aromas took her mind off the fact that Monty was sitting in James's chair.

Pearl had grabbed the chair next to Monty. She was almost on top of him, in fact, as she offered him salad. Pearl wore a brief sundress in a lime-green color that made her tan glow and set off her dark hair and eerie blue eyes. It was fairly obvious that she wore no bra, and the neckline of her dress plunged nearly to her navel.

Monty only seemed amused by Pearl. He continued to stare at Courtney.

They were almost ready to eat when Dr. V wandered in. Robin jumped up to set a place for him at the head of the table.

"Dr. Vickerey," Pearl simpered, "we've got a guest tonight. Monty Blackhorse, all the way from Kansas."

To everyone's surprise, Dr. Vickerey lifted his head and spoke. "KU med school. One of the best in the country."

"Glad you think so," Monty said. "I've known several people operated on there, with terrific results."

"You a doctor?" Dr. Vickerey asked.

"No, sir. I'm a rancher. I raise Black Angus on my family's thousand-acre ranch. But a friend of mine's father is a doctor at the med school. Walt Wright. He's a—"

"—surgeon," Dr. Vickerey cut in. "I've met him at conferences. He's good. Maybe a little arrogant."

"He deserves his arrogance, from everything I hear," Monty said. "He's saved a lot of lives."

Dr. Vickerey actually looked at Monty. He smiled. *"He deserves his arrogance.* I like that." Then he dipped his head toward his lasagna and the conversation was over.

Courtney had often wondered if Dr. V had Asperger's syndrome, but Robin had assured her he didn't. He had come out of his scientific shell long enough to court Susanna, marry her, have children, get through med school, and perform hundreds of successful surgeries. He wasn't born with any psychological defect, Robin insisted. He was simply odd, and as he grew older, he allowed himself to be as eccentric as he wanted. Courtney could recall the early years when she first came for the summer—how Susanna had patiently attempted to nudge Dr. V into a more convivial attitude. After a few years, she had given up on that lost cause.

Was Dr. V the source of the twisted little gene that brought his oldest son such pain? This afternoon, Susanna had said she wouldn't change a thing in her own biological makeup, and Courtney understood that she was also speaking of her children. Susanna's love was big enough to encompass all of her children in their various idiosyncrasies.

There were times, though, Courtney would bet, when Susanna had, over the years, wept bitterly.

And then there was tonight, when Dr. V actually smiled.

"This is delicious lasagna, ma'am," Monty told Susanna.

Pearl leaned toward Monty. "I'll bet you enjoy some amazing steaks out there in Kansas."

"We do. And I'll bet you enjoy some delicious seafood here on this island."

"Oh, we do!" Iris said eagerly. "If you stay a few more days, we'll fix something fresh from the sea for dinner."

Not to be ignored, Pearl offered, "Maybe after dinner you'd like to come down to the beach with me. It's fab at this time of day."

"You won't be able to see much with all this fog," Courtney pointed out.

Before Monty could answer, three phones pealed at the same time. Robin's cell on the kitchen counter played its little melody, Susanna's iPhone buzzed in her pocket, and the landline hanging on the kitchen wall rang.

Usually, the family didn't answer their phones once they'd sat down to dinner. But three phones at once was a signal. It heralded something significant. Something wrong?

17

Robin couldn't reach her cell from her chair, so she rose and went around the table to the kitchen counter. On the way, she bumped into Iris, who was racing to answer the kitchen landline.

The caller ID on her phone told her it was Quinn.

"Hey, Quinn. What's up?"

"There's been an accident." His breathing was shallow, his voice shaky. "The police just notified me. Christabel and James were in an accident on Milestone Road."

"Are they okay?"

"They're alive. An ambulance is taking them to the hospital. That's all I know."

"I'll meet you there."

She clicked off and met her mother's eyes. Susanna was standing in front of her plate, phone to her ear, nodding her head, saying, "Yes. Yes. Yes. We'll be there right away."

Courtney and Pearl and Monty were staring at Susanna expectantly. Robin's father was still eating.

Iris said, "Mom! That was Valerie. James and Christabel had a terrible accident! They're in an ambulance! They're being taken to the hospital."

At this, her father's fork paused. Robin studied her mother for clues to just how bad this accident was. "That was Quinn," Robin said. "He's on his way to the hospital."

They all looked at Susanna, who seemed to be undergoing a kind of invisible protective process that made her seem calm. Whatever was happening in her heart, whatever fears she had, she'd shut the door on them. She began to organize, to order and give orders.

"That was Officer Sedgewick from the police. James and Christabel have been in a car accident. The Citroën swerved off the road and hit a truck. The Citroën is totaled. James and Christabel are alive, but injured, and they've been taken by ambulance to the hospital."

Abruptly, Dr. V stood up, tossing his napkin on the table. "Let's go."

Susanna said, "I'll go in Dad's car. Robin, you drive everyone else in my minivan." She hurried from the room.

Robin lifted the car keys from their hook on the kitchen wall. "Let's go."

Monty asked, "Is there room for me?"

"Yes," Pearl told him. "Come on, we'll sit in the back."

They hurried out to the minivan and climbed in. "For god's sake, fasten your seatbelts," Robin ordered. "It's gotten foggy, and I don't want another accident."

She didn't quite perform a two-wheel scream out of the drive, but she kept her foot on the gas and an eye on the speedometer.

From the seat behind her, Courtney leaned forward as far as her seatbelt permitted. "Did Quinn say anything else? *Anything?*"

"No. It just happened, the police just notified him, he was on his way to the hospital."

"But they're both alive, Valerie said, so that's good, right?" Iris asked, needing reassurance.

"Yes. Both alive."

"Christabel's always been a terrible driver," Courtney said. "Well, she's afraid of driving off island. She's afraid of going faster than forty-five miles an hour, so I'm sure she wasn't speeding now, so the accident couldn't have been too bad."

"But the Citroën is ancient," Robin reminded her. "She had a lot of work done on it when she had it retrofitted with seatbelts and a hazard button and I don't know what else."

"But that was years ago," Iris said. "It makes terrible grinding sounds when she's driving it and half the time the battery's dead."

They were talking, Robin knew, to make the world seem normal, to fill up the threatening void of infinite possibilities with the structure of words. They didn't know what happened. They could only guess, and guessing helped them have hope.

There were only two ways to get to the hospital from 'Sconset: the twisting, slower Polpis Road, and the Milestone Road, extending in a straight line for ten miles with a forty-five-miles-per-hour limit. It was the closest thing they had to a racetrack on the island. But Robin kept the speed at a steady forty-nine mph. The fog drifted over the fields and road, lifting up and dropping down in misty white sheets that distorted the landscape and cars. In her rearview mirror, she saw her father's Jaguar approaching at its own moderate pace. Years ago, Dr. V had driven the car on the freeways around Boston and actually let the Jaguar get up to seventy miles an hour, but for the past five years, it had stayed on Nantucket and never gone over forty-five. Robin joked if the Jaguar could speak, it would say: *I'm bored.*

"Here come Dad and Mom," Robin said, looking in her rearview mirror.

"If he wants to pass you, let him!" Iris cried, twisting around in her seat to watch the Jag come closer. "He's not the best driver in the world. We don't want another accident."

"We won't have an accident, Iris." Robin kept her eyes on the road and her tone soothing. "This has to be the easiest, safest stretch of road in the world. Straight, flat, no sudden curves, and the sides of the road are flat grassland."

"Like roads in Kansas," Monty added from the backseat. "Except there everyone goes eighty miles an hour because everything is so far away from everything."

"Don't go eighty!" Iris pleaded. "It's so foggy."

"I'm holding steady at forty-five," Robin assured her sister.

"Okay, good," Iris said. "Christabel's a decent driver. She wouldn't speed, not *really* speed. So probably James and Christabel aren't hurt really badly. Maybe they broke an arm, or a leg, that would be considered 'bad' but not *awful,* not *serious.*"

Robin knew her younger sister was babbling. She was glad. Babbling was a great nervous release. This was a hideously tense time, driving to the hospital, knowing her brother and Christabel had been injured, but having no more information than that. Robin knew she could jump out of the car and run the ten miles on her nervous energy.

"Iris, you're right," Courtney chimed in. "Sometimes people are taken to the hospital by accident simply because they've gone into shock, not that I'm saying shock isn't serious, but it's relatively easy to deal with, or maybe they have concussions from the impact, or whiplash—"

Something loomed ahead on the right. As they drew closer, they could tell it was the Citroën. It had smashed head-on into the side of a gray pickup truck. A police car was angled on the grass behind the truck. Two policemen were snapping shots of the vehicles. In the distance, a tow truck headed slowly through the fog toward the accident.

Robin slowed so they could get a good look as they passed. "Head-on," she muttered. "Not good. The front end looks completely crumpled."

After that, no one spoke. Conversation seemed frivolous as they continued straight down the road toward town.

So few landmarks existed on this road to give them a clue to their location, and so much was swathed with fog. On the right, the odd little stone marked 10.1 appeared. Not long after that, the turnoff to Polpis Road cut a line of pavement into the expanse of green grass.

"We're almost there," Robin said.

They passed the turnoff to Monomoy.

Then, finally the rotary. Robin was cautious here, coming to a complete stop at the yield sign, taking her time to peer through the fog to be sure no one was coming from the left. Then she went around the rotary to Pleasant Street, and with a few more turns of the wheel, she was in the hospital parking lot. They saw Quinn's gray Volvo and slid in next to it.

Iris was out of her seatbelt and on the ground in two seconds. Courtney, Pearl, and Monty followed.

Robin opened her door. "Iris. Wait."

"What? Why?"

"Wait for Dr. V and Mom. They should be the ones to go in first. We'll follow them."

"Well, that's weird!" Iris argued, but she waited with the rest of the group.

A few moments later, the Jag pulled in next to them. Dr. V and Susanna stepped out.

Susanna ran toward them. "Have you heard anymore?"

"No," Robin said.

"But we didn't call anyone," Iris added.

"Let's go in," Dr. V ordered.

They went in through the emergency room entrance. Quinn was there, pacing, wringing his hands.

"It's her face," he said to the Vickerey group. "That's all they told me, her face. Her nose is broken and they think she's broken her jaw." He clutched Dr. Vickerey's arm. "Alastair, can't you *do* anything?"

Before Dr. V could respond, Valerie burst out of the emergency room door. She was dressed in blue scrubs and looked tense, but when she saw them, she smiled.

"They're both alive," she said. "They're not going to die. So take a few deep breaths before you all pass out and hit your heads on the floor."

Susanna silently, unobtrusively, began to cry. Iris clasped Robin's hand. Courtney hugged Robin's shoulder. Pearl and Monty stood slightly apart from the others.

"What happened?" Quinn demanded.

"Christabel swerved to miss a turtle that was crossing the road—"

"Christ," Dr. V muttered angrily. "A turtle."

"You live here," Valerie told him. "You know people are environmentally friendly. Anyway, Christabel swerved, too fast, too far, and hit the truck. Head-on. Both sustained serious injuries, but listen to me. They were both conscious when they were brought in. *They'll be okay.* James is undergoing a CAT scan now."

"Why?" Dr. V demanded.

"His blood pressure is unstable. He's bleeding internally. We think his spleen was ruptured."

"Who's operating?" Dr. V demanded, his voice low but commanding.

"Henry." Valerie folded her arms over her chest, prepared for battle.

"That won't do," Dr. V argued. "It's the height of arrogance for a surgeon to operate on a family member, and with Henry's condition, it could be dangerous to both men! How can Henry possibly achieve the necessary detached concern? And his anxiety might push him past anything his mind can handle."

Valerie squinted her blue eyes and lifted her chin. "I understand what you're saying, Dr. Vickerey. I agree with you. Henry agrees with you. But MedFlight can't get in because of the fog. If his spleen is injured as we believe the CAT scan will show and he's got internal bleeding, we will *need* to operate immediately. Henry is the only surgeon on island—well, except for you, Dr. Vickerey. I don't think you want to perform this operation."

Dr. V glared. Robin noticed with alarm that her father was trembling—with rage, with anger, and probably with fear.

Susanna put her hand on her husband's arm. "Alastair. Henry is a superb doctor. I'm glad James will be in Henry's care. Valerie, thank you so much."

Pearl stepped forward. "At the dinner table, people agreed that arrogance is a good quality for a surgeon to have."

"Fine," Dr. V conceded. "Keep us informed."

Iris shoved forward. "After the operation, will James be okay?"

"He's banged up and probably has a concussion. But we think he'll be okay."

"And Christabel?" Robin asked.

"Concussion, whiplash, broken nose, and she lost a lot of her teeth."

"Oh, no!" Iris cried. "Poor Christabel!"

"None of her injuries are fatal," Valerie reminded them all.

"I want to see her," Quinn said.

"You will. They're still working on her. The EMTs put a cervical collar on her, so that will help. We've got a call in to a dental surgeon on the Cape." She turned to go.

Quinn grasped Valerie's arm. "Is she in pain?"

"She's on a morphine drip, so no. I've got to go. I'll be back."

"When can I see her?" Quinn asked.

"Someone will come get you as soon as possible."

As Valerie headed into the emergency room, Henry came out. He immediately went to his mother and hugged her. Susanna clutched him, tears flowing down her face. "Henry, will James be okay?"

Henry kissed Susanna's forehead. "Sure he will." He stepped back. He said, "I assume Valerie's told you about James. He's got internal bleeding. His blood pressure is unstable. We've done a CT scan and his spleen is punctured. I'm going to go into the abdominal cavity and sew up the rupture. I'll check around for other injuries. But yes, Mom, James will be okay."

Robin asked what they were all wondering. "Will *you* be okay?"

Henry held out both hands to show they weren't shaking. "I'm good to go. I've been waiting for years to take a knife to my brother." Seeing his mother wince, he said, "Sorry. Bad joke. Really bad joke." He cleared his throat and drew his shoulders straight. "They're setting up for surgery now. It should take about two hours. I'll come out and tell you the minute it's over."

"Then can we see James?" Courtney asked.

"You can see him, one at a time, but don't expect him to be lucid. He'll still be hooked up to pain meds."

"Do you need me in there?" Dr. V asked.

Henry took a deep breath. "If you want to watch, Dad, you're welcome, as long as you keep silent. I mean absolutely silent. No second-guessing and absolutely no directives. I think it's better if you wait here."

Dr. V looked at his wife. Susanna put a loving, restraining hand on his arm.

"Good. Right. Good." Dr. V clapped his oldest son on his shoulder, as if cheering him into a football game.

Henry smiled and strode toward the ER. He stopped at the door and turned back.

"I've got this, you know. I've got this." He disappeared behind the doors of the ER.

"Let's sit down, Alastair," Susanna said, leading her husband toward the chairs set around the periphery of the waiting room.

"So all we can do is *sit* here?" Iris's voice almost squeaked.

Dr. V looked at his youngest child. "That's the drill." Then, to everyone's surprise, he settled Iris in the folding chair next to him and put his arm around her. "Don't be afraid. Henry is the best surgeon on the East Coast. He'll do a good job. James will be fine."

"Oh, Alastair." Susanna smiled at her husband. He met her eyes, and an invisible *something* passed between them—love, hope, gratitude, and memory, memory of times they had shared in their long life together, times both frightening and joyful.

All that in a single glance, Robin thought, feeling warmed and inspired and oddly safer, more optimistic.

Iris was twisting restlessly on her chair. "How long will we have to wait?"

Susanna was calm. "Waiting is the hardest part. We can't *do* anything. Now you know why we got so angry with you when you were in high school and came home late from parties. When you're waiting, you imagine all sorts of dreadful things."

"Like what?" Iris asked.

"Other organs could be injured," Dr. V said gloomily. "It will be bad enough if they have to do a splenectomy. The spleen is necessary for optimum functioning of the immune system and red blood cell health."

"Can a person live without it?" Iris asked.

"Yes, but statistics show a diminished response to pneumonia and other illness."

Iris bent over her cellphone and brought up the Internet. "I'm going to check it out on WebMD."

Dr. Vickerey snorted. Susanna gave him a look. Muttering to display his skepticism of Internet information, Dr. Vickerey scooted his chair closer to Iris in a show of companionship but still looked over her shoulder as she tapped into the phone, ready to correct any misinformation.

Relieved that her sister was occupied, Robin focused on her mother. "Mom, can I get you something? Coffee? A cold drink?"

Susanna shook her head. "I'm fine, dear."

Quinn, who had been standing near the group but not in it, was already in the alcove off the waiting room, buying coffee from one of the vending machines.

Monty chose a chair across from the family—available but not intrusive—and sat down. Pearl settled next to him. Robin and Courtney sat side by side at the end of the row of chairs. Courtney's right leg was jiggling up and down like a jackhammer, and her face was growing paler with each passing moment.

"He's going to be okay, you know," Robin assured her.

"I know. I know. I just feel so *responsible*."

"Why? You weren't driving that car. You weren't herding that turtle across the road."

Courtney produced a weak smile in response to Robin's attempt at humor. "If Monty hadn't come, James wouldn't have left the house with Christabel."

"Don't be ridiculous. Playing the blame game doesn't do any good and it makes us all feel terrible. We might as well say that Susanna's responsible because she invited Monty to stay with us for dinner and the night, so James had to go off with Christabel."

"Oh, no, I'd never think that!" Courtney protested.

"Don't you think Mom's thinking that? Let's just put the blame on Christabel, shall we? She's a terrible driver, and I'll bet a million dollars she wasn't paying close attention, she was blathering away at James about god knows what, and while we're at it, what the hell was that gray truck doing parked at the side of the road? Let's blame the driver for the accident!" Robin stood up and looked around the room hurriedly, as if she could catch sight of the truck driver before he got away.

"Now who's freaking out?" Courtney rose and took Robin's arm. "Let's move. Let's walk around the hospital."

Robin pulled away. "No. I want to be here when—"

"We'll stay on this floor. We'll go up and down the corridors. We'll burn off some anxiety while we're waiting."

Robin glanced at her mother, who sat very still with her eyes closed. Next to her, Dr. V was muttering to Iris, no doubt correcting every single thing Iris found on the Internet about spleens.

Pearl was asking Monty about the kinds of injuries people sustained from riding horses.

"Okay. Let's walk." Robin leaned over to get her sister's attention. "Iris? Courtney and I are going to walk the corridors. We won't be gone long, we'll check back here every few minutes."

Iris nodded, her attention fastened to her phone screen.

Robin took Courtney's hand and pulled her out of the waiting room and along the hall. "This way," she said.

Courtney strode along next to Robin, rubbing her forearms as if she were cold. "You know, I changed my mind today, but I didn't have a chance to tell James."

"Okay, you mean about children?"

"Right. Right. I did some serious soul-searching, and I decided today I want to be with James even if it means I never have his children."

"Oh, Courtney, I'm so glad! You'll join our crazy family!" Robin hugged her.

Courtney pulled away. "I wish I could be happy, too. I didn't have a chance to tell James."

"Settle down. Deep breaths. You'll be able to tell James. He'll be out of that operating room in something like sixty minutes, and conscious not long after that, and you can tell him then, okay?"

"I wish I hadn't called Monty. I had no idea he'd fly out here."

Robin picked up her pace. "But he did. And you called him. But you called him because I told you it was the right thing to do. So basically, the blame for this accident is on me."

"Don't be silly, Robin!"

"I won't if you won't." They made a right-angle turn into the longest corridor in the hospital. They passed the hospital check-in offices and the main waiting room. At this time of the day, it was quiet, after hours, no one working. "I talked with Quinn," Robin confessed.

"Oh! You mean about the whales?"

"Yes. I think I freaked him out."

"I'm not surprised."

"He said he'd make a deal with me. If I'd promise to stop visiting the whales, he'd stop pressuring me to move off island."

"What? No way!"

"Courtney, I don't think he actually believes I saw whales. He thinks I fantasized them."

"Well, it *is* hard to believe."

"Not if you've read the literature. Whales are intelligent. They're curious. They like to play, they like to make contact, they have good memories. But it's more than that, I mean my problem with Quinn. The more I think about it, the more concerned I am. I'm sure he believes, deep in his heart, that I didn't really make contact with the whales, that I'm making it up, that I'm just slightly wacky in a harmless way because I'm part of our nutty family."

"Maybe you could get him to go out with you one night to see for himself."

At the end of the corridor, they did an about-face and retraced their steps.

"I doubt it, since I promised him I wouldn't go out there ever again." Robin took Courtney's arm and drew her close, for comfort, as they walked. "I do love Quinn. I've loved him for years. And I did agree not to go out to the whales, and he did compromise and say we wouldn't have to leave the island, but I'm not happy about it. I'm beginning to realize that I'm not all that excited about being with Quinn. I'm not humming love songs. I'm . . . jumpy. Itchy. But you seem okay about your compromise with James. And what you're giving up is *huge*. And I'm glad for you both, and I feel good about you two and your decisions, but why don't I feel good about me and Quinn?"

Before Courtney replied, they reentered the waiting room area. All the Vickereys and Quinn were standing now, talking with uniformed police officers. At the edge of the group stood Monty.

Robin and Courtney joined the group. Officer Sedgewick, an extremely tall, thin man with stiff white hair and an air of authority, was talking.

"We've talked with the van driver. His name is Otto Folger."

"Oh, we know him," Susanna said. "He's an islander. Is he okay?"

"He's fine. He gave us his version of events and it all makes sense. Otto had parked on the side of the road, planning to pick up the turtle, but he was waiting for the Citroën to pass. When the crash occurred, he was at the front of his truck, so he saw everything. He immediately phoned us and an ambulance. We were at the site within five minutes. In the meantime, he checked on the passengers and found them conscious but in shock and bleeding. He didn't try to move them—he knew about the need for a cervical collar after a crash like that. He stayed next to the driver and talked to her. Gave her his handkerchief to help stanch the blood." With an embarrassed squint, he added, "He also moved the turtle into the bushes on the other side of the road."

The other officer, a large older man, added, "So the turtle wouldn't cause any more accidents. That's why he moved the turtle. It was a good thing he did. People rubberneck anyway at the scene of an accident."

Everyone in the Vickerey family stood silently listening, as if their complete attention would help James and Christabel. Courtney took Robin's hand.

Quinn spoke up. "Who did you say was driving?"

Robin gasped. Her parents stared at Quinn as if he'd slapped them across the face.

"The woman," Officer Sedgewick said. "Christabel Eliot."

"You're *sure*?" Quinn persisted. "Sometimes James drives her car."

Robin couldn't believe what she was hearing. She couldn't believe

Quinn, *her* Quinn, would ask such a question. Was he trying to pin the blame on James instead of Christabel?

"We're one hundred percent certain," Officer Sedgewick said, and his tone of voice implied that he wasn't amused by the question.

Susanna, unbelievably kindhearted, said to Quinn, "We have health insurance for the entire family. It will cover James's medical bills. I assume you have insurance for you and Christabel."

Quinn had the grace to look embarrassed. "Yes, yes, of course. I only wanted to get the picture straight."

"There will be no official charges," Officer Sedgewick told him. "It was, clear and simple, an accident."

"What will it do to Christabel's insurance rates?" Quinn asked.

To everyone's surprise, Iris spoke up. "Your daughter is sedated and my brother is on the operating table and you're wondering about *insurance rates?*"

Quinn put his hand to his forehead. "I'm sorry. I'm sorry, I apologize. To you all, I do apologize. It's just—I'm trying to make sense of it all—" He looked directly at Robin. "I'm sorry."

Robin stared at him as if he were a stranger. And, suddenly, he was.

18

After a few more words, which blurred in Courtney's ears, the police left. Courtney kept an eagle eye on Robin. Quinn's questions had practically turned Robin to stone.

"I'm going to the restroom," Robin said.

"I'll go with you," Courtney offered.

"Thank you, but no. I'm going to the *restroom*." Robin bugged her eyes out at Courtney, the way she had always done when she was younger and angry. Courtney knew the anger wasn't directed at her.

Dr. V, Susanna, and Iris gravitated toward one another in a cluster, speaking in low voices. That left Courtney and Quinn standing apart from the Vickereys.

"Maybe I said the wrong thing," Quinn said to Courtney. "Maybe I spoke too soon. But someone has to be on Christabel's side."

"I didn't realize there were *sides*," Courtney said, allowing sarcasm to edge her words. "Excuse me, my emotions are all over the place. I'm going to walk again."

She felt like an astronaut experiencing a kind of gravitational pull as she left the emergency room and began walking down the corridor. As if staying with the group would make James be all right, and for all she knew, her presence did matter.

But Quinn wasn't waiting—he was scheming. He was trying to think of a way to absolve his daughter for any guilt for the accident. And that was crazy, because none of the Vickereys were thinking about guilt—every cell in their bodies was devoted to waiting and hoping that Christabel and James would be okay.

And that Henry would perform the operation with thoroughness and his well-known superlative skill.

How odd it must be, Courtney thought as she walked, for Susanna and Dr. V to know that one son held the other son's life in his hands. Especially since they had raised those two boys, watched them turn into men, seen them at their worst, silly, or drunk, or irate, or rebellious.

As Courtney doubled back down a corridor, she let her thoughts meander toward James and her love for him. She'd come to a fairly significant conclusion today—a surrendering of all thoughts of having James Vickerey's children.

So what would their married life be like?

Okay, well, that took her breath away.

She forced herself to consider it practically, in reality. She imagined waking up in bed with him next to her, sharing meals, and laundry, and the normal annoyances like a broken drain pipe, for she would not allow herself the luxury of imagining them in a problem-free future where drain pipes never broke. First, she thought of laughter, because James could change the mood of a room with one of his smiles. She thought of how they would talk—about books, medicine, politics, movies—they had always talked a lot. She thought of living every day with him—

And *where* would that be? If she was going to insert broken pipes into her dream of a future, she couldn't allow herself to conjure a bed floating in thin air. James was here now, for the summer, but as he'd said, he would probably be based in Boston or New York. He traveled all over the world for conferences, and Courtney could easily envision going along with him. She'd love to see foreign countries!

But where would *home* be? James wanted to be based in a metropolitan region, one near a good international airport, with international companies.

For example, Boston. Courtney and Robin had stayed in the Vickereys' Back Bay apartment a few times when they wanted to see a play, a ballet, or do some serious shopping. The apartment seemed a funny old place to Courtney, who had grown up in flat country, where people built their houses low and long, because they had lots of land to build on. Her neighborhood was a forest of trees, flowers, and bushes, and one of her mother's greatest pleasures was tending to her vegetable garden. The Vickereys' Boston apartment was narrow and high, four large floors with two rooms on each floor. Sleeping in the bedroom at the top of the house felt like sleeping in a tree house, except for the noise that reminded Courtney she was in a city. At home, at night, she heard crickets, bobolinks, owls, and occasionally a passing car. She kept her window open and floated to sleep on the fragrant breeze. In Boston, they shut the windows for peace from traffic honks and sirens and adjusted the temperature on a thermostat.

In Kansas City, her rented apartment was one of several carved out of an old Victorian mansion. It had a small backyard, hedged in with privet, and Courtney liked to take her first cup of coffee out to the backyard to drink while she listened to birds sing and the breeze stir the trees. The university was only a short bike ride away, and a quick drive away the Country Club Plaza with its fabulous stores and restaurants provided all the charms of urban life. She knew there were plenty of suburbs around Boston that would make the pleasures of city and country life possible. If she married James, she could have the city and Nantucket—and of course they would visit her family in Kansas.

She turned a corner and reentered the emergency waiting room.

•　•　•

There was a television in the waiting room, set on a high shelf, and a network comedy show was flashing from the screen. It was odd, Robin thought, how it attracted her attention—and soothed her, too. It reminded her of the world out there, where people ate and laughed and worried about laxatives and teeth whiteners. She found herself staring at it, checking her watch, then jumping up and race-walking down the corridors, returning to watch the television again.

When Robin spotted Courtney, she raced up to her. "I want you to walk with me. I want you to stay with me. Cling to me like Saran wrap."

"Sure, but why?"

"I don't want Quinn to have a chance to talk to me. I'm afraid I'll say something I'll regret. I'm so damned mad at him I could scream."

They were walking now, walking fast, past the doors labeled "Lab," "Radiology," "Restroom," "Office."

"It's normal to worry about your own children," Courtney said.

"Yeah, but to try to blame James for something Christabel did?"

"I know. It's a shabby thing to do."

"And there wasn't any reason to shift the blame! The police said it was an accident! Oh, damn Quinn, he's ruined everything! Imagine how my parents must feel about him now. He was like part of our family, and now he's made it quite clear that it's only Christabel he cares about."

"I'm sure that's not true."

"Are you sure? I'm not. My parents must feel betrayed."

"Robin, I think your parents are so worried about James—and about Henry, and about Christabel. I'm sure they have no time for thinking about anything else. And in times like this, when there's a crisis, who knows what people will say. It's the shock. We're all in shock."

As they turned into the main corridor, a nurse came running up to them. Jane Hardy was an island girl. She and Robin had been in the same class in school together, but Jane had married early and they had drifted apart with their very separate lives. Still, Jane's pretty face was like a glowing light in a dark room.

"Jane!" Robin cried.

"Oh, honey, I'm so sorry, but you know he's going to be okay. He's going to be fine." Jane hugged Robin hard, then stepped back. "You're Courtney, right?"

"Yes. Hi, Jane."

"I've been looking for you."

"Me?" Courtney's heart kicked in her chest. "Is James . . . ?"

"James is still in the operating room. But Christabel is conscious now. She wants to see you."

"Me?"

"She requested that you come to her room. Only you. And not for long. I'll escort you." Jane took Courtney's arm and gently led her away from the group.

"I don't understand," Courtney said as they strode through the corridors and out a heavy door leading to the stairs.

"She can't talk, but she can write. She's on pain medication at the moment, so she's rather woozy. But she made it clear she wants to see you. You know there's an elevator to the second floor," Jane said, "but it's slow as molasses. We can climb these stairs before the damned elevator door even closes."

She pulled open another fire door and they stepped inside the second-floor hallway.

"Jane," Courtney began, but Jane answered her question before Courtney could frame it.

Jane stopped and faced Courtney, holding her hands as if she were a little girl. "Christabel looks hideous, actually, so be prepared. Her nose has been taped. Her face is swollen. She's wearing a cervical collar. She's got a nasal cannula up her nose and an IV in her arm for pain, and a saline drip for her electrolytes. She can't actually speak, so she communicates by writing. She's lucid, but slowed down by the pain meds."

"Okay," Courtney said. "This only freaks me out a little," she added with a smile.

Jane smiled back. "That's it, be cheerful with Christabel. She's going to need a lot of dental surgery, and we aren't sure when the dental surgeon can get here. But she's alive in spite of crashing headfirst into a truck."

"Does she know about James?"

"She's been told he's in surgery for internal bleeding, but he'll be fine. Which is the truth, Courtney. If she asks about him, tell her that."

They passed other patients' rooms as they walked down the hall. Courtney caught a glimpse of a wheelchair, a flickering television set high on the wall, a curtain hanging around a bed. Outside a room with a closed door, Jane stopped.

"Ready?"

Courtney paused. "I can't imagine why she wants to see me. I'm afraid I'll say the wrong thing. I don't understand why she chose me." She wanted to say: *Does Christabel love James? Is she going to tell me something extremely personal, ask me to pass a note of passionate love to him?*

Jane grinned. "I wouldn't worry. The first thing she asked when we gave her a pencil and paper was whether or not the turtle lived."

Courtney burst out laughing with surprise and then with relief. That was such an *island* thing to ask, and it made Courtney like Christabel more than she ever had.

"I'm ready."

Jane opened the door and led Courtney inside.

Christabel was in a hospital bed with the metal sides drawn up. The back of the bed had been cranked up, allowing her to sit. She was sinking into a pillow, wearing a hospital gown, covered with light blankets. The nearby table had been swung over for her to write on.

She did look terrible. Jane hadn't told her that Christabel's long blond hair would be pulled harshly back and shaved in several places so stitches could be put in her scalp. Her lovely blue eyes were puffed up and multi-colored, and the tube in her nose made her seem like a sci-fi creature.

Courtney forced herself to smile. Foolish, lovely, impish Christabel. She went to the bed, pecked a kiss on the top of her head, and pulled up a chair as close as she could get it to Christabel.

She took Christabel's hand in hers. "We're all so glad you're alive!"

Christabel pulled her hand away. For one brief moment, Courtney felt a sting of rejection. *Why did she even ask me in here if she's going to be that way?* Courtney thought, and then she saw that Christabel had taken up a pencil with that hand and was holding down a sheet of paper with her other hand.

"I'll step outside for a while," Jane said. "I'll be back, and, Christabel, you know what button to push if you need me."

It was difficult to sit still, waiting, as Christabel wrote a seemingly endless note.

Finally, Christabel shoved the note toward Courtney, staring at her with blazing raptor eyes.

Courtney picked up the paper. It read, in shaky, slanted handwriting:

Call 617 555 5345 Julian Moreau tell him 2 come now.

"I don't understand," Courtney said. "Who's Julian Moreau? Is he a dental surgeon? Shouldn't the hospital—"

A loud moaning grunt came from Christabel's throat. It obviously meant: *Why r u frustrating me, u idiot?* Snatching another piece of paper, she began to scribble again, fast.

Art dealer. Fiancé. Did not tell Dad yet. He'll be sad when I tell him I'm getting married. Leaving island. Vickereys r 2 emotional, can't keep secrets. Please do this for me.

Courtney's jaw dropped. "Get out of town!" she cried. "You have a fiancé we don't even know about? Someone named Julian Moreau? Could his name be any more fabulous? Christabel, you little sneak!"

Christabel scribbled large letters and held the paper up. *Smiling.*

"Let me get this straight. Don't be impatient, if you want me to call him, you have to satisfy my curiosity first. You met Julian when he saw your paintings at a gallery?"

Christabel wrote, *Yes. 2 years ago.*

"Where does he live?"

Boston. Art gallery on Newbury Street.

"That's just about the most romantic thing I've ever heard. Christabel, why didn't you tell us? We'll all be so happy for you!"

Wait. He's 20 years older. Married. 3 children. Getting divorced. Dad will freak.

Courtney's jaw dropped. "He's married, has three children, he's getting divorced, and he's twenty years older than you? Christabel!"

Who made you pope?

"I'm not criticizing. I'm just, well, I guess I'm trying to take it all in. It's a lot to learn, Christabel."

Christabel wrote something else and tossed the paper at Courtney. *PLEASE GO CALL HIM NOW!!!*

"Yes, sorry, sorry, yes, I'll go. I'll go right now."

Don't tell Dad or anyone.

"Okay. Look, I have to go outside to use my cell. I'll come back to tell you what he says." Courtney went to the door, then looked back, smiling. "You are full of surprises!"

Christabel made the thumbs-up with both hands and sank back into her pillows.

Courtney raced down the stairs and out a fire exit. She was far from the waiting room, so none of the Vickereys or Quinn could see her. It was still light out, though hazy, dimmed by the fog, and full of tiny drops of water that she could see settle on the leaves of the dogwood tree near her. It was very warm, still summer, and all around birds were singing their evening songs. Such a contrast from the atmosphere inside the waiting room.

Clicking on her cell, she tapped in the numbers Christabel had given her and almost immediately a man answered.

"Julian?"

He sounded wary. "Yes?"

"This is Courtney Hendricks. I'm calling about Christabel Eliot. She's been in a car accident—"

"Dear god. Is she alive?"

"Alive, yes, and she's going to be fine. Her jaw was fractured, her nose broken, she lost some teeth, but everything else is good. She can't talk but she wanted me to contact you. To tell you." Courtney couldn't help it, but she felt a tiny frisson of pleasure at being chosen to share this secret, to talk to Christabel's lover.

"It's after seven," Julian said curtly. "Too late for planes flying in from Boston. I'll charter a plane and—"

"No, the fog is terrible here. I doubt that you'd be able to land. Anyway, she's on pain medication and an oral surgeon will be here soon, or maybe tomorrow morning, we don't know yet, and also—I know this isn't my place to say anything, but her father doesn't know about you and he's out of his mind worried about Christabel."

"It's time he knew about me," Julian Moreau snapped, then softened his tone. "Very well. I'll come first thing tomorrow. Will you convey a message from me to Christabel?"

"Of course."

"Tell her I love her. I'll be there tomorrow morning. Tell her I will pray for her."

Courtney was touched by his simple message. "Yes. I'll tell her."

"Thank you for calling me, Courtney Hendricks. I look forward to meeting you."

"You're welcome. I'll go tell Christabel now."

She retraced her steps, her mind dazzled by Christabel's secret, by Julian Moreau's elegant, cultured voice. *Parents and children,* she thought, *honestly!* If Christabel didn't want her father to know because he'd be miserable if she left the island, maybe when Quinn *did* know, which would probably be tomorrow, he would feel released, he could let everyone know that he and Robin loved each other. So many secrets! Courtney was oddly cheerful as she reentered Christabel's room.

Jane Hardy was there, checking Christabel's blood pressure. "She's in pain," Jane told Courtney, her eyes focused on the digital readout in her hand. "She's getting more morphine."

Christabel's body was limp as she slid into a pain-free sleep.

"I'll go back to the waiting room," Courtney said to the nurse.

"Tell them we're still waiting for the oral surgeon. Until then, Christabel will be on a morphine drip and not lucid."

"Okay. Thanks, Jane."

Back in the hall, Courtney stood for a moment, thinking. What explanation could she give the others, especially Quinn, to explain why Christabel had chosen *her* to see?

Like the proverbial lightbulb switching on, the answer presented itself clearly: she would say that Christabel knew she looked spaced-out and she didn't want the others to see her so druggy and zonked. Every-one would believe that of Christabel; she was so vain. Courtney smiled as she headed back to the waiting room.

As if in a game of musical chairs, everyone had changed places. Pearl sat with her arm around Iris. Monty sat talking in a low voice to Dr. V. Susanna and Robin and Quinn were clustered together, talking. They all stood up when Courtney walked in.

"I just spoke to the nurse, Jane Hardy. Christabel's on a morphine drip for the pain. An oral surgeon is on his way. Christabel's asleep."

But Quinn was not satisfied by the explanation. "That makes no sense at all!" he said angrily. "I want to speak to that nurse."

"The nurses' station and the hospital rooms are on the second floor," Courtney told him.

"I know the hospital," Robin said, putting a hand on his arm. "I'll take you there."

But Quinn shook off her hand. "I know where to go." He strode off, shaking with anger.

He returned fifteen minutes later, looking ill. He fell into a chair as if his body could no longer bear his weight.

"Quinn?" Susanna went to him. "Did you see Christabel?"

"My poor child." Quinn raised his head. "She was sleeping—peacefully, the nurse said. She's on a morphine drip. The oral surgeon will come early tomorrow morning to assess her and probably to wire her mouth shut. She's lost some teeth . . ." He dropped his head again and his shoulders shook.

Susanna put her arm around his shoulders. "She will be all right, Quinn. She's in good hands. We've got good nurses and doctors here, you know that . . ."

"Not enough!" Quinn raged, lifting a red and tear-streaked face. "This is only a little hospital thirty miles out at sea. It's classified as *rural*, did you know that? And when the fog comes in as it did tonight, planes can't land, the medical flights can't get here, and we're stuck with the few overworked doctors we have!"

"But Christabel is alive. That's the main thing to remember." Susanna's voice was calm. "Just think, if we weren't on this little island, Christabel might have been driving faster."

"You're such a Pollyanna, Susanna," Quinn said, sniffing.

"Sounds like a song," Susanna replied peacefully.

Quinn snorted. He dug a handkerchief out of his pocket and blew his nose. "I apologize for my outburst," he said, addressing the entire room. His eyes lingered for a moment on Robin. "I'm not myself right now."

"We're all on edge," Susanna told him. "All we can do is wait."

19

When Courtney returned to the waiting room to give them Christabel's message, Robin said nothing, but secretly she was sure Courtney was lying. And why was that? It almost rang true that Christabel didn't want those who loved her most to see her in a damaged state—which Robin, and she was fairly certain everyone else, including Quinn—translated into Christabel not wanting anyone to see her looking less than breathtakingly gorgeous.

The Vickereys and Quinn peppered Courtney with questions—how did Christabel look, was she in terrible pain, did Courtney tell Christabel they loved her and were waiting to see her? Quinn's questions were especially intense and repetitive, but Courtney handled them well and with kindness. Finally there was nothing more to say. All they could do was wait.

"Let's walk," Robin said to Courtney.

"Give me a minute. I'm out of breath. And I'm thirsty."

"And you're lying," Robin hissed in Courtney's ear.

Courtney bit back a smile. "I don't know what you mean."

"It doesn't take that long to get such a brief message."

"But sure it does. I had to wait for Jane Hardy to check Christabel's blood pressure and all sorts of things."

"I know you're lying, Courtney."

"Christabel told me to keep it a secret."

"Keep *what* a secret? Courtney, you're my best friend in all the world, how can you keep secrets from me!"

"You've kept some from me, too," Courtney reminded her. "Come on. Let's go for a walk."

As soon as they were out of earshot of the others, Courtney said, "Christabel is in love. With a man named *Julian Moreau*. She's going to marry him, but she hasn't told her father yet."

"What? Why not?"

"He's married with three children and he's twenty years older."

"My god. I'm stunned."

"Let's go in here." Courtney pulled Robin into the main waiting room near the reception desk. The lights were low and no one was around because it was evening. "Sit down. Here." She handed Robin the note Christabel had written her.

Robin shook her head. "I don't know what to say. It's like learning a dog is a cat."

Courtney laughed. "You know what it means, don't you? You and Quinn are free now to be with each other."

Robin slumped back in the chair, sticking her legs out in front of her, gazing up at the ceiling. "I don't know if I want to do that."

"What?"

"I think I might be over Quinn."

"Because of what he said tonight?"

"Trying to put the blame for the accident on James? Well, *yeah*."

"Robin, don't act in haste. People say all sorts of unfortunate things in times of crisis."

"It's more than that. It's everything. Making me promise not to go out to the whales. That's almost like asking me to change my religion. And insisting we move off the island."

"Wait, though, Robin. Once he finds out that Christabel has a man in her life, and from the sounds of it, an older, successful, *capable* man, maybe then Quinn will be content to remain on Nantucket."

"Maybe," Robin answered listlessly. She stirred herself. "Let's go back to the waiting room. It's been almost two hours. Maybe we'll hear something."

But the waiting room was quiet. Iris sat tapping away on her phone, reading about the spleen and other organs. Monty and Pearl were talking quietly in the corner. Susanna sat as still as stone, her eyes closed, her lips moving slightly in silent prayer. Dr. V was restless, pacing the room, buying coffee from the vending machine, and tossing the cup away after one sip. He circled the room, straightening all the chairs into place. Quinn was up and walking, too, picking up magazines, tossing them down, staring up at the television, checking his watch.

Robin and Courtney sat together in chairs at the end of the row.

"I hate myself," Courtney whispered. "I should have told James I'd marry him no matter what. I wish I had, I wish I had. What if James . . ." She broke off. She buried her face in her hands.

"James isn't going to die," Robin assured her. "It's only a little operation. And Henry is a kick-ass surgeon. He'll be fine. Don't think about that—hey, think about this! Think about telling Susanna you're going to be her daughter-in-law!"

Courtney lifted her head. She was smiling, her face entirely wet with tears. "I hope that will happen. I hope James didn't change his mind because I was lukewarm."

"Were you lukewarm when you slept with him?" Robin asked.

Courtney's face blazed red. "Okay, so he probably knows how I feel about him." She dug a tissue out of her purse and blew her nose heartily. "But it's not *real* yet. Not until we talk again."

Iris stood up. She approached Courtney, holding out a bottle of Sprite. "Drink some of this. You're like me. I'm hungry and I'm tired and I'm scared and I'm freaked."

Courtney took the soft drink and sipped it. "Ah, that's refreshing. Thanks, Iris."

"What are you two talking about?"

"James and Christabel, of course," Robin told her sister. "We're worried."

Iris snorted. "Pearl doesn't seem worried. She's all over Monty."

Courtney glanced at Monty. Iris was right. Monty's total attention was focused on Pearl. And Courtney didn't feel jealous at all. She felt an enormous sense of relief.

Robin was explaining to Iris, "Everyone handles stress in his or her own way. Look at Mom. She's almost in a coma. Look at Dad. He's going to start rearranging the chairs in a circle."

Iris laughed. "Poor Dad. It's got to be hard on him not to be in the operating room, telling everyone what to do."

"It's a huge sign of respect for Henry," Robin told her sister. "Henry has James's life in his hands. Literally. And our father trusts him."

Iris cocked her head and gazed up at the ceiling. "I wonder if I could be brave enough to hold a life in my hands."

Suddenly Valerie came striding across the emergency room, beaming like an angel.

"James is out of the operating room. He's fine. We found the bleed, Henry sewed up the wound, everything else looks good. We just left the operating room. It's going to be a while before James comes out of the anesthesia." She looked at Dr. V. "You know the drill, Dr. Vickerey. When he does wake up, he's not going to be able to see all of you. I suggest two of you stay and the rest of you go home."

Susanna stood up, awake, alert, trembling with hope. "He's all right? James is all right?"

Valerie smiled. "He's as good as gold. He's going to be in your house in a couple of days, playing the invalid, driving you all crazy with requests for water, food, books, and back rubs. But really, truly, I'm serious. The operation went well. James is fine."

"How is Henry?" Susanna asked.

Valerie's face lit up. "Ah, that Henry! He's a pro. He's a magician. Except, just for fun, he left a sponge inside James." Seeing Dr. Vickerey's face, she quickly added, "Okay, that's not funny, I apologize. I was just kidding, of course. We're all a wee bit slaphappy. It's not every day a surgeon operates on his brother."

"Can we talk to Henry?" Susanna asked.

"Of course. He'll be out in a few minutes." She gestured to the window. "It's almost nine o'clock. Time to catch your breath and wind down, folks."

Susanna hugged Valerie. "Thank you, Valerie, thank you."

"You're welcome." Valerie smiled. "Yeah, Henry and I make a helluva fabulous team! I've got to take care of some things, but I'll be back and Henry will be out soon." She walked away.

Susanna went into her husband's arms and wept on his shoulder. Her husband patted her back and said, "There, there. Everything's all right."

Seeing her father display that much feeling was almost as shocking as the accident, Robin thought. She hugged Iris, who was crying like a baby, and that made Robin start blubbering. It was the relief, the blessed *relief*.

She turned to Courtney, who had gone white. "My lips are numb," she muttered.

"That's what a shocking bit of good news will do to you," Dr. V told Courtney. "Sit down and put your head between your legs."

More empathy from her father! Robin stifled a laugh. She was surprised Courtney didn't pass out on the floor right then and there from the shock of Dr. V being actually aware that she existed!

Courtney did as Dr. V told her. Robin sat on the folding chair next to her and put a friendly arm across Courtney's back.

"I'm okay," Courtney said after a moment. When she lifted her head, Robin saw that Courtney was, very quietly, crying. "If he'd died thinking I didn't love him enough . . ."

"But he didn't. He's going to be just fine." Robin handed her a tissue. "Here. Blow your nose. You'll get to see him soon, but my parents might wonder why *you* want to see him. I mean, you haven't told them about you and James."

"It's all happened so fast," Courtney reminded Robin, honking heartily into a tissue. "It's all so new."

"Is it? I think you and James have been in love with each other forever. It won't come as the world's most amazing surprise to my parents."

"Still . . . I don't want to announce anything to Susanna and Dr. V by myself. I mean, it's something James and I should do together."

"Yeah. I see that."

Valerie beckoned from the far end of the waiting room. "Susanna?"

Susanna rushed to join Valerie, and the two women disappeared around the corner.

"They won't take long," Robin said. "My dad will go next. Then I should go, but because I'm such a saintly best friend, I'll let you go in my place."

Robin watched the others. This was a different kind of waiting, and the room was buzzing with energy even though it was after ten o'clock at night. Iris was in the parking lot, calling her friends to share the good news. Dr. V had stopped pacing and stood close to the television, watching the news, his hands clasped behind his back. Pearl was standing up and stretching, of course in her own sensual, nearly pornographic way. And Monty was watching her.

Quinn had hugged Susanna and shaken hands with Dr. V when Valerie first told them James was out of the operating room and doing well. Now he sat in tense isolation, obviously worried about Christabel. Robin knew she should take pity on him. She should go speak to him, remind him that Christabel was now beginning her voyage of healing, that all would be complicated, but eventually all would be well.

But her anger and her terrible sense of estrangement held her back. She had heard songs of love at first sight. It was as if Robin was experiencing some kind of instant *unlove*. Like a thunderclap, like a jagged spear of lightning, her love for Quinn had vanished. She had changed completely. God, maybe she was only extremely tired.

Susanna returned, beaming. "He's groggy, but he's good. He's safe. He didn't speak but he squeezed my hand!"

Dr. V went off for his brief visit. He returned with shoulders straighter and his face younger, almost handsome.

"Robin?" Valerie asked. "Want to come see James for just a moment?"

"I want Courtney to go for me," Robin said.

"Too many people too soon," Dr. V grumbled. "James is your brother, Robin."

But Susanna put a restraining hand on her husband's arm. "Let Courtney go," she said.

God, Robin thought, *does Mom know everything about us all the time?*

"Thanks," Courtney said without looking at Susanna. She jumped from her chair and went with Valerie.

Because she'd seen Christabel, Courtney was prepared for the way James looked. He was pale and drowsy as he lay in his hospital bed with tubes of every kind sprouting from his body. Courtney was aware of Valerie's presence in the room, waiting by the door, trying not to intrude. *Okay,* Courtney thought, *so Valerie knows I love him. Maybe everyone knows.*

What she was not prepared for was the upswelling of emotion when she touched James's hand and met his eyes. His hand was warm, his eyes blurred with drugs, but James saw her, and he squeezed her hand *hard.* She was desperately trying not to cry, but when their eyes met, a sob escaped her throat and tears absolutely flew from her eyes and her shoulders shook and her knees went so weak she had to lean on the bars of the hospital bed for support.

"Oh, James, I love you!" she said, and she didn't care if Valerie heard it, she didn't care if she was being broadcast by hidden camera to the world. "Oh, sweetie, I'm so glad you're all right, James, I love you, I want to be with you always, and nothing else matters, nothing! I don't have to have your children. But I do have to have *you!*"

James smiled and squeezed her hand, and then his eyes closed and he fell asleep.

Courtney turned to Valerie. "He's gone all limp! He's gone to sleep! Is he okay?"

"He's only coming out of the anesthesia," Valerie said. "He stayed awake as long as his meds allowed. He's got to sleep. His body has to heal."

"Oh. Okay." Courtney wiped her eyes with her hands.

And then, to her amazement, Valerie put her arms around her and enveloped her in a warm hug. "So the other Vickerey male has captured his mate. We'll be sisters-in-law. Right now I'm telling you, please come to me anytime you want to talk. These men are strong-headed and mesmerizing, and I don't mean Henry's bipolar stuff. That only makes it more confusing."

Courtney allowed herself a moment of comfort in Valerie's arms. Then she pulled away. "We haven't told anyone yet," she said, searching Valerie's eyes. "We've only just kind of . . . come to a decision . . . ourselves."

"I understand. I won't say a word to anyone, not even Henry. But be forewarned: not much gets past Susanna." She patted Courtney's shoulder. "Come on, now, I'll show you where the restroom is so you can wash your face and put on some lipstick. You look like Kate Winslet after Leonardo DiCaprio went down from his iceberg, and you should be smiling like you just won the lottery."

"Thanks, Valerie." Courtney took a deep breath and put a lid on her emotions, even though it was like pulling the reins on a wild horse.

In the restroom, she washed her face, put on lipstick and blush, and combed her hair. *There.* She looked presentable. She found Valerie waiting for her in the hall.

"You look beat," she said to Valerie. "It must be draining, taking part in an operation on someone you care for with the man you love."

"I'm from peasant stock," Valerie said. "I can handle it." She made a muscle in a Rosie the Riveter pose. "And I think the lithium's going to help Henry a lot, which means he'll be less of a pain in the ass. I hope."

They returned to the waiting room. Courtney was surprised there weren't ruts in the floor from all the pacing and walking the Vickereys had done today.

She was confused to see everyone standing up in a circle, even Quinn. It took a moment for Courtney to comprehend, and then she saw that everyone was gathered around Henry.

Henry stood in his scrubs, and he looked like an angel. He absolutely radiated an inner light that brightened the faces of those who stood around him.

"Gosh," Courtney whispered to Valerie. "Does Henry have wings?"

Valerie laughed. "Sometimes, I think he does. At least an invisible halo. And it's not mania—I know it's not. I've seen him manic, I've seen him in every variation of the syndrome for years now, and this is not mania. This is *joy*."

Courtney looked over at Valerie, tall, blond, Wonder Woman Valerie, and saw that now she was weeping, tears streaming down her face, and Courtney's tears flowed, too. How amazing human beings are, Courtney thought, what wondrous and complex creatures, to possess the skill and the courage to cut open a loved one and save his life. Henry was recounting the operation to his father, who stared at his son with such pride he seemed about to explode—and this was Dr. V, detached, impassive, unemotional Dr. V. He was listening to his son talk about saving the life of his other son, and he was learning, and Susanna was learning, and Valerie already knew, that in spite of his manic-depression, in spite of anxiety and fear and dread, in spite of all that, Henry was what he had always intended to be, what he was every day, as *all* physicians and nurses are every day: a hero.

20

"I'm beat," Henry confessed at last. "I'm going to take a break and lie down in my office. I'm on call, and have to be here if, god forbid, there's another surgical emergency."

"I'll stay, too," Valerie said.

Susanna smiled and cocked her head. "I didn't realize Henry's office sofa was large enough for two."

"It's not," Valerie shot back with a smug grin. "But I bet I can get him to give me the sofa. He can sleep on the floor."

"Well, really!" Dr. V grumbled. "Can't you find somewhere else—"

Susanna placed a soothing hand on her husband's arm. "Alastair, *think*." And that was all she needed to say. It was enough to remind him of the days and especially the nights of his youth, when he was magnificent with energy and skill and ambition, and he'd meet Susanna in a nearby hotel to celebrate the miracle of bodies with their own young bodies.

Robin could read all this in the look they shared. She smiled. Her parents. Honestly.

Valerie and Henry hugged everyone, and they went off together.

Robin sank into a chair. She was exhausted and released from anxiety and all at once she realized that the seats of these chairs were not soft and welcoming. These were seats for temporary bottoms, she thought, and she saw that Iris was exhausted, too. Well, the whole family was, they all looked like they could simply collapse on the floor and sleep.

Robin stood up and spoke. She clapped her hands to get everyone's attention. "We need a plan. We're all happy but we're all tired. We haven't had dinner. We need food and we need beds. What do you say, can someone go get food? Can anyone go home and get some rest?"

"I'll stay here," Susanna said. "Just in case. I'd like to see James when he's fully conscious, and until then, well, I want to be here. But please, girls, go home and eat and get some sleep. Come back in the morning."

"I'll wait here, too," Dr. V announced. "Couldn't sleep if I wanted to."

"I'll stay," Courtney said.

Quinn spoke up from his chair at the far end of the room. "I'm staying."

"Well, I'm going home for a while," Robin told them. "I want to fix some sandwiches for you all." Turning to her sister, she said, "Iris, come home with me."

Iris yawned. "Mom?"

"Go home, darling. James is out of danger, and no one can see him until morning. Get some sleep. You can come back here tomorrow."

"If you need me—" Iris began.

Dr. V interrupted. "Go home. Sleep. Doctor's orders."

Iris gawked at her father, momentarily startled by his concern. "Okay," she agreed.

Iris glanced at Pearl. "Pearl? Monty?"

"We'll come, too," Pearl said, speaking as if she and Monty were already a couple.

Robin slung an arm around her sister and walked with her out of the emergency room and into the dark night. Monty and Pearl followed silently, bending over to get to the seats at the back.

"I feel like we were in there for *years*," Iris said.

"Yeah, it's that Einstein time-relativity thing." Robin opened the door of the minivan and collapsed in front of the steering wheel.

"What, you mean if you've got a relative in the hospital, time moves more slowly?" Iris joked.

"You might be right." Robin started up the minivan, hit the lights on, and they roared out of the hospital lot. Fog still laid over the island in drifting white swaths that swirled in the headlights. The road was eerily empty. It was after midnight.

Iris put her feet up on the dashboard. "So like, Courtney and James are a couple now?"

Robin's eyes flew to the rearview mirror. She wasn't surprised to see Pearl yawn and snuggle next to Monty, resting her head on his shoulder.

"Fasten your seatbelt, for heaven's sake," Robin said. "We've had enough accidents to last my lifetime." In a quieter voice, she said, "And as far as Courtney and James go, yes, they're a couple, but we need to wait until James is at least conscious before we tell anyone about it. I mean, it's their news to break."

"Hardly news," Iris said, yawning again. "Like I haven't noticed for the past few years how they look at each other. Sort of like you and Quinn look at each other sometimes."

"I'm too tired to talk," Robin said. She reached over and switched on the radio.

She liked country music sometimes, and during the ride on this dark, misty night, country music with its straight-talking, honest, and emotional ballads was absolutely what she needed. Someone was singing about being drunk on summer, and Robin realized with a shock that it was only the *beginning* of summer. All the sunshine and swimming and sailing and cookouts lay ahead.

And the whales. Summer was the best time to visit the whales.

But she'd promised Quinn she would stop going out.

On the other hand, maybe she didn't give a fig what Quinn wanted.

Maybe she'd fallen out of love with him and had landed on her feet. Perhaps tomorrow night she would run down to the beach, jump in her boat, and head out to the deep night waters.

And maybe she should try to get some sleep before she decided anything. She looked over at Iris and saw her sister already snoozing, her head leaning on the window. It was after midnight, but as Iris had noticed, time had stretched itself out of all recognition in the hospital.

Robin couldn't sleep. Even though she was tired, her veins ran with an overdose of adrenaline. She wanted a cold vodka tonic with a lot of lime.

She pulled into their driveway, still listening to the country station, idly wondering why so many songs involved girls dancing on the beds of pickup trucks. The house was completely dark.

She gently shook her sister. "We're home."

"Oh. Okay. Oh, god, I need a toothbrush and my bed." Iris leaned on Robin as they walked to the door and entered the house.

"Go to bed, sweets. Nothing else is going to happen tonight." Robin hugged her sister and Iris stumbled up the stairs to her room.

Robin headed back to the kitchen and began to make sandwiches. To her surprise, Pearl and Monty entered the kitchen.

"We thought we'd clear the dinner table, put away the lasagna and all," Pearl cooed. "Susanna goes to so much trouble making it and it's so delicious. It shouldn't go to waste."

Robin almost dropped the bread on the floor—Pearl and Monty working in the kitchen? Yes. They were clearing up the table, wrapping the lasagna and garlic bread and putting it in the refrigerator, tossing out the dressed salad. As Robin continued making the sandwiches, she couldn't help but overhear their conversation.

". . . so a heifer is a girl cow?" Pearl asked.

Robin heard Monty give out a long, low satisfied laugh. "Right. We usually keep them for breeding."

"And a steer is a cow who's been, um, fixed?"

"A steer is a calf who's been castrated. A cow is a grown female. A bull is a grown calf who can breed."

"That sounds rather complicated." Pearl's voice was wistful. "I've never seen a bull except for the statue outside the New York Stock Exchange. I don't know if I've ever seen a cow. I've lived in New York City and in the East all my life. I've been to Paris, but I've never been to Kansas."

"Do you ride?"

"Yes, I've had riding lessons and I have a riding habit, but the truth? What I care about is how sexy I look in my breeches, high black leather boots, and riding helmet."

More of Monty's low laughter.

"I know Courtney's a cowgirl—sometimes. I know she has boots and a cowboy hat. It all sounds kind of dangerous, being outside on all that land without a GPS. I'm sure I'd get lost."

What on earth is Pearl up to? Robin wondered. Whatever was going on with them wasn't simply about having a hot and steamy one-night roll in the hay. Pearl could get a man in her bed in fifteen minutes flat. And that Monty was obviously a huge sexy hunk—so what was Pearl doing talking to him about cows?

Monty took the bait. "Why don't you come out to Kansas and let me show you our ranch?"

"You know, I would love to do that!" Pearl answered. "It sounds so interesting. But you wouldn't leave me alone anywhere out there, would you?"

As Monty rumbled his reply, Robin pressed her lips together tightly to hold back her laughter. Trust Pearl to turn a ranch into a means of seduction.

And yet.

It was possible that Pearl was doing something few people had ever seen her do before. It was possible that Pearl was being nice. Even considerate. It could be that Pearl was, in her own seductive way, taking pity on Monty who was being so completely dumped by Courtney. Whether she was doing it consciously or not, she was turning what could be a sad defeat for Monty into yet another conquest.

Or it could simply be that Pearl wanted to see what he had in those jeans.

Probably that's what it was all about. But a trip to Kansas seemed like unnecessarily lengthy foreplay. And Pearl's voice rang clear and true, no simpering Jezebel ornamentation, no low sultry laughter.

Whatever Pearl was up to, Robin had to interrupt. She needed to make some sandwiches and get back to the hospital. Nantucket was such a funny old place. It had no chain restaurants, nothing that would be open after midnight, although maybe the Stop & Shop had started staying open until one for the summer, but by the time she got back to town it would be closed . . .

As she brewed Susanna's favorite peach tea and poured it into a thermos over ice, she said, "Pearl, I'm going to drive back to the hospital with the food. We all missed dinner; we're all starving."

Pearl cocked her head. "Well, if James is out of the operating room and just sleeping, why doesn't everyone come home and go back in the morning?"

Robin smiled wearily. "That's a good question. I suppose we all want to be there in case a problem arises in the middle of the night, but I think the real answer is that we feel like we're somehow helping him by staying so close to him. Like you carry a baby all the time when he's sick, only this is the grown-up version."

"I guess I understand," Pearl said.

"That's what cattle do," Monty said. "If a calf is sickly or injured, the mom, and often a lot of the other cows, stand next to her, nuzzling her with their noses, mostly just being there with her."

"Really?" Pearl asked. "That is so sweet. I'd like to see that."

Robin loaded up a couple of book bags with sandwiches, oranges, and carrots. "I don't know when I'll be back or when anyone will be back. Do you want me to call you?"

Pearl gave Robin a clear-eyed guiltless look. "No. Don't call. We'll start the dishwasher, then go to bed. I'll try to come see Christabel and James in the morning."

"Great." Robin hefted the bags. "Well, whatever you do, don't make too much noise. Remember, Iris is sleeping." Smirking, Robin went down the hall and out the door.

21

The fog was still thick as Robin drove back to the hospital. She kept her headlights on low beam and drove slowly. No cars passed in the other lane; still, this was not the time to have any kind of accident. On either side of the Milestone Road, the land was undeveloped, left natural by conservation organizations, and it stretched away in misty shadows. She loved this by day, but tonight she was eager for the warmth of other people, and she was relieved to see the lights of their small, beloved hospital shining in the dark.

The small parking lot was almost empty. The main entrance was locked, so she went through the emergency entrance into the brightly lit waiting room.

Courtney jumped up. "Can I help you carry any of that?"

"Take this." Robin handed her the book bags full of food. "Any news?"

"No. Which is a good thing, I guess."

"I've got sandwiches and peach tea." She approached her parents, who looked as if they'd aged twenty years tonight. "Mom? Dad? Quinn? A little sustenance?"

"I couldn't eat, darling, but thank you," Susanna said wearily.

"You have to eat, Mom. Keep your strength up. That's what you're always telling me." When her parents didn't respond, she coaxed them. "I'll give you the full Monty and Pearl report."

Dr. V spoke up. "He's a nice man. He'll make you a good husband, Courtney."

Robin rolled her eyes. "He'll make someone a good husband, Dad, but I don't think it will be Courtney. Here. Eat this. It's got olives and cream cheese and onions, just the way you like it."

"How's Iris?" Susanna asked.

"She's just fine. Exhausted. The last I saw her, she was dragging herself up to bed."

"And Pearl?" Susanna prompted.

"Pearl has taken charge of Monty. They actually cleaned the kitchen and put the lasagna away."

"Pearl worked in the kitchen?" Susanna laughed. "What a miraculous night!"

"She was going to show him a bed in the attic, but since she also expressed enormous fascination with Kansas and ranches, I wouldn't be surprised if"—Robin glanced at her father, who got uncomfortable when sex was mentioned—"they sat up all night talking. As I left, I heard Monty suggest she come out to his ranch and try riding."

Susanna looked puzzled. "Courtney, does it make you jealous to hear about your cowboy and Pearl?"

Courtney smiled. "I'm delighted. It will take some of the sting out of my newsflash that I don't want to marry him."

"Good," Susanna said. "He deserves a nice woman."

Robin cut in. "He does, but I can't imagine that he's thinking of Pearl as *nice*."

Susanna's smile was enigmatic. "You never know."

"Mom," Robin said, in a sweet teasing voice, "I'm coming to realize that a lot of your wisdom comes in those three words."

"Feel free to borrow them," Susanna said.

Quinn spoke up. "I'm not sure I agree, Susanna. I know everything about my daughter. I always have. It's a parent's job."

Susanna stared at Quinn, and for a moment, Robin thought her mother was actually going to say: *Quinn, you're a giant asshole.* When Susanna spoke, she said only, "Good for you, Quinn."

They all went quiet then. They nibbled at their sandwiches and drank the sweetened tea, then subsided back into their exhausted waiting. Dr. V yawned and compulsively changed the channel on the television. Quinn paced. Robin pulled a chair in front of her mother so Susanna could put her feet up. Courtney and Robin tried to doze, first leaning on each other, then leaning against the wall, using a purse as a pillow—nothing really worked.

At some point during the long night, Jane Hardy came to report that she'd checked on James and Christabel and both were doing nicely.

"Oh, my goodness," the nurse exclaimed. "What are you doing here? Come on up to the second-floor waiting room. It's much more comfortable."

They trooped together up the stairs, ignoring the elevator and preferring the climb that stretched their cramped legs and got their blood stirring. In the second-floor waiting room, there were two vinyl-covered sofas. For a while, they drank more peach tea and stared at celebrity news magazines so old that Demi Moore was still married to Ashton Kutcher. Susanna put on the sweater Robin had brought.

"Why are you putting on a sweater?" Dr. V asked his wife. "It's not as cold here as it was in the ER waiting room."

"True," Susanna said, "but there's something comforting about wrapping up in a big old sweater. I suppose it's like being a child wrapped in her special blanket."

"I'll wake you up if you start to suck your thumb," Dr. V said. Susanna laughed and the rest of the room gawked at him, shocked to hear him make an attempt at humor.

Susanna and her husband rested on one of the long sofas. Susanna kicked off her shoes, stretched her legs out, and lay her head on the plump cushy back, her sweater draped over her shoulders. Dr. V exhibited the remarkable skill of dozing while sitting upright. His chin would slowly, gradually, sink toward his chest. At touchdown, he'd give a little snort, raise his head without opening his eyes, and the process began all over again. Robin and Courtney shared the other sofa, too tired to sit properly but needing to whisper. They put some stiff sofa pillows in the middle, and lay on their backs head to head, with their knees hitting the ends of the sofa and their legs dangling down the side.

"We don't look very elegant," Courtney remarked as they made themselves comfortable.

"I don't think elegance is rated high on the scale of how you look in a hospital waiting room," Robin replied. "What did you say to James when you saw him?"

"I was in there for such a short time. He looked so terrible, all full of tubes, but I held his hand and told him I loved him and I wanted to marry him even if we didn't have children, and that I'd love him forever."

"What did he say?"

"He fell asleep," Courtney said.

"Typical male response," Robin joked.

They both giggled at that.

"It's okay to be silly now, isn't it?" Courtney asked.

"I don't know," Robin answered. "I see a poster on the wall saying 'No Smoking' and 'No Cellphones,' but I don't see one that says 'No Silliness.' "

They giggled at that, too, and for the next few minutes everything they said made them giggle.

Quinn, seated on a chair doing a paperback Sudoku, shot them a serious look.

"It's okay, Quinn," Robin told him. "We can relax."

Without replying, Quinn returned to his puzzle.

"If he only knew about Julian," Courtney whispered, "he'd be bouncing off the walls."

"I kind of am, mentally," Robin whispered. "Bouncing around, I mean. I mean, how could Christabel have so much going on—a fiancé, plans to move off island—without telling someone. If not her father, then at least me or James."

Courtney was quiet for a moment, thinking. "I can understand it. Her father's so protective, he'd probably have the FBI investigate the man before he'd let Christabel so much as date him. And if she told you, you'd have to tell Quinn. And if she told James, he'd tell me, or you, or someone. You can't sneeze in your attic without someone in the kitchen saying *Bless you*."

"I'm not so sure," Robin retorted. "You managed to make love with my brother while I, your best and closest friend, didn't know."

"Hey, what happens on the beach stays on the beach," Courtney joked. They both giggled.

After a while, they stopped talking. Courtney heard a light melodic snore coming from somewhere in the room. Probably Susanna, she decided. The snore was gentle and comforting, as if Susanna were saying even in her sleep, I'm only slightly asleep, I'm really awake and ready to help James and Christabel at a moment's notice. Courtney felt Robin's head sink deeper into the pillow. Courtney's pillow had been hand cross-stitched with a Nantucket scene. It was artistic, but it itched her skin. Still, it gave support to her head as she closed her eyes and let go and relaxed and slept.

The hospital sprang to life at six A.M. As the Vickereys and Courtney and Quinn shuffled off to the bathroom, sounds surrounded them: nurses and doctors briskly coming and going, the ping of the world's slowest elevator arriving on the second floor, a cart of some kind rolling down the hall. Lured by the aroma of freshly brewed coffee, they went out to the cart and helped themselves. After a few sips of the strong, fragrant dark brew, they woke up, smoothed their wrinkled clothes and their tangled hair, and walked around the hospital waiting room, stretching, yawning, and eager to see Christabel and James.

Erica Carr, another island nurse, stepped into the room, looking crisp and bright and wide awake.

"Courtney Hendricks?" she asked.

"Yes?" She was glad she'd washed her face—it made her feel more alert.

"Christabel would like to see you now." Before Quinn could object, she informed him, "Your daughter will see you in a moment. The oral surgeon's on his way. He'll be working on her this morning, but Christabel will definitely see you before that."

Courtney followed Erica out of the room, down the hall, and into Christabel's room. Christabel looked even worse today. Some of the bruises on her face were displaying a rainbow of colors that no human face should wear. And she still looked woozy, no doubt from the pain medication.

Courtney went to the side of the hospital bed and took Christabel's hand. "I spoke to Julian. He said to tell you he loves you. He couldn't get over last night—the fog, no planes, no ferries. But he's coming first thing this morning."

Christabel scribbled: *Thank you.*

"I didn't tell your father. I thought you should do that."

Christabel scribbled: *Groan.*

"Yes, but what's going to happen when Julian arrives here to see you? This hospital's too small for them not to run into each other. Your poor father, Christabel, you've got to warn him."

Christabel scribbled: *U do it.*

"Oh, thanks very much, but come on, Christabel, it's not my place to tell him."

Christabel scribbled: *Sorry. Fading. Can't talk now.* She closed her eyes. Her hand went limp and the pen rolled away from her fingers onto the bed table.

"Christabel. I know you're faking it. You can't leave this kind of responsibility with me. You've got to grow up and tell your father yourself!"

Erica Carr, who had been standing silently in the corner, came forward. "We should let the patient rest."

Frustrated, Courtney nodded and stepped away. She went out into the hall and returned to the waiting room. As she came in, Quinn went out, following the nurse who was taking him to see Christabel.

"While you were there," Robin said, "a nurse came in and told us that James is resting comfortably. All signs good." She cocked her head. "What?"

"Let's go outside," Courtney said. "I need some fresh air to wake me up."

They trotted down the stairs and out the heavy fire door. The air was sparkling and fresh, as if it were carbonated. For a few minutes, they didn't talk but walked around the hospital, letting their gazes—and their minds—rest on the flowers of the dogwood tree and the impatiens planted in profusion by the front door. Traffic buzzed up and down Surfside Road and they saw a couple of early-bird bikers pedaling along Vestal Street.

"The world is going on as usual," Robin said. "It's kind of unsettling, isn't it? Inside the hospital, everything's shrunk down to one—or two—people and their tiny cells and veins and muscles."

"James's muscles aren't tiny," Courtney insisted.

"Oh, you know what I mean. Out here, the world is limitless. We can hear birds singing. And all this luscious green grass." Robin spun in a circle, arms out.

"You are kind of a freak, you know," Courtney said wryly.

"That's probably true," Robin answered, without taking offense. "But, Courtney, I feel so *free* today. So relieved!"

"You mean about Christabel? And what about you and Quinn? If you still feel things are over between you, I think you need to have a conversation with him. I know it's hard."

"You're right." Robin sagged. "Gosh, what a way to begin the summer."

"Hang on." Courtney held up her hand. "Phone."

"Miss Hendricks? This is Julian Moreau. I'm boarding Nantucket Airlines shortly. I'll arrive on the island a little before eight o'clock. Shall I rent a car or will you be able to pick me up?"

"I'll pick you up," Courtney said. "I'll be in a white minivan."

"What?" Robin demanded.

Courtney checked her watch. "Julian will be here in twenty minutes. I told him I'd pick him up."

"Holy moly. Courtney, you've got to say something about him to Quinn. You've got to prepare him."

"*I* do? *You* do."

"No, listen to me. Christabel broke the news to you because she knows you are the least entangled in this whole mess. Come on, Quinn might get all emotional if *I* tell him. He's bound to be more restrained with you, and truly, that's a kindness to him, to prevent him from making some kind of scene he'd be embarrassed about later."

"You really should work for the State Department," Courtney said. "You've got the instincts of a diplomat!"

"But I'm right. You know I'm right."

"So I've got twenty minutes to tell Quinn something that will explode his mind, and then I've got to go get Julian?"

"Yes, and I'm going with you. I'll be with you when you tell Quinn, but then I'll want to get away from him as soon as possible."

"Coward," Courtney said mildly.

Robin strode toward the front door and held it open. "Come on. Let's get it over with."

Invigorated by the fresh morning air and their anxiety, they raced up the stairs to the second floor and hurried to the waiting room.

"Quinn?" Courtney stuck her head in the door. "We need to speak to you."

"Actually, I changed my mind. We need to speak to you all." Robin brushed past Courtney and stepped into the waiting room. "It's not going to be a secret in about twenty minutes. And Dad and Mom can help Quinn deal with it."

"What else could I possibly need to deal with?" Quinn stood up, looking puzzled.

Courtney pulled the door shut. "When I went in to see Christabel last night, she wrote me a note. She told me that she's been seeing an art dealer from Boston, Julian Moreau, for two years. She's kept it secret because he's married, with three children, and he's in the process of getting divorced."

Quinn glared at Robin. "What is Courtney talking about? I know no Julian Moreau."

Robin's heart swelled with sympathy. "It's true, Quinn. She's not making it up. Christabel wrote Courtney a note last night telling her this."

Quinn swayed. "I—I—Why didn't she tell me?"

"Christabel said she was worried that you'd object. He's twenty years older than she is.'"

Quinn looked at Robin. "That would pose no problem for me. But that he's married, that she's been seeing a married man . . ." He put his hand on his forehead. "I can't take it in. I can't believe it."

"I'm sorry to be the one to tell you all this," Courtney said. "But there's more. I called Julian last night—because Christabel asked me to. He just called and I'm picking him up at the airport in about fifteen minutes."

"More like ten minutes," Robin said. She touched Courtney's arm. "We've got to go."

"This is too much," Quinn said. "This is too much." He fixed his gaze on Robin, as if waiting for her to say something.

Robin jangled the keys. "Come on, Courtney."

They left the room and trotted down the stairs and outside.

"You really don't love him, do you?" Courtney asked Robin. "If you did, you couldn't leave him now when he's had such shocking news."

They jumped in the minivan with Robin behind the wheel. "I don't love him, Courtney. It's the oddest thing. I mean, I was sure I loved him, I *did* love him, but first he insisted we move off island and then he objected to my visits with the whales. It's like my love for him was a loose tooth and it got looser and looser and then last night when he wanted to blame James for the accident, it simply fell out."

Courtney burst into laughter. "Trust you to compare love to a loose tooth."

"Well, whatever it is, I am completely no longer in love with Quinn. You should understand. You've just kissed off that hunky cowboy."

"I never loved Monty the way you loved Quinn. I loved him like a brother. We were best buddies for years."

"Yeah, and I'm sure you never noticed his manly cowboy charm," Robin teased.

She slowed as she turned into the airport road. In front of the terminal stood a man wearing a light linen suit, white duck shoes, a blue shirt, and a white tie.

"That has to be Julian Moreau," Courtney said.

"He looks like Tom Wolfe, you know, the writer."

"Like a dandy, you mean. Oh, god, Robin, look at his hair. Look at his face! He could be a double for Quinn."

"No, he couldn't! What a gross thing to say." Robin parked the car in the loading zone. "You go get him. You're the one he's been talking to."

Courtney stepped out onto the sidewalk. The day was getting brighter and warmer and she felt slightly dizzy from lack of sleep.

She approached the man. "Julian?"

"Yes. You must be Courtney. Thank you for fetching me."

"You're welcome." As she slid the door open to the backseat, she said, "Robin's driving. She's one of Christabel's friends. We've been at the hospital all night."

Julian set his heavy leather case on the floor of the backseat, climbed in, and settled. "Hello, Robin. Thank you for your help."

Courtney returned to the front seat and Robin put the car in gear.

"How is Christabel?" Julian Moreau asked.

"She's being operated on by an oral surgeon," Courtney said. "I saw her this morning, before her operation, and I told her I'd spoken to you. I let her know you were coming."

"We also told her father about you," Robin said. She kept her eyes fixed on the road as she spoke. "He was shocked. I mean, we *just* told Quinn about you. So he's got a lot to absorb. The accident. Christabel needing oral surgery. Now, you."

"How soon can I see Christabel?"

"I don't know, whenever the oral surgeon's done with her. Until then, you can do what we've been doing—waiting."

22

R obin couldn't explain exactly why she took Julian up to the second floor in the elevator. Courtney didn't object, and Julian obviously thought this was normal, and it *was* normal, but to Robin going
up in the elevator seemed almost ceremonial and certainly more digni-
fied than running up the steps two at a time, the way she'd been doing.
Maybe there was something theatrical about the elevator, too — the way
the doors opened, like curtains in a theater.

She had expected that Quinn would be pacing the hallway, and he
was. Her parents, she could see, were seated in the waiting room, allowing Quinn to meet Julian Moreau in privacy.

The elevator pinged when it stopped at the second floor. Julian
stepped out. Robin and Courtney followed. Robin couldn't breathe.

Quinn approached his daughter's fiancé and held out his hand.
"You must be Julian Moreau. I'm Quinn Eliot, Christabel's father."

Quinn was so *civilized*! Robin thought. He didn't seem upset or
critical, and it was eerie how much the two men resembled each other.
They could be brothers.

"I'm happy to meet you," Julian said as the two men shook hands. "How is she?"

"Probably sedated at the moment," Quinn said. "She's being worked on by an oral surgeon. The nurse told me Christabel has to have her mouth wired shut because of her broken jaw. She will need to drink out of a straw for the next six weeks. Then she will need new teeth implanted." Quinn gave the other man an appraising look. "Eventually, she'll be as good as new, but she will need a lot of care."

Julian nodded. "I see. Okay, then, how can I help?"

Quinn raised his eyebrows. "I'm not sure. I would assume Christabel should remain on the island for a while after this operation. The dental surgeon lives here."

"I'll rent a house," Julian said. "That way I can come to your house whenever you or Christabel want me there."

Robin stared at Courtney, who stared back, both of them openmouthed with shock.

"My divorce has been finalized," Julian continued. "I'm a free man, and I want to marry your daughter. I want to be here for her. I can run my business from anywhere I can get Wi-Fi, although I will need to make a few quick trips to Boston. My children are in Europe traveling with their mother this summer. They know about Christabel and they're happy for me."

"There's no need for you to rent a house," Quinn said. Turning, he continued, "Let's walk. We have a lot to talk about."

As soon as the men had gone around the corner, Robin said, "Oh my god! Quinn is being more than polite! He's being *friendly*."

"It seems like he's good with the idea of another man taking on the care of Christabel," Courtney said with a grin.

In the waiting room, they found Susanna standing up, smoothing her clothes, finding her purse.

"What's up, Mom?" Robin asked.

"Your father and I got to see James while you were off at the airport. He's sound asleep—"

"Which he should be," her father interrupted, "given the amount of pain medication pumping through him. It's a violation of the body, you know, to be cut open, and the body needs its rest to recover and renew. He's not going to be able to converse until this evening at the earliest."

"But he's okay?" Courtney asked.

"He's okay," Susanna answered. "I couldn't have gone home last night and slept, not with James in the hospital. There's something about the night, the dark . . . I can't explain it. It's as if, during the night, when everyone is sleeping, everyone is vulnerable, more vulnerable than in the day. So your father and I needed to stay here, close by, dozing, but waking often, our minds and hearts sheltering James through the silent mysterious empty hours. And you two girls, you helped, too, being here."

Dr. V grumbled, "We stayed because we needed to be here in case James's vital signs changed. If necessary, I could always step in."

"Of course, dear." Susanna patted her husband's arm. "But I'm exhausted, and I need a shower and a nap. I'll come back this afternoon to relieve you girls, and we can all be here this evening. I think—your father thinks—James will be able to talk a little tonight. And you'll call us if anything happens?"

"Of course. Go get some rest," Robin said.

After her parents left, Robin said to Courtney, "Okay, they're both whack jobs and I can't decide which one's craziest."

"Actually, Robin, I think your mother's right, about night and day. I love being around her, hearing her say stuff like that."

"What about *your* mother?" Robin asked as they settled on the long sofa.

"What about her? You met her at Easter. She's the opposite of Susanna. Rarely speaks her feelings."

"Still, if you marry James, I can't see you living in Kansas. Won't your mother miss you?"

"Really? I doubt it. Mom and Dad are like moss on a tree—what's that word? *Symbiotic*. They're so close to each other that in their own way they are dependent on each other. They have their routine, and they like it never to change. Dad runs the pharmacy, Mom hides in the back and does the books. She reads while he watches sports. They never go to, oh, Kansas City to a play or a baseball game. They've never traveled anywhere, except to Colorado on their honeymoon."

"But still . . . Monty's such a huge catch. Did they ever think you'd end up with him?"

Courtney grinned. "I doubt it. Remember, Monty hung around our house when he was thirteen. They probably think he's like a brother to me. If they think about it at all." Courtney put her arms around a pillow and leaned forward. "I love my parents, but they wouldn't be upset if I decided to move to China. Not every family is like yours, Robin."

"Thank god for that."

Courtney laughed. "I mean, your family is so close. You take people in. Susanna actually adopts children—her 'summer children.' My parents aren't like that. I'm not saying one is good or one is bad, no judgment here. Anyway, never mind about me. *You* have to have a conversation with Quinn."

"Not today," Robin decided. "I don't want him to have two shocks on the same day."

"Mmm," Courtney agreed sleepily, adjusting the pillow behind her head.

"I should at least wait until Christabel's out of surgery. Or home, or something . . ." Robin leaned her head against the sofa and closed her eyes.

They were awakened by the tantalizing aroma of cheeseburgers. Julian and Quinn came into the waiting room, both carrying brown paper bags.

"Lunch!" Quinn announced, moving the magazines aside and setting the food out on the coffee table. "Comfort food. Cheeseburgers and hot turkey Reubens."

Robin sat up, rubbing her eyes. "What time is it?"

"It's twelve-thirty," Quinn told her. "We have both been in to see Christabel, who is resting comfortably. We decided we needed sustenance, so we went to the Downy Flake. We brought enough for Alastair and Susanna." Quinn looked around, obviously wondering where they were.

"They went home to shower and rest," Courtney told them. "They'll be back this afternoon and then we can go home and shower."

"Great!" Quinn handed out the food.

Robin was certain she felt too wound up to eat. But when she bit into her warm, rich, tasty cheeseburger, it calmed every corpuscle in her body.

Julian pulled a chair closer to the table. He gobbled up a turkey Reuben and drank soda from a paper cup—something that amused Robin, who thought he seemed way too elegant for paper cups.

"I'll go peek at Christabel after I eat," Robin said, wanting to put off the talk with Quinn as long as possible.

"You'll be shocked," Julian said. "Because her jaw's been wired, she can't open her mouth and they had to do a tracheotomy so they could insert a breathing tube."

"Oh, no!" Courtney cried. "That sounds painful."

"It's not," Quinn said. "And it's necessary. She'll be here, on an IV for a couple more days, until she's stabilized."

"After a week or so at home, we can move her to my place in Boston," Julian said. "The change of scenery should cheer her up."

Courtney exchanged glances with Robin. So Quinn would be alone for a few weeks. What did that mean for Robin?

"Let's go see James!" Robin announced, crumpling up her sandwich wrapper.

"Don't go into Christabel's room," Julian said. "She's sleeping. The nurse told us to let her rest until tonight. We can see her then."

Robin watched Quinn as Julian spoke. Julian was politely marking Christabel as his territory, and Quinn merely continued eating his cheeseburger.

"Can it get any weirder?" Courtney whispered as they walked down the hall toward the patients' rooms.

They peeked into James's room. He was flat on his back, sleeping soundly.

"Darn," Robin said.

"Why? It's like your father said. He's resting."

Robin lightly kicked at the molding on the hospital wall. "I guess I feel antsy. I don't think I can go back into that room with those two men and just sit until Mom returns."

"Then *don't*," Courtney told her. "Go outside. Take a walk. Breathe fresh air. The men are here for Christabel. I want to go in and sit with James."

"He's sleeping."

"Yeah, but maybe he'll sense that I'm there. It will make me happier, just to watch him breathe."

Robin smiled and kissed Courtney's cheek. "Okay, then. I'll go for a walk! I've got my cell, so you can get in touch with me if you need to."

Courtney went into James's room. For a long time she only stood looking at him. A day's growth of beard bristled along his jaw and around his mouth, such a good, healthy sign of life. She really wanted to touch it. Bending over the bed, she lightly drew her fingertips along the bristles, almost shivering at their prickliness. Oooh, she loved this man.

He had a breathing tube up his nose and IVs in each arm and what looked like a giant plastic paper clip on one of his fingers. Courtney maneuvered a chair next to his bed and sat in it, putting her hand on the sheets, but not heavily, not trying to wake James. She wanted to tell him about Julian Moreau. She had a gut feeling that James would be completely delighted that Christabel, whom he loved like a sister, had a man who wanted to marry her.

Once, James had been Christabel's best friend, boyfriend, lover, and partner in crime. As they grew older, James became sort of a guardian for her. Did Christabel have a genetic kink, a physical syndrome to explain her fey, eccentric personality? Christabel was part exhibitionist, part little girl, part sex goddess. An enticing mix, especially since she was so lovely to look at. Perhaps that troublesome beauty was a genetic gift from her mother, who had left Christabel to be with her lover. Whatever the reason, it was worrisome to think of Christabel ever having her own children. She was often much like a child herself. Courtney hoped that Julian was as good as he appeared, that he would be able to care for Christabel and help her constant need to seduce. Help her become a mature, and happy, woman. At twenty-seven, Christabel did not yet seem like a woman. Maybe this accident, this trial before her when she would have her jaw wired together, maybe, Courtney hoped, this would serve as a kind of chrysalis for Christabel. She could emerge as a new and better self.

And maybe Courtney was punch drunk on lack of sleep. Courtney yawned and stretched. She walked to the window, looked out at the bright day, and yawned again. She would go for a walk when Robin returned. Until then, she would sit and stare at the man she loved.

They would marry. They would travel to wonderful, exotic locales. Maybe someday they would adopt a child, or children—there were so many who needed homes. She would—

James opened his eyes.

"Oh!" Courtney took his hand and leaned over him. *"James."*

He appeared woozy from his drugged sleep. He couldn't seem to quite focus his eyes. After blinking a few times, he managed to focus on Courtney. He smiled.

"Hey, James," Courtney said, gently squeezing his hand. "How do you feel?"

James said, "Henry."

"Henry is the hero of the hour! He's so proud of himself he's about to burst. And we're all so proud of him."

"Good," James said, and promptly closed his eyes and fell asleep again.

The rest of the day passed in a blur of coming and going, interrupted naps and phone calls. Courtney took a walk. By the time she returned to the hospital, Susanna and Dr. V were there, wearing fresh clothes and looking much more optimistic. Robin and Courtney went to the Vickerey house to shower and nap. They returned, Iris along with them, to the hospital while Pearl and Monty—*Pearl and Monty!*—went to the Stop & Shop and bought bags and bags of groceries to carry the household over for a few days. Pearl had frozen the lasagna Susanna had made, so she created, with her own sophisticated city hands, a casserole of chicken and vegetables that would sustain a crowd.

"I think Pearl's trying to impress that Monty guy," Iris said from the backseat as the three women drove toward the hospital. "I mean, has Pearl ever cooked before? I didn't know she *could* cook."

"Fasten your seatbelt." Courtney laughed. "From what I've seen of Monty—and I've seen a lot—by the time he's spent another day with her, Pearl will be cooking a homemade apple pie."

Visiting hours were from five to seven. Time with Christabel or James was limited, and time alone with James was impossible. A nurse told them James was awake, and the family and Courtney crowded into the room together. Julian stationed himself by Christabel's side throughout all the other visits.

When it was time to leave, Robin went through the waiting room, gathering up used paper cups, plates, and napkins. When she turned to drop them in the waste basket, Callum was standing in the doorway.

Robin jumped and gave a little scream. "Callum!"

He grinned. "Am I that frightening?"

"No, no, sorry. I'm a mess of nervous energy with all that's been going on, and I haven't had two full hours of sleep for what seems like a week but has actually been only about a day. What are you doing here?"

Callum stared at Robin.

"Oh! You're here to see James, of course. Sorry, my brain is not working correctly. But how did you know?"

"Valerie called me this morning. I had to attend to some work matters, and then I flew down here. How's James?"

"He's good. He's awake. Come and see him. He'll be so glad to see you." Without thinking, Robin reached out and took Callum's hand in order to lead him to James's room. Something—some warmth, some buzz, some brightness—passed between her and Callum. She almost asked, "What was *that*?" But Callum was here to see James, and visiting hours were almost over, and she knew she was overreacting to every single thing that happened. She said nothing but pulled him toward James's room.

James was exhausted from all his visitors, but he brightened when he saw Callum.

"Lookin' good," Callum said, punching James very lightly in the shoulder. "Got some cute nurses taking care of you?"

"Yeah, but don't tell Mom," James joked, because Susanna was sitting right there.

It was almost a relief when the family was told visiting hours were over. Both patients were doing well, resting comfortably; James might be allowed to go home tomorrow if he promised not to exert himself and to spend most of his time in bed. Christabel was definitely going home tomorrow.

"All I want to do," Robin said as she staggered out to the car with Courtney, "is eat an enormous bowl of macaroni and cheese and watch *Game of Thrones.*"

"I get that totally," Courtney replied. "It will make your family seem like it's normal."

"Yeah," Robin said. "Plus, I like the dragons."

23

For the next few days, such coming and going took place at the Vickerey house; it was almost as if they were all back in college.

James was informed that on Thursday he would be released from the hospital, with a sheaf of notes on his incision care, pain medications, restrictions on movement, and exercise.

Before James came home, Courtney knew she wanted Monty gone. Okay, he'd been helpful buying groceries, and he hadn't pestered Courtney, but still, he should go.

So, two days after the accident, Courtney sought Monty out. It wasn't hard. She'd slept in Robin's room with her last night—just in case Monty thought if he found her alone he could persuade her to change her mind. But when she pulled on her white shorts and a blue tank top and trotted down the stairs for coffee, she found Monty already up, out on the patio having coffee with Pearl.

She poured her own coffee, slugged back half a cup for courage, and went out to join them.

She said hey to both Monty and Pearl—Pearl, who was mouthwateringly sensual in a simple yet stunning slip dress of watermelon silk. Then she said, "Monty, I need to talk to you."

"I'm sittin' here all ready to listen," Monty said, seeming cheerful and even friendly.

Courtney glanced at Pearl, who was idly swirling her fingertips on Monty's hand. Courtney pulled another chair up to the round patio table and sat down.

"James is coming home today. We'll have to get the house ready for him. He'll have to sleep down in the family room so he won't have to climb stairs. We'll need to keep the house quiet for a few days, while he recovers."

"So you want me to leave," Monty said.

"If you would be so kind."

"Oh, I believe I can be *so kind.*" Monty's voice mocked her formality.

"And the house will be really quiet," Pearl said, "because I'm going with him."

Courtney sighed. She did not have the energy for this. "Pearl, I'm not sure that's such a good idea."

"Why?" Pearl arched one perfect eyebrow. "Are you afraid Monty's toying with innocent little me?"

"He *is* a good seven years older than you are."

"Yeah, but maybe I like that about him. Maybe I enjoy being with a man who knows a thing or two."

"Have you talked to your parents about this?"

"Why should I?" Pearl rolled her pale blue eyes. "I don't even know where they are this week. Besides, I'm twenty-two. An adult. I can make my own decisions."

Courtney looked back at her former suitor. He had a great big cat-who-ate-the-canary grin on his face. "Monty. Come on."

"What's your problem?" Monty inquired, a slight edge to his voice. "Pearl has been to Paris and Mexico, but she's never been to Kansas. She's never ridden Western. She might enjoy the ranch. If she doesn't, she's free to leave. But for all we know, she might want to stay."

She knew from the look in his eyes that he wasn't going to back down. She returned her attention to Pearl.

"Have you told Susanna? Or Iris?"

"Iris knows. She's fine with it. Don't worry so much, Courtney. I know you've seen me every summer, but you have no idea what sorts of things I do in the winter, in the city."

"Monty's ranch won't have a Starbucks nearby," Courtney warned her. "Or a five-star Thai restaurant or Hermes."

Pearl let her head fall back, her silky black hair hanging down, and she laughed. "Courtney, I promise you, I'll be fine. Plus, Monty's going to show me Kansas City, and from what he's said, it's a great place, with that fabulous Rockhill Nelson Art Museum." Straightening up, Pearl surprised Courtney by reaching over and taking her hand. "You're sweet to worry about me, but I'm a big girl now. I'm going to be fine." A sideways grin crept over her lips. "For all you know, *I'm* going to be the one toying with *Monty*."

Courtney surrendered. "Fine. I'll go make reservations—"

"Already done," Monty said. "We fly to Boston at eleven-thirty and catch a flight from there to KC. And we're flying first class."

Courtney took a moment to study Monty, this huge, handsome, fascinating man she had cared for, this man whose pride was as big as the prairies, and who was acting fairly elegantly for being dumped. She wanted to apologize again, but she knew that was the wrong thing to do.

So she smiled and said, "Everything is first class with you, Monty."

She drove Pearl and Monty to the airport in James's rented Jeep. The sky was blue, the wind calm, and no fog was predicted, which meant the planes would be flying on time. Which also meant Courtney didn't have to hang out in the terminal, waiting to be certain they were good to go.

So instead of parking in the large short-term lot, Courtney slid the Jeep into place in a ten-minute loading zone close to the entrance. Monty and Pearl had chosen to sit together in the backseat, and they unbuckled their seatbelts and almost jumped out of the Jeep. Courtney got out, too, more slowly, and stood on the sidewalk watching as Monty unpacked his leather bags and Pearl's Louis Vuitton luggage set. She watched as Monty spoke to Pearl—did they have everything? Was she ready to go?—and allowed a moment of regret to pass over her like a shadow, like a drift of incense, a pinch of memory. Monty was really a lovely man. It was possible that he'd met his match in complicated, devious Pearl. Or maybe Pearl would love him. She hoped so.

"Goodbye, and thanks for the ride!" Pearl was not floating in space like Courtney. She was clearly planted in the here and now, and loving it. She blew a kiss in Courtney's direction and took Monty's arm.

Monty gave Courtney a long, slow, unreadable look. Then he tipped his cowboy hat at her and turned away, pulling Pearl's roll-on, hefting her other luggage on his right shoulder and his own on his left, with Pearl holding on to his arm. The couple disappeared into the terminal.

Courtney thought: *James*. This afternoon James would be home.

James, slightly zonked out on pain medication, returned home, which meant several trips to the pharmacy and grocery store and several more trips up and down the stairs, because it was decided to put James in the family room pullout bed, which had a television and was next to the bathroom. Pillows, linens, blankets, and a pile of pajamas and other clothing were carried down. James spent most of day one sleeping and talking to people, but the second day home, he insisted on being able to use his computer for work—he had masses of emails to answer. So down came his laptop, and Susanna brought out her white wicker bed tray to set over his legs to hold the computer. They stuffed pillows behind his back to support him. He also needed his iPhone, and the chargers for the computer and phones.

Callum stayed over, sleeping on the living room sofa, in case James needed something in the night. This allowed Susanna and Dr. V to shut themselves off in their bedroom for a restorative night of sleep.

The next day, James, still in pajamas, was allowed to walk around the house. He played a game of chess with Callum. That night, he sat at the dinner table with everyone else as they finally ate Susanna's delicious lasagna. Henry and Valerie came for dinner, and even Dr. V emerged from solitude, so it was a very Vickerey family kind of meal, with people laughing and teasing and reaching across the table for the bread because if they waited for a pause in the conversation to ask for it, they'd never get it.

After Robin brought out dessert—peaches and ginger snaps—a momentary lull fell over the table. Iris took the opportunity to make an announcement.

"Hey, guys, guess what. I'm going to be a nurse!"

"You what?" Robin asked, stunned.

"I'm going to be a nurse. I've already spoken to Elena Murphy when I was waiting to visit James and Christabel. I have most of the science requirements. I can take a course online this summer, after I register, and I'll go to Boston this fall to attend classes at Northeastern."

"Wow, sis, that's awesome," James said.

Valerie leaned forward. "Iris, I'm going to be the devil's advocate here. Just pretend I'm Pearl, because I know this is what she would say: *Oh, gross, that means you'll have to clean up vomit and bring people food and wipe people's asses.*"

Susanna laughed. "Rather like being a mother."

Courtney met James's eyes. "Or like having Pearl for a roommate."

"Why don't you want to be a doctor?"

Dr. V had asked the question, and the table fell silent in surprise that he had spoken.

"Because I've decided nursing is more important. I've read up on it, and I've talked to nurses like Elena. Nurses get to know their patients. They touch them, they talk to them, they comfort them, they change their IVs, they wipe their asses, and they do this with care. Doctors are one step removed. Their pedestals aren't as high as they were thirty years ago, but they've still got power and they have to concentrate on the details of their profession—the technological changes, the pharmaceutical innovations. I don't want to do that. I want to be there, helping people."

"Well, I, for one, think that's absolutely wonderful," Henry said. "This world needs more dedicated nurses. Here's to you!" He raised his water glass in a toast.

Courtney raised her wine glass. "Yes, Iris, here's to you." Tears brimmed in her eyes. She had the oddest sensation that it was her own sister she was toasting, and she supposed in a way that was true. Iris was certainly her summer sister.

After dinner, Callum helped James out to the patio and gently lowered him into place on a lounge chair. Most of the others came out, too, to relax, to hear the birds in the bushes, to watch the sun progress in its stately way toward the horizon.

Robin insisted on cleaning the kitchen herself. She waved away any offers of help. This kind of work helped her think, she said, and it was true. Putting material items in order—the dishes in the lower rack, the glasses in the upper rack, the utensils in their basket—gave her time to feel in charge of *something* when she knew she wasn't in charge of anything at all.

Robin felt she had to talk to Quinn. She hadn't spoken to him for two days. Susanna had phoned to ask how Christabel was; she'd relayed the good news to the family: Christabel was recovering nicely, her color was good, but she'd need to be in the hospital for a few more days. Quinn and Julian were taking turns visiting her, but the dangerous period had passed, and the men could leave her safely asleep at night.

It would be a long and arduous road for Christabel, back to her normal life, but eventually, after the oral surgeon had implanted new teeth, she would be fine. Robin was still having trouble wrapping her head around the sheer existence of Julian Moreau. The man clearly loved Christabel. And Robin was delighted about that, and even grateful to whatever fate had brought the art dealer into Christabel's life. But that Christabel could keep such an enormous secret—well, that was something that would take Robin a long time to recover from. She had thought she was fairly adept at reading people. She had been wrong.

Also, *Quinn.* While Robin had been out dutifully and happily buying groceries at Stop & Shop, and wine and beer at Hatch's, and fresh vegetables at Moors' End, and picking up prescriptions at the Nantucket Pharmacy on Main Street, she'd played music on the radio.

Played it loudly, to drown out any possible thoughts. She'd carried James's smallest printer down to the family room and hooked up the cables so he could print off what he'd needed, and she'd taken his mail to the post office for him.

She'd kept herself so busy she was almost exhausted, but at night, when she showered and sprayed her pillow with lavender scent to help her fall asleep, when she lay down on her soft sheets with the window open and a light summer breeze drifting over her, when she closed her eyes to sleep, her disobedient, fretting little mind started all over again, asking her: When are you going to talk with Quinn? What are you going to say? What's the best time to talk to him? Should you wait until Christabel has left the island with Julian, or do it more quickly?

She was driving herself crazy. She was also making herself miserable. As each hour passed, she felt a bit more trapped, as if the walls and ceiling were closing in on her.

So when the phone rang and she saw Quinn's number on the caller ID, she left the dishwasher only half loaded and answered the phone.

"Robin, it's Quinn. Listen, could we talk? Now? I mean just the two of us?"

"Of course. Do you mean on the phone?"

"No. Let's meet at the 'Sconset beach. Christabel's sleeping at the hospital. Julian and I have had dinner at the Seagrille. I can be out at 'Sconset in fifteen minutes."

"I'll see you there."

She dreaded the thought of an intimate conversation with Quinn, but she knew it was necessary. She might as well get it over with.

She stuck her head out the back door. "Mom? Courtney? I'm going to walk down to the beach." With a wave, she was off. She didn't bother to comb her hair or put on lipstick. She wanted to look her worst when she told Quinn it was over between them.

She took the bluff path toward the brick walk down the hill and through Codfish Park. She waved hello to families who were settling in for the summer and admired the pots of petunias or cherry tomatoes set out in the sun.

And here she was, at the beach, and there was Quinn's reliable gray Volvo, parked in the small parking lot.

She waved at him. "Hey, Quinn! Isn't it a beautiful night?"

He unfolded himself from the driver's seat and stepped out. "Robin."

They embraced. She felt him kiss the top of her head, but he made no moves toward her mouth, maybe because they were in a public place.

"Let's walk," he said.

She kicked off her sandals so she could walk barefoot on the beach. Quinn was wearing sneakers and he kept them on.

"Are you exhausted?" she asked.

"More dazed than anything else," Quinn said. "The accident was shocking, but the presence of Julian—well, it's difficult to believe I'm not dreaming."

"He seems so in love with Christabel."

"He is. I've sat up with him the past two nights and we've talked, about everything. His ex-wife. My ex-wife. Christabel's trauma from her mother's abandonment—although she'd already told him all about that. I offered him my point of view. Julian believes Christabel's got a future as an artist. He admires her work tremendously. Of course I do, too, but I would, I'm her father." Quinn stopped walking. He bent over to pick up a shell, an ordinary scallop shell with purple streaks inside. "He loves Christabel very much. He wants to marry her. They'll live together, in Boston."

"That's wonderful, Quinn. I'm so happy for her."

"Yes. It will be a whole new world for her. Boston, and a loving, devoted husband, her art, a gallery. Perhaps she can be free of her everlasting fascination with the Vickerey family."

Robin swallowed. She turned, facing the waves, gathering her thoughts. "But of course we'll still all be friends," she said.

"That's true. I hope that will continue to be true."

Quinn sat down on the sand, facing the ocean, and patted the ground next to him, inviting her to join him. So they sat side by side, not touching, watching the rise and fall of the waves. Robin's mind was racing. She wanted to break off with Quinn, but she wanted to do it gently, sweetly, without causing him pain, and yet here she was next to him, feeling obscurely angry at him, insulted by him: *her everlasting fascination with the Vickerey family.*

"Quinn," she began. "I need to tell you something."

"And I need to tell you something."

Robin laughed. "Okay. You go first." The little voice in her conscience said: *Coward.*

"I don't know if you can comprehend what the past few days have meant to me. Robin, I'm happy. No, I'm *ecstatic.*"

"Yes, I'm glad, too, that the accident wasn't—"

"No, Robin, that's not what I mean. What I mean is that without having to take care of Christabel, I'm free to do what I want!"

Oh, god, here we go. Wedding plans coming straight toward me. "About that," Robin began.

In his newfound enthusiasm, Quinn railroaded right over her. "And what I want to do most in the world is travel through England."

"You what?"

"I've always wanted to spend time there, but either I was teaching, or I had to be there for Christabel. Not that she's incapable, we both know she's not, but she can be so—*imaginative.*"

"That's one word for it. *Impetuous* might be another."

"True. But now Julian has convinced me that he loves Christabel exactly as she is. He wants to marry her as soon as possible. He adores her."

"That's wonderful, Quinn. I can see how this will change your life. But I need to tell you—"

Quinn turned abruptly, rising onto his knees as he moved in the sand. He took both of Robin's hands in his. His face was serious as he gazed steadily into Robin's eyes.

Oh, dear Lord, don't let him say that now we can get married, Robin prayed.

"Robin, you know I have loved you very much over the past few years. With all my heart, I don't want to cause you any pain. But the moment I met Julian, and while we were talking, I experienced the most amazing sense of *liberation*! I'm in my late forties, after all. I've been a teacher all my life. I've never even taken a sabbatical, and I have at least one due to me, probably two if I check into it. I'm going to travel at last. I'm going to take a year, and maybe two years, to travel around England. I'll find a cottage—my god, how fabulous a thought that is! *A cottage!* Who lives in a cottage these days?"

Robin pulled her hands away. "Quinn, you sound like you've been eating pot brownies."

"I know! But I'm high on life." Taking Robin by the shoulders, he said earnestly, "Robin, you have been such a light in the darkness to me the past few years. Your company, and your passion, your kindness— believe me when I say you have saved my life. I never thought Christabel could live on her own. Of course I don't mean to imply that she has the kind of serious issues *your* family has, and I'm impressed and astonished that Henry, with all his emotional glitches, managed to pull off that surgery on James—"

Robin shook her shoulders out of Quinn's grasp. "How can you speak that way about my family? Henry's a talented surgeon and a wonderful man!"

"Well, then, there's you and your fantasy about whales," Quinn shot back.

Robin's hand flew to her mouth, as if physically holding back all the words she wanted to say. After a moment, she spoke quietly, softly. "Quinn, we shouldn't say anything now that we'll regret. If I'm reading you right, you're saying you want to break off with me."

Quinn nodded. "Yes. I am so sorry, Robin. I've given this great thought, I've never been in such a quandary. I don't want to hurt you, I'd never want to hurt you. But you're a lovely young woman and I know many men will love you. I know you'll find that certain someone someday and—"

Robin touched his lips with the tips of her fingers. "No need to say any of that. We've been there for each other. I hope we can still be friends."

"Yes, of course we can still be friends." With a puzzled glance at Robin, he said, "You seem to be taking this remarkably well."

Robin smiled gently. "My mind's in a whirlwind. It's going to take me a while to come to terms with everything."

"Of course." Quinn stood up, stretching, gazing at the far horizon. The setting sun turned the sky gold and cast a glow over his face. "My god, Robin, the freedom I feel now—it's as if shackles have fallen from me!"

Robin stood up. She brushed sand off her shorts as she said, "I'm glad for you, Quinn. I'm truly glad for you."

Reaching out, Quinn brought Robin against him in a warm embrace. "You are a beautiful, intelligent, lovely woman. I know you'll meet many men who will be better for you than I could be."

Robin couldn't help it. She really was in the most peculiar mood, and so she replied, "And if I don't meet a man who's better than you, I'll always have the whales."

24

James had been home for a week. His incision was healing nicely—everyone in the house had been treated to a viewing of the puckered scar. He spent more time working at his computer and less time sleeping. He no longer needed Callum to help him to the shower.

The household settled back into its normal drowsy summer state. Susanna drove into town for meetings with the various committees holding fundraisers in July or August. Dr. V retreated to his study. Robin took care of the household matters and spent a few hours each day helping her father. Iris traveled up to talk to the director of the direct entry nursing program at Northeastern University. She agreed to stay in the Vickereys' Boston apartment, as long as her father swore he would not come up or make any phone calls, write any letters, or in any way try to influence anyone to help get Iris into Northeastern. The same thing, she insisted, held true for Henry and Valerie. Iris wanted to do it all on her own.

Henry and Valerie managed to synchronize their schedules so they worked most of the same hours and had most of the same hours off.

Sometimes they wandered down to the house from Henry's apartment over the garage to join everyone in a meal, but usually it was Sunday afternoons that they spent with the family, going for a sail or a picnic. Henry got all huffy if anyone asked him how he liked the lithium, but Valerie had reported to Susanna, who had told everyone else, that in fact he was finding the lithium extremely helpful. He felt clearheaded, not depressed, not manic—he felt like himself.

Courtney was frustrated, never having one long, uninterrupted period of time to talk with James. He always had people around him, helping him, bringing him iced tea, checking on his incision, taking his temperature, asking if he wanted help getting out to the patio or something special to eat.

But after a week, he was well enough to move upstairs to his room, where not only his bed and clothes and general stuff lived, but also his larger, more complicated printer and fax machine. Once he was in his own room, he could shut the door and have some privacy.

And then, Courtney could wait no longer. It was ten days after the accident. She entered his bedroom, shut the door, and locked it. The June afternoon was bright and hot. James's bedroom windows were open, and a lazy sea breeze puffed the curtains out. James wore board shorts and an old T-shirt, and he'd shaved off the beard that had grown during his recovery. Courtney was kind of sorry about that. She had liked that beard.

James turned from his desk and grinned at her. "Locking the door? Are you planning to have your way with me?"

"Yes. That's exactly what I'm going to do. No, don't get up. I want to talk with you. You can stay right where you are."

She pulled an old leather armchair from the corner of the room close to him, facing him. She removed the piles of manuscripts, journals, and books from the chair and set them on the floor, resting them against the wall. She sat down in the armchair, ignoring the way the springs had given out so that the seat was tilted sideways. She leaned forward, in order to gaze directly into James's eyes, and also to give him a good look down the front of her sundress.

For a moment, she couldn't speak. She had so much to say to him, and it mattered so much.

James watched her patiently, a slight smile on his face.

Finally, she blurted, "James, I want to marry you and live my life with you even with the clear agreement that we won't have *your* children." He started to speak. She put up her hand to stop him. "I decided this *before* the accident, it's not some emotional freaked-out bargain I made with God or fate that if you lived, I'd agree to your condition. I didn't have the chance to tell you, although I did tell you when I first saw you in the hospital, I was afraid you might—that you weren't going to—I wanted you to know how much I love you, so I told you even though you weren't really conscious, but I hoped somehow you'd hear me." She stopped talking, breathless.

"Hey," James said. "Come here." He reached out for her. "Let me hold you."

She felt so vulnerable. "I can't sit on your lap," she protested. "I weigh so much, I'll pop all your stitches."

James laughed. "I'll risk it." He pulled her onto his lap.

She laid her head against his shoulder. He stroked her arm. "God, I love you," he whispered. "How have I lived for ten days without this?"

She sighed with relief, with pleasure. She was *here*, with the man she loved, the healthy, healing man she loved. "Because I wanted you to recover. I didn't want you to rush things. Plus, it seems you never had any time when someone wasn't checking in on you."

"You don't have to worry anymore. I'm fine. More than fine." He nudged Courtney so that she was sitting straight, so that she could see him as he spoke, but he kept his hands on her arms. "No. I didn't hear your thoughts about children when I was in the hospital. But that's okay, because while I was there, I came to a decision of my own."

"Oh?"

"I want to marry you, Courtney, and I want to have *my* children with you. Two. Or three. Maybe four, like Mom and Dad. *Vickerey* children."

Stunned, Courtney choked out, "Really? *Why?*"

"Part of it was the accident. That time, those few minutes, in a way they flashed past. In a way, it all happened in slow motion."

"Tell me." She could feel his heart beating faster, harder, she could see his face change, taking on a tightness, his entire body tensing as he remembered. She moved back to her chair.

James was facing her now, but it wasn't Courtney he was seeing. "I could see it coming at us, the pickup truck, only of course *it* wasn't coming at *us*, *we* were speeding toward *it*. I had the thought that I should take control of the wheel from Christabel and wrench it to the left. But we hit. The impact was . . . I suppose it was like a bomb going off. Even though I knew it was coming, it was a shock, it was like an insult, like it hit me on purpose. The force knocked me backward, and we rocked back and forth and shuddered. I heard this terrifying shriek of metal and all this crunching. The windshield shattered. Christabel screamed, she kept screaming, and then I couldn't move, and I looked down at my seatbelt because it hurt. I saw blood coming out of my side. Lots of blood. And I thought, *Don't let me die. Let me live. I want to be with Courtney, I want a full life with Courtney.*" James's cheeks were flushed with emotion, and his breathing quickened.

"James, oh, how frightening."

"It was. It was terrifying, and the ride to the hospital in the ambulance with the EMTs was surreal—I knew both the guys. I wanted them to tell you I love you, but they were sticking tubes up my nose and in my arm so I couldn't speak. By then the shock had kind of passed and I was in pain, bad pain, there on my left side. All I could say was, *Oh, fuck, fuck, it hurts!*"

Courtney reached out to stroke his face. "Oh, *James.*"

"Then I was in the hospital, and people were all around me. I couldn't see much, flashes of a white coat or blue scrubs. A nurse was bending over me, telling me I was going to be just fine, and I tried to tell her about you, to tell you I loved you, but she said, 'He's getting incoherent now.' And they stuck me with some kind of injection, and I got all woozy. They wheeled me into the room where the CT scanner was, and that was creepy, I mean, I had no control, none. I hate not having any control. And my feet were cold. I think I was going in and out of consciousness. They wheeled me into that horrible elephantine old elevator and I was sure I'd die before we made it to the second floor, but finally we were there. They wheeled me through some swinging doors into the operating room, and the light was so bright it hurt my eyes. People were muttering; I couldn't understand what they were saying. Someone put another IV in my arm. I felt myself sinking, falling backward down into this blackness, and I was really, really afraid."

James closed his eyes. For a few seconds he sat there simply breathing, calming himself down. Courtney waited, not speaking, not interrupting him.

"But then it changed. Everything changed—suddenly *Henry* was there. It was like the ferry touching the dock after a storm, like stepping safe onto a firm shore. I looked up and saw his face. *My big brother's face.* He was smiling at me. God, Courtney, Henry was *smiling* at me. He cracked a joke sort of like, 'I've always wanted to do this,' or something equally lame and I heard the nurses laughing. He bent down over me, so I could see his face clearly, his mask was down around his neck, but he had on his operating scrubs and that silly shower cap. He put his hands on my cheeks and held my face steady. He said, 'James, I'm going to put you to sleep for a while. Then I'm going to cut you open and stop the bleeding. Then you're going to wake up and be as good as new. 'Cause I'm a kick-ass surgeon and you're my little brother, and I'll take care of you.' I felt safe. I knew I could give it all up. I fell asleep, knowing my brother was there."

Tears welled up in James's eyes. His cheeks were flushed. Courtney waited. Outside the window, a seagull cried. The curtains drifted in and out with the breeze.

James shook himself. "Well, that was embarrassing."

"That was beautiful," Courtney said. "I'm honored that you shared that with me. Have you told Henry?"

"Henry and I have talked. We have more talking to do, someday when we're alone. It's easier to joke when other people are around." James took Courtney's hands in his. "God, that sucked. I hate talking about the accident. But I needed to tell you, I need you to know that I had a lot of time to think when I was in the hospital, and I kept thinking about how important my family is to me. We're weird, all of us, but together, we're kind of wonderful. And you fit right in. And I do want *my* children with you. It all became crystal clear to me. I want to marry you and live with you and make you pregnant and go through all the scary, boring, cool stuff of having children. A family. Whatever we can get. And we'll visit here a lot, and Robin and Iris will be the coolest aunts, and I was thinking, if it was all right with you, we could ask Henry to be godfather." He paused. "I sound like I'm manic, but I'm not. I'm alive, and I know exactly what I want." He took a deep breath. "What do you want, Courtney?"

Courtney's lower lip was trembling. "I want to hold you."

"I want to hold you just as much, but this typing chair isn't made for two." James grinned. "Anyway, I think it would be much better for me, as an invalid, if we lay down in bed."

"Absolutely."

They walked to the bed, James bent over slightly to the left, favoring his wound, not wanting to tear anything. They lay down together, face-to-face.

James stroked her hair. "So the point of all that blather—"

"*Not* blather." She scooted as close as she could get to him, wrapping her arms around him, so they were touching all up and down.

"Do you like my idea?" he asked. "You having *my* children?"

"Of course I like your idea," she told him. "I love your idea!"

"Well, then." James took her hand in his and brought it to his crotch, which was swelling nicely inside his jeans. "Why don't we start trying now?"

25

Robin spent part of the afternoon with her father in his study. Mostly, she wrote emails and downloaded messages on his computer, because her father, for all his talent and skill with the tools of his trade, hated the computer. He found it perverse, tricky, as if the computer were full of imps especially designed to drive him, personally, mad.

She set about making dinner, an easy task because they still had so many casseroles and cakes dropped off by friends. Her mother returned from town, bringing local gossip to share as they ate. Henry and Valerie joined them, but Courtney and James didn't appear. Robin grinned to herself about that. Callum was there, and Robin was glad. Without Courtney, James, Iris, Christabel, and Quinn, the table seemed almost sad, almost abandoned. She was glad she'd cut the last of the tulips to put in the middle of the table.

It was a good, relaxing meal, with no one bursting in with breaking news. A few knowing smiles broke out when everyone else also realized James and Courtney hadn't shown. Her father was his usual taciturn self. After the meal, Henry and Valerie retreated to his room above the garage. Callum went up to see if it was possible to intrude on James for a brief visit. Susanna helped Robin clean up the kitchen, although there wasn't a lot to do.

"Want to watch a movie?" Susanna asked Robin.

"No, thanks. I think I'll go down to the beach for a while."

"It will be dark soon."

"I know. I like it that way."

Susanna went to join her husband in their bedroom, where they would probably watch *Homeland* or *House of Cards* on their Netflix DVDs. Her dad was so peculiar about those shows. He refused to stream them, insisting on waiting for the DVDs to arrive in the mail, as if there were something more genuine about the DVD. Robin laughed to herself, thinking about it. She snatched a beach towel hanging from a hook in the back hall, and stepped out into the twilight. All the huge luminous world enveloped her, and her breathing deepened as she entered the dazzle of the outdoors.

She paused at the top of the steps to watch a spectacular sunset unfold itself in a majestic array of color. Then, when the sky was still lavender and the stars were beginning to show, she went down the zig-zag stairs, walked along the beach, spread out the towel, and sat down.

She was alone. That was okay. That was fine. Quinn had phoned her and texted her, asking to see her again, but he'd spoiled it for her by phrasing his words so that it was clear that he was worried about her, concerned that she might be depressed by his announcement that he wanted to travel, that he didn't want to be with her.

She hadn't answered or responded. She couldn't be bothered. She didn't want to insult him, but she was so over him.

What a summer this was, and it was only June! Robin wrapped her arms around her knees and stared out at the blue ocean as infinite and unknowable as her own future. Iris had texted that she'd talked with Pearl, who was having a grand time on Monty's ranch and learning to ride Western style. That blew Robin's mind. She imagined Pearl on a horse, in a saddle, wearing capris and sapphire earrings and Manolo Blahnik high heels. She laughed at the image.

She sat there, listening to the waves roll steadily in, loving the scent of salt and the caress of night air. Probably, she thought, that was the only caress she'd be getting for a long while, if not forever. She was alone, and that was okay. She supposed she missed Quinn, but her heart wasn't broken. More than anything, she felt relieved. Set free.

She heard footsteps coming down the zigzag stairs. Glancing over, she saw Callum walking toward her in the sand.

"Mind if I join you?" he asked.

"Oh," she said, surprised. "Sure. Have a seat."

He settled in the sand, not touching her, and yet the heat of his body radiated toward hers, and she felt an answering warmth in her heart.

"It's nice being out here with you," Callum said.

From the top of her head to the very end of her toes, Robin's skin broke out in goosebumps. Her heart leapt. She was terrified, she was amazed, she was dazzled with hope. She felt as if a fairy godmother had touched her with a wand.

"I have a confession to make," Robin said, almost whispering because what she was going to say could bring about such enormous and unknown consequences. "I often come out here in the middle of the night. I motor and row far out from shore, then cut the engine. Then I wait and . . . sometimes whales gather around the boat." When Callum didn't laugh, she continued, more bravely, "I think—I know, it sounds crazy, but it's true—I think the whales know me. I think they visit me."

For a few moments, Callum didn't respond. Robin's breath caught in her throat.

Then Callum said, "How extraordinary. But then you are an extraordinary woman."

"*Oh*," Robin said. "Thank you, Callum."

"Could I go with you sometime?" Callum asked.

"Absolutely," she told him. "But they don't always come, you know."

"Could we go out tonight?"

"I'd like that," Robin said.

Callum rose and held out his hand to Robin. Together they walked down the beach to her rowboat. Robin was delighted at how easy it was to shove the boat into the water with someone helping her. She jumped in, and Callum joined her.

He took the oars and rowed until they were in deep water, then started the motor. It puttered along reliably away from the shore.

"Look," Robin said, pointing. A fat white moon was lifting itself up into the sky, streaking the calm ocean with dazzling light. Behind her, the land receded until the lights of the house were mere sparkles no larger than the diamond-point sparks of the stars coming out in the black velvet sky.

"Here is good," she told Callum when she thought they were far enough out. "I never know exactly where I am when I come out. I've timed it with my watch, but the tides and wind make it difficult to calibrate."

Callum cut the motor. Except for the slight slapping of the waves against the boat, all was silent. All around them was darkness, the dark sky, the dark water.

"It's kind of eerie out here, isn't it?" Callum asked. He spoke quietly, as if he didn't want to disturb the silence. "In a good way."

Robin nodded. "It's their world out here, not ours."

"Are we intruding?"

"I don't think so. I think we're *visiting*. I think—" She held out her hand. "Listen!" she whispered.

Around them, the water bubbled with movement. A wave rocked the boat.

"Look!" Robin said. "There she is! She came to see us!"

Next to the boat, a dark, enormous shape emerged. From a mass of gray spotted with white, an eye looked at Robin. A wave rocked the boat as the whale floated closer to Callum.

"She's looking at me!" Callum whispered.

Robin smiled. "Tell her hello."

Callum looked at Robin, and then down into the water. "Hello," he said. "I'm Robin's friend."

The whale floated next to them for a few more moments, its dark skin only scarcely visible in the dark water. Then it sank, and bubbles frothed up around the boat.

"She's gone," Callum said, disappointed.

"She might come back," Robin told him. With a smile, she reached over and took his hand. "Sometimes it pays to be patient."

With great care, Callum moved to sit next to Robin. "I've been very patient," he said.

"You have. And I'm glad." Robin kissed him, lightly, and then not so lightly. And then she said, "Wait. Stop. *Listen.*"

Low notes, like those from a cello, floated into the air, joined by higher, flute-like, answering notes. It was as if someone was calling to them from another world. A third note sounded, a bubbling shrill echoing. And a fourth, deep and sonorous.

The whales were singing for them.

about the author

NANCY THAYER is the *New York Times* bestselling author of *The Island House, The Guest Cottage, An Island Christmas, Nantucket Sisters, A Nantucket Christmas, Island Girls, Summer Breeze, Heat Wave, Beachcombers, Summer House, Moon Shell Beach,* and *The Hot Flash Club.* She lives on Nantucket Island.

nancythayer.com
Facebook.com/NancyThayerBooks

about the type

This book was set in Electra, a typeface designed for Linotype by renowned type designer W. A. Dwiggins (1880–1956). Electra is a fluid typeface, avoiding the contrasts of thick and thin strokes that are prevalent in most modern typefaces.